Praise for t...
Sherry...

"Sherryl Woods writes emotio...
family, friendship and home. Truly feel-great reads!"
—#1 *New York Times* bestselling author Debbie Macomber

"Woods is a master heartstring puller."
—*Publishers Weekly* on *Seaview Inn*

"Woods's readers will eagerly anticipate her trademark
small-town setting, loyal friendships, and honorable mentors
as they meet new characters and reconnect with familiar
ones in this heartwarming tale."
—*Booklist* on *Home in Carolina*

"Once again, Woods, with such authenticity, weaves a tale
of true love and the challenges that can knock up against
that love."
—*RT Book Reviews* on *Beach Lane*

"In this sweet, sometimes funny and often touching story,
the characters are beautifully depicted, and readers…will…
want to wish themselves away to Seaview Key."
—*RT Book Reviews* on *Seaview Inn*

"Woods…is noted for appealing character-driven stories
that are often infused with the flavor and fragrance of the
South."
—*Library Journal*

"A reunion story punctuated by family drama, Woods's first
novel in her new Ocean Breeze series is touching, tense and
tantalizing."
—*RT Book Reviews* on *Sand Castle Bay*

"A whimsical, sweet scenario…the digressions have their
own charm, and Woods never fails to come back to the
romantic point."
—*Publishers Weekly* on *Sweet Tea at Sunrise*

SHERRYL WOODS

THE
CALAMITY JANES
Cassie & Karen

MIRA®

ISBN-13: 978-0-7783-1791-3

Recycling programs for this product may not exist in your area.

The Calamity Janes: Cassie & Karen

Copyright © 2015 by Harlequin Books S. A.

The publisher acknowledges the copyright holder of the individual works as follows:

Do You Take This Rebel?
Copyright © 2001 by Sherryl Woods

Courting the Enemy
Copyright © 2001 by Sherryl Woods

For questions and comments about the quality of this book, please contact us at CustomerService@Harlequin.com.

www.MIRABooks.com

Printed in U.S.A.

Dear friend,

When I first conceived the idea for the Calamity Janes series years ago, I knew I wanted to write about a group of friends who'd been a bit of a disaster back in high school, then taken very different paths. Now they're back in Wyoming for their class reunion and the chance to catch up on their lives. In a lot of ways, these women were the predecessors of the Sweet Magnolias. I'm so delighted that new readers will have a chance to get to know them.

Back then, in addition to writing about strong friendships, I also wanted to attempt a group of books set in a parallel time frame. In other words, even though these are very separate stories, the plots overlap during the big class reunion. Only the final book continues past the last dance. It was an interesting writing challenge. As you read the five stories, you'll have to decide if the experiment worked.

I hope you'll have as much fun with the Calamity Janes as you've had through the years with the Sweet Magnolias and that you'll enjoy the Wyoming setting as much as I enjoyed visiting that part of the country to do research for the series.

With all good wishes for lasting friendships in your life.

Sherryl

CONTENTS

DO YOU TAKE THIS REBEL?   9

COURTING THE ENEMY   259

DO YOU TAKE THIS REBEL?

Prologue

The thick white envelope had all the formality of a wedding invitation. Cassie weighed it in her hands, her gaze locked on the postmark—Winding River, Wyoming. Her hometown. A place she sometimes longed for in the dark of night when she could hear her heart instead of her common sense, when hope outdistanced regrets.

Face facts, she told herself sternly. She didn't belong there anymore. The greatest gift she'd ever given to her mother was her having left town. Her high school friends—the Calamity Janes, they'd called themselves, in honor of their penchant for broken hearts and trouble—were all scattered now. The man she'd once loved with everything in her... Well, who knew where he was? More than likely he was back in Winding River, running the ranch that would be his legacy from his powerful, domineering father. She hadn't asked, because to do so would be an admission that he still mattered, even after he'd betrayed her, leaving her alone and pregnant.

Still, she couldn't seem to help the stirring of anticipation that she felt as she ran her fingers over the fancy
calligraphy and wondered what was inside. Was one
of her best friends getting married? Was it a baby announcement? Whatever it was, it was bound to evoke
a lot of old memories.

Finally, reluctantly, she broke the seal and pulled out
the thick sheaf of pages inside. Right on top, written
in more of that intricate calligraphy, was the explanation: a ten-year high school reunion, scheduled for two
months away at the beginning of July. The additional
pages described all of the activities planned—a dance,
a picnic, a tour of the new addition to the school. There
would be lots of time for reminiscing. It would all be
capped off by the town's annual parade and fireworks
on the Fourth of July.

Her first thought was of the Calamity Janes. Would
they all be there? Would Gina come back from New
York, where she was running a fancy Italian restaurant? Would Emma leave Denver and the fast track she
was on at her prestigious law firm? And even though
she was less than a hundred miles away, would Karen
be able to get away from her ranch and its never-ending, backbreaking chores? Then, of course, there was
Lauren, the studious one, who'd stunned them all by
becoming one of Hollywood's top box-office stars.
Would she come back to a small town in Wyoming
for something as ordinary as a class reunion?

Just the possibility of seeing them all was enough
to bring a lump to Cassie's throat and a tear to her eye.
Oh, how she had missed them. They were as different

as night and day. Their lives had taken wildly divergent paths, but somehow they had always managed to stay in touch, to stay as close as sisters despite the infrequent contact. They had rejoiced over the four marriages among them, over the births of children, over career triumphs. And they had cried over Lauren's two divorces and Emma's one.

Cassie would give anything to see them, but it was out of the question. The timing, the cost…it just wouldn't work.

"Mom, are you crying?"

Cassie cast a startled look at her son, whose brow was puckered by a frown. "Of course not," she said, swiping away the telltale dampness on her cheek. "Must have gotten something in my eye."

Jake peered at her skeptically, but then his attention was caught by the papers she was holding. "What are those?" he asked, trying to get a look.

Cassie held them out of his reach. "Just some stuff from Winding River," she said.

"From Grandma?" he asked, his eyes lighting up.

Despite her mood, Cassie grinned. Her mother, with whom she'd always been at odds over one thing or another, was her son's favorite person, mainly because she spoiled him outrageously on her infrequent visits. She also had a habit of tucking money for Jake into her dutiful, weekly letters to Cassie. And for his ninth birthday, a few months back, she had sent him a check. There'd been no mistaking how grown-up he'd felt when he'd taken it into the bank to cash it.

"No, it's not from Grandma," she said. "It's from my old school."

"How come?"

"They're having a reunion this summer and I'm invited."

His expression brightened. "Are we gonna go? That would be so awesome. We hardly ever go to see Grandma. I was just a baby last time."

Not a baby, she thought. He'd been five, but to him it must seem like forever. She'd never had the heart to tell him that the trips were so infrequent because his beloved grandmother liked it that way. Not that she'd ever discouraged Cassie from coming home, but she certainly hadn't encouraged it. She'd always seemed more comfortable coming to visit them, far away from those judgmental stares of her friends and neighbors. As dearly as Edna Collins loved Jake, his illegitimacy grated on her moral values. At least she placed the blame for that where it belonged—with Cassie. She had never held it against Jake.

"I doubt it, sweetie. I probably won't be able to get time off from work."

Jake's face took on an increasingly familiar mutinous look. "I'll bet Earlene would let you go if you asked."

"I can't ask," she said flatly. "It's the middle of the tourist season. The restaurant is always busy in summer. You know that. That's when I make the best tips. We need the money from every single weekend to make it through the slow winter months."

She tried never to say much about their precarious

financial status because she figured a nine-year-old didn't need to have that burden weighing on him. But she also wanted Jake to be realistic about what they could and couldn't afford. A trip to Winding River, no matter how badly either of them might want to make it, wasn't in the cards. It was the lost wages, not the cost of the drive itself, that kept her from agreeing.

"I could help," he said. "Earlene will pay me to bus tables when it's busy."

"I'm sorry, kiddo. I don't think so."

"But, Mom—"

"I said no, Jake, and that's the end of it." To emphasize the point, she tore up the invitation and tossed it in the trash.

Later that night, regretting the impulsive gesture, she went back to get the pieces, but they were gone. Jake had retrieved them, no doubt, though she couldn't imagine why. Of course, Winding River didn't mean the same thing to him as it did to her—mistakes, regrets and, if she was being totally honest, a few very precious, though painful, memories.

Her son didn't understand any of that. He knew only that his grandmother was there, the sole family he had, other than his mom. If Cassie had had any idea just how badly he missed Edna or just how far he would go for the chance to see her again, she would have burned that invitation without ever having opened it.

By the time she found out, Jake was in more trouble than she'd ever imagined getting into, and her life was about to take one of those calamitous turns she and her friends were famous for.

1

Nine-year-old Jake Collins didn't exactly look like a big-time criminal. In fact, Cassie thought her son looked an awful lot like a scared little boy as he sat across the desk from the sheriff, sneaker-clad feet swinging a good six inches off the floor, his glasses sliding down his freckled nose. When he pushed them up, she could see the tears in his blue eyes magnified by the thick lenses. It was hard to feel sorry for him, though, when he was the reason for the twisting knot in her stomach and for the uncharacteristically stern look on the sheriff's face.

"What you've done is very serious," Sheriff Joshua Cartwright said. "You understand that, don't you?"

Jake's head bobbed. "Yes, sir," he whispered.

"It's stealing," the sheriff added.

Jake's chin rose indignantly. "I didn't steal nothing from those people."

"You took their money and you didn't send them the toys you promised," Joshua said. "You made a deal and you didn't keep your end of it. That's the same as stealing."

Cassie knew that the only reason the sheriff wasn't being even harder on Jake was because of her boss. Earlene ran the diner where Cassie worked, and Joshua had been courting the woman for the past six months, ever since Earlene had worked up the courage to toss out her drunken, sleazebag husband. The sheriff spent a lot of time at the diner and knew that Earlene was as protective as a mother hen where Cassie and Jake were concerned.

In fact, even now Earlene was hovering outside, waiting to learn what had possessed Joshua to haul her favorite little boy down to his office. If she didn't like the answer, Cassie had no doubt there would be hell for the sheriff to pay.

"How bad is it?" Cassie asked, dreading the answer. She didn't have much in the way of savings at this time of year with the summer tourist season just starting. The total in her bank account was a few hundred dollars at most. That paltry sum was all that stood between them and financial disaster.

"Two thousand, two hundred and fifty dollars, plus some change," the sheriff said, reading the total from a report in front of him.

Cassie gasped at the amount. "There has to be some mistake. Who in heaven's name would send that much money to a boy they don't even know?" she demanded.

"Not just one person. Dozens of them. They all bid on auctions that Jake put up on the internet. When the time came to send them the items, he didn't."

Cassie was flabbergasted. The internet was something she had absolutely no experience with. How on earth could her son know enough to use it to con people?

"I started getting calls last week from people claiming that a person in town was running a scam," the sheriff continued. He shook his head. "When the first person gave me the name, I have to tell you, I almost fell off my chair. Just like you, I thought it had to be some mistake. When the calls kept coming, I couldn't ignore it. I figured there had to be some truth to it. I checked down at the post office, and Louella confirmed that Jake had been cashing a lot of money orders. It didn't occur to her to question why a kid his age was getting so much mail, all of it with money orders."

Ignoring the dull ache in her chest, Cassie faced her son. "Then it's true? You did do this?"

Defiance flashed briefly in his eyes, but then he lowered his head and whispered, "Yes, ma'am."

Cassie stared at him. Jake was a smart kid. She knew that. She also understood that his troublemaking behavior was a bid for attention, just as hers had been years ago. But this took the occasional brawl at school or shoplifting a pack of gum to a whole new level. His behavior had gotten worse since she had refused to consider going to Winding River so he could spend some time with his grandmother.

"How did you even get access to the internet?" she asked him. "We don't have a computer."

"The school does," he said defensively. "I get extra credit for using it."

"Somehow I doubt they'd give a lot of credit for running cons on some auction site," the sheriff said dryly. He glanced at Cassie. "Unfortunately, there's nothing to keep a kid from putting something up for sale. Most sites rely on feedback from customers to keep the sellers honest. As I understand it, most of Jake's auctions ran back-to-back within a day or two of each other, so by the time there was negative feedback, it was too late. He had the money. The auction site manager called this morning, following up on the complaints they had received, and looking for their cut, as well."

"What kind of toys were you promising these people, Jake?" Cassie asked, still struggling to grasp the idea that strangers had actually sent her son over two thousand dollars. That was more than she earned in tips in several months.

"Just some stuff," Jake mumbled.

"Baseball cards, Pokémon cards, rare Beanie Babies," the sheriff said, reading from that same report. "Looks like he'd been watching the site. He knew exactly what items to list for sale, which ones would bring top dollar from kids and collectors."

"And where is this money?" Cassie asked, imagining it squandered on who knew what.

"I've been saving it," Jake explained, his studious little face suddenly intense. "For something real important."

"Saving it?" she repeated, thinking of the little metal box that contained his most treasured possessions and those dollars that his grandmother sent. Had he been socking away that much cash in there? All of his friends knew about that box. Any one of them could steal the contents.

"Where?" she asked, praying he'd put it someplace more secure.

"In my box," he said, confirming her worst fears.

"Oh, Jake."

"It's safe," he insisted. "I hid it where nobody would ever find it."

There was a dull throbbing behind Cassie's eyes. She resisted the temptation to rub her temples, resisted even harder the desire to cry.

"But why would you do something like this?" she asked, still at a loss. "You had to know it was wrong. I just don't understand. Why did you need so much money? Were you hoping to buy your own computer?"

He shook his head. "I did it for you, Mom."

"Me?" she said, aghast. "Why?"

"So we could go back home for your reunion and maybe stay there for a really long time. I know you want to, even though you said you didn't." He regarded her with another touch of defiance. "Besides, I miss Grandma."

"Oh, baby, I know you do," Cassie said with a sigh. "So do I, but this…this was wrong. The sheriff is right. It was stealing."

"It's not like I took a whole lot from anybody," he insisted stubbornly. "They just paid for some dumb old cards and toys. They probably would have lost 'em, anyway."

"That's not the point," she said impatiently. "They paid you for them. You have to send every penny of the money back, unless you have the toys to make things right."

She figured that was highly unlikely, since Jake spent his allowance on books, not toys. She met the sheriff's gaze. "You have a list of all the people involved?"

"Right here. As far as I know, it's complete."

"If Jake sends the money back and writes a note of apology to each one, will that take care of everything?"

"I imagine most of the people will be willing to drop any charges once they get their money back and hear the whole story," he said. "I think a lot of them felt pretty foolish when they realized they were dealing with a third-grader."

"Yeah, well, Jake is obviously nine going on thirty," Cassie said. At this rate he'd be running real estate scams by ten and stock market cons by his teens.

This was not the first time she had faced the fact that she was in way over her head when it came to raising her son. Every single mom struggled. In all likelihood, every single mom had doubts about her ability to teach right and wrong. Cassie had accepted that it wouldn't be easy when she'd made the decision to raise Jake on her own with no family at all nearby to help out.

And it should have been okay. They might never be rich, but Jake was loved. She had a steady job. Their basic needs were met. There were plenty of positive influences in his life.

Maybe if Jake had been an average little kid, everything would have been just fine, but he had his father's brilliance and her penchant for mischief. It was clearly a dangerous combination.

"If you'll give me that list of names, Jake will write the notes tonight. We'll be back in the morning with those and the money," she said grimly.

"But, Mom," Jake began. One look at Cassie's face and the protest died on his lips. His expression turned sullen.

"Jake, could you wait outside with Earlene for just a minute?" the sheriff said. "I'd like to speak to your mother."

Jake slid out of the chair and, with one last backward glance, left the room. When he'd gone, Joshua faced Cassie, eyes twinkling.

"That boy of yours is a handful," he said.

"No kidding."

"You ever think about getting together with his daddy? Seems to me like he could use a man's influence."

"Not a chance," Cassie said fiercely.

Cole Davis might be the smartest, sexiest man she'd ever met. He might be the son of Winding River's biggest rancher. But she wouldn't marry him if he were the last chance she had to escape the fires of hell. He'd sweet-talked her into his bed when she was eighteen and he was twenty, but once that mission had been accomplished, she hadn't set eyes on him again. He'd gone back to college without so much as a goodbye.

When she'd discovered she was pregnant, she was too proud to try to track Cole down and plead for help. She'd left town, her reputation in tatters, determined to build a decent life for herself and her baby someplace where people weren't always expecting the worst of her.

Not that she hadn't given them cause to think poorly of her. She'd been rebellious from the moment she'd discovered that breaking the rules was a whole lot more fun than following them. She'd given her mother fits from the time she'd been a two-year-old whose favorite word was *no,* right on through her teens when she hadn't said no nearly enough.

If there was trouble in town, Cassie was the first person everyone looked to as ringleader. Her pregnancy hadn't surprised a single soul. Rather than endure the knowing looks and clucking remarks, rather than ask her mother to do the same, she'd simply fled, stopping in the first town where she'd spotted a Help Wanted sign in a diner window.

In the years since, she had made only rare trips back to visit her mother, and she'd never once asked about Cole or his family. If her mother suspected who Jake's father was, she'd never admitted it. The topic was off-limits to this day. Jake was Cassie's alone. Most of the time she was justifiably proud of the job she'd done raising him. She resented Joshua's implication that she wasn't up to the task on her own.

"Are you saying Jake wouldn't have done this if his father had been around?" she asked, an edge to her voice. "What could he have done that I haven't? I've taught Jake that it's wrong to steal. The message has been reinforced in Sunday school. And, believe me, he will be punished for this. He may well be grounded till he's twenty-one."

Joshua held up his hand. "I wasn't criticizing you. Kids get into trouble even with the best parents around, but with boys especially, they need a solid male role model."

Cassie didn't especially want her son following in Cole Davis's footsteps. There had to be better role models around. One was sitting right in front of her.

"He has you, Joshua," she pointed out. "Since you've been coming around the diner, he's spent a lot of time with you. He looks up to you. If anyone represents authority and law and order, you do. Did that help?"

"Point taken." He regarded her with concern. "Are you going to take that trip Jake was talking about? Obviously, it's something that he really cares about."

"I don't see how we can."

"If it's a matter of money, the way the boy said, it could be worked out," he said. "Earlene and I—"

"I'm not taking money from you," she said fiercely. "Or from Earlene. She's done enough for me."

"I think you should consider it," Joshua said slowly. His expression turned uneasy. "Look, Earlene would have my hide if she knew I was suggesting this, but I think you might want to give some thought to staying in Winding River when you do go back there." He said it as if their going was a done deal despite her expressed reluctance.

Cassie stared at him in shock. "Are you throwing us out of town?"

Joshua chuckled. "Nothing that dramatic. I was just

thinking that it might be good for Jake to have more family around, more people to look out for him, lend a little extra stability to his life. It would be a help to you and maybe keep him out of mischief. This latest escapade can't be dismissed as easily as some of the others. Sometimes even kids need a fresh start. I've heard you tell Earlene yourself that he gives his teachers fits at school. Maybe a whole new environment where no one's expecting the worst would help him settle down. Better to get him in hand now than when he hits his teens and the trouble can get a whole lot more serious."

"I know," Cassie said, defeated. Nobody knew better than she did about fresh starts and living down past mistakes. Even so, it wasn't as easy as Joshua made it sound. She didn't bother to explain that her mother was all the family they'd have in Winding River and that friends there were few and far between. She had a stronger support system right here. Unfortunately, Joshua clearly didn't want to hear that.

"I'll think about it," she said eventually. "I promise."

But going home for a few days for a class reunion was one thing. Going back to live in the same town where Cole Davis and his father ruled was quite another.

Unfortunately, though, it sounded as if circumstances—and the well-intentioned sheriff—might not be giving her much choice.

"Blast it all, boy, I ain't getting any younger," Frank Davis grumbled over the eggs, ham and grits that were likely to do him in. "Who's going to run this ranch when I die?"

Cole put down his fork and sighed. He and his father had had this same discussion at least a thousand times in the past eight years.

"I thought that was why I was here," Cole said. "So you could go to your eternal rest knowing that the ranch was still in Davis hands."

His father waved off the comment. "Your heart's not in this place. I might as well admit it. It could fall down around us for all the attention you pay it. You spend half the night locked away in that office of yours with all that fancy computer equipment. For the life of me I can't figure what's so all-fired fascinating about staring at a screen with a bunch of gobbledygook on it."

"Last year that gobbledygook earned three times as much as this ranch," Cole pointed out, knowing even as he spoke that his father wouldn't be impressed. If it didn't have to do with cattle or land, Frank Davis didn't trust it. Cole had given up expecting his father to be proud of his accomplishments in the high-tech world. He got higher praise when he negotiated top dollar for their cattle at market.

"All I have to say is, if I'd known then what I know now, I wouldn't have been so quick to break up you and that Collins girl. Maybe you'd have been settled down by now. Maybe you would have a little respect for this ranch your great-grandfather started."

Cole was not about to head off down that particular path. Any discussion of Cassie was doomed. He remembered all too clearly what had happened the minute his father had learned that the two of them were getting close. He had packed up Cole's things and shipped him off to school weeks before the start of his junior year.

To his everlasting regret, there hadn't been a thing Cole could do about it. At that point he'd wanted his college diploma too much to risk his father's wrath. That diploma had been his ticket away from ranching. He'd sent a note to Cassie explaining and begging for her understanding. Her reply had been curt. She'd told him it didn't matter, that he could do whatever suited him. She intended to get on with her life.

Ironically, the ink had barely been dry on his diploma when his father had suffered a heart attack and pleaded with him to return home. Now here he was, spending his days running the ranch he hated and his nights working on the computer programming he loved. It wasn't as awful as it could have been. The reality was he could design his computer programs anywhere, even in a town where he had to dodge old memories at every turn.

By the time he'd come back to Winding River, Cassie Collins had been gone, and no one was saying where. Up until then her mother had been kind to him, standing in for the mother he'd lost at an early age. But when he'd gone to see her on his return, Edna Collins had slammed the door in his face. He hadn't understood why, but he hadn't forced the issue.

Over the years he'd heard Cassie's name mentioned, usually in connection with some wild, reckless stunt that had been exaggerated by time. He'd debated questioning her best friends when they occasionally passed through town, but he'd told himself that if he'd meant anything at all to Cassie, she would have responded differently to his note. Maybe she'd just viewed that summer as a wild fling. Maybe he was the only one who'd seen it as something more. Either way, it was probably for the best to leave things as they were. Wherever she was, she was no doubt happily married by now.

When he was doing some of his rare soul-searching, Cole could admit that the romance had been ill-fated from the beginning. He and Cassie were as different as two people could be. Until they'd met, he'd been the classic nerd, both studious and shy. Only an innate athletic ability and the Davis name had made him popular.

Cassie, with her warmth and exuberance and try-anything mentality, had brought out an unexpected wild streak in him. He would have done anything to earn one of her devastating smiles. The summer they had spent together had been the best time of his life. Just the memory of it was enough to stir more lust than any flesh-and-blood woman had for quite some time.

He brought himself up short. Those days were long past, and it was definitely best not to go back there.

"Well?" his father demanded. "Don't you have anything to say about that?"

"Leave it alone, Pop. The quickest way to get rid of me is to start bringing up old news."

"I hear she's coming back to town for this big reunion the school has planned," his father said, his expression sly. "Is that news current enough for you?"

Cole didn't like the way his pulse reacted to the announcement. It ricocheted as if he'd just been told that his company had outearned Microsoft.

"That has nothing to do with me," he insisted.

"She's not married."

Cole ignored that, though he was forced to concede that his heart started beating double time at the news.

"Has a son she's raising on her own," his father added.

"You know, I think you missed your calling," Cole said. "You should have started a newspaper. You seem to know all the gossip in town."

"You saying you're not interested?"

Cole met his father's gaze without flinching. "That's what I'm telling you."

Frank gave a little nod. "Okay, then. How about a game of poker tonight? I could call a few men. Have 'em out here in an hour."

Though he was relieved that his father had suddenly switched gears, Cole's gaze narrowed suspiciously. "Why would you want to do that?"

A grin spread across Frank Davis's face. "'Cause a man who can lie with a straight face the way you just did is wasting it if he's not playing a high-stakes game of cards."

2

As she and Jake drove through the Snowy Range toward Winding River two months later, Joshua Cartwright's words played over and over in Cassie's head like the refrain from some country music tune. Going home, even temporarily, wasn't nearly as simple as he'd made it sound, which was why she'd flatly refused to pack up everything she owned and bring it with her. Once she decided whether to stay—*if* she decided to stay—she would go back for the rest of her belongings.

Meantime, with every familiar landmark she passed, her pulse escalated and her palms began to sweat. Time hadn't dulled any of her trepidation.

Jake, however, had no such qualms. He was literally bouncing on the seat in his enthusiasm, taking in everything, commenting on most of it until she wanted to scream at him to be quiet. Nerves, she told herself. It was just nerves. Jake wasn't doing anything wrong. In fact, it was good that he was so excited. There had been far too few adventures in his young life. And it had been four years, she reminded herself. He'd been only five on their last brief visit. This all seemed as new and exciting to him as it was terrifying to her.

"How far now?" he asked for the hundredth time.

Cassie managed a thin smile. "About ten miles less than the last time you asked. We'll be there by lunchtime."

"And all these ranches, the great big ones, belong to people you know?"

"Most of them," she conceded.

She dreaded the moment when the wrought-iron gate for the Double D came into sight. Frank Davis had named it that the day his son was born, anticipating the time when the two of them would run it together. He'd never envisioned his son bringing home the daughter of a woman who took in mending. If anything, he'd wanted Cole to marry someone whose neighboring land could be added to the holdings of the Double D.

Unfortunately for him, Cole had never looked twice at their neighbors' daughters. She wondered, though, if that had changed, if Frank had gotten his way.

As the road twisted and turned, the snowcapped mountains gave way to rolling foothills. Black Angus cattle dotted the landscape. Bubbling streams and a broader, winding river cut through the land, the banks lined by thick stands of leafy cottonwoods.

Eventually the road dipped, went over a narrow span of bridge, and there it was, the town in which she'd grown up, complete with the water tower she'd once climbed and repainted shocking pink. It was a pristine white now, with flowing blue script proudly spelling out Winding River and, beneath that, in bolder letters: WELCOME.

A sign by the side of the road proudly announced the population at 1,939. If she decided to stay, would it soon be altered to say 1,941? Cassie wondered. Or would the ebb and flow of births and deaths, departures and new arrivals, keep it forever the same?

"Mom, look," Jake said in an awestruck tone.

"What?"

"Over there," he said, pointing to something she'd never seen before.

It was an airstrip, not much by big-city standards, but there were half a dozen very fancy private planes parked outside the hangar. Obviously over the past ten years some folks with money had settled in Winding River. Years ago a few of the ranchers, Cole's father among them, had kept small planes for making rapid inspections of their far-flung land, but nothing like these.

"Awesome," Jake declared, his eyes as big as saucers.

"Awesome," Cassie was forced to agree, even as she wondered at the implication.

Her mother hadn't mentioned anything to suggest that big changes were taking place in town, but then Edna Collins wasn't the kind to take stock of her surroundings or to comment on them. She stayed mostly to herself, spending her time on the mending she did to make ends meet and on church work. Because she was relieved to no longer be the target of it herself, she didn't indulge in gossip. Cassie regretted not asking more questions since her last trip home. Even her mother had to have noticed an influx of wealthy newcomers.

"Can we drive through town before we go to Grandma's?" Jake pleaded. "I've forgotten what it was like. Besides, I'm starved. Grandma won't have anything but peanut butter and jelly."

"Which she is expecting you to eat," Cassie reminded him, grateful for the excuse to put off the moment when she would have to start seeing people, facing their curious stares and blunt questions.

"We'll go into town after lunch," she promised, grinning at him. "You can have ice cream for dessert."

The promise was enough to pacify Jake, and it bought her some time…time to ask questions, time to brace herself for the possibility of running into Jake's father.

Time to get used to the increasingly likely possibility that this was going to be home again.

Cole was mending fences near the highway when the old blue sedan sped past. It said a lot about his state of mind that he even looked up. Usually his concentration was intent on the task at hand, but ever since his father's sly comment about Cassie's return, passing cars had caught his interest.

This time there was no mistaking the thick brown hair caught up in a ponytail and pulled through the opening of a baseball cap. Cassie had worn her hair exactly that way on too many occasions, making his fingers itch to free it and watch it tumble to her shoulders in silky waves. His belly tightened and his hand trembled unmistakably, either at the memory or the glimpse of her. Maybe both.

He forced his attention back to the fence, aimed his hammer at the nail with too much force and too little concentration and caught his thumb instead. His muttered expletive carried across the field to his father, who stared at him with that smug expression that had become increasingly familiar lately.

"See something interesting?" his father inquired tartly.

"Not a thing," Cole insisted, though the image of Cassie with the breeze stealing wisps of hair to tease her cheeks was firmly planted in his head. If a glimpse could tie him up in knots, what would seeing her up close do to him? He didn't want to find out.

He just needed to make himself scarce for a few days and she'd be gone again, back to wherever she lived, taking that mysterious boy of hers with her. Then his life would return to normal. His days would be uncomplicated. His nights…well, they might be boring from a social perspective, but they would be rewarding financially. He did his best work in the middle of the night when the day's stresses faded and his mind could wander.

"You going into town this afternoon?" his father asked, his expression neutral.

"Hadn't planned to."

"We could use an order of feed."

"Then pick up the phone and order it," Cole retorted, refusing to take the less-than-subtle bait.

"Just thought you might have other business to see to."

"I do," he agreed, tossing his tools into the back of the pickup. "If you need me, I'll be at the house."

His father stared at him with a disgusted expression. "Working on that blasted computer, I suppose."

"Exactly."

With any luck he could create a computer game in which the meddling owner of a ranch was murdered by his put-upon son and nobody caught on.

From the moment she drove into the driveway at her mother's place, Cassie was taken back in time. Nothing had changed. The little white house, not much more than a cottage, really, still had a sagging porch and needed paint. As always, there was a pot of struggling red geraniums in need of water on the steps. A swing hung from a sturdy but rusting chain. The white paint had long since chipped away, leaving the swing a weathered gray.

Inside, the walls were a faded cream, the drapes too dark and heavy, as if her mother was determined to shut out the world that had never been kind to her. A sewing basket, overflowing with colorful threads, sat beside the worn chair where her mother liked to work under a bare hundred-watt bulb.

They left Jake glued to the TV and went down the hall with the luggage. Cassie discovered her room still had posters of her favorite musicians on the walls and a Denver Broncos bedspread on one twin bed. She'd bought that navy-blue and orange spread as a rebellion against the pink paint and ruffled curtains her mother had insisted on. The second bed still had a frilly, flowered spread on it. Cassie suspected its mate was still shoved in the back of the closet, where she'd put it years ago.

"I haven't changed anything," her mother said, twisting her hands nervously. "I thought you'd like to know that home was always going to be the way you remembered it."

Cassie didn't have the heart to say that some things were best forgotten. Instead she gave her mother a fierce hug. For all of her flaws this woman had done her best to give Cassie a good life. She'd lost her husband in a freak accident at a grain elevator when Cassie was little more than a toddler, but she'd found a way to be a stay-at-home mom and keep food on the table. And despite her private disapproval of her daughter's behavior and the occasional long-suffering sighs, she hadn't turned her back on Cassie, not ever.

"Thanks, Mom," she said, finally acknowledging what was long overdue.

Her mother looked startled and faintly pleased, but her face quickly assumed its more familiar neutral mask. "Will you and Jake be okay in here? You won't mind sharing a room?"

"Of course not. This will be fine. We're just glad to be here."

"Are you?" her mother asked, peering at her intently. "It's been a long time."

"Too long," Cassie agreed, studying her mother's face and seeing new wrinkles. There was more gray in her hair, too. "Jake and I have missed you."

That pleased look came and went in a heartbeat. "Will your friends be home for the reunion?" Edna asked, retreating as always to a less emotional topic.

"I haven't spoken to any of them recently. I hope so. It would be wonderful to see them again."

Her mother shook her head. "I can't imagine what Lauren must be like. Do you suppose all that fame has gone to her head? She certainly hasn't spent a dime of the money she's making on her folks. That house of theirs is tumbling down around them."

"Don't blame Lauren," Cassie said. "Her parents wouldn't take anything from her. They said an acting career was too precarious and she needed to save every last cent in case it didn't last. Lauren hired a carpenter and sent him over, but her parents just sent him away."

"That father of hers always was a stubborn old coot," Edna said. "Still, all the attention she gets from TV and the newspapers must have changed her some."

Cassie chuckled. "Lauren never cared about fame or money. I'm sure she's as surprised as the rest of us about the turn her life has taken."

"Well, Hollywood has a way of changing people. That's all I'm saying," her mother replied, disapproval written all over her face.

"Not Lauren," Cassie said with absolute confidence. If any of them had her head on straight, it was Lauren. She was always the one to express caution when a prank threatened to get out of hand, always the one who came up with a thoughtful gesture to make amends when someone's feelings were hurt.

"I suppose you know her better than I do," her

mother said, though her doubts were still evident. "Are you hungry? I've made some sandwiches, and there are cookies. Mildred brought them by this morning. Oatmeal-raisin. Your favorite, if I'm not mistaken."

"Mildred's oatmeal-raisin cookies were always the best," Cassie enthused. And their neighbor had always come up with excuses for bringing over a plateful to share with a little girl whose own mother rarely baked. Those treats had earned Mildred a special place in Cassie's heart. "I'll have to stop by later to thank her."

"She'd like that. She doesn't get out much these days. Her arthritis makes it difficult for her to get around. Jake can stay with me while you and Mildred visit."

Cassie's gaze narrowed. "Don't you think Mildred would like to see your grandson?"

"There's nothing for a boy to do over there. He'd be bored," Edna responded.

She said it in a hurried way that told Cassie she was only making up hasty excuses. "Mom, I can't keep Jake hidden away in the house while we're here."

For an instant her mother looked ashamed. "No, of course not. I never meant to imply that you should."

"Surely people have gotten over what happened by now."

"Yes, I'm sure you're right. It's just that…"

Cassie met her gaze evenly. She had known they were going to have to face this. Now was as good a time as any. "What?" she asked, prepared for battle.

"He looks so much like his father now."

That was the last thing Cassie had expected her

mother to say, but it was true. Jake did look like Cole, from his sun-streaked hair to his blue eyes, from those freckles across his nose to the shape of his mouth. Even the glasses were a reminder of the ones Cole had worn until high school, when he'd finally been persuaded to trade them for contacts.

Cole had been a self-described skinny, awkward geek until he'd gone away to college. There he'd begun to fill out, his body becoming less awkward and lanky. And after a summer at home working the ranch, his lean body had been all hard muscle by the time they'd started dating in earnest. Cassie imagined the same thing would happen to Jake one day, and that he would be breaking girls' hearts just like his daddy had.

The shock, of course, was that her mother could see all that. "You know," Cassie said flatly.

It was her mother's turn to look startled. "Did you think I didn't?"

"You never said a word."

Her mother shrugged. "There was nothing to say. What was done was done. No point in talking about it."

Cassie sank down on the bed, her thoughts in turmoil. All this time her mother had known the truth. She met Edna's gaze.

"Is Cole...?" Her voice trailed off.

"He's here," her mother said tightly. "Has been ever since college. He came back to help out when Frank had a heart attack. If you ask me, the man talked himself into getting sick just to manipulate that boy, but they seem to be getting on well enough out there."

Another secret kept, Cassie thought, just as she'd kept Cole's identity a secret from Jake. Why did it surprise her that her mother could be reticent about something so important? Edna had always kept her own counsel, never saying more than the situation required for politeness. Even now she didn't elaborate. If Cassie wanted to know more, she was going to have to ask directly.

"Is he married?" she asked, not sure she wanted to hear the answer.

"No."

Relief warred with surprise. Cole must be the county's prize catch. How had he managed to elude all the single women of Winding River and their ambitious parents, especially with Frank Davis no doubt pressuring him to produce an heir?

It didn't matter, she told herself sternly. It had nothing to do with her, except that it complicated her situation that Cole was still living right here. How could she possibly keep him from finding out that Jake was his son if he was practically underfoot? And if he did figure it out, what would his reaction be? Would he pretend ignorance or would he want to claim his son? She wasn't sure which thought terrified her more. Explaining to Jake that his father was here when she'd always been so elusive about his whereabouts wouldn't be any easier.

"Hey, Mom, can we eat? I'm starved."

Jake's voice cut into her thoughts. Struggling with the unexpected taste of fear in her mouth, Cassie stayed silent a minute too long, drawing a puzzled look from her son and an understanding one from her mother.

"I'll get him his sandwich," her mother offered. "You spend a few minutes unpacking and getting settled."

She followed Jake from the room, then turned back. "Give some thought to what I said. The Davises are powerful people, and Cole's got a streak of his daddy in him—no matter how you once thought otherwise. They take what's theirs."

Cassie understood the warning and all its implications. If Emma, now an attorney, was coming to the reunion, Cassie would talk to her the second she arrived. Surely Emma would be able to give her some advice on how to protect her rights where Jake was concerned.

And if what her friend had to say wasn't reassuring, Cassie would take her son and leave. Perhaps she couldn't go back to work for Earlene, but they could move someplace entirely new. Cheyenne, maybe. Or Laramie. Maybe all the way north to someplace like Jackson Hole. A fresh start in a whole new town wouldn't be easy, but if it was necessary to keep her son away from Cole, Cassie would do it and never look back.

Just then the phone rang, and a moment later her mother poked her head into the bedroom. "It's Karen. She heard you were back. Somebody in town must have seen you drive through."

A smile spread across Cassie's face as she walked down the hall to the little alcove where the old-fashioned black phone still sat on a rickety mahogany table. The first of the Calamity Janes was checking in.

"Hey, cowgirl, how are you?" she asked Karen. "And how's that handsome husband of yours?"

"Working too hard. We both are."

"But you'll be here for the reunion?"

"I wouldn't miss it."

"And the others? Have you heard from any of them?"

"They're all coming. In fact, that's why I'm calling. Lunch tomorrow at Stella's. I've told her to put a reserved sign on our favorite table in the back. Can you be there at noon?"

"I can't wait," Cassie said truthfully. "You have no idea how much I've missed you guys."

"Same here," Karen said. "And we're counting on you to think of something outrageous we can do to make this reunion as memorable as all our years in high school."

"Not me," Cassie said fervently. "I'm older and wiser now."

"And a mother," Karen said quietly. "How's Jake?"

"He's the best thing I ever did."

"And Cole? He's here, you know."

"I know."

"What will you do if you run into him?"

Cassie sighed. "I wish I knew."

"Maybe it's time to tell him the truth. I always thought you were making a mistake in not doing that in the beginning. He loved you."

"He used me."

"No," Karen said. "Anyone who ever saw the two

of you together knew better than that. How you could miss it is beyond me."

"He left me without a word," Cassie reminded her.

"A mistake," Karen agreed. "But you compounded it."

"How?"

"By giving up on him. By never asking what happened. By running away. For a girl who had more gumption than anyone I knew, you wimped out when it really counted."

It was an old argument, but it still put Cassie on the defensive. "I had no choice," she insisted.

"Oh, sweetie, we all have choices," she said, sounding suddenly tired.

The hint of exhaustion was so unlike the ex-cheerleader that it startled Cassie. If she'd been a ringleader, Karen had always been her most energetic sidekick, always eager for a lark.

"Karen, are you okay? Is everything all right at the ranch?"

"Just too much work and too little time."

"But you and Caleb are happy, right?"

"Blissfully, at least when we can stay awake long enough to remember why we got married in the first place." She sighed. "Don't listen to me. I love my life. I wouldn't trade it for anything. And I will tell you every last, boring detail when I see you tomorrow."

"Love you, pal."

"You, too. I can't wait to see you. Bring Jake along. I want to see if he's as handsome as his daddy."

"Not tomorrow. Can you imagine a nine-year-old

listening to us talk about old times? Besides, it might give him ideas."

"Meaning?"

"Meaning he gets into enough mischief without getting any tips from us. And I'll tell you *that* story when I see you."

As she hung up the phone, she suddenly felt as if all her fears and cares had slipped away. The Calamity Janes were getting together tomorrow. Let Cole find out about Jake and do his worst. She had backup on the way. And together, the Calamity Janes were indomitable.

3

The door to Cole's home office burst open, and his father charged in as if he were on a mission. Normally Cole would have protested the intrusion into his private sanctuary, but he was too exhausted. He'd been up all night putting the finishing touches on a program that would revolutionize the way businesses interconnected on the internet. His gut told him it was going to be the most lucrative bit of technology he'd ever created.

"What?" he asked as his father loomed over him, a frown on his face as he studied the computer screen.

"Is that supposed to make sense?" Frank asked, leaning down for a closer look.

"Not to you, but to another computer it's magic," Cole said.

"Guess I'll have to take your word on that."

"I'm sure you didn't barge in here to talk about computers," Cole said dryly. "What's on your mind? You're usually in town at Stella's at this hour swapping lies with all your buddies."

"Been there. Now I'm back."

"I see," Cole said. "And you're what? Reporting in with the latest Winding River gossip?"

"Don't sass me, son. I did happen to pick up a little bit of news I thought might interest you."

"Unless it's a way to squeeze eight hours of sleep into the two hours I have before I meet with Don Rollins about that bull you want, I doubt it."

Undaunted, his father announced, "Cassie and her friends will be at Stella's at noon today. Stella's about to bust a gusset at the thought that a famous movie star is going to be dining in her establishment. That's what she said, 'dining in my establishment.' Talk about putting on airs. She's talking about little Lauren Winters. We've known the girl since she was in diapers. I can't see what all the ruckus is about."

He shook his head. "Well, never mind about that. The point is that Cassie will be there."

Cole's pulse did a little hop, skip and jump, which he resolutely blamed on exhaustion. "So?"

"Just thought you'd want to know."

"And now I do." He stared evenly at his father. "Are you waiting for some sort of reaction?"

"As a matter of fact, I am. Any hot-blooded son of mine would take a shower, shave, splash on a little of that fancy aftershave women like and haul his butt into town. Now's your chance, son. Don't waste it."

"I'm confused about something. When did you become such a big fan of Cassie's?"

Guilt flickered in his father's eyes for an instant

before he shrugged. "The point is *you* cared about her once."

"A long time ago. You saw to it that it came to nothing."

"Well, maybe I regret that."

"Do you really?" Cole asked doubtfully, then shook his head. "Look, forget it. I have an appointment, anyway."

"I can buy my own blasted bull," his father retorted. "Seems to me like you ought to have better fish to fry."

Cole raked a hand through his hair, spared one last glance at the computer screen before shutting it down, then stood up.

"A shower sounds good," he conceded. "As for the rest, if I were you, I'd be real careful about telling me how capable you are of managing without me. I might get the idea that I could leave this ranch and Winding River and you wouldn't even miss me."

His father began to sputter a lot of nonsense about not saying any such thing, but Cole ignored the protest and headed upstairs for a long, hot shower to work out the kinks in his neck and shoulders. Given the state of his thoughts about Cassie Collins, he probably should have let the water run cold.

An hour later, feeling moderately more alive, he left the house and headed into town. Not to satisfy his father, he assured himself. Not even to catch a glimpse of Cassie. Just to grab a decent meal that he didn't have to cook himself, maybe pick up a few things at the feed and grain store. If Cassie happened to be around, well, that was pure coincidence, the kind of thing that hap-

pened in small towns. People bumped into people all
the time, exchanged a few words, then went on about
their business. It didn't have to mean a thing.

Yeah, right. He sneezed as he caught a whiff of
that aftershave he'd splashed on at the last minute. He
yanked a handkerchief out of his pocket and rubbed at
his cheeks, but the scent stayed with him, mocking his
avowed intentions about this trip into town.

He glanced in the rearview mirror of his truck,
assured himself that no one was behind him, then
slammed on the brakes right there in the middle of
the highway. He could quit lying to himself right now,
turn around, go back to the ranch and take that nap he'd
been craving before his father had shown up. And if
he wanted to salvage a lick of pride, that was exactly
what he ought to do.

"Do it," he muttered. "Be sensible for once in your
miserable life."

But the lure of seeing Cassie again was too much to
ignore. It had been a long time since he'd let temptation get the better of him. Surely he could be forgiven
a single lapse.

With a sigh he took his foot off the brake and kept
going, heading straight for trouble.

"Oh, my word, I never thought I'd see all of you
back together again," Stella Partlow said, hands on her
ample hips as her gaze circled the table at the back of
her diner. "These class reunions always take me right
back. Not a one of you has changed a lick."

"Not even Lauren?" Cassie asked the woman who

had given her her first job as a waitress back in high school. Stella had ignored the gossip and patiently gone about the business of turning Cassie into a responsible employee.

At Cassie's question, Stella peered intently at Lauren, then shook her head. "Nope. She was always a beauty. Back then she just didn't make the most of the looks God gave her. I've always said a good haircut and a few beauty products can turn the plainest woman into something a man can't resist."

"You still selling Avon?" Emma teased.

"Well, of course I am," Stella retorted. "But right this second I'm pushing hamburgers. How about five with the works, just the way you used to like 'em?"

"And fries," Karen said with a gleam of anticipation in her eyes.

"And chocolate milk shakes," Cassie added, all but licking her lips. Nobody anywhere made shakes as thick and rich as Stella's. Not even Earlene had the knack.

"Except for me," Lauren corrected.

"I imagine you'll be having a cherry cola, same as always," Stella said, giving her a wink. "Coming right up. You all try to keep the noise level down back here. I've got tourists, and they like a little peace and quiet while they eat."

"I'll bet if you point out that they're in the presence of a gen-u-ine movie star, they won't care how much racket we make," Gina told her.

Lauren frowned. "Stop it, you guys. Acting's a job.

It's not who I am. If anybody ought to know that, you should," she reminded them.

Cassie thought she detected an edge in her friend's voice, but Lauren laughed just as hard as the rest of them at the teasing comments that followed. And when they plagued her with questions about her leading men, her responses were as ribald as the discussions they'd had about boys in high school.

When their drinks came, Cassie raised her glass. "A toast. To the Calamity Janes—may all our troubles be behind us."

Just as the others joined in, Cassie's glance strayed to the window looking onto Main Street. Cole Davis was standing on the sidewalk staring right back at her, his hands jammed in the pockets of his faded denims, his jaw set and an unreadable expression in his eyes.

"Uh-oh," Karen murmured. "Looks as if that toast came too late. Trouble is about to come calling."

All of the women followed Cole's progress as he strode to the door and entered the diner.

Cassie swallowed hard and prayed that she wouldn't make a complete fool of herself. It was just a chance meeting with an old flame. Nothing more. Nothing to cause this churning in the pit of her stomach. There was no reason for her heart to slam against her ribs or her pulse to ricochet wildly. Jake was safely at home with her mother, so there was no reason for this little lick of fear that was sliding up the back of her throat.

Get a grip, she told herself mentally as she lifted her gaze to meet his. Those unflinching blue eyes were just as devastating as ever. Her stomach flipped over.

Her heart pounded. Her pulse ricocheted. Reason apparently had nothing to do with anything where Cole was concerned, not even after ten long years.

Tension swirled as she felt four gazes pinned on her, waiting to see what she would do. She drew in a deep breath and reminded herself she was a grown-up woman—a mother, in fact. She could handle a simple little exchange with a man, even if he did happen to be the father of the child she'd kept from him…even if she'd spent years nurturing her hatred of him.

"Cole," she acknowledged with a slight nod.

"Cassie."

His voice was as low and sexy as she'd remembered, his face more mature, his lips in that same straight line that had always dared her to try to coax a smile from him. His blue eyes were as cold as a wintry sky, though why they were eluded her. *He* was the one who'd walked out on *her*. If anyone had a right to be fuming mad, it was she. He ought to be on his knees apologizing, which was about as likely as the sun starting to rise in the west.

When it looked as if the conversation had run into a dead end before getting off the ground, Karen, ever the peacemaker, jumped in.

"How's Frank?" she asked, as if the tension weren't already thick enough without bringing up Cole's father.

"Same as ever. Cantankerous," he said, bestowing the smile on her that he'd refused Cassie.

"Still grumbling about getting you married off?" Karen teased. Cassie poked an elbow sharply in her ribs.

"The topic does come up now and again," Cole said, amusement tilting the corners of his mouth.

"Your father always gets his way in the end," Gina chimed in. "I don't see why you don't just get it over with. The way I hear it from my folks, every female in ten counties is after you."

Cole grinned at her, a full-fledged smile, capable of breaking hearts. "Including you? How about it, Gina? Are you available?"

Cassie scowled as she waited for her friend's reply.

"If you'd asked a week ago, I'd have turned you down flat," Gina said. "Now, who knows?"

The flip remark drew stares from the others. Something wasn't right with Gina, either. Cassie had sensed it from the moment they'd sat down, but there hadn't been time to get into it. Whatever it was, it had to be serious for her to even joke about a willingness to leave her beloved New York and stay in Wyoming.

Cassie couldn't give the matter any more thought just then, though, because she glanced up and spotted Jake and his grandmother coming across the street. After their talk yesterday, Cassie had thought there was no way her mother would bring the boy into town, but she'd clearly underestimated Jake's powers of persuasion. He'd been pestering them for ice cream ever since Cassie had reneged on her promise of it the day before.

A sense of dread filled her as she watched their progress. She did not want Cole meeting her son—not today, not ever—though that was likely to be tricky if she decided she was back home to stay. After the awkwardness of the past few minutes, she was beginning to see that staying in Winding River might not be feasible. She couldn't live with the kind of panic that had streaked through her when she'd seen Jake unwittingly heading straight toward his daddy.

"You guys, I have to run," she said, dropping some money on the table and slipping out of the booth. "I have to get home."

"But our food…" Lauren began, then glanced outside and fell silent.

Cassie circled around behind Cole, giving him a wide berth, hoping that her friends would keep him occupied just long enough for her to catch Jake and her mother and detour them away from the restaurant.

"I'll call you," Karen said.

"And we'll see you tomorrow night," Lauren added.

"Absolutely. I can't wait," she said before dashing off to intercept her son.

She was dismayed when she realized Cole had fallen into step beside her. Just outside the door, he gazed down into her eyes, his expression vaguely troubled.

"Why the sudden rush, Cassie? I didn't scare you off, did I?"

His tone mocked her, but there was that contradictory flicker of concern in his eyes. She didn't know what to make of either, and right now she didn't have time to grapple with it. Disaster was less than half a block away.

"Of course not," she said a little too sharply. "I just have to get home, that's all. I promised my mother I wouldn't be gone long."

His expression softened. "How's your mother doing?" he asked with apparent sincerity.

Cassie thought back to the special bond Cole and her mom had shared. It, too, had died when Cole abandoned Cassie. If she were a more generous person, Cassie mused, she might regret that. Cole, who'd lost his own mother at an early age, had basked in the attention Edna had given him.

Cassie glanced down the street and saw that her mother was disappearing through a door down the street. Apparently she'd caught a glimpse of Cole and wisely hurried Jake toward the trendy new restaurant and coffee bar Cassie had noticed earlier. Cassie breathed a sigh of relief and turned her gaze back to Cole.

"Fine," she said. "My mother's just fine."

He seemed startled by that. "Really?"

Something in his voice told Cassie he knew something she didn't. She stared at him intently. "Why did you say that like that?"

He evaded her gaze, his expression suddenly uneasy. "Like what?"

"Stop it, Cole. Don't play games with me. Is there something going on with my mother that I don't know about? Is she keeping something from me?"

"You'll have to ask her that."

All thoughts of Cole's near-miss encounter with his son fled as she stared at him and tried to read his deliberately enigmatic expression. He was hiding something. It was plain as day. "Dammit, Cole. Tell me."

"I just inquired after your mother, Cassie. I was

being polite," he insisted mildly. "Don't read anything more into it."

"Nothing with you is ever that simple."

"You're a fine one to talk."

Her temper flared, and her gaze clashed with his. "What is *that* supposed to mean?"

"Nothing. Never mind. There's no point in dredging up old news." He bit back a curse, then shook his head. "I knew coming into town today was a mistake."

Cassie was startled by the note of betrayal in his voice. "Have you been rewriting history, Cole? *You* left *me.* It wasn't the other way around."

"Wasn't it?" he asked with unmistakable resentment.

Her own bitter memories, always just beneath the surface, bubbled up. "How can you ask that? One night you were making love to me, telling me how incredible I was, the next day you were gone."

"I explained that."

"Explained it?" she repeated incredulously. "When was that? Until you walked through the door at Stella's a few minutes ago, I hadn't seen or heard from you since the night you stole my virginity."

He winced. "Dammit, Cassie, it wasn't like that. I didn't steal anything. We made love. It was a mutual decision. Besides, I left you a note. I know you got it, because you sent me an answer. Do I have to remind you what was in it? You said you wanted nothing more to do with me, that I should go back to college and forget all about you. You said you intended to get on with your life and that I was no longer a part of it."

Disbelief washed over her. This was ridiculous. Why would he make up such an absurd lie? No doubt to soothe his own conscience.

"I never wrote such a note and you know it."

"Really?" he said scathingly. "Remind me to show it to you sometime. I've kept it all these years as a reminder not to trust a woman's pretty words of love, especially when she says them in my bed."

Before she could recover, he turned on his heel and walked away, leaving Cassie staring after him, wide-eyed with shock. Not one single word he'd said made a lick of sense. She'd never gotten any letter from him. Nor had she sent a reply. But it was clear that Cole believed otherwise.

She felt a blast of cool air as the door to Stella's opened behind her. "You okay?" Gina asked, draping an arm around her shoulders.

"I'm…" She thought about what had just happened. "Confused, I guess."

"About what? Your feelings for Cole?"

"No. He said some things. Things that didn't make any sense."

Gina's gaze narrowed. "What things? If he upset you, I'll get the others and we'll beat him up for you."

The comment drew a weak smile. They would do it, too. "I don't think that will be necessary," Cassie said. "But I love you for offering."

"Come back inside and eat your burger."

"I can't. I need to find Jake and my mother. I want to make sure that Cole didn't catch a glimpse of them." She thought then of his odd reaction to her claim that her mother was fine. "I need to talk to Mom about something else, too."

"But you'll be at the party tomorrow, right?"

"I'll be there," Cassie promised. She met Gina's gaze evenly. "You and I need to have a long talk."

"About?"

"Whatever's going on with you."

"Don't worry about me," Gina said, giving her a hug.

"Then what was that remark to Cole all about? You sounded as if you might actually consider hanging around Winding River instead of going back to New York. I can't believe you would ever walk away from your restaurant."

"I was joking," Gina insisted. "Surely you didn't think I would seriously consider marrying your guy?"

"Cole's not my guy, and that wasn't the point. You might have been joking about that, but you sounded serious about the rest, about staying here."

"So?" Gina said, her expression defiant. "It's home. Are you telling me that the thought of staying here hasn't crossed *your* mind since you've been back?"

"That's different."

"How?"

"It just is," Cassie said. She looked up and saw Jake and her mother emerge from the restaurant down the block carrying ice cream cones. They caught sight of her and headed in her direction.

"We'll finish this conversation tomorrow," she warned Gina. "I'm not buying a word you've said so far."

"And I'm not buying for a second that you're over Cole Davis," Gina retorted. She waved at Cassie's mother, then retreated inside Stella's.

Cassie sighed. Gina was right. If she'd learned nothing else in the past half hour, it was that she was a long, long way from being over Cole Davis.

4

"Mom!"

Grappling with the discovery that her feelings for Cole were as powerful as ever, Cassie barely registered Jake's cry. Then she felt an impatient tug on her arm and gazed down into her son's eyes, eyes the same shade of blue as those of the man who'd just dropped a bombshell, then strolled away.

"What, Jake?" she asked, still distracted by her realization that not even years of bitterness had dimmed what she'd once felt for Cole Davis. Add to that Cole's charge that she'd been at fault, that he hadn't abandoned her at all, but rather *she* had turned her back on *him,* and it was little wonder that she was confused. How could he have gotten it so wrong?

"Mom!" Jake said impatiently. "You're not listening."

"I'm sorry," she said, turning her attention to him.

"Do you know who that was?" Jake demanded, his cheeks flushed with excitement, his eyes sparkling.

Her heart seemed to slam to a stop. "Who?" she asked cautiously, fighting panic.

Had Jake guessed? Had he seen the resemblance between himself and the man with whom she'd been talking? Would a nine-year-old be intuitive enough to guess that a stranger was his father?

A quick glance at her mother reassured her. Her mother gave a slight shake of her head, indicating that so far her secret was safe, both from Cole and her son. No, this was about something else, though she couldn't imagine what.

"That man you were talking to," Jake explained. "Do you know who he is?"

"Of course I know. He's a rancher. He's lived here all his life."

"And you know him?" Jake demanded, clearly awe-struck.

"Yes," she said slowly. Clearly she was missing something. "How do *you* know him?"

"He's Cole Davis," Jake said. "*The* Cole Davis."

When she failed to react, her son regarded her with exasperation. "Mom, you know, the guy who makes all the neat computer programs, remember? Like I told you I wanted to do someday. He's, like, the smartest guy in the whole tech world. I've told you about him, remember?"

She had a vague recollection of that, but it couldn't possibly be the same man. This Cole, *her* Cole, was a rancher, not a computer programmer. Or was he? She had no idea what he'd studied in college. Back then they'd been far too caught up in their hormones to spend a lot of time talking about Cole's plans for the future.

"Are you sure, honey? Cole's from a ranching family. His father owns the biggest spread in this county."

"I know. I read all about it on the internet. It is so awesome that you actually know him." He turned to his grandmother. "Do you know him, too?"

She nodded, looking distraught.

"Will you introduce me?" Jake begged Cassie.

"No," she said so sharply that Jake's eyes filled with tears.

"Why not?" he asked, practically quivering with indignation.

Because she couldn't risk it. If Cole was furious with her because of a letter she'd known nothing about, how would he react to the news that she'd kept his son from him? And then there was Frank Davis. How would he react to the news that a Davis heir had been kept from *him*?

"Because we're not going to be here long enough," she said, making up her mind that staying in Winding River was impossible. "Besides, if what you say is true, I'm sure he's a very busy man. I doubt we'll even bump into him again."

The crestfallen look on Jake's face cut straight through her. He asked for so little, and she was denying him something that was evidently very important to him.

"I'm sorry, Jake."

"You're not sorry," he shouted, letting his ice cream cone tumble to the ground. "You're not sorry at all."

He took off at a run, blindly heading in the very same direction in which his father had gone only moments before. Dear God, what if Cole hadn't left? What if he were in a store and chose that precise moment to exit? Jake would take matters into his own hands. He would force an introduction.

Cassie raced after Jake, commanding him to stop.

He was at the end of Main Street before his pace faltered. She caught up with him there. Breathless, she tilted his chin up to gaze at his tear-streaked face.

"I'm sorry, baby. I truly am." She wrapped her arms around her son and let him sob out his unhappiness, regretting that she couldn't grant his seemingly simple request. How much worse would his anger at her be if he ever discovered the truth—that she was not only keeping him from a hero, but from his own father?

"I don't get it," Jake whispered. "If you know him, why can't I just meet him? It's not like I'd pester him with a million questions."

Cassie actually found herself grinning at that as she brushed the hair back from his forehead. "Oh, no? You *always* have a million questions."

"But I wouldn't ask them. I swear it."

"Sweetie, if I could make it happen, I would."

His expression turned mulish again. "You could. You just don't want to. And you said we were gonna stay at Grandma's a long time, so there's plenty of time."

Apparently, he hadn't picked up on her earlier comment about leaving…or else he'd chosen to ignore it because it hadn't suited him.

"I've been thinking about that," she admitted slowly. "I think we should leave right after the reunion." She forced a smile. "How about going to Cheyenne? Wouldn't you like to live in a big city for a change, Jake? Just think about it. It's the capital of the state, and in the summer there are Frontier Days. You've asked about that."

Jake pushed away from her, that look of betrayal back in his eyes. "No. I don't want to live in Cheyenne. I want to stay here. You promised. When you said goodbye to Earlene, you said you weren't ever coming back except to pick up our things. That meant we were gonna stay here."

"I didn't promise. I said it was something we might consider. I've thought it over, and I think it's a bad idea."

"Don't I get a say?"

"Not about this."

"Well, I won't go. You do whatever you want. Grandma will let me stay with her."

Cassie knew better, but she let it pass. Once Jake calmed down, she would make him see how exciting it would be to move to Cheyenne, even though she dreaded the prospect herself.

"Come on. Let's go find Grandma," she said, taking his hand. He yanked it away, but he did come with her.

She could see her mother still waiting in front of Stella's, leaning against the bumper of a pickup, her face pale except for too-bright patches of color in her cheeks. There was a sheen of perspiration on Edna's brow. Cole's offhand remarks flooded back to Cassie. She studied her mother.

"Mom, are you okay?"

"I'm fine. It's just a little hotter out here than I thought."

Was it that or something more? Was her imagination running wild? After all, it *was* hot. She was perspiring herself. "Let's go inside and get you something cold to drink," Cassie suggested.

"No, I'd rather go home. If you'll get the car..." Edna's voice trailed off.

Cassie regarded her worriedly. The request was a totally uncharacteristic sign of weakness. "Of course I will. Where did you park?"

"I can show you," Jake said.

"No, you stay right here with your grandmother in case she needs anything. I'll find the car."

"It's just around the corner," her mother said, handing her the keys.

Cassie ran all the way to the car. She hadn't liked the way her mother looked. Worse, Edna Collins never admitted to an illness of any kind. She had borne everything from colds to appendicitis with stoic resolve during Cassie's childhood. For her to ask Cassie to get the car, rather than coming along with her, was an incredible admission.

Cassie found the car parked in front of Dolly's Hair Salon, whipped it out of the tight parking space and was back at Stella's in less than five minutes. Her mother all but collapsed into the front seat.

"That air-conditioning sure feels good," she said to

Cassie. Then, as if determined to reassure her daughter, she added, "The heat just got to me for a minute. I promise that's all it was."

Cassie let the remark pass. She had no intention of discussing her mother's health with Jake sitting in the backseat, tuned in to every word. The minute they were alone, though, she was determined to get some straight answers. And if she didn't like them, she was going to call their longtime family physician and get the truth from him.

Unfortunately, her mother seemed to anticipate her intentions and scooted straight to her room, where she all but slammed the door in Cassie's face.

"What on earth?" Cassie murmured, staring at the door.

She picked up the phone and called the doctor, only to be told he was away until the following week. Frustrated, she had barely hung up when the phone rang. She answered distractedly, then froze at the sound of Cole's voice.

"Cassie?" he repeated when she remained silent.

"What?" she said finally.

"We need to talk."

"I don't think so."

"Well, I do. I'm coming over."

She glanced at Jake, who was back in front of the TV. "No, absolutely not," she said fiercely. "I don't want you here."

"Why not, Cassie? What are you hiding?"

"I'm not hiding anything. It's my mother. She's not feeling well," she said, grasping at straws. "The last thing she needs is to have the two of us fussing right under her nose."

"Then meet me. You pick the place."

"Didn't you hear a word I said? My mother's not feeling well."

"Of course. You need to stay there for now."

He had given up too easily. That only made Cassie more suspicious.

"I'll see you at the party tomorrow night, then," he said. "We'll find some time to talk there."

"You're coming to the party?" she asked, not even trying to hide her dismay. "You weren't in our class."

He chuckled at that. "It's a small town. The reunion's a big deal. Everyone will be there, if only to get a glimpse of our big movie star."

"But…" Why had she never considered that possibility? What had ever made her think she could go to a reunion in Winding River and not bump into Cole everywhere she turned?

"My being there won't bother you, will it? Ten years is a long time. Whatever was between us is surely dead and buried, right?"

She heard the unmistakable taunt in his voice. "Absolutely," she responded. "It is definitely dead and buried. Just one question, though."

"What's that?"

"If it's dead and buried, then what could you and I possibly have to talk about?"

"Just putting one last nail in the coffin to make sure it stays that way," he said dryly. "I'll see you tomorrow."

Now there was something to look forward to, she thought dully as she hung up the phone. The prospect should have terrified her, and on one level it did. His taunts should have filled her with outrage, and to a degree they did.

So why was her pulse scampering wildly out of control? Why was she suddenly wondering if there was one sexy outfit packed in her luggage? Why did she feel as if not one of the outrageous, dangerous things she'd done in high school could hold a candle to what might happen tomorrow night back in that same high school gym?

Something told her she didn't dare spend a whole lot of time considering the answers to those questions. If she did, and if she was smart, she might pack up everything and head for Cheyenne tonight.

Cole couldn't imagine what had possessed him to call Cassie, much less announce his intention of going to the reunion party. It was the last place he wanted to be. In fact, he'd ignored the invitation, though he doubted anyone would turn him away at the door as long as he showed up with the price of admission.

He blamed his last-minute change of heart on that encounter with Cassie in the street. It wasn't just the fact that her skin still looked as soft as silk. Nor did it have anything to do with the way her body had added a few lush curves over the years. And it wasn't because her hair was shot through with fire when the sunlight caught it. No, it was none of that.

It was that damnable lie she'd told him with a perfectly straight face. If he hadn't known the truth, he would have believed her—she'd been that convincing. Which meant, he concluded, that she'd believed every word she'd spoken.

Somewhere along the way something had gotten all twisted around, and he wanted to know how. Once he knew that, he could put the past to rest, put that last nail in the coffin of their love affair, just as he'd told her. Maybe she didn't care about what had happened back then, but he did. God help him.

In fact, he was so anxious to get the difficult conversation over with that he got to the gym the next night before seven, while the reunion committee was still setting up its tables outside the doors. Mimi Frances Lawson took one look at him and latched on to his arm with a death grip.

"I need you inside, Cole," she announced, dragging him along behind her. "The streamers are falling down around us, and I don't have time to deal with it. The ladder's over there." She pointed it out. "Here's a roll of tape. I don't know what Hallie used when she put them up, but it's not holding."

She leveled a look straight into his eyes, the somber look of a general sending troops into battle. "I'm counting on you to fix it."

"Yes, ma'am," he said, amused and somewhat relieved to have a task that was actually within his capabilities and not fraught with the emotional repercussions of his anticipated confrontation with Cassie.

"I mean it," Mimi Frances said with an authority that came from being class president for three years running, or maybe from being the mother of five rambunctious boys. "I'm counting on you, Cole."

"These streamers won't budge before next Christmas, Mimi Frances," he assured her. "Now go on with whatever you need to be doing and leave this to me."

She nodded. "I'll send someone in to help as soon as I can spare them."

The fact that she thought he needed help rankled a bit, but Cole ignored it and went to work. He was at the top of a ladder, balanced precariously, when he realized he was no longer alone. He looked straight down into Cassie's familiar green eyes. She stared back unhappily.

"So, Mimi Frances recruited you, too," he said mildly, all too aware that she wasn't one bit happy about being stuck with him, even in this very public setting.

"That woman could run the entire U.S. government without breaking a sweat," Cassie muttered. "I'm fairly certain I told her I was not climbing any ladders."

"Then it's fortunate she paired you up with me. I'm not scared of heights," Cole said, trying not to stare too hard at the sexy little black dress that revealed way too much cleavage, at least from this angle.

"I'm not scared of heights, either," Cassie retorted, indignant patches of color promptly flaring in her cheeks. "I beat you to the top of the town water tower, if I remember correctly."

"So you did," he agreed, grinning. "Then what's the problem?"

"I'd like to see you climb anything in this dress."

"Honey, if I were in that dress, we'd have bigger problems at this reunion than the falling streamers."

A chuckle erupted, just as he'd intended, but she was quick to choke it back. Clearly, she wasn't quite ready for a thaw in the icy distance between them.

He gazed down at her. "Don't stop. I always liked hearing you laugh."

Her gaze narrowed. "Don't go there, Cole."

"Go where?"

"You know."

"To the past? Isn't that what this reunion is all about? Can you think of a better time to think about what used to be?"

"I suspect you and I have very different memories about what used to be."

He nodded. "Based on our conversation yesterday, I'd say you're right about that."

He was about to use the opening to pursue the topic, when Mimi Frances bustled up.

"Stop chatting," she ordered briskly. "We only have a few more minutes."

"Everything is going to go beautifully," Cassie reassured her. "The gym looks sensational. And Cole only has one or two more streamers to secure. Go outside, Mimi Frances, and take a deep breath, then sit back and enjoy yourself. You've outdone yourself. It looks prettier in here than it did on prom night—and that's saying a lot."

"I don't have time to enjoy myself," Mimi Frances snapped, refusing to bask in the praise or take the advice. "Somebody has to see to all the details. I'd like to know who it's going to be, if not me."

"Delegate," Cole advised. "You got me on this ladder, didn't you?"

Mimi Frances looked flustered for a second, then a smile spread across her face. "Yes, I did, didn't I? Well, let me just go outside and see who's lurking about with nothing to do. Thanks, Cole."

He gave her a wink. "Anytime, Madam President."

Mimi Frances went off in search of more recruits. Cole came down the ladder, slid it a few feet across the floor, then turned to Cassie. "Okay, your turn."

"My turn?" she echoed blankly. "To do what?"

"You were assigned streamer duty, too. So far, I'm the only one who's done a lick of work. How could you stand there and look Mimi Frances in the eye, knowing that you hadn't done a blessed thing she asked you to? That woman is counting on us. The success of this entire reunion rests on our shoulders."

"Oh, please," Cassie said with a groan. "Besides, you're doing a fine job. I'll hold the ladder."

"Not that I don't trust you, darlin', but I think I like the idea of *me* holding it for *you* a whole lot better." He handed her the tape, plucked her off the ground and set her on the first rung. "Climb." He paused, his gazed locked with hers. "Unless you really are scared of heights."

She frowned at him, then dutifully kicked off her shoes. She was halfway up, seemingly oblivious to the fact that her dress had hiked a good three inches up her thighs, when she paused and scowled down at him. "If I catch you looking up my skirt, Cole Davis, you're a dead man."

"The thought never crossed my mind," he lied cheerfully, then dutifully averted his gaze, at least until her back was turned.

"You can't have changed that much," she retorted, shooting daggers at him when she caught the direction of his gaze.

"Maybe I have," he said. "You haven't spent enough time with me to find out."

"And I'm not likely to," she told him, slapping a wad of tape on the streamer, then sticking it to the wall before descending.

Cole stood right at the bottom waiting for her, just far enough back to give her a little room to maneuver her way toward the floor. Then he braced one arm on either side of the ladder so that when she reached the last step she was all but in his arms.

"Want to place a bet on that?" he taunted, his mouth next to her ear. She almost tumbled off the bottom rung and into his waiting arms, just as he'd anticipated. He was starting to enjoy keeping her off balance, literally and figuratively.

"Back off," she commanded.

Cole recognized the heat in her tone. Cassie had always had a temper. It was slow to flare out of control, but once it did, it was as lively as the fireworks the town had planned for the Fourth of July. He'd missed that kind of excitement in his life.

He stood his ground. "Not just yet."

She looked over her shoulder and straight into his eyes. "Why are you doing this?"

For the longest time he just lost himself in the depths of her furious, flashing eyes. He ignored the whisper of dismay in her voice, the cry of old wounds in his soul. Finally he sighed.

"I wish to hell I knew," he said softly.

Then and only then did he take a step back and, after one last lingering look, turn and walk away.

It was a strategic retreat, nothing more, he told himself. He needed to spend a little time getting his head together before he had that confrontation with her he'd been thinking about for the past two days.

Otherwise he was liable to spend the time kissing her senseless, instead of getting the answers he wanted.

5

Cassie hadn't felt this jittery since her first date with Cole more than ten years earlier. After he'd walked away, when she finally managed that last shaky step from the ladder, her knees all but buckled. She grabbed her shoes and fled to the ladies' room. She was splashing cold water on her overheated cheeks when Karen wandered in.

"Here you are. Cole said you were around. How long have you been here?"

"Too long," Cassie muttered.

"What?"

"Oh, never mind. I never should have come back to Winding River."

Karen's gaze narrowed. "Is Cole giving you a rough time? He hasn't seen Jake, has he?"

"Not yet, but wouldn't you know my son spotted him yesterday and knew exactly who he was. Apparently Cole is some hotshot computer guy, total hero material to a tech-savvy nine-year-old. Jake is furious because I won't introduce them."

"Oh, my," Karen said, regarding her with sympathy. "That *is* a problem. Will Jake let it drop?"

"Not a chance, which is why I'm getting out of town first thing next week."

"But your mom," Karen began, then fell silent.

Cassie seized on the inadvertent slip. "What about my mother?"

"Nothing." Karen turned away to concentrate on touching up her lipstick.

Cassie regarded her with impatience. "Dammit, not you, too. Cole started this same tight-lipped routine with me yesterday. What is going on? The doctor's out of town, so I haven't been able to get any answers from him."

Karen sighed, then stepped away from the mirror to give her a fierce hug. "Talk to her."

Cassie's heart began to thud dully. There was only one thing that would have Cole and one of her dearest friends tiptoeing around. She held on to Karen and looked straight into her eyes.

"She's sick, isn't she?"

"Just talk to her," her friend repeated, then fell silent. A moment later, before Cassie could even attempt to persuade her to open up, Karen subtly sniffed the air.

"School's been out for a month. How is it possible that it still smells like sweaty gym socks in here?"

Cassie chuckled despite herself, then gestured to the array of air fresheners around the room. "Don't tell Mimi Frances. She'll die of embarrassment. Evidently she thought she'd solved that particular problem."

Karen wrinkled her nose. "Not by a long shot."

She grabbed Cassie's hand. "Come on. Let's get out of here before the others come crowding in to see what's wrong. I don't know about you, but I do not intend to spend an entire evening in a room that stinks, not when there's fresh air in the gym and a great band playing all our old favorites. I get my husband to myself too seldom as it is. I intend to make the most of it."

Back in the gym, they found most of the Calamity Janes already dancing. Caleb gave Cassie a quick kiss on the cheek, then snagged his wife's hand.

"Come on, angel, let's see if you've still got those moves I remember," he said.

Cassie watched enviously as he spun Karen onto the dance floor. At least one of her friends had settled into a happy relationship, she thought. Caleb might be older than his wife, but it was evident that their match was heaven made. Once Karen had set eyes on the rancher, all her dreams of traveling the globe had taken a backseat to her desire to become his wife.

Feeling blue and alone, Cassie wandered over to the bar and ordered a soda. Something told her she was going to need a clear head tonight, if not to deal with Cole, then certainly for that dreaded conversation with her mother.

The fast song ended, and a slow, oldies ballad began. Memories of another night, hot and sultry and filled with promise, stole over her. She felt a hand on her waist, felt the whisper of warm breath against her cheek and knew it was Cole behind her.

"Does it take you back?" he asked.

To a place she didn't want to go, she thought but

didn't say. "Nostalgia's a funny thing," she said instead. "It tends to take away all the rough edges and leave you with pretty images."

"Anything wrong with that?" he asked.

"It's not real. It's not the way it was. Not all of it, anyway."

He stepped in front of her, his gaze steady. "Dance with me, Cassie."

"Cole…" The protest formed in her head, but she couldn't seem to get the words out.

"For old time's sake."

Drawn to him, caught up in the very nostalgia she'd decried, she slipped into his arms and rested her head against his chest. The feel of him, the clean, male scent, the weight of his arms circling her waist—all of it was incredibly, dangerously familiar. Their bodies fit together perfectly, moving as one to the music, connected in a way that hinted of another, far more intimate and never-forgotten unity.

"God, I've missed you," he said, his voice ragged and tinged with regret.

Was it regret for time lost, though, or for emotions he couldn't control? Cassie wondered.

The music played on for what seemed like an eternity, but when it ended at last, she thought it hadn't gone on nearly long enough. Cole released her, then captured her hand in his.

"Come on. I'll buy you a drink." He regarded her questioningly as they approached the bar. "Another soda?"

She nodded. When he had her cola and his beer,

he led her outside. She didn't resist. She couldn't. It seemed they were both caught up in some sort of spell. Reunions had a way of doing that, she supposed. They were intended to take you back in time, to a simpler era when nothing mattered but football victories and school dances. Unfortunately, for her those times were far more complicated.

The heat of the day had given way to a cool breeze. The summer sun was just now sinking below the horizon in the west in a blaze of orange. They stood silently, side by side, watching as the sky faded to pale pink, then mauve, then turned dark as velvet.

"Quite a show," Cole observed.

"God's gift at the end of the day, if you take the time to enjoy it," Cassie said.

"Do you?"

"Do I what?"

"Take the time to enjoy it? What have you been up to for the past ten years, Cassie?"

"Working."

"Doing what? Where are you living?"

Now there was the question of the hour, she thought. "I've been in a small town north of Cheyenne," she said.

"Doing?"

"The same old thing," she said, unable to hide a note of defensiveness. "Working in a diner."

"You were always good at that," he said with what sounded like genuine admiration. "You had a way of making every customer feel special, even the grumpy ones."

She shrugged. "Better tips that way."

"Why do you do that?" he asked, regarding her with a puzzled expression. "Why do you put yourself down? There's nothing wrong with being a damn fine waitress."

"No, there's not," she agreed.

He grinned. "That's better. Besides being a waitress, what have you been up to? I imagine raising your son takes most of your time."

She swallowed hard. Obviously he knew about Jake's existence, so there was little point in denying it. "Yes."

"I saw him, you know."

Fear made her stiffen. "You did? When?"

"The day you drove into town. I saw you go speeding past the ranch. He was with you."

She breathed a sigh of relief. Only from a distance, then. He couldn't have seen much, a glimpse at most.

"How old is he?"

"Nine."

"Then you must have had him not long after we broke up," he said, his expression thoughtful. Then, as if a dark cloud had passed in front of the sun, his eyes filled with shadows. His gaze hardened. "You didn't waste a lot of time finding somebody new, did you?"

She wanted to deny the damning conclusion to which he'd leaped, but it was safer than the alternative, safer than letting him make a connection with the timing of their relationship. "Not long," she agreed. She studied him curiously. "I didn't think it mattered what I did, since you were long gone."

"So, we're back to that," he said, his tone cold. "I wrote to you. I explained that my father insisted I go back to college right then. I asked you to wait, told you I'd get home the first chance I got."

"And I'm telling you that I never got such a letter," she said. "If I had, I would have waited." She started to add that she had loved him, but what was the point of saying that now? Whatever she had felt had died years ago.

"I would have understood," she told him, her voice flat.

"Oh, really? That wasn't how it sounded in the letter I got. You sounded as if you didn't give a rat's behind what I did."

She looked him straight in his eyes as she made another flat denial. "I never wrote to you. How could I? I didn't even know where you'd gone."

"I have the letter, dammit."

"I didn't write it," she repeated.

He studied her unflinching gaze, then sighed. "You're telling me the truth, aren't you?" He stepped away from her and raked his hand through his hair in a gesture that had become habit whenever he was troubled. "What the hell happened back then?"

Suddenly, before she could even speculate aloud, he muttered a harsh expletive. "My father, no doubt. He had something to do with it, you can be sure of that. He forced me to go, then made sure my letter never reached you. I'm sure he was responsible for the letter I got, as well."

"Wouldn't you have recognized his handwriting?"

"Of course, but he wouldn't write it himself. He'd have someone else do his dirty work."

If that was true, Cassie didn't know how she felt about it. It would be a relief to know Cole hadn't abandoned her after all, but it didn't change anything. Too much time had passed. And there was Jake to consider. Cole would be livid if he found out the boy was his.

"It doesn't matter now, Cole. It was a long time ago. We've both moved on with our lives."

He scanned her face intently. "You're happy, then?"

"Yes," she said. It was only a tiny lie. Most of the time she was…content. At least she had been until Jake's mischief had made it necessary for her to leave the home she'd worked so hard to make for them.

"You didn't marry your son's father, though, did you?"

"No. It wouldn't have worked," she said truthfully. "Jake and I do okay on our own."

He smiled. "That's his name? Jake?"

She nodded.

"I like it."

She had known he would, because they had discussed baby names one night when they'd allowed themselves to dream about the future. Cole had evidently forgotten that, which was just as well.

"He's a good kid?"

"Most of the time," she said with a rueful grin.

"Being your son, I'll bet he's a handful. What sort of mischief does he get into?"

She found herself telling him about the computer scam, laughing now that it was behind them, admiring—despite herself—her son's audacity. "Not that I would ever in a million years tell him that. What he did was wrong. That's the only message I want him to get from me."

"We did worse," Cole pointed out.

"We certainly did not," she protested.

"We stole all the footballs right before the biggest game of the season, because I was injured and the team was likely to lose without me."

Cassie remembered. She also remembered that they'd been suspended from school for a week because of it. In high school she had loved leading the older, more popular Cole into mischief. It was only later, when he'd come home from college, that their best-buddy relationship had turned into something else.

Thinking of the stunts she'd instigated, she smiled. "That was different. No one was really harmed by it. And they played, anyway. The coach went home and found a football in his garage. The team was so fired up by what we'd done, by the implication that they couldn't win without you, that they went out and won that game just to prove that they didn't need you to run one single play."

Cole laughed. "It was quite a reality check for my ego, that's for sure."

"Okay, so we chalk that one up as a stunt that backfired," she said. "Anything else you remember us doing that was so terrible?"

"There was the time you talked me into taking all the prayer books from the Episcopal church and switching them with the ones at the Baptist church." He grinned. "Why did we do that, anyway?"

She shrugged. "It seemed like a good idea at the time. And I think I was mad at my mom, because she kept pointing out prayers she thought I ought to be learning to save my soul from eternal damnation. I was tired of hearing the same ones over and over again, so I thought a switch would give her some new material."

The mention of her mother snapped her back to the present and the worries that had been stirred up about her health, first by Cole, tonight by Karen and even by that incident in town.

Suddenly she simply had to know the truth. She handed Cole her glass. "I have to go."

"Where?" he asked, his expression puzzled.

"Home. I want to talk to my mother before it gets to be too late."

The fact that he simply nodded and didn't challenge her abrupt decision to leave confirmed her fear that something must be terribly wrong. Moreover, Cole obviously knew what it was. There was too much sympathy in his expression.

"Give her my regards," he said quietly.

She considered trying to question him again about what he knew, but it was pointless. Cole could keep a secret as well as anyone, and it was evident he intended to keep this one out of loyalty to her mother.

"I will," she said.

She started across the parking lot, but he called out to her. "Cassie?"

She turned back. "Yes?"

He lifted his glass in a silent toast. "Thanks for the dance."

"Anytime," she said.

He grinned. "I'll hold you to that. There will be a great country band at the picnic tomorrow, and I haven't had a decent Texas two-step partner in years."

"You might still be saying that after tomorrow," she retorted. "I haven't been dancing in years."

And then, because she was far too tempted to go back and steal a kiss as she once would have done without a thought, she turned on her heel and strode away without another backward glance.

At home Cassie kicked off her shoes in the living room, then noted with relief that there was still a light on in her mother's room. She padded into the kitchen and brewed two cups of tea, then carried them upstairs. In her bedroom Edna was reading her Bible as she had every night before bed for as long as Cassie could remember.

"I made some tea," she announced.

Startled, her mother's gaze shot up. Worry puckered her brow. "You're home awfully early. Weren't you having a good time seeing all your friends?"

"Cole was there," she said, as if that explained everything.

"I see." Her mother set aside her Bible and patted the edge of the bed. "Come, sit beside me." She smiled. "I remember when you used to come in here after one of your dates and tell me everything you'd done."

"Almost everything," Cassie corrected dryly as she

set the teacups on the nightstand and sat beside her mother.

"Some things a mother doesn't need to know."

Cassie leaned down and pressed a kiss to her mother's cheek. "I'm sorry I made things so difficult for you."

"You were testing the limits. It was natural enough. So, tell me, did you and Cole talk tonight?"

"Some, but I don't want to get into that right now." She took her mother's hand in her own, felt the calluses on the tips of her fingers put there by mending countless shirts, sewing on hundreds of buttons and hemming at least as many skirts, month after month, year after year. "I want to talk about you."

"Me?" Her mother withdrew her hand and looked away, her expression suddenly nervous. "Why would you want to talk about me?"

"Because of that spell you had in town and because twice in the past few days people have said things, things that didn't make any sense to me."

"About?"

"You." She studied her mother's face. "Are you okay, Mom? Is there something going on that you haven't told me?"

A soft smile touched her mother's lips. She raised her hand to tuck a wayward curl behind Cassie's ear. "I'm glad you're home for a visit."

The evasion only made her impatient. "Mom, tell me."

Her mother drew in a deep breath, then blurted out, "I have cancer."

There it was, that single, plainspoken word with the power to instill terror. Cassie was devastated. For a full five minutes after her mother said the words, Cassie simply stared at her in shock.

"But you don't look sick," she whispered finally, her voice catching on a sob. "Except for that little spell yesterday afternoon, you've looked just fine since I got here."

"They tell me I'm going to look a whole lot worse before they're through with me," her mother said, managing to inject an unexpected note of wry humor into the solemn discussion. "And that spell was because of the heat, not the cancer."

Tears spilled down Cassie's cheeks as she reached for the woman who'd had to endure so much by having a daughter who was always causing trouble.

"I want to know everything the doctors said. When did you find out?"

"I found the lump in my breast two weeks ago and had a needle biopsy that was positive. They wanted to operate right away, but you were coming home. I told them they'd just have to wait."

Cassie was appalled. "You haven't even had the surgery yet?"

"There will be time enough after you've gone back home."

"Don't be ridiculous. I'm not leaving you here to go through this alone."

"You've made a life for yourself," her mother countered. "You can't know how grateful I am that you and Jake are doing well. I won't disrupt that."

"You don't have a choice," Cassie said decisively. "We will call the doctor first thing next week and schedule the surgery. You'll need someone here when you're going through treatment, too. Will you be having radiation? Chemotherapy?"

"That will depend on what they find when they operate, but I have plenty of friends who will stand by me," her mother insisted. "I'm sure that's how Cole and Karen know. People are already rallying around with offers to drive me wherever I need to go. I don't want you turning your life upside down on my account, especially not with Cole snooping around. Who knows what sort of trouble that man and his father might stir up?"

Cassie's gaze narrowed. She had never heard her mother say a harsh word about Cole. In fact, she had always treated him as if he were her own son. Of course, if she had known all along about Cole being Jake's father, that would have colored her opinion of him.

"Cole's not important right now," Cassie said fiercely. "The only thing that matters is getting you well." Tears stung her eyes again. "Oh, Mom, you're going to beat this. I know you are."

"Yes," her mother said confidently, "I am. I intend to see my grandson grow into a fine man, one that both of us can be proud of."

"Then, no more arguments. Jake and I are staying right here with you. I'll make a quick trip to get the rest of my things, and I'll talk to Stella tomorrow about going back to work for her. If she can't take me on, I'll try the new restaurant."

"But how on earth can you keep Jake and Cole apart?" her mother asked worriedly. "I won't be responsible for Cole figuring out that the boy is his. What if he decides he wants to be a part of Jake's life? What if he asks for custody? Frank Davis will push him to, I know that much. The man is desperate for an heir for that ranch of his. It grates on his nerves that Cole only gives it half his attention."

Cassie couldn't deny that staying was a risk, but weighed against the prospect of her mother battling cancer all alone, she had no choice. "Mom, I want to be here. I owe you. You were always there for me when I needed you, even when I didn't deserve it. You are not going to face this ordeal without your family standing beside you, and that's that."

Just that easily—just that heartbreakingly—the decision to stay was made, and this time it was irreversible. Only time would tell if she would be able to live with the consequences.

6

When Cassie finally left her mother's room, it was almost midnight. As she went to take their untouched, full teacups into the kitchen, she thought she noticed a movement on the front porch. She set the cups on a table in the foyer, slipped quietly up to the door, flipped on the overhead light and saw Cole sitting in the swing, idly setting it in motion. She wasn't nearly as surprised by his presence as she should have been, nor as dismayed.

She stepped outside, closing the door behind her. "What are you doing here?" she asked, aware that her voice was ragged and her eyes red rimmed from crying.

He turned to face her, his expression sympathetic. "I thought you might need a friendly shoulder."

"I could use one," she agreed. But his? How could she possibly turn to him? How could she let him back into her life at all?

He patted the swing. "Come on over here and tell me how your talk with your mom went."

At the moment she needed comfort more than she needed to maintain a safe emotional distance from this man who represented such a huge threat to her and her son. She sat beside him, careful to keep as much physical distance between them as the swing allowed. Cole was having none of that, though. He slid closer and draped his arm around her shoulders as he had dozens of times in the past.

She turned and met his gaze. "How did you know? I'm sure she didn't share it with you."

"It's a small town. Word gets around, especially about something like this. There have been prayers at church. Everyone wants to help out. How's she doing?"

"Better than I am," Cassie said honestly. "She thought she'd just postpone the surgery until after I was gone and I'd never have to know a thing. She didn't want me worrying. Well, she was right about one thing—I am worried. I'm scared silly, in fact."

Cole simply let her talk, his silence giving her permission to voice all of the fears she hadn't been able to express to her mother.

"I know all the statistics, but I always thought breast cancer was something that happened to other people, not to me, not to my mom. It's not just the surgery. These days they treat cancer aggressively—she's likely to have both radiation and chemo. She'll lose her hair, more than likely. She'll be exhausted. She doesn't have any kind of medical insurance. And she thought she could go through all of this alone, that she could manage. What does that say about our relationship? She's sick, really sick, and she didn't think she could count on me."

"I don't think it was that," Cole said. "Your mom's always had to be strong to face the adversities in her life. She's always had to rely on herself. She simply figured she'd deal with this the same way."

Cassie turned her tear-filled gaze on him. "But, Cole, she could *die*."

Cole's expression suddenly turned bleak. "Breast cancer survival rates are better these days than they used to be," he said stiffly.

Only then did she remember that Cole had lost his own mother to breast cancer years ago. She cursed herself for her insensitivity. How could she have forgotten that he'd been little more than a boy when he'd had to face what she was facing now? How much more terrifying it must have seemed to him. And his father, with all his power, hadn't been able to change the outcome. Nor had he ever gotten over the loss.

She touched a hand to his cheek. "I'm sorry. I should have thought. You shouldn't have to listen to me go on and on about this. It's bound to bring up a lot of very painful memories."

"Stop it," he said, clasping her hand in his. "I'm the one who came over here, remember? Nobody understands better than I do what you're going through, but I'll say it again, the odds are in her favor. And stop worrying about the expense. Just put it out of your mind. I don't cared who she's seen already, we'll see to it that she has the best surgeon and the best oncologist around."

"We?" she echoed.

"Of course I'm going to help."

"But why would you do that?" she asked, genuinely bewildered by the offer.

"Because she's your mother," he said simply. "Besides, for a time she was the closest thing I had to a mother, too. It hurt to lose her, when I lost you. I don't want either of us to lose her forever."

"Oh, God," Cassie whispered as the panic rose inside her again. "We're not going to, are we?"

"Not if I can help it," Cole said with grim determination.

Cassie felt some of the tension leave her body. It was as good as a promise, and at one time she had trusted Cole's promises with total confidence.

There might be a million things left for them to work out where the past was concerned, but just for tonight she wanted to believe in him again. Because he was all that stood between her and despair.

He shouldn't have promised Cassie that her mother would live. Cole paced his office, portable phone in hand, as he waited for yet another so-called expert— men who were recommended by friends—to deliver an opinion about Edna Collins's chances of survival. He'd spent the day looking for guarantees, but so far none had been given.

He told himself he was doing it as a courtesy to a woman who'd once been kind to him, but he knew better. He was doing it for Cassie. He'd recognized that bleak expression on her face, that panic she hadn't been able to keep out of her eyes. He'd seen it reflected time and again in the mirror years ago.

While his father had ranted at the doctors and cursed God, it had been left to Cole to pray, to sit and hold his mother's increasingly frail hand as she slipped farther and farther away from them. No matter that Cassie was older than he'd been, no matter what he thought of her, he didn't want her to go through that, not if he could help it.

"Why are you mixed up in this?" his father asked, his gaze speculative. "Edna Collins won't take kindly to your interference."

"What would you know about Edna Collins? You always looked down on her."

"I did not. She's a fine woman. I just thought her daughter wasn't the right woman for you—not back then, anyway."

"And now?"

"Now I'm maintaining an open mind."

"Not likely," Cole muttered. "But whatever your agenda is, Dad, keep it to yourself. Cassie and I were over and done a long time ago, and you know precisely why that is. You did your damage, and it's too late to fix things."

He needed to convince his father of that, if only to keep him from meddling and ruining whatever chance Cole might have to patch things up. This time no one would have an opportunity to interfere.

"It's never too late as long as there's breath in your body," his father said fiercely, clearly undaunted by

Cole's remark. "If there's a second chance for the two of you, don't be bullheaded and waste it."

Was there a second chance? Cole wasn't certain yet. A part of him wanted there to be. To be sure all of the old feelings—that quick slam of desire—were as powerful as they'd ever been, stronger, in fact, now that they were a man's, not a boy's.

Funny how at twenty he'd thought he was so mature, so grown-up. Yet he'd let himself be manipulated and controlled. He'd given up one thing he wanted for another, never asking if the price was too high. Only later, when he'd realized Cassie was gone for good, did he consider the cost.

And then it had been too late.

The Calamity Janes had spread a half dozen quilts across the grass. Each of them had brought a cooler filled with drinks, sandwiches and a variety of desserts. There was more than enough food for themselves and most of their class, but none of them had eaten a bite.

"I can't believe it," Gina said. "Your mom was always such a skinny little thing. She looked as if a strong wind would blow her away, but she had this unmistakable strength."

"And that's exactly what's going to get her through this," Karen said, giving Cassie's hand a squeeze as she shot a warning glance at Gina. "No more talk of gloom and doom. I'm so glad you're going to stay to help out. I know how much that must mean to your mom."

"She fought me on it," Cassie admitted.

"And we all know why that was," Lauren chimed in.

"Sweetie, I know you feel you need to be here, but let's think about this. What about Jake and Cole?"

"I'll just have to do whatever I can to keep them apart," Cassie said. It was going to be more easily said than done, given Cole's determination to help out with her mom's treatment in any way he could. She doubted that meant merely writing a check and steering clear of the house or whatever hospital she went to.

"You'd barely been in town for a day, and they almost ran into each other," Gina reminded her. "How can you help your mom if you're worried every second about Cole figuring out that Jake is his?"

"I think she should just tell Cole and get it over with," Karen said.

"Tell Cole what?" the very man in question inquired, making Cassie's heart thump wildly.

"Where did you come from?" she asked irritably. "You shouldn't sneak up on people when they're having private conversations."

"If you don't want anyone to overhear, then you shouldn't be having a private conversation in the middle of an event in a public park," he retorted mildly. He sat down beside her, deliberately crowding her, deliberately ignoring her scowl.

Her friends exchanged knowing looks, then one by one excused themselves to play badminton or horseshoes or baseball. Even Lauren, who'd never had an athletic bone in her body except when it came to horses, declared a sudden urge to join the women's baseball team being formed to challenge the men.

When they were all gone, Cassie looked Cole

squarely in the eye. "Don't you want to play? I'm sure the men could use you."

"I'm where I want to be," he said, picking up an apple and taking a bite.

Cassie was suddenly struck by an image of Adam in the garden of Eden, tempted into sin by a seductive Eve. "Cole, you aren't imagining that you and I..." Her voice trailed off as color flooded her cheeks.

He grinned. "That we're going to have ourselves a fling for old-time's sake?"

"I wouldn't have put it like that, but yes."

"Would it be so terrible?"

"It would be a disaster," she said with feeling.

"Why? We're consenting adults now. It would be nobody's business but ours."

She knew he probably wasn't even serious, that he was deliberately baiting her, but she couldn't let it pass. "Do you actually think that would stop anyone from making it their business? You're the one who said it last night. This is still a small town. People love to talk. Just seeing us sitting here together now will raise eyebrows. It won't be five minutes before someone makes a call to your father to report the latest."

He seemed totally unconcerned. "Let them. My father doesn't run my life."

"Since when?"

"A lot's changed since the last time we were together," he said mildly. "We'll get into it one of these days."

"No, we won't. This is impossible."

"Nothing's impossible if you want it badly enough."

She frowned at him. "My mother's already been through enough. I won't have her embarrassed by my actions ever again, especially not with everything else that's going on."

"So it's only because of your mother that you're turning me down?" he inquired, a glint of amusement in his eyes.

"No, of course not," she snapped. "It's a bad idea all the way around."

"Then you don't find me the least bit attractive anymore?"

She knew she could never lie convincingly enough to tell him no, so she settled for saying, "It doesn't matter whether I do or I don't. *Nothing* is going to happen."

He shrugged. "If you say so." An infuriating, smug smile tugged at his lips.

"I say so," she said firmly.

"That's that, then." He tossed his apple toward a nearby trash can. It went in neatly. An instant later he was on his feet, his hand held out. "Come on. If we can't have sex, we might as well play ball."

Ignoring the outrageous comment and his outstretched hand, Cassie stood up, but before she could take a single step, he snagged her wrist and held her still. His gaze locked with hers and sent her heartbeat tripping.

Before she could guess his intention, his mouth settled on hers, the touch as light as a butterfly's, as devastating as ever. The world went spinning, but when she would have reached out to steady herself, he was already stepping away, apparently satisfied that she was completely off balance.

"Interesting," he commented, as if it had been nothing more than an experiment.

Still shaken, she stared at him. "What?"

"You taste exactly the way I remembered. I guess there are some things in life we can't forget, no matter how hard we try." That odd note of regret was back in his voice again.

"Try harder," she snapped, then stalked off to the sound of his laughter.

There was just one problem with that advice, she conceded as she joined the others on the ball field. There wasn't a snowball's chance in hell that she could forget it, either. Cole's kisses were as memorable now as they had been ten years ago. Hard and demanding or soft and sweet, they had always taken her by surprise, always sent her senses reeling. Time hadn't dulled that.

Okay, she admitted, she might not be able to forget. That didn't mean she couldn't steer clear of any more stolen kisses, minimize the risk, prevent disaster from striking again. It would just take some fancy footwork and plenty of polite excuses for never spending a single second with him alone.

"You okay?" Karen asked, studying her worriedly. "You look a little flushed."

"It's hot out here," she said with an unmistakable trace of defensiveness.

"It's cloudy and barely seventy," Karen pointed out.

"Do you always have to take everything so literally?" she grumbled.

Karen grinned. "Ah, this is about Cole, then. I should have known."

"Oh, go suck an egg."

"Can't. I'm next up to bat. If you want to get in the lineup, see Emma. She's managing the team."

Despite herself, Cassie chuckled. "Why am I not surprised?" Despite the rough time they had given her, Emma had always taken charge. Now that she was a big-shot attorney, no doubt she was more of a control freak than ever.

Cassie glanced at the field and reacted with amazement when she saw that Lauren was on second base. "Lauren got a hit?"

"No," Karen said, chuckling. "The pitcher got so flustered when she started moving her hips up at the plate, he walked her. She stole second when the catcher got distracted by her moves down at first. I think she's going to be our secret weapon to win this game."

"Men are so predictable," Cassie noted.

"Even Cole? I thought he'd always kept you guessing."

"Unfortunately, he's the exception." She sighed. "I could really do without an exception in my life right now."

"My advice? Go with the flow. Let the man make up for lost time if he wants to."

"And then what? Wait for the fireworks when he discovers I've spent the past nine years keeping him from his son? I don't think so. Besides, he's offered to help with my mother's medical expenses. She'll probably pitch a fit, but I don't see that we have any other choice. I can't risk having him change his mind."

"He would never renege on that commitment, and you know it."

Cassie glanced across the field and spotted Cole. He'd taken his place at second base, but he was actually ignoring the Hollywood superstar who was standing on it.

"He's really oblivious to Lauren, isn't he?" she said to Karen, feeling ridiculously pleased.

"Because there's only one of us he's ever had eyes for. That's you, honey. Don't be so quick to dismiss the possibility of getting back together with him." Her gaze narrowed. "Unless you don't love him anymore. Is that it? Have you stopped loving Cole?"

"Honestly?"

"Of course."

She did a little soul-searching, then thought of the kiss they'd just shared and almost touched a finger to her lips. "I don't know what I feel anymore."

"Then keep an open mind and find out."

"Hey, Karen, do you intend to bat anytime today?" Emma called out impatiently. She tapped a pen against the hastily scrawled lineup on her legal pad.

"She brought a legal pad with her to a picnic?" Cassie murmured.

"Oh, yes," Karen replied. "And her cell phone. And her day planner. I think there's an entire set of law books in the trunk of her car."

Cassie gazed at Emma with dismay. "Sweet heaven,

the woman's going to have a heart attack before she hits thirty."

"I've mentioned that. I've also reminded her that she has a little girl to think about." Karen shrugged. "She stares at me as if I'm speaking Swahili."

"Karen!" Emma's tone was sharp.

"Coming!" She winked at Cassie. "If I don't get a hit, I'm dead meat."

"Yes, I can see that. I think I'll go find myself a nice shady spot and rest. All this fun you're supposedly having sounds a little too stressful for me. I can't be around Emma when she gets that manic, winner-take-all glint in her eyes."

She cast a last, lingering look at Cole, but he was busy taunting Karen, trying to distract her just as the pitcher threw the ball. Cassie laughed when Karen slammed the ball in a little blooper that sailed right past him and dropped into center field. Karen reached first base, turned to Cole and stuck out her tongue.

"Way to go," Cassie shouted, then wandered off in search of shade and a little peace and quiet to recover from the traumatic news she'd received the night before. She doubted she would actually sleep, but even a few minutes alone sounded good.

Unfortunately, it seemed as if she'd barely closed her eyes and taken a deep, relaxing breath, when noise erupted from the ball field and everyone began trailing back in search of drinks and food.

"Hey, Sleeping Beauty," Cole said, dropping down beside her.

"I wasn't asleep."

"Oh, really?" he said, his expression amused. "How many innings of ball have we played since you took off?"

Cassie glanced toward Karen, but there was no help there. She was feeding plump strawberries to her husband. "I wasn't paying attention," she finally conceded.

"Five," he said. "And you slept through every one of them. You missed my home run and Emma's tantrum when Mimi Frances failed to touch third base and was declared out."

If she had slept, it hadn't done any good. She certainly didn't feel rested. "Who won?"

"The women, of course," Lauren said haughtily, sitting down beside Cole.

"Only because you used that body of yours shamelessly to distract us," Caleb accused.

"You're married. You're not supposed to be looking at Lauren's body," Karen chided, but there was amusement dancing in her eyes.

"A man would have to be dead not to notice the way she was wiggling around," he retorted.

Lauren feigned innocence. "I did nothing of the kind. I just took my turn at bat like everyone else."

"I haven't seen hips move that much since Marilyn Monroe strutted across a screen," one of the other men said.

"Are you complaining?" Gina inquired. "Seemed to me like you were all but drooling."

"I was not," he protested.

Cole leaned down and whispered in Cassie's ear, "I have no idea what all the fuss was about."

She risked meeting his gaze and saw the twinkle in his eyes that was at odds with his pious expression. "Oh, really?"

"I only have eyes for one woman here," he insisted.

"Oh? And who would that be?"

"You."

A shiver washed over her, despite herself. "Cole, don't."

"I just want you to know where I'm coming from." His expression sobered. "There's unfinished business between us, Cassie. You know there is. I think it's about time we dealt with it."

"I can't think about that now. I can't think about you," she said fiercely, scrambling to her feet.

"Where are you going?"

"For a walk."

"I'll come with you."

"No," she said, her scowl keeping him in place.

"I'll still be here when you get back," he reminded her mildly. "And nothing will have changed."

Cassie didn't care. She needed space now. She needed time to figure out why Cole could still get to her, even when she desperately wanted him not to matter at all.

"You do whatever you want to do," she told him. "You always have."

That said, she fled, but though Cole didn't follow, he stayed right smack in the middle of her thoughts. That was okay, though, she finally concluded. Thinking about the man couldn't get her into that much trouble. *Being* with him could be disastrous.

7

"Mom, Grandma says there are going to be fireworks tomorrow night for the Fourth of July," Jake said eagerly over breakfast two days later.

The class reunion had bumped smack into the town's annual holiday festivities, so people had lingered after the weekend. Unfortunately, the one person Cassie wanted most to avoid lived right here in town. Cole wouldn't be going anywhere, not anytime soon. And unless times had changed, he would be at the fireworks. His father, always a benefactor of the event, would no doubt be grand marshal of the parade. Avoiding the two of them would be next to impossible.

"Can we go, please?" Jake pleaded. "And there's a parade, too. There will be hot dogs and all sorts of neat stuff. Grandma told me all about it."

Cassie cast a startled look at her mother, who shrugged.

"He asked if anything special was going on for the Fourth," she explained. "I guess I got carried away."

"Mom, can we go?" Jake begged. "The Fourth of July is my very favorite holiday."

Cassie chuckled at that. "And right before Thanksgiving you always say *that's* your favorite because you love turkey and pumpkin pie. And then there's Christmas with the tree and Santa and all the presents."

"But they're not for months and months. This is my very favorite because it happens *now*. We've gotta go. Maybe I'll meet some other kids. If we're gonna be here even for a little while, I've gotta have friends."

Cassie hated the thought of denying him, but what about Cole? How could she manage to keep them apart? Or was it simply time to get used to the idea that she couldn't, not and stay here in Winding River?

"Give me a little time to think about it," she said, praying she could come up with a reasonable solution that would balance Jake's needs and her fears.

Jake's face fell. "You're going to say no, aren't you? You never want me to have any fun. You're still mad about what happened before we left home. You said when we came here I wouldn't be grounded anymore, but I might as well be if I can't do anything and I don't have one single friend to play with."

"Sweetie, it's not that," Cassie told him. "I swear it. I would love to take you. And I do want you to get to know the other kids in town." She thought desperately, trying to come up with a believable excuse for her hesitation. She could hardly tell him the truth—that she didn't want him anywhere near his father.

"It's just that your mother knows I haven't been

feeling all that well," Edna broke in, throwing Cassie a lifeline. "It might have to be a last-minute decision."

Worry immediately creased Jake's brow. "You're sick?" he asked, wide-eyed.

"Nothing serious," Edna insisted, keeping to her agreement with Cassie to keep the truth from Jake for as long as possible. She fell back on the incident he had seen for himself. "But the heat bothers me some. You saw that in town the other day."

He scrambled off his chair and snuggled close to her side. "I'm sorry. We don't have to go," he said bravely, though his chin quivered ever so slightly as he made the concession.

His grandmother gave him a fierce hug. "You are such a thoughtful child. Thank you. Now why don't you go on out to the garage and see if you can get that old bike in shape to ride. Once you've got some wheels, you'll be able to get around and meet those kids." She gave him one last squeeze. "Now, go on."

Jake gave her one last worried look, then left.

"Thank you for bailing me out," Cassie said, breathing a sigh of relief when he'd gone.

"It was my fault he got his heart set on it in the first place. I just remembered how you used to love the parade and the hot dogs and the fireworks, and the next thing I knew I was feeling nostalgic and telling him all about it."

"I wish I could take him," Cassie said wistfully.

"Then do it," her mother said staunchly. "Maybe we've been going about this all wrong, keeping him from Cole. If you're determined to stay here, you can't keep Jake locked up in this house. He shouldn't be punished because of something that's not his fault."

Cassie had been thinking the same thing herself just moments earlier, but the fear the idea stirred was tough to conquer. "You know all hell will break loose if Cole adds two and two together and figures everything out."

"It might," her mother conceded. "But that child needs a father. He could do worse than Cole." Her mother seemed to be oblivious to the fact that her attitude was a major turnaround.

"That's quite a change of heart," Cassie noted.

"Not really," her mother denied, looking guilty.

"Oh? You'll have to explain that to me."

"I always thought he was a fine young man. What you told me after he left the other night, that he's willing to pay my medical expenses is proof of that. Back then I just thought things got a little out of hand between the two of you, especially with you being so young. Then when he left and you turned out to be pregnant, naturally I blamed him."

"There were two of us to blame," Cassie said, finding herself taking Cole's side as well.

"Well, of course, but he was older. I thought he took advantage of you. And, then…" She shrugged and fell silent.

"Then what?"

"Nothing. It's water under the bridge now."

Before Cassie could press her, she heard a masculine voice outside. "Oh, my God," she said, leaping up. "What if that's Cole?"

"Then you go out there and act perfectly natural,"

her mother advised. "Anything else will make him suspicious. Until you decide you're going to admit the truth to him, you have to keep those two apart, but you have to do it as subtly as possible. He won't see what you and I see when we look at Jake, because he won't be expecting it."

Cassie knew she was right, but that didn't stop the panic from clawing at her as she stepped outside and saw Cole bending down to help Jake tighten a bolt on the bicycle he'd retrieved from the garage. Her heart slammed to a stop at the sight, then resumed beating at a more frantic pace.

Jake looked up at her with shining eyes. "Mom, Mr. Davis is helping me fix the bike."

"I see that. Does Mr. Davis actually have any idea what he's doing?"

Cole frowned up at her with feigned indignation. "Hey, lady, are you questioning my mechanical skills?"

She forced a grin. "You bet. I seem to recall an electric coffeepot that blew up after you'd tinkered with it."

Cole tapped the wrench against the bike. "No electricity involved here, just nuts and bolts and chains."

"True, but I'm sure you didn't stop by to do bike repair," she said. "I'll help Jake later."

"But, Mom," Jake wailed.

"I said I'd help later. Cole, why don't you come on inside? I know Mother is anxious to thank you for what you're doing for her."

"Is she really?" Cole asked, his expression skeptical.

Cassie did grin at that. "Well, she will thank you right after she tells you how she can't accept, that Edna

Collins doesn't accept anyone's charity, et cetera, et cetera."

Cole got to his feet. "Now that sounds more like it. I guess I'll just have to dust off my charm."

That ought to do it, Cassie thought as he held out his hand to her son for a grown-up handshake. Certainly one member of the Collins family was under his spell. Okay, two, she conceded reluctantly. She might not hold out any hope for their future, but that didn't stop her from indulging in the occasional fantasy, the one in which she, Jake and Cole somehow put aside all the lies and deceit of the past and became a happy family.

As soon as Cole left and she could get away, Cassie invited her mother to come into town with her and Jake to have lunch at Stella's. Eager for an outing of any kind, Jake had already raced ahead to the car.

"I need to talk to Stella about that job," she explained to her mother. "This is as good a time as any. And maybe it will pacify Jake. He's still smarting over the fact that I didn't let Cole spend the whole morning helping him with that bike."

"Then you're determined to stay?" her mother asked. "Even with Cole showing up here earlier and sending you into a tizzy?"

Cassie couldn't deny that she'd been thrown, but a promise was a promise. "I told you I would. Besides, there is nowhere else I could be right now. You need me."

Her mother nodded, and what might have been relief passed across her face. "That's that, then," she said giving Cassie's hand a squeeze. "It'll be good to have the two of you here. The house gets awfully quiet sometimes."

"I thought you'd be grateful for that after all the ruckus I raised as a kid."

Her mother smiled. "I was for a time, but no more. Having Jake running in and out, having you to talk to now that you're a grown-up woman yourself, it's a real blessing, Cassie. I'm grateful."

"I don't need your gratitude, Mom. I belong here, especially now. Go on and get your purse. I'm going to buy you the biggest sundae Stella can make."

"Oh, my, I couldn't possibly," her mother said, but she looked tempted as she followed Cassie to the car.

"Of course you can," Cassie said as she checked to make sure everyone had fastened their seat belts. Then she grinned at her mother. "And you can have it before lunch."

Her mother looked horrified. "Heavens, no. It will ruin my appetite."

"So what?" Cassie said as they made the quick trip to Main Street. "Why can't we have dessert first every now and again on a special occasion?"

"And what occasion would that be?" her mother asked as Cassie pulled into a parking spot in front of the diner.

"My homecoming, of course."

A rare and full-fledged smile spread across her mother's too-pale face. "Now that really is worth celebrating."

She said it with such genuine emotion that Cassie

had to blink back tears. Maybe she'd had it wrong all these years. Maybe her mother really had missed her.

"Can I celebrate, too?" Jake asked from the back.

"Absolutely," Cassie agreed.

"And we're really going to stay here?" he asked. "You're not going to change your mind again?"

"I'm not changing my mind," Cassie said firmly.

He pumped a fist into the air. "All right!"

When they were settled into a booth at Stella's, Cassie beckoned her old boss over. "We need three large sundaes, two hot fudge." She glanced at her mother. "Caramel or strawberry?"

"Definitely strawberry," her mother said.

Stella reacted with shock. "No main course? Not even a burger?"

"Not yet," Cassie said.

"Anything else?"

"How about a job?"

Stella's mouth gaped. She stuck her order pad in her pocket, then scooted into the booth next to Cassie. "You're looking for work?"

Cassie nodded.

"Well, hallelujah! That must mean you're home to stay."

"I am."

"Then you can start tomorrow. With the parade and all, it's going to be a zoo in here, and the teenage girl I had working for me announced today that she intended to spend the Fourth with her boyfriend whether I liked it or not."

"Did you fire her?"

Stella chuckled. "I will now. Irresponsible kids need to be taught a lesson." She patted Cassie's hand. "Didn't take long for you to catch on, did it? One warning had you in here right on time every single day you were scheduled."

"I liked the perks," Cassie said with a grin. "All the ice cream I could eat."

"It was a small price to pay for a reliable worker," Stella replied.

After she'd gone off to fix their sundaes, Jake left his grandmother's side to squeeze in next to Cassie. "If we're gonna stay, that means I can spend more time with Mr. Davis, doesn't it? My friends back home will be so jealous when I tell them I know him. I mean, he's almost like a celebrity."

"In that case you should understand that you can't go bothering him. I'm sure he has lots and lots of work to do," Cassie said.

"But I asked him if he would explain to me about computers and how they work and stuff, and he said he would." Jake regarded her with an earnest, hopeful expression. "He said he wouldn't mind at all."

Cassie exchanged a helpless look with her mother. Leave it to Jake to take matters into his own hands.

"We'll see," Cassie said evasively.

"I think we should go after lunch, before he forgets," Jake said.

"No, not today," Cassie told him firmly.

"When?"

"I'll talk to him and work something out," she said, grateful when Stella appeared with their sundaes.

The ice cream distracted Jake for maybe five minutes before he began to badger her again.

"If you don't drop this right now," Cassie said finally, "you won't see him at all."

"But—"

"I said to drop it."

Tears welled up in Jake's eyes, but he fell silent, shoving the rest of his sundae away in protest. Cassie's appetite disappeared, as well. Only her mother continued to enjoy her sundae, or at least pretended to.

Was this what it was going to be like living in Winding River, a constant tug-of-war with her son over his hero worship of a man he didn't even realize was his father?

By the time they left for home, Cassie had a splitting headache and a knot the size of Wyoming in her stomach. At this rate she was going to wind up in a hospital bed right next to her mother's.

Naturally Jake didn't take her decision as final. Nor did the concession she made, allowing him to attend the parade and fireworks, appease him. She had to admit that had gone well enough. If Cole had been around, she hadn't spotted him. And Jake's delight had been worth every second of nervousness she'd experienced.

But by the next morning the treat had been forgotten, and Jake was back on the subject of going to see Cole. Her repeated warnings that she didn't want to hear another word about it seemed to fall on deaf ears.

He continued to pester her for the rest of the week

about going out to the Double D. He'd gotten his stubbornness and willfulness from her, no doubt about it.

She steadfastly continued to refuse to take him to visit Cole, making up excuse after excuse, but Cassie could see that they were wearing thin. Even so, she was stunned when Jake disappeared on Saturday morning. She searched high and low, but finally had to admit there was no sign of him.

"Mom, have you seen Jake?"

"Not since breakfast. Why?"

"He's not in the house. He's not working on the bike, and nobody on the block has seen him. I've looked everywhere I can think of."

"You don't suppose he's gone out to Cole's ranch, do you?" Edna asked, as aware as Cassie of her grandson's obsession.

That was exactly what Cassie feared. "How would he get there, though?"

"I imagine it wouldn't be all that difficult to get somebody to give him a lift. Half the ranchers in town on a Saturday take that road back home. All the boy would have to do is ask one of them."

"Should I call out there?"

"Why not ride around town first and see if anyone's seen him," her mother suggested. "No point in getting Cole involved if the boy's just wandered off to get an ice cream cone or something."

But no one in town had seen Jake. Cassie was about to reach for the phone to call Cole when it rang.

"You looking for Jake, by any chance?" Cole asked without preamble.

"Oh, my God," Cassie murmured. "He *is* with you. Is he okay?"

"He looks fine to me, but I thought you might be worried. He was pretty evasive at first when I asked how he got here and whether he had your permission to come. I got the feeling he didn't tell you before he hitchhiked out here."

"He *what?*"

"Pete gave him a ride on his way back from Stella's," Cole explained. Then he assured her, "He's okay, Cassie."

"That's not the point. I'm going to wring his scrawny little neck. I'll be there in twenty minutes."

"Take your time and cool off a little. Keep reminding yourself that there's been no harm done."

"Don't tell me what to do where my son's concerned," she snapped, and slammed down the phone.

"He's with Cole?" her mother asked.

"Oh, yes."

"Should I come with you?"

She shook her head. "No. Cole was right about one thing. I do need to calm down before I get out there. No telling what I might say."

Cassie made it to the Double D in less than the twenty minutes it usually took. The front door was standing open as if she were expected, so she went straight in. Oblivious to the grandeur of the antiques that generations of Davises had collected over the years, she went in search of her son.

When she finally found the two of them in Cole's office, heads bent over the computer keyboard, her blood ran cold. Jake looked happier than she'd seen him in ages. Just thinking about the bond the two of them were obviously forming made her knees go weak. She had to lean against the doorjamb for support.

"Look right natural together, don't they?" Frank Davis remarked, slipping up quietly to stand at her shoulder in the doorway.

Something in his voice alerted her. She stepped away from the room and turned to study the man who had probably come between her and Cole.

Frank Davis had a powerful build. His shock of dark-brown hair was streaked with gray now, but there was still plenty of spark in his blue eyes, and he wore that same arrogant, superior expression that had intimidated her as a girl. Oddly she discovered that he didn't scare her now. She met his gaze without flinching.

"What are you saying?" she asked in a cool, deliberate tone.

Her reaction seemed to amuse him. "I'm saying I know."

"Know what?"

He smirked. "One look is all it takes to know that boy is my grandson. Even if your mama hadn't told me the truth years ago, I would have seen it right off."

Despite her determination not to let the man get to her, Cassie felt faint for the second time in just a few minutes. This time she had to will herself not to lean against the wall for support.

"My mother told you?" Her mother had never said a single word to Cassie about her suspicions, but she had discussed them with Cole's father? What had she been thinking?

"She thought I had a right to know."

More likely her mother had been desperate for advice from the one person she'd assumed had as big a stake in keeping the secret as she did. *Oh, Mom, what have you done?* Cassie thought as she stared into that confident gaze. *And why didn't you warn me?*

"Does Cole know?"

"Not unless he's figured it out in the last half hour."

"Why haven't you told him?" Understanding dawned. "You haven't hold him because even now you don't think I'm good enough for him, because you don't want him to know that I had his child. You're afraid he'll insist on marrying me. That's why you came between us years ago, sending him back to school, then getting someone to write him a note saying I was breaking it off for good. That was you, wasn't it?"

Color rose in Frank's cheeks, but he didn't deny the accusation. "You two were way too young to get involved. Your mother and I did what we thought was best."

His words delivered yet another blow. The two of them had conspired, even before they had known about the pregnancy? She felt as if she were standing on a slippery slope and beginning to skid. Nothing seemed certain anymore.

"My mother?" she repeated, needing to understand, praying she was mistaken. "What did she have to do with it?"

"Who do you think wrote the note that Cole got?

And who kept his note from you? No way I could keep
Berta Smith from delivering it. She takes her duties at
the post office real serious. But your mama got it out
of the box and ripped it up."

"Oh, my God," she whispered, brokenhearted at
the thought of the betrayal that had changed not just
her life and Cole's but their son's, as well. Maybe they
wouldn't have married if Cole had known about the
pregnancy, but they'd never had a chance to decide
things for themselves. Each had been convinced of
the other's betrayal. As a result the choices had been
taken out of their hands.

"Well, the lies are over now," Frank said, a compla-
cent expression settling on his face. "Cole will know
about his son soon enough, and if I know my boy, he'll
be furious that you kept such a secret from him. He'll
fight you for custody."

Cassie felt sick to her stomach as she realized that
even now the man was scheming against her. "That's
what you're counting on, isn't it? That he'll reject me
but claim Jake?"

His eyes glittered with satisfaction. "That's exactly
right. You won't stand a chance of keeping the boy, not
in this state."

If she hadn't been filled with such white-hot fury,
Cassie might have been chilled by his threat or by the
triumphant expression on his face. Instead, poking him
in the chest, she backed him up against the opposite
wall, oblivious to the difference in their sizes, oblivious to anything beyond the outrage that his smug remark had stirred.

"You will never take my boy from me," she said in a low tone, praying it wouldn't carry down the hall. "Never. Not if I have to see you in hell first."

She must not have gotten the right note of warning in her voice, because she could still hear Frank's chuckle echoing after her as she stormed into Cole's office to claim her son.

8

Cole had heard Cassie's raised voice in the hall but couldn't imagine what she and his father had to fight about, especially since his father had been giving so much lip service lately to the prospect of Cole getting back together with her.

Then their voices had dropped, and he hadn't given the subject much thought since the boy sitting beside him was hurling questions at him so fast his head was spinning. The kid clearly had an insatiable curiosity when it came to computers, and he was smart, too. Cole didn't have to talk down to him. Given what Cassie had told him about the trouble Jake had gotten into on a computer, he probably shouldn't have been surprised, but he was.

When he finally glanced up from the screen and spotted Cassie, his pulse took another one of those wicked lurches. She was wearing a sundress that showed off the satiny skin of her shoulders and her long, shapely calves. Her cheeks were flushed with color and her eyes sparkled dangerously. Whatever she and Frank had been discussing, it had rankled.

"Jake Collins!" she said sternly, avoiding Cole's gaze altogether.

The boy glanced up at Cole, then gave a resigned shrug. "Yes, ma'am."

"Do you have any idea at all how much trouble you're in?"

"A lot?" he said hesitantly.

"Oh, yes," she said. "You know you are not supposed to be here, that you are not supposed to hitch rides with strangers and that you are always supposed to tell me where you're going."

"You wouldn't let me come," Jake said, as if that were excuse enough.

"I had my reasons," she said direly. "And that's all that matters. You disobeyed me, and I won't have it. Am I getting through to you yet?"

Cole saw Jake's shoulders slump and immediately felt sorry for the kid. He knew what the boy had done was wrong, but no harm had come out of it. Shouldn't Cassie be thankful for that, at least? Ignoring the temper flashing in her eyes, he decided he'd better intercede.

"He's already assured me that nothing like this will ever happen again," he said, gazing directly at the boy. "Right, Jake?"

Clearly sensing a powerful ally, Jake nodded eagerly. "I'll get permission next time."

"Not likely," Cassie muttered. She leveled a stern

look at Jake. "There will not be a next time, period. End of discussion."

Cole stared at her, curious about what had infuriated her so much. Was it Jake's disobedience? Panic over what could have happened to a kid out hitchhiking, even in this relatively safe community?

Or did it specifically have to do with him? This was the second time he'd gotten the feeling she didn't want him spending time with her son.

There could be any number of reasons for that, of course. A lot of responsible single mothers tried to keep some distance between their children and the men in their lives, at least until they knew if the relationship was going to lead somewhere. That didn't seem to apply here, since he and Cassie weren't exactly having a relationship and she'd stated quite clearly that she didn't intend for that to change.

Maybe it was just a case of protecting the boy from being disappointed by a man who had disappointed her in the past.

Still trying to figure it out, Cole gave her a penetrating look, but her face was giving away nothing. Because he found that annoying, he deliberately set out to provoke an honest answer out of her.

"What was that you said, Cassie?" he taunted mildly. "Something about there not being a next time?"

She gave him a sweet, completely insincere smile. "That's right. Jake knows he shouldn't be bothering you."

"I don't mind."

"Well, I do," she said, her look meant as a warning

that he wasn't to contradict her. "We have to leave now. Jake, go to the car. I'll be there in a minute. Cole and I have a few things we need to clear up."

Cole could hardly wait to hear what those were.

"But, Mom—"

"Go," she repeated in a way that had her son scrambling from the chair.

Jake skidded to a stop as he reached the door. "Bye, Cole. Thanks."

"Anytime," he said, deliberately defying Cassie, his gaze locked with hers.

There was no mistaking the storm brewing in her eyes. He felt a rare spark of anticipation. He'd been itching to get into a good old-fashioned, rip-roaring fight with her for days now. It was the only time she let down those rock-solid defenses of hers. This seemed as good a battle as any, especially since she appeared as eager as he was to start it.

The minute Jake was out of sight, Cassie marched up to the desk, then leaned down until her face was just inches above his. The effect was ruined somewhat by the way her sundress gaped, but she was clearly oblivious to that. She would have been appalled had she known.

"I will not have my son out here, do you understand me?" she snapped. "Where he goes and what he does are my decisions."

"You are his mother," he agreed.

She scowled at him, then added, "He is *my* son and *my* responsibility."

"No question about that," he said, then locked gazes

with her. "Where's his father? How much say does he have in things?" He'd let that issue pass once before, but he'd concluded it was time to get it out in the open.

Dismay flickered briefly in her eyes, then vanished. "None of your business. All you need to know is that when it comes to Jake, I make the rules." She shook her head, regarding him with evident distaste. "I can't understand how I overlooked this years ago. You Davis men are all alike."

He stared at her, startled by the very real venom in her voice. Clearly he'd missed something. "What the hell does that mean?" he demanded. "Does this have something to do with the argument you and my father were having out there in the hall?"

Something that might have been panic registered in her expression for just an instant, long enough to betray the fact that she wasn't nearly as calm as she pretended to be when she shrugged. Then that cool mask he'd come to hate slid back into place.

"Just a difference of opinion," she said mildly.

"About?"

"I don't want to get into it now."

"I do."

"Then this will be just one more instance in life when you don't get what you want. Get used to it," she said.

The woman had developed a lot of spunk over the years; he had to give her that. Back when they'd been dating, she had been all brash bravado. Few people had ever seen past it to the vulnerable girl inside. Cole had.

Now, though, her feistiness ran deeper, carried more conviction and self-confidence.

Still, he couldn't seem to shake the memory of that tiny, fleeting glimpse of fear he'd caught earlier.

"I'm sorry if my father said something to upset you," he offered, treading carefully, still hoping to get an honest explanation.

"He didn't," she insisted. "Your father doesn't scare me. He never has."

"But he tried to," Cole guessed. What he couldn't understand was why his father would do such a thing. For days now he'd been doing everything in his power to bring the two of them together. Was he just trying a different tactic with Cassie? Maybe a little reverse psychology, since his blatant scheming obviously hadn't worked on Cole?

"I have to go," Cassie said, ignoring his question. "I need to get out there to Jake before he gets it into his head to hitchhike back home."

"I imagine my father's keeping him company."

The color drained out of her face at that. "All the more reason for me to go. I don't want him influencing Jake in any way."

"Are you suggesting he did a lousy job with me?" Cole said.

She shrugged. "If the shoe fits..." Her expression turned intense. "I meant what I said earlier, Cole, I don't want Jake out here. And I don't want you encouraging him to come. Are we clear about that?"

Her implication—that he and his father were somehow lousy role models for her son—grated. Added to the heat and tension that swirled in the air every time he and Cassie got together, it was more than Cole could take. He was overcome by a need to do something about it, to rattle her so badly she would lose that distant, disdainful expression.

Before he could consider the ramifications, he reached out and hauled her into his lap and settled his mouth over hers, muffling her gasp of protest.

She tasted of cinnamon and maybe a lingering hint of mint. Her lips were as soft as he'd remembered, if not nearly as willing as they had been even the other day at the picnic. She struggled in his arms, bit down on his lower lip. He winced at the taste of blood, became more determined than ever to tame her, to remind her of the way she had once melted in his arms.

He framed her face with his hands, looked long and deep into her flashing eyes, waited for the anger to die, then slanted his mouth over hers once more.

This time she shuddered, then relaxed in his embrace before kissing him back. Temper gave way to passion, chilly disdain turned to fiery acceptance.

They were both breathless and panting when he finally released her with a great deal of reluctance. She stared back at him with dazed eyes. Slowly her gaze cleared and the temper came roaring back. It was like watching water come to a boil, simmering slowly at first, then suddenly bubbling up and over.

"Damn you," she murmured, then shot to her feet. "I won't let you do this to me, not again."

She whirled around and stalked from the room without another word. A smile crept across Cole's face as he watched her go.

"When it comes to you, Cassie, and most of those rules you're so intent on reminding me of," he said softly, "they were made to be broken."

"And then he kissed me," Cassie told Gina, all but quivering with outrage. "Can you imagine?"

"The man's a cad," Gina agreed, barely containing a grin.

"Are you laughing at me?"

"Never," Gina denied, though her smile spread.

"You *are* laughing at me."

"It's just that the whole time you're trying to sound so outraged, there's a very becoming blush on your cheeks."

"Because I'm furious."

"Why? Because he kissed you or because you liked it?"

"I did not like it," Cassie said emphatically.

Gina looked skeptical. "He's lost his touch?"

"I never said that. It's not important whether or not he's a good kisser. The point is that he had no business kissing me in the first place. We were fighting. It was a sneaky, low-down way to make me forget that."

"He wants you back," Gina said.

"Don't be crazy. He doesn't want me back any more than I want him."

"If you say so."

Cassie scowled. "I do," she said, even though her conviction was weakening.

"Okay, then. There's nothing to worry about. You're not going to be swayed by a few harmless little kisses, then, are you?"

There had been nothing harmless about those kisses. They had been devastating, Cassie admitted to herself. She could deny it to her friend from now till doomsday and it wouldn't change the truth. She sighed. Everything was so blasted complicated.

"Let's forget about Cole," she said.

"Okay by me."

"I want to hear about you. Who is that handsome man you were with over the weekend? I've never seen him before. Is he a friend from New York?"

Gina suddenly looked uncomfortable. "I have no idea who you mean."

"The man who was following you around like he'd never met such an exotic creature before."

"Oh, him," Gina said, then shrugged. "He's a nuisance. Nothing more. He's probably gone by now."

"I don't think so," Cassie said, glancing pointedly outside, where the very man under discussion was lurking on the sidewalk.

Gina followed the direction of her gaze, then sighed heavily, her expression miserable. "Well, hell," she muttered under her breath.

Cassie studied her intently, saw the genuine worry in her friend's eyes. "Gina, what's really going on? Who is he?"

"Nobody important," her friend said staunchly, but she slid out of the booth. She gave Cassie a hug. "See you later. If you ask me, you ought to consider what Cole's offering."

The comment was enough to throw Cassie and keep her from asking all the other questions on the tip of her tongue as Gina left Stella's. She watched idly as Gina marched up to the man, appeared to exchange words with him, then took off alone in the direction of her car. Another example of true love not running smoothly, perhaps?

And speaking of that, what the heck had Gina meant with that comment about taking what Cole was offering? As far as Cassie could see, he wasn't offering a blessed thing. A few stolen kisses didn't add up to anything…except maybe trouble. And frankly she had more of that in her life these days than she could possibly cope with.

Dismissing that and Gina's odd behavior, she went back to work. Stella's was as busy as ever at lunchtime. Cassie was on the run until almost two.

"Go," Stella said, taking her last order from her. "I know you have to get your mother to the hospital. And I don't want to see you anywhere near here in the morning. I can manage. You stay right there until she's out of surgery and you know how she's doing."

"Thank you, Stella. You're an angel."

"Good heavens, don't be spreading that around," the older woman pleaded. "The only way I keep my customers in line is having them think I'm a tyrant."

Cassie laughed. "I hate to tell you this, but you don't have anyone in town fooled."

Stella looked genuinely disappointed. "Well, shucks.

I guess I'm just going to have to work a little harder at it. Now, scoot."

"Hey, how about getting that burger over here before I starve to death?" Hank Folsom hollered.

"Keep your britches on, Hank," Stella shouted right back. "If you don't like the service in here, you can just march right through the door and get your lunch someplace else." She winked at Cassie. "How was that?"

"Tough as nails," Cassie assured her. "Unfortunately, it's an idle threat. There is no place else in town to get a burger."

"I know," Stella said with satisfaction. "Works out real nice, don't you think?"

Cassie was still chuckling over that when she got home and found her mother sitting on the sofa in her best dress, her suitcase sitting beside her. Jake hovered nearby, looking worried. They had told him about the surgery the night before, talking about it only in the most upbeat and positive way, but it had clearly rattled him.

"I'm going to the hospital with you," Jake said, shooting a defiant look at Cassie.

"I made arrangements for you to stay next door."

"Well, I'm not going to."

"Let him come," her mother said. "He'll just worry if he stays here with Mildred, and he'll be company for you."

Cassie finally relented. "Okay, give me two seconds to change and we'll head on up to Laramie to the hospital."

The screen door banged open just then. "She's not

going to Laramie," Cole said. "I've made arrangements for her to go to University Hospital down in Denver. The doctor there has consulted with her doctor. Her records were sent to him yesterday once your mother okayed it."

Cassie's mouth dropped open. "What right did you have to do that?" Cassie demanded finally. She looked at her mother. "You knew about this?"

"I knew it was a possibility," Edna said.

Cole regarded Cassie evenly. "I told you at the beginning that I was going to see that she had the best care possible. We're going to Denver. I've got my plane all fueled up."

Jake's eyes widened, oblivious to anything except Cole's announcement. "We're going in a real plane? One of those ones I saw at the airport on the way into town?"

Cole grinned at his enthusiasm. "That's right. If you're good, I'll even let you take the controls for a minute."

"Over my dead body," Cassie said at once.

Before that could erupt into a full-fledged battle, her mother said quietly, "I think if Cole's gone to all this trouble, then we should do as he says. We're certainly not going to drive all that way."

Cassie stared at her. "Mom, you've always sworn you would never set foot in an airplane."

"This is different."

"How?"

"I'm sure Cole knows what he's doing."

"He just told a nine-year-old he could operate the controls," Cassie pointed out.

"It's not as if I'm going to nod off and take a nap while Jake flies us to Denver," Cole said mildly. "And I know you want your mother to have the very best chance she can have. The surgeon in Denver comes highly recommended."

"Why didn't you say anything about this before?" Cassie asked.

"Because he didn't have an opening in his schedule until yesterday. The minute he called me, I spoke to your mother and made the arrangements."

Cassie felt as if the entire situation, already terrifying enough, was spinning wildly out of control. It wasn't just that the four of them would be stuck in close quarters in that tiny plane, it was the fact that Cole clearly intended to be right by her side all through her mother's surgery. On the one hand the gesture was both generous and kind. On the other, it would inevitably tighten the bond between them. Worse, it would keep him and his son in close proximity for hours, if not days.

In the end, though, Cassie knew she had no choice. The only thing that mattered was getting her mother the finest treatment available. And while the doctor in Laramie was surely good, the one in Denver would have greater experience and perhaps a more experienced support staff, as well.

Swallowing her pride—and her fear—she finally nodded. "Let's go, then."

In the plane Cole was true to his word. He allowed

the awestruck Jake to take over the controls, if only for a few minutes. It was an experience Cassie knew her son would never forget. By the time they landed in Denver, his case of hero worship was stronger than ever.

They checked her mother into the hospital, then saw her settled into the private room Cole had arranged. When the surgeon came in to speak to her, Cassie was impressed with his warmth, his reassurances and his detailed explanations about what her mother could expect in the morning. In his early fifties, he was clearly both experienced and compassionate. For the first time since she had learned of her mother's diagnosis, Cassie could see hope in her mother's eyes.

"He seemed like a nice man," her mother said, following the surgeon with her gaze as he left the room.

"We couldn't have found a better doctor," Cole said.

"Nice-looking, too," Cassie teased her mother. "No wonder there's a little color in your cheeks."

"Stop with that," her mother said, clearly flustered. The pink in her cheeks deepened. "All I care about is how good he is with that scalpel of his."

A few minutes later a nurse came in. "We're going to give your mother a little something to help her relax and get a good night's sleep."

"Then you all might as well run along," Edna said. "I'm in good hands." She reached for Cole's hand. "And it's all thanks to you. I don't know how I'll ever repay you."

He bent down and kissed her cheek. "All you need to do for me is get well and live a long and healthy life."

"I'm going to do my best." Her gaze locked on Cole's. "Keep an eye on my girl for me, okay?"

Cole glanced Cassie's way. "Always," he said softly.

Trying to ignore the fluttery feeling in the pit of her stomach caused by Cole's promise, Cassie gave her mother a kiss. "See you in the morning, Mom. I love you."

Now that the time had come to leave, Jake looked shaken. He edged close to the bad. "I don't want to go, Grandma."

She brushed the hair out of his eyes. "I'm going to be just fine," she reassured him. "Go with your mom and Cole. Get something good to eat and see the sights. This time tomorrow you can come back here and tell me all about them."

Jake still looked reluctant. Cole squeezed his shoulder. "Come along, son."

Even though he spoke casually, in a way men spoke to young boys all the time without it meaning a thing, Cassie froze. Hearing him call Jake *son,* no matter the context, made her tremble. How long? she wondered, exchanging a look with her mother. How long would it be before Cole realized that the boy he was addressing really was his son?

Cole did his best to relieve Cassie's tension over a quick dinner in a fast-food restaurant. He enumerated all of the surgeon's qualifications and cited all of the latest cancer recovery statistics. But nothing he said seemed to get through to her. She listened, she nodded, but her fingers continued to shred napkin after napkin until there was a pile of white fluff on the table in front of her.

Finally he reached across the table and placed his hand over hers. "Enough," he said gently. He glanced pointedly at the normally effusive Jake, who had grown increasingly silent as the meal went on, clearly picking up on her mood.

Cassie's gaze flew to her son. "Sweetie, are you okay?"

He shook his head. "I'm scared," he admitted.

"You heard Cole. Grandma's doctor is the best. She's going to get well."

Jake regarded her hopefully. "You believe that?"

"With all my heart," she said fervently.

"Then how come you're acting like you're scared, too?" He pointed to the mound of shredded napkins.

Cassie stared at them, looking vaguely startled. "Oh, dear, I guess my mind was on all sorts of things."

"What things?" Jake promptly wanted to know.

She forced a grin. "Cabbages and kings."

"Mom!"

Cole wanted to protest, as well. He'd hoped Jake might get a straight answer out of her. He doubted *he* could. If it wasn't her mother that had her looking so worried, then what could it be?

Only after they'd gone to the hotel near the hospital and settled Jake in bed did Cole get a chance to ask. He was pacing the suite's living room when Cassie finally joined him. He hadn't been at all sure that she would. He had the oddest feeling that he was the cause of her nervousness, though why that should be he couldn't imagine. And surely that kiss they'd shared hadn't rattled her so badly that she was scared to be in the same room with him. It wasn't as if he was likely to try to ravish her on the eve of her mother's surgery.

"Jake asleep?"

She nodded.

"How are you?"

"Scared, just like he said."

"About your mother?"

She shot him a startled look, then glanced away. "Of course," she said hurriedly. "What else?"

"That's what I was wondering." He studied her intently. "You're not scared of me, are you? Of being here in a hotel room with me overnight?"

A glimmer of a smile passed across her face as she gestured around the suite. "It's not as if we're in cramped quarters, Cole. We won't even be sleeping in the same room."

"More's the pity," he murmured.

She frowned at him. "Why would you say that?"

"Because it's true."

"Cole, we can't go back."

"Then how about going forward?"

She shook her head without giving the notion a moment's consideration. That grated on him more than he could say.

"You always were too blasted stubborn for your own good."

"Then I'm surprised you'd want to bother with me."

"Unfortunately, you're still the only woman who's ever fascinated me."

"Cole!"

The protest was only halfhearted, which he considered encouraging. "It's true," he said, stepping closer until he could lift his hand to her cheek. Her skin was like cool satin, but it warmed beneath his touch as if he'd stirred a fire to life below the surface. He rubbed the pad of his thumb across her lips and felt her shudder.

It took every bit of willpower he possessed not to claim her mouth and satisfy the urgency already building inside him. Not tonight, he warned himself. Taking advantage of her vulnerability was no way to win her heart. It would just give her more ammunition to use against him.

Slow and steady, he reminded himself. Like the tortoise. Winning, not speed, was the goal. In fact, in the past few weeks he'd begun to wonder how he'd ever lost sight of that goal, even for a single second.

9

Cassie alternated between pacing the hospital waiting room and huddling miserably in a corner, trying not to look at the other families. Each time she did, she saw her own fear reflected in their faces. It was more than she could bear.

Instead of thinking about what was going on in the operating room, she forced herself to think about Cole. He was the only distraction that stood a chance against the weight of her concern for her mother. Right now he and Jake were off on a shopping expedition, ostensibly to find something suitable for her mother.

"Just a little get-well gift," Cole had assured her. "It will keep Jake's mind off everything."

She couldn't fault him for wanting to do that for her son. In fact, there was very little she could fault him on these days. He had been nothing but kind and utterly thoughtful. It reminded her of why she'd fallen in love with him years ago.

It was driving her nuts.

Even the night before, when she had thought for sure he was going to take advantage of both proximity and her fragile emotional state, Cole had behaved like a perfect gentleman, backing off before things could get too heated.

His consideration was like a magnet. She wanted so badly to lean on him, to accept the comfort he was offering, but the past had taught her that the only person she could count on was herself. And her mother, of course.

Now, though, it was because of her mother's health that she needed someone to help her be strong. And it would be folly to let Cole be that person, even for a second.

"There she is," a familiar voice whispered.

Cassie's gaze shot up to see her four best friends hovering in the doorway of the waiting room. Tears stung her eyes, then rolled down her cheeks. *These* were people she could trust, women who had always been there for her. When times got tough, the Calamity Janes had always hung together.

"You guys," she murmured, crossing the room to be enfolded in a fierce group hug. "What are you doing here?"

"Did you honestly think we were going to let you go through this alone?" Karen chided.

"No way," Lauren declared.

She was wearing jeans and a faded blouse and hiding behind a pair of oversize sunglasses and a floppy hat, but none of that could disguise the fact that she was the glamorous one among them. Hollywood had taught her too much for her ever to be the plain Jane of the group again.

"The Calamity Janes stick together through thick and thin, remember?" she said to Cassie.

Cassie gave her a watery smile. "I remember."

"Any word yet?" Emma asked.

"Nothing. She's still in surgery."

Gina squeezed her hand. "Where's Jake?"

"With Cole."

Three pairs of eyes regarded her incredulously. Even Lauren removed her sunglasses long enough to stare.

"He volunteered to keep Jake occupied. What could I do?" Cassie asked defensively.

"Why is he even here in the first place?" Emma demanded in her best ready-to-charge-into-battle voice.

"He made the arrangements for Mom to be treated here, instead of in Laramie. In fact, come to think of it, how did you find out where we were? It all happened so fast I never even had a chance to call and let you know."

"Lauren waved her magic wand and, *poof,* information was forthcoming. Then a jet appeared. The woman has contacts," Gina said respectfully. She feigned an exaggerated bow. "I am in awe."

"One of the few perks of stardom worth having," Lauren said with a distinct edge to her voice. Then, before anyone could question her, she tucked an arm around Cassie's waist. "Come on. Let's sit down over here where we won't be the center of attention. You doing okay, sweetie?" She whipped open a bag, and cups of gourmet coffee appeared for all of them.

"Hanging in," Cassie said, taking the cup and

breathing in the aroma. Hazelnut. "I thought I'd know something by now, but it seems like it's been forever and there's still no word."

Lauren nodded and set aside her own coffee. "Then let me see what I can find out."

As soon as she'd gone, Emma shook her head. "I don't know how she does it. Even incognito, she has a way of commanding respect. You should have seen her down at the information desk. The poor volunteer kept trying to tell us that only family was permitted up here, but Lauren finally persuaded her that we were as close to being family as anybody could be. She did it in a Southern voice straight out of *Gone with the Wind.* I kept looking around to see who was talking. Next thing you know we're on an elevator with a little map showing us precisely where the waiting room is located. If I could do what she does, I'd never lose a case."

"You never lose a case, anyway," Karen pointed out.

Emma frowned. "That's not true. I've lost some."

"How many?" Gina teased. "One? Two?"

"Four," Emma retorted.

Gina rolled her eyes. "Out of how many?"

"I don't know."

"Hundreds, I imagine," Gina countered.

"The point is, Lauren is very good at what she does," Emma said.

"Then why does she look so unhappy?" Cassie wondered.

"I've been asking myself the same thing," Karen said, her expression thoughtful. "And I know she wanted to stick around for your mom's surgery, but she's showing no inclination at all to get back to her glamorous life in Hollywood. Every time I bring up anything about her career, she puts me off."

"Well, it can't be because she's having trouble getting roles," Cassie said. "I saw on TV the other night that there are two producers who are counting on her starring in their next films."

"Which producers? What films?" Gina asked with the starstruck fascination of an old movie buff.

"I don't remember, but I do recall that both admitted she hasn't committed yet."

The discussion of Lauren's apparent unhappiness ended when she came back into the waiting room with a triumphant expression and the bemused surgeon in tow.

"Look who I found," she announced happily. "And the news is good." She beamed at him. "I said that straight off, because you doctors always hem and haw before you get to the bottom line."

He regarded her with a dazed expression. "Who are you again?"

"Just a friend of the family."

He still looked puzzled. "But you look so familiar."

She sighed dramatically. "See what I mean about dillydallying. Come on, Doc. Tell Cassie how her mom's surgery went."

He gathered his composure and faced Cassie. "Everything went exactly as I'd hoped it would. The cancer appeared to be contained. We did a lumpectomy and I'll be recommending a course of chemotherapy and radiation, but there's no reason to think she will have anything other than a full recovery. There will be regular checkups after that to make sure there hasn't been a recurrence, but I'd say the prognosis is very good."

For the second time that morning, Cassie's tears flowed unchecked. She clasped the doctor's hand. "Thank you."

"No need. I was just doing my job."

"Can I see her?"

"She's still in recovery. Why not go and have your lunch, then come back. She'll be in her room by then. I'll check in on her later. If all goes as I anticipate, she'll be released in the morning."

Cassie and her friends were exchanging joyful hugs when Cole and Jake arrived.

"Good news?" Cole asked, his gaze on Cassie.

She nodded. "The best. The surgeon expects her to make a full recovery."

Genuine relief washed over his face. "I'm glad."

"Grandma's going to be okay?" Jake asked as if he didn't dare to believe it. "Really?"

Cassie gave him a hug, wanting to believe in that as much as he did. "Absolutely," she said with confidence. If a positive outlook and the support of family and friends had anything to do with it, her mother would not only survive, she would thrive. "She'll have some treatments for a while, but that should do the trick."

"I propose we all go out and celebrate," Cole said. "My treat."

"I never turn down a man with a credit card in his hand," Gina teased. "Especially when the alternative is hospital cafeteria food. Let's do it."

They found a lovely restaurant just a few blocks away from the hospital. Cassie actually managed to eat with enthusiasm for the first time in several days. Not even the sight of Jake sitting side by side with his father could take away the relief she'd felt when the doctor had given his report.

Her mother was going to survive. She had said the words, had tried not to let her faith waver for a single second, but until the surgeon had spoken with such optimism, she hadn't really dared to believe it.

"You okay?" Cole asked, leaning close to whisper in her ear.

"I am now," she said. "Thank you for arranging for her to come here."

"It was the least I could do."

"But you didn't have to do it."

"Yes, I did," he insisted. "For a lot of reasons, not the least of which is that she's your mother."

Cassie refused to let herself read anything at all into that. She was just grateful that everything had turned out as well as it had so far.

"I need to call Stella. If she doesn't object, I'd like to stay tonight, then Jake and I can go back tomorrow with my mother. If you need to get home, I'm sure Lauren will take the three of us back. She chartered a plane."

"I'm staying," Cole said flatly. "I've already made arrangements to keep the suite another night. And if the doctor says your mother should have her chemo and radiation here, when the time comes we'll reserve the suite for as long as necessary."

Cassie hadn't even considered what arrangements might have to be made for the follow-up treatments. "Cole, we can't keep imposing on you like that. I'm sure whatever she needs can be done in Laramie."

"She's going to have the best," he insisted. "We'll let the doctor decide."

Because there was no way she could knowingly accept less than the best for her mother, she reluctantly nodded her agreement. She was already in Cole's debt. It would be foolish to turn down his offer out of stubborn pride.

"Thank you," she said stiffly.

"Like I said, I owe you."

But for what, she wondered. For betraying her? He claimed he hadn't done that, or hadn't meant to, at any rate. Even though he knew his father had likely had some hand in it, he still didn't know the whole truth, that it was his father and her mother who had done the conniving. Would he be so eager to help her mother if he knew that?

She pushed all of that aside when Karen raised a glass in a toast. "To long, healthy lives for all of us and for those we love," she said.

It was a toast that would come back to haunt them. Three hours later, just as Karen, Lauren, Emma and Gina were about to return to Winding River, a call came that Caleb had collapsed at the ranch. By the time they reached the hospital in Laramie, Karen's husband was dead of a massive heart attack at thirty-eight.

The next few days passed in a blur. Cassie alternated between caring for her mother and sitting with her friend, whose pale complexion and glassy, dazed eyes were frightening to behold. None of them were able to reach Karen, no matter how they tried.

Karen got through Caleb's funeral without shedding a single tear. She politely thanked everyone who attended the services, served food to the mourners who visited the ranch, then went about the ranch chores with sporadic surges of frenzied activity, refusing all offers of help. She'd reacted only once—to the arrival of Grady Blackhawk, a man who'd made no secret of the fact he wanted to buy their ranch. Caleb had hated him. Karen had almost lost it when she'd seen him. Cole had escorted him away from the house.

"She can't go on like this," Lauren said, watching her worriedly after most of the guests had left.

"She needs to cry, to let it out," Gina added. Gina had always been the one most in touch with her emotions—the quickest to cry but also the fastest to laugh.

"I think she's afraid to start," Cassie said. "I think she's terrified that once the tears come, she won't be able to stop. To be honest, I feel that way myself. How could this happen to Caleb? He was so young. A thirty-eight-year-old isn't supposed to be having a heart attack, much less dying from it. There were so many things they planned to do together. They wanted to start a family. It's not fair."

"I feel as if that boy traded his life for mine," her mother said, her expression gloomy. She had insisted on attending the funeral, then stopping by the ranch to offer her condolences.

"Mama, don't you dare say that," Cassie said. "It doesn't work like that."

"Well, it just breaks my heart to see Karen this way," her mother said. "The burden of running this ranch was heavy enough on the two of them. How she'll keep up alone is beyond me. Of all you girls, she was the one I thought was set for life with a nice, steady man by her side. No offense to you, Emma, or you, Lauren, but Caleb was the kind of man all of you should have been looking for."

"No question about that," Lauren agreed. "I certainly had a knack for picking losers."

"Mick wasn't a loser, but he wasn't exactly the dependable, steady guy that Caleb was," Emma said of her own ex.

"What's that about a steady man?" Cole inquired, coming up behind Cassie. He rested his hands on her shoulders, massaging gently.

Ever since they'd gotten the news about Caleb, Cole had been a rock for Karen and all the rest of them. Leaving Cassie and Jake overnight with her mother in Denver, he had accompanied Karen and the others to the hospital in Laramie, then handled all of the funeral arrangements. He seemed to anticipate what needed to be done and took care of it without waiting to be asked. The only thing Karen had refused was his offer to send over help for the ranch.

She had been adamant about that, insisting that the ranch was her responsibility and that she needed to learn to deal with the work on her own. Nothing anyone said could dissuade her.

"I don't like the way she looks," Cassie said worriedly. "She's exhausted. She can't stay here by herself, and that's that."

"Well, we know she's not going to leave, so I'll just have to move in," Lauren said. "I imagine I can still do a few ranch chores."

They all stared. "You?"

"Why not me?" she asked indignantly. "I grew up on a ranch. It hasn't been that long. I still know one end of a cow from the other."

"But, Lauren," Emma protested, "what about your career?"

Lauren waved off the question. "It'll be there when I get back or it won't. I already have more money than I can ever spend. I'm staying here, and that's that."

Gina and Emma agreed to stay that night, as well, so Cassie left with her mother and Cole for the hundred-mile ride back to Winding River. It was late when they arrived, and her mother went straight to bed, but Cassie lingered on the porch with Cole. Jake was spending the night next door, so they were alone.

"Do you honestly think Karen will be able to manage that ranch on her own?" she asked Cole, settling into the swing.

He sat next to her and set the swing into a slow, easy motion. "Ranching is difficult work under the best of conditions. She's going to need help. I get the impression she doesn't have the money to hire on additional hands, and she flatly refused my offer to send one of my men over, even temporarily."

"Maybe she should consider selling. She always

wanted to travel. In high school that's all she ever talked about." Even as she said it, though, she knew Karen would never sell the ranch that Caleb had loved. Even if it drained her financially and physically, she would keep it because it had been his dream. But Karen's misplaced sense of loyalty could wind up killing her.

"She won't sell," Cole said with certainty.

Cassie sighed and met his gaze. "I know, but it might be better if she did."

He tucked a curl behind her ear. "We don't always do what's best, even if it's plain as day to us what that is."

Something in his voice told her he was no longer talking about Karen. "What would you do differently if you could?"

"Fight for you," he said without hesitation.

Cassie's breath caught in her throat at the regret she heard in his voice. "Would you?"

His gaze locked with hers. "I should have done it back then. I knew it the second I left town, but by then it was too late. Then I got that note and, well, all I could do was hate you for what I thought was an even worse betrayal than my own."

Cassie debated telling him what she had learned from his father. Part of her was reluctant to stir up the ashes of the past, but he deserved to know the truth, especially after all he had done for Edna Collins in recent days. "My mother wrote that note," she said flatly, praying that it wouldn't change his commitment to helping with her medical expenses.

Shock washed over his face. "How do you know that?" he demanded.

"Your father told me. He admitted that they conspired to keep us apart."

Cole stood and began to pace. Suddenly he stopped and slammed his fist against a post. "Dammit! I should have guessed."

"How could you have guessed? I certainly never imagined it."

"I saw them with their heads together back then," he explained. "But your mom and I had always gotten along so well, I couldn't believe that she would be involved in splitting us up. I only saw my father's less-than-subtle touch all over it."

"Well, unless your father lied, which I seriously doubt, she was involved," Cassie said flatly. "I haven't spoken to her about it, but I will, once things settle down and she has her health back."

Her voice caught at the end, and she put her hands over her face as the tears, never far from the surface, flowed again. Cole sat back down and reached for her.

"It's okay," he murmured. "Don't cry. She's going to be fine."

"I know, but..." She looked at him, feeling an overwhelming sense of sorrow. "But Caleb won't be. Karen's lost him forever. How can I be so glad about my mother, when my best friend's husband is dead?"

"One has absolutely nothing to do with the other. Karen understands that. She's as happy as you are that your mother's prognosis is good. She would never begrudge you that. And she knows that you care about her and her loss. She's going to need all of you more than ever. It's good that you've come home. Even better that you and Lauren, at least, intend to stick around."

She dared to meet his gaze then and saw something else in his eyes, something she hadn't dared to hope for in years and years. There was tenderness and longing and hope.

"*I'm* glad you're back to stay," he said softly.

They were words she had longed to hear. His eyes promised things that she had yearned for. And yet she couldn't allow herself to be swept off her feet, caught up in a dream of what might be, now that she was back in Winding River. Not with Jake and the secret of his paternity standing between them.

Because if Cole knew the truth, that she had kept his son from him all these years, whatever fantasy he was spinning about their future would crash and burn under the weight of his justifiable fury. He might eventually forgive his father's actions, but he would never forgive her for keeping such a secret. Never. And if he was inclined to, Frank Davis would have quite a lot to say about having the Davis heir kept from them.

"I have to go in," she said, pulling away, putting a safe distance between them.

"Why? It's not that late."

"But I have to be at Stella's for the morning shift tomorrow," she said.

"Come on," he chided. "Surely you don't need that much beauty sleep."

"You'd be surprised."

"Then have dinner with me tomorrow night, you and Jake."

"No," she said, more harshly than she should have.

He regarded her quizzically. "Why not?"

"Because I need to go to the ranch to see Karen," she said at once, praying that he would accept the excuse.

"Then I'll drive you."

If she refused him, he would want to know why, and she didn't have a single answer that he would accept without dissecting it.

"Fine," she said with undisguised reluctance.

"Thank you, Cole," he mocked.

She sighed. "I'm sorry. I do appreciate it, really I do. You've been a rock through all of this. I know Karen is grateful, too."

He regarded her doubtfully, but let it go. "Then I'll see you about three. Does that give you enough time after your shift ends?"

"Three will be fine."

"Maybe I'll stop by earlier and spend some time with Jake."

Cassie's heart skidded to a stop. "I...I don't think that's a good idea," she said, scrambling to come up with a reason he would buy. None came to mind.

Cole studied her quietly for what seemed to be an eternity, then asked, "Is there a reason you don't want me around Jake? This isn't the first time I've sensed that you'd just as soon I steer clear of him."

"I just don't want him to start to count on you. It's hard on a boy if men come and go in his life."

His gaze narrowed. "Have a lot of men come and gone in Jake's life?"

"No, because I have been very careful not to let that happen."

"I won't let him down," Cole said.

"You say that, but you can't guarantee it."

"Any more than you can," he replied. "We're all human. We all disappoint the people we care about from time to time, even with the best intentions. But I swear to you, Cassie, I would never knowingly hurt him."

"You wouldn't mean to," she agreed. "But it's inevitable."

"You would rather deprive him of my company than risk having me hurt him?"

"Yes," she said flatly. "That's how it has to be."

"For a woman who once thrived on risks, you've grown up to be a cautious woman."

"I was burned," she said simply. "I learned my lesson."

He studied her with a disconcerting intensity, then asked, "Who did that to you, Cassie?"

She regarded him incredulously. "You have to ask?"

"It wasn't just me. It couldn't have been. Was it Jake's father? Did he disappoint you badly, too?"

"Yes," she said, seizing the explanation. He had no idea how true it was. "Jake's father made it impossible for me ever to trust another man."

Cole leveled a look into her eyes that burned right through to her soul. "I'm going to change that," he vowed. "Just wait and see."

But he couldn't, she thought as he dropped a tender kiss on her forehead and walked away. Of all the men in the world, Cole Davis was the one least likely to be able to change the way she felt about trust.

And if he knew the truth about Jake, he'd feel the exact same way about her.

10

Cole took Cassie's reluctance to let him get too involved in her son's life as a challenge. Not only did he intend to convince her she was wrong about that, he intended to win her heart again.

Of course, trying to court a woman whose mother was ill and whose best friend was in mourning required a bit of inventiveness. Overt attempts to sweep her off her feet would, no doubt, be met with dismay. That left subtlety, something the Davis men were not known for. He'd inherited his father's inclination to go after what he wanted, no holds barred. Restraining that impulse was going to be tricky, but he could do it. He had to. The stakes were too high to risk losing.

As promised, he arrived at Cassie's promptly at three to drive her to Karen's. He came with a new computer game for Jake, flowers for Mrs. Collins and nothing at all for Cassie. A faint flicker of disappointment in her eyes was his reward. Next time he knew she wouldn't be so quick to turn down whatever token offering he brought for her.

Meantime, Jake was staring at the computer game with a mix of excitement and unmistakable frustration that Cole couldn't quite interpret.

"Anything wrong, pal? I thought you'd like that game. It's just hit the market. You don't have it, do you?"

Jake shook his head. "It's great, but..." He shot a condemning look at his mother, then muttered, "I don't have a computer. Mom won't get me one, especially after what happened where we used to live."

"Jake Collins, don't you dare imply that I refused to buy you a computer out of spite or something," Cassie said. "You know perfectly well it's not some sort of punishment. We simply can't afford one, though I have to admit you didn't display any evidence that you can use one responsibly."

Cole was about to speak, but one look at her face kept him silent. If he made an offer to buy the computer, it was evident she wouldn't appreciate it. Besides, he understood why she might be reluctant for the boy to have a computer after the trouble he'd gotten into on the internet.

"Maybe we can think about getting a computer for Christmas," Mrs. Collins said.

"But that's months and months away," Jake protested. "This game is so cool. I want to play it now."

Cole locked gazes with Cassie. "How about if I loan you an old computer I have at the house for now? We can leave off the modem so there will be no internet hookup."

"I don't know," she said, clearly hesitant.

"Mom, please," Jake pleaded.

"It's just a loan," Cole insisted. "And it's just gathering dust out at the ranch."

She sighed. "Okay, if you're sure you have it to spare. And definitely no modem."

Little did she know that he had half a dozen tucked away, thanks to the rapidly changing technology and his own need to be on the cutting edge of the industry. He could have supplied her with one that was state-of-the-art without batting an eye, but he resolved to provide an older model that wouldn't get her dander up.

"No internet," Cassie said pointedly. "Understood?"

Jake sighed heavily. "Okay."

Cole gave the boy's shoulder a squeeze. "I'll bring it by tomorrow, Jake. How will that be?"

"All right," the boy said eagerly. "And you'll show me how to write a program?"

"Sure, if you want to learn," he said, then cautioned, "It's a lot of work."

"That's okay. Someday I'm going to start my own computer technology company just like you." He grabbed Cole's hand. "Come look at my room and we can decide where the computer should go when you bring it."

Cole found Jake's budding case of hero worship touching. After living for the past few years with his own computer-illiterate father, a man who had absolutely no appreciation for his work, it was nice to have someone so eager to understand it and share in it. Jake was a good kid. Cassie had done a terrific job raising him on her own. Cole reminded himself to tell her that.

But when he tried to bring up the subject on the ride to Karen's ranch, Cassie's response was as touchy as always when he mentioned Jake. Cole told himself that her reaction was simply that of an overly protective single mom, but he was having difficulty believing it. Calling her on it would accomplish nothing. He'd already tried that, and she had only become more defensive.

Maybe he would ask Mrs. Collins. Her attitude toward him seemed to be mellowing lately. Maybe she would give him a straight answer. If not, he would just have to count on the fact that one of these days, Cassie would trust him enough to be completely honest with him. By nature, she wasn't a secretive person.

At least she hadn't been ten years ago, he reminded himself. Ten years was a long time, especially when most of that time she had been raising a child on her own. The truth was, he had no idea how Cassie might have changed. He just knew that plenty of things about her were the same, enough to fascinate him all over again.

He glanced at her, distressed to see that she was staring out the window with a distant, sad expression on her face. Maybe she was merely thinking about her friend's loss, but he doubted it. He had caught that same expression even before Caleb's death. Something—or someone—had stolen her youthful vibrancy and optimism, and Cole wouldn't rest until he knew how that had happened.

* * *

Over the next few weeks Cassie lived in terror that Cole was going to learn the truth. It had become evident that he suspected that she was keeping something from him. And he also seemed to sense that it had to do with Jake. When he'd first tried to pin her down about her reasons for wanting to keep them apart, pure panic had washed through her. She'd had to force herself to calm down and respond as if her behavior was merely the reaction of a single mom.

She had thought at the time that Cole had bought her explanation about not allowing Jake to start counting on anyone who wasn't likely to be around permanently. She'd also tried to be less overt about keeping the two of them apart, finding legitimate excuses to get Jake out of the house whenever Cole was likely to stop by. She'd been pleased by her success.

But then Cole had brought over that blasted computer, and it was clear that he intended to stick around and teach Jake to use it. When she'd tried to protest, the look he'd given her told her that nothing she said was going to be convincing. He was on to her, and sooner or later he was going to demand answers.

If her own determination to keep silent were the only thing at issue, she was sure the secret of Jake's paternity would be safe enough, but there was Frank Davis to consider. She didn't trust Cole's father not to tell him everything. It had been evident during their confrontation that he wanted, in fact expected, Cole to claim Jake as the Davis heir. She doubted he would patiently wait forever for that to happen.

As it had ever since her return home, the debate over what to do raged in her head, setting off yet another dull, throbbing headache.

"Cassie, are you okay?" her mother asked weakly.

She forced a smile and turned back to the bed where her mother was resting after her first radiation treatment. The trip to Denver was more tiring for her than the treatment itself.

"I'm fine," Cassie fibbed.

"You're worried about the amount of time Jake and Cole are spending together, aren't you?"

"I've done everything I can to keep them apart," she admitted. "I don't know what else to do, short of telling Cole the truth."

"Why not do that?" she said. "Face it, Cassie. He's going to figure it out sooner or later. Wouldn't it be better if the truth came from you?"

Cassie knew her mother was right, but she simply hadn't been able to work up the courage to say the words. "I don't know how to tell him, not after all this time."

"Would you like me to do it?"

She shook her head. "No, I have to be the one." She faced her mother, grateful for this opening. "There's something I don't understand."

"What?"

"Why are you and Frank Davis both so eager for the truth to come out, when years ago you couldn't wait to break us up?"

What little color there had been in her mother's

cheeks faded. "Why..." she began, but her voice faltered. "Why would you say something like that?"

"I know, Mom. Mr. Davis told me all about the letter you kept from me, the one in which Cole explained why he had to leave. He also told me about the letter you wrote to Cole telling him I didn't want him in my life anymore."

Tears tracked down her mother's cheeks. She reached for Cassie's hand. Her frail grasp was icy cold. "I'm sorry. We thought it was for the best."

"You mean Mr. Davis thought it was best."

"No," her mother said sharply. "We agreed. You were both too young."

"But I was having a baby, and you've already admitted that you knew it was Cole's. Things might have been so different."

"No," her mother said just as adamantly. "Nothing would have been any different. Frank would never have approved of a marriage between the two of you. He would have found a way to stop it. Once I knew about the baby, I told him—in fact, I begged him—to let you and Cole work it out, but he refused. I would have gone to Cole myself, but I didn't know where he was. Frank gave me the money for your medical expenses. He promised me more if I let things be, but I never took another dime."

She squeezed Cassie's hand. "Not another dime," she repeated.

"Oh, Mom," Cassie whispered wearily. "You should have gone ahead and taken the money. The damage was done."

"I couldn't. I already felt guilty enough. I could barely look you in the face. When Jake was born, I thought of all we could have done for him with that money, but by then it was too late. And that wasn't the worst of it. When Cole came by here to visit, to ask after you, I slammed the door on him. I couldn't bear to face him after what I'd done to keep you apart, to keep him from his own son."

Her mother sighed. "I shudder to think what would have happened to me if he knew all of that. He certainly wouldn't have offered to pay my medical expenses."

"Yes he would," Cassie reassured her. "And he does know, because I told him that much at least. I told him about the letters."

"When?"

"A few weeks ago, right after your surgery."

"And he never said a word," her mother said, looking amazed. "And all this time he's been paying for my radiation treatments and taking me to Denver."

Cassie nodded.

"That should tell you something, then."

"What?"

"If he can forgive me, then surely he'll be able to forgive you."

Cassie wanted desperately to believe that, but what she had done wasn't the same. It wasn't the same thing at all. She had once professed to love Cole, and yet she had kept their child a secret from him…and was continuing to do so.

Despite all of Cassie's warnings and her threats of dire punishments, she knew that Jake was still trying to come up with ways to sneak off to the Davis ranch. Maybe it was simply the lure of the forbidden. More likely it was hero worship.

So far she'd caught Jake half a dozen times on the outskirts of town, riding the bike he'd repaired. At this rate the boy was going to be grounded until he hit thirty. It didn't seem to faze him, though. He simply tried a more inventive approach the next time.

As if that weren't nerve-racking enough, since Jake wasn't going to him, Cole continued to stop by her house unannounced, bringing thoughtful treats for her mother and disconcerting kisses for her. She hadn't figured out a way to get the man to keep his hands and his mouth to himself. He had history on his side. She hadn't been able to do it ten years ago, either.

She had just kicked off her shoes and propped her feet on the porch railing, when Cole's car turned into the driveway. He emerged in a pair of faded jeans that hugged his hips, and a T-shirt that stretched taut over his broad shoulders. It was hard to imagine that this was the same man whose computer company had just reported earnings in the millions. She sighed when she thought about it. If they had been a lousy match ten years ago, there was an even greater divide between them now. He was a college-educated business whiz. She was a waitress with a high school diploma.

"Why are you here?" she inquired testily.

Undaunted by her attitude, he shot her a grin. "To improve your mood, for starters."

"Exactly how are you planning to do that?" she inquired warily.

"I'm going to take you away from all this. Get your bathing suit."

"Why?"

"This is an impulsive moment, darlin'. Stop asking so many questions. I never used to have to work so hard to persuade you to come with me. I seem to recall a time when you couldn't wait to sneak off to be alone with me."

"I'm older and wiser now."

"More's the pity." He nudged her bare, aching feet off the railing. "Get a move on."

"Maybe I don't enjoy swimming," she said grumpily.

"Since when?"

"Since right this second."

He sighed heavily and sat beside her. "Okay, spill it. What's really going on here? Did somebody sneak out of Stella's today without paying the bill? Did somebody stiff you on your tip?"

"Everything at work went just fine."

"Then this grouchiness has to do with me?"

Him, the situation, the lies, everything. Her life was a mess. Not that she admitted any of that. Unfortunately, he seemed to interpret her silence as agreement.

"What did I do?" he asked.

"Nothing," she admitted. "You've been great."

"But?"

Finally she leveled a look straight at him and repeated her earlier question. "Why are you here?"

"To take you swimming."

"But why?"

"Because it's a hot day and I thought we could cool off in the river, then have a picnic. That used to be your favorite way to spend a summer evening."

It had also been what had gotten them into trouble. Being alone and scantily clad had led to steamy kisses and eventually, on that one memorable night, to making love. He wasn't fooling her one bit. That was exactly the way he saw the evening ending tonight, too.

"I'm not as young and foolish as I once was."

He frowned at that. "What is that supposed to mean?"

"I am not interested in letting you seduce me."

She had expected anger or at the very least irritation, but instead he chuckled.

"Okay, then, *you* can seduce *me,*" he said cheerfully. "I'm easy."

"No seduction, period."

He shrugged, as if it didn't matter a bit to him one way or the other. "Suit yourself. Bring Jake along as a chaperone."

As if he'd been lurking just inside the door waiting for a chance to join them, Jake stepped onto the porch and let the screen door slam shut behind him.

"Bring me where? And what's a chaperone?"

"You are grounded, young man," Cassie said, regarding him sternly. "You're not going anywhere. And eavesdropping is not polite."

"But, Mom…"

"Inside," she said, gesturing in that direction. "You know the rules."

"You're ruining my whole summer," he protested. He inched closer to Cole. "Tell her."

Though Cole looked as if he wanted to ask a whole lot of questions, he merely shrugged. "She's your mother. You do as she says."

"But it's not fair. What did I do that was so wrong? I just wanted to go over to see Cole. He said I could." He gazed up at Cole. "Didn't you? You said I could come anytime."

"With your mother's permission," Cole reminded him. "Is that what this is all about? You were sneaking off to the ranch again?"

"More than once," Cassie told him before facing Jake. "Inside now, or I swear I'll add another day to your grounding."

Tears welled up in Jake's eyes. "I hate you!" he shouted. "I hate you and I wish we'd never come here!"

The words cut through her like well-aimed knives, but she couldn't relent. She simply couldn't. What she was doing was for the best.

But then Jake whirled away from her, and instead of going inside as she'd ordered, he threw himself at Cole. "I wish you were my dad. Then I could come and live with you."

Dismay welled up in her throat. She wanted to cry out, to protest. She didn't think she'd reacted aloud, but she must have, because Cole's gaze shot to hers and suddenly she saw that he knew, that in that instant he'd guessed the truth she had been trying so desperately to hide.

She also saw the cold rage in his eyes as it stripped away the warmth she'd come to yearn for.

"Son," he said, his voice faltering ever so slightly. His hand rested for just an instant on Jake's head. Finally he added, "Do as your mother asked, Jake. Go inside."

Jake seemed to sense that the mood on the porch had shifted in some way. Though his expression remained sullen, he went into the house, but not without slamming the door emphatically behind him.

Cassie waited, frozen, for Cole to say something, anything.

His gaze was damning.

"Is it true?" he asked eventually. "Is Jake my son?"

She tried to speak, tried desperately to find the right words, but none came. Finally she just nodded.

"And all this time you never said a word," he said, regarding her with disbelief. "Not one single word."

"You'd left me," she reminded him. "What was I supposed to do, run after you?"

He winced at that, but his expression didn't soften. "Yes," he said. "You were supposed to come after me. I had a right to know."

"You left me," she repeated. "You had no rights. None at all."

"That boy in there is my son," he all but shouted. At her frantic glance toward the house, he lowered his voice. "I had rights, dammit! And so did he. He had the right not to be born a bastard. He had the right to have my name, my love."

"It wouldn't have happened that way," Cassie said

flatly, knowing that his father would have prevented it. Her mother had been right about that. Frank Davis had admitted as much himself. His attitude now might have changed, but back then he would never have permitted a marriage between his son and a girl with no education and no well-connected family. Even now he wanted Cole to claim Jake, not her.

"Well, we'll never know that now, will we?" Cole said bitterly. He regarded her as if he'd never seen her before. "I thought I knew you."

"You knew the woman I used to be, the girl. I've changed, Cole."

"Obviously," he said derisively.

"Because I've had to. While you've been off making your millions, I've been struggling to make ends meet. Instead of going off to college, I had a baby. Instead of being right here in Winding River with family and old friends, I've been living with strangers. I've been doing the best I could to see that my son was loved and fed and educated."

"*Our* son, dammit. *Ours!*"

Something beyond the words, something in his tone, terrified her. It had gotten proprietary.

"Jake is mine," she repeated fiercely. "In every way that counts, he is mine. Biologically, you might be his father, but you've never done anything for him, never stayed up when he was sick, never read him a story, never comforted him during a storm."

Cole's eyes blazed with fury. "And whose fault is that? Don't start throwing that in my face, Cassie," he warned. "It won't hold up. If I've failed as a father, it's because I was never given the chance to be one, and the blame for that lies with you, no one else. Just you."

She was going about this all wrong. Every word out of her mouth was making him angrier, reminding him that she had cost him nine years with his son.

"Maybe…maybe you should leave now," she suggested tentatively. "Go home and think about this. You'll see that I had no choice."

At least she prayed that he would.

But Cole wasn't finished with her yet. "You know," he said, "even if I were to accept that back then you were young and scared, that you thought I'd abandoned you, it wouldn't explain the past few weeks. We'd cleared up the old misunderstandings. We both knew the truth about how we were manipulated by our parents. We were starting to build a future together— at least that's what I was hoping for. And still you kept silent."

"I was afraid," she admitted.

"Of what?"

She didn't dare voice it. She couldn't tell him that she was terrified that he would do as his father expected, that he would want to claim his son, that he would try to take Jake away from her. Saying the words might plant the idea in his head.

"I just was," she said, leaving it at that.

Cole regarded her with disgust. "The old Cassie would never have given in to fear. The old Cassie would have trusted me with the truth."

"But don't you see?" she said softly. "The old Cassie doesn't exist anymore."

Cole sighed heavily. "And it's plain that I don't know the new one at all."

11

How could he have been so blind?

Cole asked himself that a hundred times on the drive back to his ranch. Now that he knew the truth, he could see that the boy was the spitting image of him, not just in looks, but in interests and attitude.

The photo albums at the Double D were probably stuffed with pictures of him at Jake's age, all taken shortly before his mother's death. He'd bet that any one of those would have shown the unmistakable resemblance. Of course, all those albums were gathering dust in the attic and had been for years. His father wasn't an especially sentimental man.

Still, Cole should have seen it. It had been so clear in that split second between the time Jake had uttered his wistful cry about wishing Cole were his father and Cassie's own cry of dismay. He hadn't needed to look into her eyes to know the truth, but he had, and it was there, plain as day.

And if he were being honest, he had also seen the

genuine fear, and a part of him understood it, even sympathized with it. He didn't want to, but he did. Davis men took what they wanted. His father's reputation for ruthlessness was widely known. Cassie had no reason to believe that he was any different. Though she hadn't said it, it was evident that she was terrified that he was going to take her son away from her.

"What are you going to do?" she'd asked just as he'd walked off. There had been no mistaking the fear, the vulnerability, behind the question, or the slight hitch in her voice.

He'd turned and faced her, his thoughts in turmoil, his heart aching. "I don't know," he'd told her honestly.

Until tonight he had truly believed they were getting past all the old hurts and betrayals and building something solid this time, something that could last. It was what he had desperately come to want over the past few weeks. Years ago they had loved with the reckless passion of youth. Since Cassie's return, he'd started to anticipate a future built on the more mature love of two adults who knew their own minds and hearts, two people who would no longer let anything or anyone stand in their way.

Now he'd discovered his fantasy had been spun from a web of lies and omissions. It was the latter that were the most painful to bear. For weeks now his own son had been right under his nose and he hadn't known, hadn't had a clue. Shouldn't he have had at least an inkling, a tiny suspicion? He blamed himself for that, but he blamed Cassie for more—for nine long years he'd lost forever.

He thought of all the suspicions he'd had, the evidence that Cassie had been trying her level best to keep him and Jake apart. Now he knew why, but it was the one reason that had never once crossed his mind, because a deception of such magnitude had seemed impossible. Cassie had always been the one person who was unfailingly straight with him, the one person he could count on to say exactly what she meant. His father? That was another story, but Cassie had always spoken from the heart. That was why he had taken that letter at face value years ago.

When he walked into his house after the long drive home from Cassie's, all he wanted was a stiff drink and some time to himself, time to wrestle with this new turn of events.

Instead, his father greeted him. "You look like something the cat dragged in. You and Cassie have a spat?" he asked, zeroing in on the problem with unerring accuracy.

"Something like that," Cole said wryly. It was definitely a massive understatement.

His father's gaze turned sharp. He studied Cole's face, then gave a little nod of satisfaction. "She finally told you, then?"

As understanding dawned, Cole stared at him. "You know? You know that Jake is my son?"

"Well, of course I know," he boasted, clearly oblivious to Cole's barely concealed surge of anger.

"How long?" Cole asked, his voice deadly calm as he grappled with this newest revelation.

"I suspected it years ago, after you'd left to go back

to school, but I didn't have any proof. Not at first, anyway. Then, finally, I got Edna Collins to admit it. Took a whole lot of persuading, I'll tell you that. The woman would have taken the information to her grave, if I hadn't dangled some cash in front of her."

Leave it to his father to buy what he wanted. "When was that?" Cole asked.

"A month or so after Cassie left town. I guessed she was pregnant. Why else would the girl turn her back on her only family?"

"But you saw no reason to share that with me?"

"No," he said, regarding Cole evenly. "For a time I let myself believe it was better to leave things the way they were. You would have wanted to do the right thing, no matter what kind of mess it made of your life. So I took care of the girl's medical expenses. I offered more, the same as you would have done, but Edna turned me down flat."

"You offered more," Cole repeated derisively. "Money, I imagine."

"Well, of course. What else?"

"You didn't consider offering marriage, maybe righting the wrong I had done by getting Cassie pregnant in the first place?"

His father scowled. "I told you, I wasn't going to let you mess up your life."

"I don't see how taking responsibility for my own actions would have messed up my life. It might have taught me a lesson. And of course there was the fact that I loved the boy's mother."

"That girl was no good for you, that much was plain

as day. She was a nobody." At Cole's muttered expletive, he backed down. "At least, that's how I viewed
it then."

Cole regarded him curiously, wondering about the
kind of logic his father used to justify his actions. "And
now?"

"I've been forced to reevaluate," he conceded.

Which explained the attempts to push him and
Cassie together. "And why is that?"

"You weren't showing any signs of getting over the
woman. You haven't had a single serious relationship
in all the years you've been back. When I heard Cassie
was coming back, I decided enough was enough. I
couldn't sit by and let the Davis heir be raised as a bastard right under our noses."

Suddenly all of the evening's stress boiled over. Infuriated, Cole grabbed a fistful of his father's shirt and
dragged him close until they were practically nose to
nose. "How dare you?"

"I did what I had to do."

"Then this is all about your choices, your decisions?" It took every bit of restraint he possessed to
keep from shaking his father. "That boy was mine—
hell, he was *your* grandson—and you kept it to yourself. What were you thinking?"

Not bothering to wait for an answer, he released his
father and backed off before he could take the swing at
him he so desperately wanted to take. "You're the same
manipulative, controlling son of a bitch I left home to
escape ten years ago."

His father drew himself up, seemingly unfazed by

Cole's anger. "I'm your father, and I'll thank you to show a little respect," he commanded.

"Then you'll have to work damn hard to prove you deserve it. Right now I don't see it," Cole snapped, then whirled and headed up the stairs.

In his room he dragged out a suitcase and began haphazardly filling it with clothes. He had no idea where he was going, but he knew he had to get away. He heard his father huffing and puffing as he climbed the stairs, but he ignored it.

"Dammit, boy, where do you think you're going?" his father demanded, hanging on to the doorjamb as he caught his breath.

"Away from here."

"You've just found out you have a son and you're leaving?" the old man asked incredulously.

"I have to think, and I sure as hell can't do it here under your roof."

"I'd like to know why not? The Double D is your home. It's your heritage."

"Not because I want it," Cole pointed out. "Because you insist on it. If I stay, I'll never know if what I decide is right or what you've deliberately set out to plant in my head."

"That boy belongs here with us. It couldn't be any clearer," his father said.

"To you, maybe." Then the full significance of what his father had said sank in. "*Jake* belongs here? Not Cassie? Is that what you're saying? Even now, knowing that she's the mother of my child, you still don't think she's good enough?"

"Hasn't she proved that by lying to you?"

Cole couldn't argue the point, not successfully, when he was still spitting mad over that himself. He let it go and continued packing.

"Cole, don't do this," his father pleaded. "Don't give Cassie time to get herself an attorney, maybe even to take off again. Stay here and claim what's yours."

Cole silently closed the suitcase, then turned to face his father. "Jake is mine, not yours. The decision is mine, too. I want you to steer clear of him and stay the hell out of it. You've already done more than enough."

His father shook his head. "You're making a mistake."

"It's mine to make."

That said, he left the room and the house. He had to wonder, as he drove away from the Double D, if he would ever be able to come back, knowing the part his father had played in everything that had happened.

Cassie sat on the front porch, trembling and sick at heart, long after Cole had left. When Jake crept outside to sit beside her, she wrapped him in a hug and clung to him until he protested.

"Mom, why did you and Cole fight?" he asked when she reluctantly released him. "I could hear you."

Her blood ran cold. "How much did you hear?"

"Not the words, just that he sounded real mad. Was he mad?"

"Very," she admitted.

"How come?"

"I...I kept something from him that I shouldn't have."

Did she dare tell Jake the rest? Not yet, she concluded, not until she and Cole had worked things out, if that was even possible. She needed to know what he wanted, how much a part of Jake's life he intended to be, how much of a fight she might have on her hands.

"I like him, Mom. He's been teaching me stuff, and he doesn't talk down to me like I'm a dumb kid."

"I know. He thinks you're pretty special. He's said so."

Jake regarded her worriedly. "I didn't mean what I said before about hating you."

She managed a faint smile. "I know that."

"You're the best. And I like being here with Grandma, too. I don't want to leave Winding River. We aren't going to, are we?"

No, Cassie thought, for better or worse, they were here to stay. She wasn't going to run again. Why bother, when Cole had the resources to find her wherever she went, anyway? And he would hunt her down. She had no doubts about that.

The next day, though, she was stunned to discover that Cole had left town.

"Went out to Silicon Valley," one of Frank's friends reported when he showed up for breakfast at Stella's. He regarded her speculatively. "I don't suppose *you* know anything about that?"

"Not a thing," she said honestly, not certain whether to be relieved by the news or not.

Adding to the puzzle was the fact that Frank himself was a no-show at Stella's. He hadn't missed a day there in forty years or more.

"Frank took it real hard," Pete reported as Cassie poured his coffee. "Despite all his grumbling, he dotes on that boy. I stopped by the ranch on my way here, but he wouldn't even get out of bed. Said if Cole was gone for good, he didn't have any reason to live."

"That's nonsense," Cassie said.

"That's what I told him, but you know Frank. He's always been the dramatic type. Likes to control things, too. He'll moan and groan for a few days, then come out swinging like always."

No one knew that better than Cassie. "Yes, I'm sure he'll pull himself together," she agreed. "I'll get your eggs now, Pete."

"Don't forget the bacon and hash browns."

She grinned at him. "As if I could. You've been having the exact same breakfast for the past twelve years."

"More than that," he said, grinning back at her. "Started before your time. Of course, I have to have it here at Stella's. If my wife found out, she'd have my hide."

"I imagine she guessed your little secret years ago."

Pete sighed. "Probably so. Never could keep a thing from that woman. That's the basis of a good marriage, you know, keeping everything out in the open. Remember that when your wedding day comes along, and you won't go wrong."

Unfortunately, it was too late for that advice to do Cassie any good at all.

The discovery that his father knew the truth and had chosen to hide it had been the final bitter blow on the worst night of Cole's entire life. After driving aimlessly for most of the night, he took off for Silicon Valley and a round of business meetings he'd been postponing for months. He left word on his father's answering machine that that's where he'd be until further notice.

He'd expected the change of scenery to give him some perspective. He'd also hoped that the steady lineup of strategy meetings and technology discussions would keep him focused on work. He didn't want to think about Jake or Cassie or his father. The wound was still too raw.

Unfortunately, he'd never been much good at avoiding tough decisions. Facing things squarely and dealing with them was the way he conducted business.

He managed to prolong his stay in California for a month, but Cassie was never far from his thoughts. Was his father right? Would she bolt with Jake now that the truth was out? She was certainly terrified enough to try. His only consolation was that the world wasn't big enough to swallow her up so completely that he couldn't find her again. Few people vanished without a trace, and Cassie wasn't clever enough or rich enough to be one of them.

Of course, she had been clever enough to keep his son away from him for nine long years. He'd missed Jake's birth, his first step, his first word. Things that he could never get back. The lack of memories weighed on him. Eventually the prospect of missing so much as a minute more of his son's life had him reaching for the phone, something he should have done days or even weeks earlier.

When Cassie picked up on the first ring, he breathed a sigh of relief. "You're there," he said.

"Where else would I be?"

She sounded resigned.

"I wasn't sure you'd stick around."

"Running would have been pointless," she said, all but admitting she'd considered it. "Besides, my mother and Karen need me here."

"And that's the only reason you stayed?"

She remained silent so long he thought she might not answer.

"No," she said at last. "We have to deal with this for Jake's sake."

"I'm glad you realize that."

"I've always had my son's best interests at heart."

Cole barely bit back a sharp retort. "Now's not the time to debate that," he said. "I'll be home in a few days. We'll talk then."

He hung up without waiting for her reply. He'd discovered two things by making that call—one reassuring, one disconcerting. He now knew that Cassie would be waiting when he returned to Winding River. And, God help him, he also knew just how much that mattered to him.

When Cole drove into Winding River a few days later, his mind was made up at last. He'd lost the first nine years of his son's life. He didn't intend to lose the next nine or any thereafter. This wasn't about revenge or even justice. It was about a father forming a bond with his son, a bond he'd been denied up until now.

He arrived on Cassie's doorstep prepared to start the custody fight to end all custody fights.

She greeted him with pale cheeks and frightened eyes, then stepped onto the porch and closed the door securely behind her. He couldn't help noticing that she had lost weight she could hardly spare in the month he'd been gone. Even so, she was the most beautiful woman he'd ever known, and his heart lurched into the familiar rhythm of desire.

"What are you going to do?" she asked straight-out, not even trying to mask her fear.

One look into her eyes and his determination faltered. He knew he couldn't do what he'd planned. He couldn't take her son—their son—away from her. Whatever else he thought of her, she'd been a good mother and Jake loved her. Separating them would be a hollow victory.

Besides, there was no denying that even after all that had happened, he wanted her. Bitterness wasn't quite enough to bury lust. The heat of anger felt awfully damn close to the heat of passion.

"Marry me," he said before he could stop himself.

Clearly taken by surprise, she blinked hard, then shook her head. "No, not if this is just some way for you to claim your son."

"You don't have a choice," he said mildly.

"Of course I do."

"If you don't marry me, I'll fight you for Jake—and I guarantee you, I'll win. There are some perks to being a Davis in this state, and that's one of them."

"You would use your father's power?" she asked in

a whisper, then shook her head. "What was I thinking? Of course you would. And I imagine you have a fair share of power yourself these days. Everyone warned me, but I wanted to believe you were better than that."

"Once upon a time I thought so, too," he said wearily. "Not anymore. Just remember, darlin', you started this when you kept Jake from me. I'm just playing by the winner-take-all rules you set."

"But marriage?" she said. "It would be a mockery. Surely there has to be another way. We could make an arrangement of some kind."

"So that I can spend a few hours each week with my son?" He shook his head. "Not nearly good enough. Marriage is my best offer. Take it or leave it. Otherwise I sue for custody."

She stared at him with such a look of despair that he almost wavered, but not quite. He knew he was bullying her, but at the moment he didn't really give a damn. He told himself that she would like the alternative even less.

"I need some time," she whispered finally.

"Time for what? To think it over? To run?"

Her chin came up at that. "I've already told you, I'm not running."

"Good. I'm glad you see the futility in that. Okay," he said, relenting, "you can have a few days to think it over. Go to Emma if you want to and ask her legal opinion about whether I can force you to do this."

When she winced, he knew he had been dead on about her intention.

"She'll only tell you that my case for custody is very strong, whether I use my influence in this state or not."

"You've already consulted an attorney, then," she said, her voice flat.

"Did you honestly think I wouldn't?"

"I was hoping we could work this out between the two of us without getting a bunch of lawyers involved."

"We can," he said. "All you have to do is marry me. Then you and I will raise Jake together. We'll be a family."

"Will we?" she asked, regarding him with skepticism. "Exactly what kind of family can we have if the only reason we're together is your determination to be a real father to Jake?"

"I don't know," he said honestly. "I don't have a whole lot of experience with picture-book family life. I grew up with a manipulative father who has done his utmost to control me. I fell in love with a woman who kept my own son a secret. Obviously, I've missed a few lessons on what it takes to make a family."

He leveled a look straight into her eyes. "By the same token, I can tell you a whole lot about lies and deceit."

She weathered the attack without flinching. "Cole, this will be a disaster," she said, a pleading note in her voice. "Can't you see that?"

"Then we'll just be living up to those low expectations everyone had for us years ago," he said without emotion. "Seems to me like a fitting end to our so-called love story, don't you think?"

Her complexion went even paler at his mocking remark, but to her credit she didn't shed a single tear.

"I'll give you my answer on Sunday," she said at last. And then, as if to get in a mocking blow of her own, she added, "Right after church."

Unfortunately, Cole was relatively certain that no matter how many prayers were uttered, there were no heavenly answers for the two of them. Their sorry fate had been decided a long time ago by people right here on earth.

12

Cassie felt sick to her stomach. Marrying Cole—once her most powerful fantasy—was now nothing more than a way to keep her son. How could she go through with such a travesty? How could Cole?

But, judging from his cold, distant demeanor, he had no intention of backing down. He saw this as a generous gesture…and maybe, under the circumstances, it was. She couldn't help thinking, though, that it was little better than blackmail.

Maybe she didn't deserve any better after what she'd done, Cassie thought, but she couldn't seem to stop the regrets from adding up until she felt smothered by them.

"Oh, God, how can I do it?" she murmured, hands over her face. And suddenly the tears she had refused to give in to in front of Cole cascaded down her cheeks.

That was how her mother found her, still leaning against the door, sobbing as if her heart would break.

"What on earth?" Edna said, hurrying to her daughter's side. "Cassie, what happened? Is it Jake? Is he hurt?"

Only the very real panic in her mother's voice snapped her out of her desolation. "No, no, Mom. Jake is fine. Mildred is baking cookies, and he's over there hoping for samples."

Her mother pressed a hand to her chest. "Thank goodness. You had me scared for a minute. Now come on over here and sit down and tell me what has you so upset. I woke up from my nap and heard you in here crying."

Cassie followed her mother to the sofa, but when she was seated she couldn't seem to make herself explain what had happened. Her mother would blame herself that it had come to this, and she didn't need the stress.

"Cassie?"

"I just saw Cole," she said finally.

"He's back, then. How is he?"

"Still furious."

"That was to be expected. He'll calm down soon enough, and then you two can deal with this rationally."

"I think it's too late for that," Cassie said ruefully.

Her mother's gaze narrowed. "Oh?"

"He expects me to marry him."

Even her mother gasped at that. "Now? After all that's happened?" Her expression brightened just a little. "Has he forgiven you, then?"

"Hardly. He says it's that or a custody fight." She sighed. "Not exactly the proposal of a lifetime, is it?"

"What is he thinking? That's absurd. He can't make you do that."

"Can't he?"

"What did you tell him?"

"That I would give him an answer on Sunday."

"You're not seriously considering this, are you? I know you still have feelings for him, and I honestly believe he has feelings for you, but the timing couldn't be worse. You need to work through your differences before you even consider getting married."

"I don't think Cole is interested in working through anything," Cassie said honestly. "He wants his son. This is his way of getting him. I just happen to be part of the package. He's willing to put up with me."

"I don't believe that. The man loves you. He can't admit it to himself right now, but he will forgive you. He just needs some time."

"If I believed that, then it wouldn't be so hard to say yes, but, Mom, what if you're wrong? What if he really does hate me? What if he can't forgive me? How can we possibly live under the same roof?"

"You can't and that's that," her mother said grimly. "You'll just have to stall him until you can figure out how he really feels."

"I don't think Cole is in any mood for my stalling tactics. He pretty much said I either do this his way or I take my chances in court."

"Have you talked to Emma? She's in town, isn't she?"

Cassie nodded. Emma had come back to take a controversial case that no lawyer in town would touch. Just last week Cassie had gotten the impression that no matter how that case went, Emma might be back to stay.

"I'll call her first thing in the morning," she said.

"Call her now," her mother urged. "It's not that late, and you won't sleep a wink if you don't get some answers tonight."

"You're right," she agreed, and went into the kitchen to call.

Emma sounded wide-awake when she answered. "Cassie? What's wrong? You sound like you've been crying."

"It's been a difficult evening," she said, putting it mildly. "Do you have a few minutes?"

"For you? Of course. What's this about?"

"Custody of Jake."

"I'm coming over," Emma said at once.

"You don't have to…" Cassie began, but she was wasting her breath.

"I'm on my way," Emma said, then hung up before Cassie could argue.

Cassie looked up to meet her mother's worried frown. "She's on her way."

"Good. I'm sure she'll have sensible advice."

"I don't need sensible," Cassie said. "I need the advice of a legal shark who takes no prisoners."

Her mother managed a faint grin. "Then you've called the right person. Our Emma didn't earn her reputation in Denver by being anybody's patsy."

Cassie was startled by the observation. "How do you know so much about her reputation in Denver?"

"Ever since she took that case here, the paper's been running stories about how tough she is. I have to admit

I was surprised. When you were girls, you gave her an awful lot of grief, and she took it without so much as a whimper."

"Maybe that's what toughened her up," Cassie said.

She was beginning to feel the first little hint of optimism by the time the doorbell rang. Emma swept in with eyes blazing and a determined jut to her jaw. She gave Cassie a fierce hug, then plunked her briefcase on the dining room table and pulled out a chair.

"Start at the beginning. I want to know everything Cole said to you."

As Cassie talked, Emma took notes, never once flinching, not even when Cassie summed up that night's conversation and the proposal that was Cole's alternative to a custody battle. When Cassie had concluded, Emma sighed and rubbed her eyes.

"We can give him a fight, if that's what he wants," she said, then clasped Cassie's hand. "But I won't lie to you, he has a good case. I don't think he could get sole custody of Jake, but he could certainly get visitation rights and perhaps even some form of joint custody. You have absolutely no grounds for accusing him of being unfit, especially since he never had a chance to demonstrate his parenting skills."

Cassie drew in a deep breath. "Then I have no choice. I have to marry him."

"That's up to you, of course." She touched Cassie's cheek. "It doesn't have to be a fate worse than death, you know. You do love him."

"A lot of good that does."

Emma smiled. "Not that you could prove it by me, but I've heard that love can perform miracles."

"Well, I'm certainly about to put it to the test, aren't I?"

Cole took a room in a hotel while he awaited Cassie's decision. When news of his return reached his father, Frank Davis came striding into the hotel lobby demanding to see him. At the commotion just outside the door to the hotel coffee shop, Cole glanced up from behind his newspaper and sighed.

"Over here, Dad," he said.

His father crossed the small lobby and headed straight for his table. He sank down opposite Cole. "It's about time you got back here. Why aren't you at the ranch?"

"Do you even have to ask?"

"Are you planning on staying in this place?" his father asked, glancing around at the shabby furnishings, the tiny coffee shop that had only a handful of scarred tables.

"That depends."

"On?"

"What happens this Sunday."

His father regarded him with exasperation. "Stop talking in riddles. Are you back here to stay or not?"

"I'll keep you posted."

For just an instant his father looked older than his years. He looked defeated. "I suppose I might as well put the ranch on the market. I can't manage it anymore on my own."

Cole scowled at him. "Don't pull that with me. You recovered from that heart attack years ago. You could run the whole state if you were of a mind to, never mind one little cattle ranch."

"Fifty thousand acres isn't little," his father said heatedly. "It's a demanding job, and I just don't have the heart for it anymore. Not if there's no one to leave it to."

"Leave it to your grandson."

"How am I supposed to do that? The boy doesn't even know we're related. If it's left up to his mother, he never will."

"That will change," Cole said grimly. One way or another.

"Oh?" His father's expression brightened. "You going after custody?"

"No. Not the way you mean, anyway."

"What then?"

"I'll tell you on Sunday." He would know how this was going to play out by then.

His father struggled to his feet, looking disgusted. "You're wasting time, son. I would have had this settled long ago."

"Probably so," Cole agreed. "But for once I'm doing things my way."

And they'd better work out, he thought, or he'd never hear the end of it.

For once Cassie wished the preacher's sermon would go on and on. Instead, Pastor Kirkland spoke for only a few minutes, citing the late-August heat and lack of air-conditioning as the reason for his brevity.

"No point in talking if no one can hear me over the fluttering of those fans you're waving," he said. "You can all give thanks to the Lord for that and we'll call it a day."

The congregation laughed appreciatively, sang one final, rousing hymn, then began to file out. Cassie was one of the last to go. When she reached the church steps, she spotted Cole at once, leaning against the fender of his car, his eyes shaded by sunglasses and the brim of his Stetson.

"You've made up your mind, then?" her mother asked, clinging to her hand. "There's nothing I can say to change it?"

"Nothing," Cassie said grimly. "This is what I have to do."

As she crossed the street, she wished she could feel one tiny little surge of joy, one little spark of hope, but Cole's somber expression wasn't encouraging. He was there to make a deal, not a love match.

He opened the car door for her without speaking, then got into the driver's side and started the engine. He glanced her way once, then focused on the road. Not until they were parked in a secluded spot along the river did he face her.

"Well?"

"I'll do it," she said. "I'll marry you."

He responded with little more than a nod of satisfaction. "Will next weekend suit you?"

Cassie bit back a cry of dismay. What had she

thought, that he would allow her time to plan something lavish? Had she honestly expected him to let her carry out the charade that this was the wedding of her dreams, the start of a happy life for two people deeply in love?

"Fine," she said tersely.

"At the church or at town hall?"

Cassie didn't think she could bear either one. "At home, in the garden," she said, ready to fight for that much at least. "I'll speak to Pastor Kirkland about it."

"What time?"

She had always dreamed of a wedding at sunset with color splashed across the western sky. "Seven-thirty," she said, allowing herself this one romantic touch, even if it would mean nothing at all to the man beside her. She hesitated, then asked, "Will you be inviting your father?"

Cole nodded. "I can't see any way around it."

"Anyone else?"

"No."

"I'll want my friends there."

"Whatever," he said, looking completely uninterested in the details now that the decision had been made.

It seemed as if there was nothing else to discuss, not about the ceremony itself, anyway. But there was one thing—the most important thing—that couldn't be ignored.

"Cole, how do I explain this to Jake?"

His hands tightened on the steering wheel until his

knuckles turned white. "Why not try the truth? It's about time, don't you think?"

"He's nine. He won't understand the truth, not all of it, anyway."

Cole sighed. "No, I suppose not." He turned slightly toward her, removed his sunglasses and met her gaze directly for the first time all afternoon. "He needs to know I'm his father. We can tell him together, if you'd like."

She nodded. "That would be good, I think. And I want him to know that we loved each other back then," she said fiercely, regarding Cole defiantly, prepared to fight for that, too. "I don't want him to think for a single second that he was a mistake. Nor do I want him to figure out that this marriage is nothing more than a bargain I made with the devil."

"The devil, am I? I've been called worse." For an instant Cole's expression softened. "I suppose it won't be much of a lie, telling him that we loved each other. Back then what we had was pretty special."

Her heart flipped over at the wistfulness in his voice. "Do you think…? Can we get that back again?"

He didn't answer right away. Eventually he slid his sunglasses back into place and looked away. "I honestly don't know," he said in a voice devoid of emotion.

Determined now, she put her hand on his arm, felt his muscle jerk beneath her touch. "We have to try, Cole," she said urgently. "For Jake's sake, if not our own."

Cole's only response was to reach for the key and start the car, his gaze straight ahead. His silence told her all she needed to know. He was nowhere close to forgiving her. In fact, it seemed as if he might not even intend to try.

Saturday dawned under a blazing sun. As wedding days went, Cole supposed this one was picture-perfect, but there was none of the joy he'd once expected, none of the anticipation. In fact, all he felt was an aching sense of loneliness, accompanied by the certainty that a few words spoken today at sunset were unlikely to alter that feeling in any way.

Refusing to dwell on his dark mood, he spent the morning working at his computer, then headed for Cassie's. To her mother's dismay, they had dismissed the traditional superstition about the groom not seeing his bride before the wedding and agreed that today was the perfect time to tell Jake the truth about Cole being his father. At least he would have a few hours to get used to the idea before the ceremony. Cole also intended to ask his son to be his best man.

When he arrived at the house, he was surprised by the whirl of activity going on. Flowers and chairs were being carried into the backyard, a small tent was being set up with tables beneath it. Lauren, wearing shorts, a T-shirt and rollers in her hair, was directing traffic. Cole grinned despite himself.

"You'd better hope there are no paparazzi around," he teased. "The tabloids would pay a fortune for this picture. You are not at your glamorous best."

"If you only came over here to harass me and get in the way, you can leave," she said, frowning at him.

"Why anybody would insist on having a wedding in less than a week is beyond me."

"We didn't want a lot of hoopla," he said defensively, aware that she must not know the whole story.

"Maybe you didn't, but Cassie deserves a lot of hoopla, and, by golly, she's going to have as much of it as we can pull off on short notice."

Cole withstood the icy glint in her eyes and the barely concealed criticism. One of the things he'd always admired about Lauren and the others was their fierce loyalty to each other. He'd never had friends like that…except for Cassie. Somewhere along the way, through no fault of his own, he'd lost that. Among the regrets in his life, that one was right at the top of the list.

He sighed at the thought and went in search of his bride-to-be. He found her in the kitchen getting a manicure. Pink flooded her cheeks when he walked in, but Gina barely spared him a glance.

"You're not supposed to be here," she said, and went right on painting Cassie's neatly filed nails a pale shade of pink.

Cassie cleared her throat. "Actually, he is. We're supposed to talk to Jake, explain things."

"Well, you can't do it now," Gina said briskly. "I'm not finished." She waved Cole away. "Go in the living room or out back and make yourself useful. I'll let you know when she's free."

Cassie shrugged. "Better do as she says. I've given up fighting with them."

Amused despite himself, he nodded. "Yes, I can see why it would be a waste of breath. Where's Jake?"

"Hiding out in his room, if he's smart," she said dryly. "Lauren brought him a tuxedo."

So that's the way it was going to be, then, Cole concluded. They were going to make this wedding into a special occasion for Cassie's sake, or die trying.

"I'll look for him," he said.

Alarm flared in Cassie's eyes. "You won't say anything, though, not till I can get up there?"

"No," he promised. "I won't say anything."

He found Jake in his room, staring not at the computer screen as Cole had expected, but out the window at the frenzied activity down below. He glanced up when Cole came in, but his expression was bleak.

"Hey, kiddo," Cole said, joining him at the window. "What's up?"

"You and Mom are gonna get married today, right?"

"That's right." Something in Jake's voice alerted him that the boy found the news troubling in some way. He studied him intently, then asked, "Is that okay with you?"

"I guess," Jake said, then regarded Cole with a serious expression. "How come I didn't know anything about it till practically the last minute?"

"That's when we decided," Cole said. "I thought you might be happy about it."

He regarded Cole earnestly. "I think it's pretty cool that you're going to be around all the time," he admitted, then added, "but there's something I don't get."

"What's that?"

"Nobody seems really excited, not even Mom. In fact, she looks kinda sad."

Cole winced. "I think maybe it's just a little overwhelming," he said. "It all happened so fast, and there was a lot to do."

"But Grandma keeps crying. I heard her tell Mom that this was all her fault." His brow puckered with a frown. "But I don't know what that means. How can having a wedding be anybody's fault?"

Cole put his hands on the boy's shoulders and gave him a reassuring squeeze. "It's just some grown-up stuff. It's nothing for you to worry about, pal."

"You love my mom, though, right? I mean that's why you're getting married, isn't it?"

Cole closed his eyes against the tide of pain that that innocent question sent through him. There was no easy answer. A part of him, a part he had worked like the dickens to bury, did love Cassie.

"Yes," he said, giving Jake the answer he needed to hear, even if it was only half-true, even if the whole truth was far more complicated. If he couldn't understand it, how could this nine-year-old boy?

Jake nodded, looking relieved. "I thought so." Suddenly he threw his arms around Cole and hugged him. "I can't wait till we're a real family."

Cole sighed. Would the bond being formed a few hours from now ever be that clear and that simple?

"Cole, can I ask you something else?"

"Anything, pal."

"Do you think maybe I could have a baby brother? I

guess it wouldn't be my real brother, but almost, right? That would be so cool. I'd even take a sister."

For the first time since he'd put this plan into motion, Cole realized the full ramifications. Jake, if no one else, was expecting a real marriage, complete with brothers and sisters. How in heaven's name was he supposed to get around that? For the last week he'd been moving ahead with caution, taking one day at a time. Now with a single innocent question Jake had forced him to gaze into the future.

"I think maybe we'd better discuss that another time," Cole said, aware that his voice sounded vaguely choked up. He cleared his throat. "It's a little soon to be talking about babies."

He heard Cassie's muffled gasp and realized she had arrived just in time to hear his comment. Even out of context, she had obviously guessed the general direction of the conversation.

"It certainly is," she said, stepping into the room and giving Cole a questioning look.

"Jake's looking ahead."

"Obviously." She sat on the edge of the bed and beckoned her son over. "Sit with me. We want to talk to you."

Jake went to her readily. "What about?"

"There's something you need to know before Cole and I get married today." Her gaze sought Cole's and held. "A long time ago he and I were very good friends."

"When you were kids, right?" Jake asked.

"Exactly. We were very young and for a long time we were just good friends, but then we fell in love."

Jake's eyes widened. "Really?"

"That's right," Cole said. "But then some things happened and we were separated. I didn't know that your mom was having a baby."

"You mean me," Jake guessed.

"Exactly." He took a deep breath, then added, "I didn't know that she was going to have my son."

For a minute Cole's words hung in the air. Jake looked from Cole to his mother and back again, a puzzled look on his face.

"Cole is your father," Cassie explained quietly. "But he never knew that until a few weeks ago."

Cole reached out to touch his son's cheek, but pulled back before making contact. "Nothing could have made me happier, Jake. I am very proud that you're my boy."

Jake swallowed hard, clearly struggling to comprehend the announcement. "You're my real dad?" he whispered at last. He looked at Cassie. "He is? For real?"

She nodded. "He really is."

"Oh, wow," Jake said, awestruck. "Then we really are gonna be a family. I'm gonna have my mom *and* my dad." He bounced up. "Does Grandma know? I've gotta tell her."

He raced out the door, then turned around and ran back, throwing himself at Cole before taking off again.

Cole met Cassie's gaze and allowed himself a faint smile. "He seems to be taking it well."

"You've just made his dream come true. He's finally got his real dad in his life."

But, gazing into her despondent eyes, Cole had to ask himself if the price he and Cassie were paying for uniting Jake's family was too high.

13

The ceremony went off without a hitch. Cassie actually managed to say her vows around the lump in her throat. She hadn't been able to meet Cole's gaze, though. It would have been too hard to look in his eyes and not see the love shining there that every bride had a right to expect on her wedding day. Just thinking about what was lacking had her blinking back tears as the minister pronounced them man and wife.

Then there was that awkward moment when Pastor Kirkland had announced that Cole could kiss the bride. She had stood there waiting, panicked that he would refuse and embarrass them both. But finally he had lowered his head and touched his lips to hers. It hadn't been a passionate kiss, but it had lingered, and there had been heat in it, more than she'd had any right to expect.

Her friends made every effort to pretend that this was a perfectly normal wedding. Lauren had outdone herself to turn the garden into a perfect setting. She had had exotic flowers flown in, along with a designer wedding dress. Cassie had almost wept when she'd seen the delicate lace and organza confection. Never in her wildest dreams had she ever imagined wearing such a gown.

But then, never in her wildest dreams had she imagined a wedding day that was such a sham.

Not that anyone was acknowledging that. Everyone was painfully polite, determinedly upbeat. Frank Davis was acting as if he'd been looking forward to Cassie's marriage to his son for years. Her mother's tears could be dismissed as typical of the mother of the bride. If her proud smile seemed a little forced, no one commented on it. And exhilarated by the discovery that Cole was his real father, Jake scooted from one guest to another to share that incredible news.

Meanwhile, her friends were offering up toasts with French champagne and snapping pictures as she and Cole cut the gorgeous three-tiered wedding cake that Lauren had had flown in from Beverly Hills along with the caterer himself. The man had moaned when he'd seen her mother's kitchen, then gone to work whipping up the most amazing hors d'oeuvres under Gina's watchful gaze. Though Gina grumbled at not being allowed to do the job herself, Cassie noted that she seemed happy enough taking surreptitious notes on the recipes. It was the first interest she'd shown in anything related to her restaurant business since arriving in Winding River weeks ago.

Studying the small gathering, Cassie concluded that everyone except the bride and groom seemed to be having a blast. They were all happily caught up in the illusion of happily-ever-after that weddings always evoked.

When she could stand it no longer, she went looking for her new husband. She found him all alone on the front porch, an untouched glass of champagne dangling from his fingers and an unreadable expression on his handsome face.

"Quite a day," he said without looking up when she joined him.

"It was a dream wedding," she said, unable to keep the wistful note out of her voice. If only the bride and groom had been happy, she thought.

"Yeah, too bad it was such a farce, huh?"

Hearing him voice it hurt as badly as being a part of the subterfuge. Some part of her had obviously been hoping against hope that the occasion, or maybe the wedding vows themselves, would soften his attitude, that he would want all of this to be real.

"I need to get out of here," she said stiffly. "I don't think I can bear it for another second."

"Anxious for your wedding night?" he taunted.

She swallowed hard and fought tears. "Hardly." In fact, she hadn't anticipated a wedding night at all. She was positive that Cole intended this to be a marriage in name only, if only to punish her. Maybe even to punish himself for being foolish enough to marry her.

He glanced at her. "I've arranged for you to have your own suite at the hotel until we decide what we're going to do," he said, confirming her guess and stripping away any lingering hope she might have harbored that it would be otherwise.

She stared at him blankly. "What we're going to do?" she repeated. "What does that mean?"

"Whether we're going to leave Winding River," he explained. "I can set up shop in California or anywhere else, for that matter."

The explanation—the very prospect of leaving—was too much. The thought of running away once more, essentially in disgrace—even if she was the only one who understood that—was overwhelming. She bounced off the swing.

"I am not leaving here," she said, scowling down at him. "I've gone along with everything you wanted, but not that."

He didn't seem the least bit disconcerted or distressed by her vehemence. "I just thought it might be easier to start fresh in a new place, where no one knows our history. We'd be just like any other couple who's grown apart. No one would know we'd never really been together in the first place."

"No, Cole," she said, standing up to him on this as she hadn't on anything else. "We did this to give Jake a family. That means a whole family, including your father and my mother."

"Heaven help the kid," he said grimly, but he nodded. "Okay, then, we stay. You can start looking for a house tomorrow."

"I gather you don't want to live at the Double D?"

"Not a chance."

She breathed a sigh of relief. The prospect of living under Frank Davis's thumb had been daunting. Maybe she and Cole would have half a chance to work things out if they were on their own.

"In town? Or would you prefer a ranch?" she asked.

"Not a ranch," he said at once. "Though buying some property outside of town and building would be okay. That way we'll get exactly what we want, a place with plenty of room."

So they would barely have to speak, much less spend time together? she wondered. How had it come to this? How could there be such a terrible distance between two people who had once shared everything? Of course, the answer was plain enough. She was responsible. She had no one to blame but herself for destroying the trust that they had once felt.

"Building would take time," she pointed out, even though her imagination was already at work on all the possibilities. She wondered if he even remembered that once upon a time they had spun their fantasies about what their dream house would look like. It had been spacious but cozy, with lots of fireplaces, overstuffed furniture and a king-size bed for the two of them. That bed had been the centerpiece of all their daydreams. Her cheeks burned at the memory. Now there would be separate beds, separate rooms, if Cole had his way.

"We have the time," he said, his gaze locked with hers.

For a heartbeat she thought she saw affection, at least, in his eyes, maybe a promise that as the weeks and months passed, they would work things out.

Then he had to go and ruin it by lifting his champagne glass and adding in a sarcastic tone, "After all, isn't this the first day of the rest of our lives?"

Deliberate cruelty had never been in Cole's nature. As he heard himself taunting Cassie repeatedly on their wedding day, he wondered if this new pattern of behavior was tapping into an uncontrollable dark side of him, a side far too much like his father in the early days after his mother's death. He hated the hurt that darkened her eyes, hated that he was responsible, but once his bitterness had been unleashed, he hadn't been able to stop.

Cassie's mother had insisted on keeping Jake with her for a few days while Cole and Cassie settled into married life. Obviously, she was determined to keep up the charade that this was a real marriage. And because he cared about her, had always cared about her, he let her have her illusions. He even went so far as to take Cassie's hand as they ran to the car that her friends had decorated with painted slogans and strings of empty cans.

At the hotel, though, he left Cassie at the door to her adjoining suite, then retreated to the bar, where he nursed a drink and his dark thoughts for hours.

This was the part he hadn't considered when he'd made his impulsive decision to marry her rather than fight her for custody of his son. He hadn't imagined what it would be like to know that Cassie was upstairs, dressed in something slinky and sexy, perhaps, wondering if there was to be a real wedding night. He hadn't thought ahead to how it would feel to know that she was his wife, that legally, at least, they were bound together.

He muttered a harsh expletive and tossed some money on the bar, then headed upstairs. Until he reached the door to his own room, he'd thought he was going to bed—alone. But that image of Cassie wearing lace wouldn't quit, and his body didn't seem to understand that she was the enemy, the betrayer.

He took a few steps toward her door, then backtracked to his own, then cursed himself for a fool. He went back to hers and hammered on it.

"Yes?"

Her voice was muffled and sleepy and so damn sexy it made his blood roar.

"It's me," he said tightly.

She opened the door and destroyed his illusions. She was wearing an oversize T-shirt that skimmed her knees. Her hair was rumpled, her cheeks streaked with dried tears, her eyes filled with distress. All the same, she was so blasted desirable it made him ache.

If she'd been waiting for him, though, she had long since given up. Cole raked a hand through his hair and bit back another curse.

Still, she was his wife now...if he dared to claim her. He thought about it, then sighed, defeated by his own conscience.

"Sorry," he mumbled. "I thought you might be awake."

"I was until a few minutes ago," she said. "Do you want to come in?"

"No," he said, then, "Yes."

A faint smile touched her lips, then faded. "Can't make up your mind?"

"I shouldn't be here."

"Why not? We *are* married. I have a paper that says so."

"Yeah, but we both know..." His voice trailed off.

"What? That it's not real?"

He nodded. What amazed him right now, though, was that it felt real, even though it wasn't supposed to. He wanted her. He wanted all the things they had once talked about...a future, a family, a home. He wanted to make love to Cassie Collins Davis and prove that she was finally his.

He gazed into her eyes, saw the little spark of desire, caught the way her lips parted as if she was about to speak...or about to welcome his kiss. He steeled himself against his own traitorous desire and took a step back.

"I'm sorry. I shouldn't have disturbed you," he said stiffly.

"Cole—"

"No, Cassie. I am not coming in there." He said it as if she were the one who'd set out to tempt him, rather than take responsibility for his own actions in coming to her door.

"Then why are you here?"

"I wish to God I knew."

She nodded at that. The hope that had been in her eyes dimmed, then died. Her expression hardened. "Then do me a favor," she said quietly. "Don't come back until you do."

He wanted to argue that she was his wife and that he'd damn well come and go as he pleased, but what was the point? She was right. He had no business being here, not unless he was willing to forgive and forget, and he was far from ready to do that. He wasn't sure he would *ever* be able to do that.

But as he turned and walked away, as he heard the whisper of her sigh as the door clicked shut behind him, he wondered if he hadn't just consigned them both—not just her, but the two of them—to a life of pure hell.

Cassie hadn't thought it was possible to be any more miserable than she had been waiting for Cole to decide what he wanted from her, but she'd been wrong. This so-called marriage was worse. Much worse.

To be so close to a man she loved and know that he didn't trust her, that, in fact, he all but hated her, was sheer torment. Whatever hope she had felt when he'd held her in his arms just a few short weeks ago at the reunion dance was gone. The hunger and heat stirred by his touch was little more than cold ashes now. All of it had been lost due to her years of deceit.

The day after the wedding she got up, got dressed and waited for some sign from Cole of what he expected. When he hadn't come by nine, she ordered breakfast in her room. She was tempted to change clothes and go to work, but Stella would have been appalled, and tongues all over town would have wagged. Cassie felt the same way about going to church. To arrive alone on the morning after her wedding would have stirred all sorts of comment.

By noon, though, she was going stir-crazy. Grabbing her keys, she went downstairs, got in her car and headed for Karen's. If ever there was a time to be with her best friends, this was it.

She found all four Calamity Janes seated around the kitchen table debating the merits of various gourmet coffees. Well, Lauren and Gina were debating them, anyway. Karen and Emma were exchanging amused looks. All of them looked up, clearly startled, as Cassie walked in.

"Any of that coffee left for me?" she asked as if her arrival was nothing out of the ordinary. "And I don't care what kind it is, as long as it's strong."

Karen jumped up, pulled out a chair for her and poured the coffee, as the others simply stared.

"Stop it," Cassie ordered. "I haven't grown two heads overnight, have I?"

"It's just a surprise," Gina began cautiously. "You got married yesterday. I thought—we all thought…"

"Well, you thought wrong," she said succinctly. "Where's Cole?"

Cassie shrugged. "Beats me. I haven't seen him since last night."

Emma scowled. "The man walked out on you right after your wedding night?"

"Only in the loosest interpretation of that," Cassie said mildly. "Technically there was no wedding night. And he never walked in, much less out."

Gina clasped her hand. "Explain," she ordered. "Then we can go strangle him."

Cassie opened her mouth, but the words wouldn't

come. Instead, all the hurt and humiliation bubbled up from deep inside. Great choking sobs emerged, taking her and the rest of them by surprise.

For an instant her friends just sat there. Then they were all around her, patting her back, handing her tissues and describing Cole in such unflattering terms that eventually even Cassie began to smile.

"He is not meaner and uglier than a hound dog," she said, sniffing. "That's the trouble. I'm only getting what I deserve."

"Don't be absurd," Emma snapped. "You don't deserve to be treated like this, abandoned on your wedding night."

"You, of all people, know why we got married. This wasn't a love match."

"Oh, of course it was," Lauren retorted, haughtily dismissing the claim. "And the sooner the two of you realize it, the sooner you can get on with the business of being married. Cole's just being bullheaded."

"I lied to him," Cassie reminded her.

"And you've apologized. Jake's in his life now. Cole needs to get over the past and move on."

"Otherwise, I'll be down at the courthouse first thing tomorrow filing for an annulment," Emma threatened.

"I think I'm the one who'd have to do that," Cassie teased, amazed at how much better she felt knowing these women were on her side. That they knew the whole story—or most of it—and loved her anyway.

Emma frowned. "You know what I meant. He is not going to get away with tormenting you."

Karen, silent up until now, reached for Cassie's hand. "Do you still love him?" she asked quietly.

"Of course I do," she said without hesitation. Only in the past few days with misery building at the distance between them had she realized just how much.

"Have you told him that?"

"Not in so many words."

"Why not?"

"Because he'd throw the words back in my face."

Karen shook her head. "I don't think so—but so what if he does? You just keep saying 'em till he gets the message. Don't let pride stand in your way, Cassie. Life is too short to waste a single second of it."

The message was powerful enough on its own, but coming from Karen, who'd so recently lost her beloved husband, it carried additional weight.

"Talk to him," Karen insisted. "And do it now. Hanging around here with us isn't solving your problem."

Cassie wasn't so sure about that. Being here with her friends had given her a sense of peace. Karen's advice had solidified her resolve to make this marriage work. She stood up and gave each of her friends a hug.

"You guys are the best," she said. "I knew if I came here I'd feel better."

"Now go back there and give him hell," Emma said.

"Tell him you love him," Karen corrected, poking Emma in the ribs.

Emma sighed. "Whatever. But call me if you want to nail the guy's hide in court."

"Emma, you really do have to learn to express yourself less subtly," Gina teased. "No one can ever figure out what you're thinking."

"Emma's just a passionate defender of the under-dog," Lauren said. "There's nothing wrong with that. It's why she's so good in court. Now leave her alone."

"Yeah, leave me alone," Emma said. "I'm not the same little wimp you guys used to walk all over."

"Really?" Gina asked with exaggerated shock.

Cassie chuckled at all the bantering and left Karen's with her heart lighter and her determination renewed. No matter how long it took, she was going to win Cole's heart again.

Unfortunately, as the first weeks of her marriage crept by with no thawing of Cole's attitude, Cassie slowly sank into despair again. Though the three of them—she, Cole and Jake—frequently shared meals, Cole made it a point never to be alone with her. Their conversations were limited to plans for the house and anything concerning their son. He didn't discuss his work or his days, and he never asked about hers. The wall between them was getting thicker and thicker with each passing week. She began to think it would take a wrecking ball to break it down.

Thankfully, though, Cole's chilly attitude didn't extend to Jake. The time he spent with his son, making up for all the lost years, was the only thing that kept Cassie going. Their bond was growing stronger day by day, and Jake was flourishing with all of the male attention.

Coming back to the hotel after her shift at Stella's, which she had refused to give up, she glanced into

Cole's office and saw them, their heads bent over the computer keyboard. Jake was peppering Cole with a thousand questions, which he answered with an endless supply of patience.

Cassie sighed heavily. Would her own relationship with her husband ever reach that stage again? Would there ever be the easy camaraderie they'd once shared? Only one thing gave her any hope at all. Despite Cole's cold attitude, she could tell that he still wanted her. From time to time she caught him watching her, his gaze hooded. On occasion he reached out, as if to touch her, only to withdraw without making contact. It was evident that the embers of their passion hadn't entirely cooled.

Even without Karen's advice still ringing in her ears, she knew she had a choice to make. She could endure this marriage and keep her pride, or she could risk her heart to change it. She had opted for pride once and nearly lost everything. This time she wouldn't make the same mistake.

Sex wasn't love, but it was a means of communication, an undeniable form of intimacy, of sharing. Slowly she would turn Cole's desire into need.

And over time she prayed she could turn it into love.

14

Cassie was driving Cole crazy. First there had been the constant hurt in her eyes, which left him filled with guilt.

Then there'd been unmistakable signs of anger. That had stiffened his resolve, prepared him for a battle that hadn't come.

Now lately she had been doing everything in her power to seduce him. The changes were keeping him dizzy and off balance, wavering between guilt and yearning.

He'd tried telling himself that this last, sly attempt to seduce was merely wishful thinking on his part, but there was no mistaking the intent of her glancing touches, the subtle perfume, the suddenly provocative attire on a woman who'd always preferred denim to lace. She wanted him and she intended to get him, by fair means or foul.

And he, blast it all, was losing the battle. How could he hold out against a woman he'd spent the past ten years wanting?

"Cole?"

"Hmm?" he responded distractedly. When she stroked his cheek with a lingering caress, his gaze shot up. Where had she come from? She rarely entered his room without knocking, but here she was, lips moist, color high. He eyed her suspiciously. "What?"

"Do you have a minute?" she asked, her expression all innocence as her hand fell away.

She was wearing white shorts and some skimpy little triangle of fabric that pretended to be a blouse. Aside from a few bows holding it all together, her back was bare, as were her feet. Rather than her usual pale-pink, she had painted her toenails a kick-ass red. Staring down at those erotic little toes, he lost his train of thought completely.

"Cole, do you have a minute?" she repeated, amusement threading through her voice.

"I suppose," he said uneasily. "Is there a problem with Jake?"

"No. He's fine. He's spending the night with my mother. He won't be back till after lunchtime tomorrow."

Uh-oh, he thought. They were alone. She was in his room, not her own, and she was wearing that sexy scent again, the one that made his pulse pound.

"The house?" he asked, sounding a little desperate even to his own ears. He cleared his throat. "Is there a problem with the house? I, um, I could call the contractor." He reached for the phone, clung to it as if it were a lifeline.

She smiled. "Nope. It's coming along right on schedule."

That left what? he wondered, battling panic as he reluctantly set the phone aside. What the dickens did she want? Besides him, of course. Oh, she definitely wanted him, he concluded, meeting her gaze and discovering the heat there.

"Then what's on your mind?" he asked, resigned to a really tough test of his willpower.

She edged closer, sat on the corner of his desk, her gaze locked with his, her very bare thigh nudging his. Even through his own jeans, he could feel the temperature of her skin soar. His body reacted predictably with a rush of blood straight to his groin.

This was a dangerous game she was playing. He wondered if she realized it. One glance into her smoldering eyes answered that. She knew, all right. And she was enjoying every single second of making him sweat, of watching him struggle with himself to do the right thing. She was deliberately trying to blast his conscience right out of the water.

"Cassie?" he prodded, a hitch in his voice.

A purely female smile came and went. "I'm not making you nervous, am I?"

Nervous? Hell, no. He was coming unglued. He was about to go up in flames.

"This…" He cleared his throat yet again. "This isn't wise."

He sounded like a cranky, sixty-year-old prude. Evidently she thought so, too, because she chuckled, a low, throaty sound that danced down his spine like a flame.

"Really? Why not?"

"Do I really have to explain it?"

She regarded him thoughtfully for a second, then nodded. "Yes, I think you do."

"Because we have issues," he began, then all but groaned. Not a sixty-year-old prude. Maybe ninety— and a stiff-necked psychiatrist to boot.

She nodded, acknowledging what he said, but she didn't look swayed. Nor did she budge one millimeter away from his thigh.

"Care to talk about them?" she asked, her tone only mildly curious.

Now there was a loaded question, if ever he'd heard one. If he said yes, he would be opening up the whole blasted can of worms he'd been trying so hard to ignore. If he said no, he was pretty sure she had some other way for them to spend the time.

He swallowed hard, cleared his throat, then shrugged. "What's the point?" he asked, proud of himself for coming up with a third option, an evasion that might annoy her enough to convince her to leave.

"Oh, I don't know. It might clear the air," she said, sounding amused perhaps, but definitely not annoyed.

He, however, was getting downright irritable. Her attitude was exasperating. Her proximity was arousing. The conflicting messages were roaring around in his head…and elsewhere.

"It. Would. Not. Clear. The. Air." He bit the words out from between clenched teeth.

She swung her legs, deliberately letting her calf brush his. "Oh, I don't know," she said, her expres-

sion serious, even thoughtful. "We won't know unless we try."

He narrowed his gaze and studied her. "Is that what
you really want?" he asked skeptically. "A nice, polite
discussion, a chance to make a few excuses, maybe
even some promises?"

A spark of anger flashed in her eyes, and he thought
for a second she might really explode, tell him to take
his sarcasm and shove it. Instead, she leaned over until
her gaze was level with his, until he could feel the
soft whisper of her breath against his cheek. His heart
raced.

"No," she said in that same quiet, intense tone. "This
is what I want."

Before he could even catch his breath, her mouth
was on his, sweet and urgent and hot. Her tongue
skimmed his lips, then slid inside, tangling with his.
And Cole was pretty sure his entire body was going
to go up in flames.

For one tiny, fleeting second, he considered a protest, ordered himself to utter it, in fact, but the moment
passed in a frenzy of need. *This* was what he'd missed,
this was what he and Cassie could be together if only
he could let go of his anger and his stiff-necked pride.
All it would take was the little matter of forgiving her,
of letting go of the past. Right now he was too caught
up in the moment to give a hang about anything, the
past included.

He groaned and claimed her, deepening the kiss,
blanking out all of the arguments against what was
happening and seizing the pulse-pounding moment.

She slid into his lap, all willing and eager and hot as a winter fire, just the way he remembered. When he would have moved beyond the devastating kisses for more, she held him still, savoring the mating of their mouths, discovering the amazing nuances possible in a kiss.

His hand drifted to her thigh, skimmed along warm, supple skin until he reached the core of her heat. He hesitated there, knowing that they were crossing the point of no return. If he touched her intimately, if she let him, there would be no going back. He would have to bury himself inside her. He would have to discover if reality matched fantasy, if the present could equal the memory. He would have to rediscover every texture, every taste, every throbbing response. He would have to make her his.

And he would be hers. Forever. Without denials or recriminations or regrets. Forgiveness might be a struggle for some time to come, but this, *this* would be a given, a habit too hard to break for a second time in his life.

He sighed and held still, waiting for the panic to wash through him, waiting for the anger to resurface and destroy desire. He waited and waited, but it didn't happen.

Instead, anticipation built…along with soul-wrenching need and astonishing heat.

And then she smoothed her hand across his brow as if to wipe away the worry, the distress that had kept him—kept them—from moving on. He was lost, caught up in the magical spell of her touch, in the powerful pull of her tenderness.

"I want you," he admitted at long last. "You have no idea how much I want you."

"I think I do," she soothed, beginning to work the buttons of his shirt.

Her knuckles skimmed lightly across his chest, and then her mouth was there, clever and damp and eager. Her touch turned the wanting to a persistent ache.

Cole thought he might finally understand what it was like to be ravished, to be taken completely and not have the will to fight it, just to go along for the astonishing ride. He was on sensory overload, climbing to a peak that he had no intention of reaching alone.

He reached for Cassie's hands, stilled them, then shifted to evade her lips. "Enough," he commanded, his voice ragged.

Startled smoky eyes met his.

"I am not making love with my wife for the first time since the wedding in an uncomfortable, straight-backed chair," he said, scooping her into his arms and standing up.

He carried her to the bed in the next room. There were a dozen times along the way when he could have allowed sane, sensible thoughts to crowd in and end this, but he ignored everything but the feel of the woman in his arms, the need pounding through his veins.

Tomorrow would take care of itself, he told himself. Tonight was about him and the woman whose memory had burned in his heart for years. If it was all they ever had, he told himself that tonight would be enough.

Cassie hadn't been nearly as sure of herself as she'd wanted Cole to believe. There had been moments, more than she could count, when she'd wanted to dash from his room rather than risk the rejection she feared was coming. Only grim determination and the terror that this might be her one and only chance had kept her there when he'd made it plain he wanted her to go.

Now, as he held her in his arms, as he made steady, deliberate progress toward his bed, she began to allow hope to flare along with desire. Surely this would be the beginning. Surely after tonight the barriers would come down and they would be able to communicate as they once had, as friends *and* as lovers. Not perfectly, not without setbacks, but with the commitment of two people who'd finally figured out what mattered most in their lives.

Inside the room dominated by that great expanse of bed, Cassie felt a moment's triumph. She had gotten them this far. She had taken control of her life—not by running, but by staying. If there had been time, if Cole's clever hands hadn't been busily stripping away her clothes, she would have taken the time to pat herself on the back for finally maturing enough to stay the course, no matter how difficult.

But Cole clearly didn't intend to give her—or himself—time to think. His touches, like hers earlier, were meant to excite. His kisses became deeper and more urgent. When his mouth closed over her breast, a wild-fire burst into flame inside her.

This was the way it had been ten years ago—pow-erful, all-consuming need, frenzied caresses and a buildup so sweet, so intense, that she was sure she would die from it. Instead, just when she thought she could go no higher, when it seemed likely that her body was about to shudder in a wild, cataclysmic release, Cole found some way to ease her down before lifting her back to a new and even higher peak.

Beneath him, she moaned, straining, desperate and awash in sensations, frantic for him to bury himself in-side her. His work-roughened hands were gentle, skill-ful and oh, so devious—tender one second, demanding the next. His muscles, hard from working the ranch, bunched beneath her touch. The body that had invaded her dreams, filling her head with erotic images, was even better in reality. Ten years had added strength and agility, had turned awkward, if delicious, fumbling into skillful lovemaking.

She might have had the will and the incentive to take the initiative tonight, but Cole was in control now, setting the pace, destroying her with his devas-tating kisses, his tormenting touches. She wanted… she *needed*…

"Cole, please," she begged. "Now. I want you in-side me now."

His eyes glittered with satisfaction. His hands cupped her face, and his gaze locked with hers.

Then, oh, so slowly, he entered her at last, sinking

deep inside her, filling her. She gasped at the pleasure of it, at the sense of fulfillment that stole over her.

But then he was moving and her body was soaring until together they climbed to the highest peak yet. This time there was no retreat, no blessed relief, just this building urgency, this frantic, fevered yearning that grew hotter and wilder until it exploded through her, then him in shuddering waves.

Cole murmured her name over and over as they clung together, trembling, then slowly...slowly returned to earth...to his bed...to reality.

And to all the problems that couldn't be resolved so easily.

Cassie banished that thought as soon as it dared to creep in. She wouldn't allow it, wouldn't allow anything to spoil this moment. She had waited too long— not just since her wedding night, but years. Illusion or not, she deserved this sweet oblivion.

She sighed and cuddled more tightly against Cole. His arm held her securely, his hand rested on her hip. His breathing grew steadier, whispering against hot, fevered skin, cooling it.

"That was—" she began.

Cole touched a finger to her lips. "Don't say anything."

It was part command, part warning. "Why?" she asked as tension crept in to steal the serenity.

"Just let it be what it was. If we start examining it, things will only get complicated."

Rather than quieting her, the request to leave things be stirred more questions. "Complicated how?"

This time Cole sighed heavily and pulled away, retreating from her not just physically but emotionally. She could feel the sudden chill in the air as surely as if the air-conditioning had kicked on. She gathered the sheet and wrapped herself in it before facing him.

"Cole, talk to me. Don't you dare shut me out now."

"What's the point?"

It wasn't the first time he'd asked that since she'd walked in on him earlier, but it was more devastating now. The hurt and anger she'd been living with for weeks bubbled back to the surface. "The point is that you and I have just made love—using no protection, I might add. We could have made another baby here today."

An expression of such dismay crossed his face that Cassie's heart sank. What she had viewed as a hopeful beginning Cole obviously saw as nothing more than another lapse in judgment. Rather than solving anything, tonight had only complicated their lives, perhaps more than either of them was ready to cope with.

"I assumed you were on the Pill," he said stiffly.

She shivered as ice formed where only moments before there had been fire. "Why would you assume such a thing?" she asked. "I haven't been involved with anyone. You certainly haven't come near me since the wedding. Why would I be on the Pill?"

An unreadable mask slid over his face. "Because it would be the mature, responsible thing to do if you intended to come into my room and seduce me."

"And the way you've been behaving is mature?" she snapped, losing patience. "You married me, Cole. For better or worse. Did you do it just so you could punish me till the end of time?"

He stiffened at the accusation, but he didn't deny it.

She stared at him incredulously. "You did, didn't you? Well, I don't intend to live like this." She leaped out of the bed and started grabbing clothes and putting them on haphazardly, not worrying with buttons or snaps, just the most basic decency so she could get from his room to her own.

"Oh?" he said with deadly calm, his gaze hooded as he watched her. "What will you do? Run?"

"Only across town," she said. "I'll take Jake and—"

"You won't take Jake anywhere," he said. "Jake stays with me."

"Not until a court says he does," she retorted.

He leveled a look at her that might have daunted her if she hadn't been so furious.

"Are you willing to take that chance?" he asked. "Are you willing to risk losing your son? I won't go about this halfway. I'll go after full custody."

She met his gaze and saw that he was absolutely serious. Fury died as fear crept back in. She wouldn't let him see that, though. She couldn't.

"Why do you want to keep me trapped in marriage, Cole? Have you asked yourself that? I think it's because a part of you loves me, a part of you wants to know that I'm yours anytime you get around to forgiving me. You like dangling the prospect of forgiveness in front of me just to torture me, just to get a little revenge for what I did to you."

He didn't deny any of it, not even her claim that he

loved her. He couldn't, because they both knew it was true. The last hour had proved that. More than sex had been involved. They had made love. For a little while anger and hurt had slid away and their hearts had spoken. Cole had wanted this as desperately as she had. He just couldn't make himself admit it.

Cassie might have pitied him for that, but right now she had no pity to spare. She was fighting not just for her son but for her marriage.

"If I stay," she said firmly, her gaze clashing with his, "*if* I stay, then both of us have to work to make this marriage real. We have to do whatever it takes, see a counselor if we can't figure things out on our own. The time has come for drastic measures, Cole. I'm willing." She challenged him with a steady look. "Are you?"

He studied her warily. "Meaning?"

"No more separate bedrooms. No more separate beds." She was adamant about it. There would be no compromise. "I love you. I always have. And I'm sorrier than I can say that I kept your son from you, but the truth is out now. You know. Either we deal with it and move on, together, as a family, or I take Jake and move back in with my mother and we go to court."

Taking such a stance was a risk. She knew it even as the words left her mouth, but she had no choice. She would not live in emotional limbo. Maybe if Cole hadn't mattered to her, she could have done it, but he did matter. He was the love of her life, the father of her son, and the distance between them was killing her bit by bit, day by day. It was worse than when they'd been separated, when she'd thought he had abandoned her.

He gave her a measured look, then said with a degree of bemusement, "You've changed."

"I hope so. I'm not a teenage girl anymore."

"No, I mean in the past few weeks. You're stronger."

Stronger? She wasn't so sure about that. But she did recognize that this was no way to live. If she didn't fight for her future, who would?

"I love you," she said quietly. "If I'm stronger, it's because I've stopped denying that. Maybe there's a lesson in there for you, too. Loving me doesn't make you weak, Cole. It takes a strong man to forgive."

Before he could respond to the challenge of that, she walked out of his room and headed back to her own for what she prayed would be the last time. She would give him until tomorrow to come for her, to say that he was willing to try.

And just in case he stayed stubbornly away, she would begin to pack her bags.

15

Cole spent a long, lonely night after Cassie left his bed. He cursed himself for letting it come to this, for weakening his stance, for letting his determination slip.

He debated with himself for hours, wanting one thing, needing another and hating himself because of it. She had betrayed him. She wasn't to be trusted. It was as simple—as black-and-white—as that.

But it wasn't. It was murky as hell. Maybe there weren't any rights or wrongs. Maybe there wasn't any such thing as justice when emotions were involved. Maybe what was in his heart was all that mattered.

If only he knew precisely what that was. Until today he'd been able to convince himself that he'd married Cassie only so he wouldn't have to fight her for custody of Jake. He'd seen himself as the magnanimous one. Practically a saint, he thought wryly.

But, holding her in his arms, burying himself deep inside her, he had known better. He was no saint. Far from it. Just as she'd said, he had married her because he couldn't bear the thought of losing her for a second time.

But that was exactly what was going to happen if he didn't get over the anger that ate at him during every waking minute. He'd seen the determination in her eyes last night and again this morning before she'd left for work. She would go, even if that meant a court fight. That she would risk so much proved to him just how serious she was. She wanted all or nothing.

There was only one problem. He wasn't at all sure he could give her what she wanted, not without resentment bubbling up. What chance would they have if it was always there, just below the surface, something to throw in her face whenever they hit a rough patch?

Just let it go, forgive and forget. If he'd asked a half dozen people, five of the six would have told him that was what he needed to do. The sixth would tell him to cling to the anger, to remember it, so she could never hurt him again. That would have been his father's advice—which made it suspect right off.

Frank Davis hadn't let up once since the wedding. Despite the show he'd put on during the reception, he hadn't gone out of his way to welcome Cassie any more than Cole had. He seemed to have forgotten all about his own role in keeping Cassie and his son apart.

At the same time, he was doing everything in his power to turn Jake into the rancher that Cole himself refused to be. It frustrated Frank no end that Jake showed more interest in Cole's computers than he did in cattle.

"You're ruining that boy," Frank grumbled when he

stopped by the hotel the morning after Cole's argument with Cassie and found father and son squinting at the computer screen.

His arrival was a good distraction. It meant Cole wouldn't have to deal with Cassie and the feelings that had come roaring to life the night before. He could ignore them for a little longer, put off having to make the decision he'd spent the night debating.

Jake, unaware of the undercurrents or the depth of his grandfather's disapproval, regarded the older man with innocent excitement. "But this is so cool. Cole's letting me write a real program for a game, one I made up myself. One of these days every kid in America will play it," he said with complete confidence. "Cole said so."

Frank scowled. "What are you doing calling your daddy Cole?" he demanded, seizing on that, rather than commenting on the game that had his grandson so excited.

"Leave it be," Cole said tightly, though it bothered him some, too, that Jake hadn't started calling him Dad.

Jake blinked rapidly at his grandfather's criticism, then gazed up at Cole. "Can I?"

"Can you what?"

"Call you Dad?"

Cole's heart crept into his throat. "Of course you can."

A smile spread across the boy's face. "You never said, so I wasn't sure, and I didn't want to ask Mom, 'cause she looks kinda sad a lot, especially when you and I spend a lot of time together."

"She needs to get over it," Frank grumbled even as Cole shot a warning look in his direction.

"I'll speak to your mother," Cole promised. "I'm sure she won't have any objections." How could she? he thought. There was no denying the relationship. The whole town knew about it by now.

The things he and Cassie needed to discuss were adding up...and most of the topics promised to be uncomfortable.

"Jake, why don't you come out and spend the night at the ranch with me?" Cole's father asked. "That horse I bought for you needs to be ridden."

"I'm not very good," Jake protested.

"And you won't get any better by avoiding it," Frank said.

"Okay, enough," Cole said, frowning at his father. "Don't push him."

"I want to learn to ride," Jake said, regarding his grandfather earnestly. "But that horse is too big, and he doesn't like me."

"Part of learning to ride is learning to control the horse. You'll get the hang of it," Frank insisted.

"Maybe he should start out on Buttercup," Cole said. He grinned at Jake. "She was my first horse."

That was recommendation enough for Jake. "Could I?" Jake begged his grandfather.

"Absolutely," Cole said, not giving his father a chance to refuse or to label the boy a sissy because of his preference for a gentler horse. "Shall I come along?"

"I'm perfectly capable of giving the boy a riding lesson," his father grumbled, clearly understanding Cole's unspoken message. "On Buttercup, if that's the way you want it. The poor old mare can barely make it out of the barn, though."

"Which means she's not likely to run off with him," Cole said. He winked at Jake. "Take her an apple, and she'll do whatever you ask of her."

Jake ran to grab one from the basket of fruit the hotel had sent up. "Okay, Grandpa, I'm ready."

Frank looked momentarily taken aback by his eagerness, but he finally gave him a gruff pat on the back. "Let's go, then."

"Jake, shouldn't you get your toothbrush, at least?" Cole asked.

"I don't need one. Grandpa gave me one last time. And there are some jeans and shirts and stuff in my room at the ranch."

Cole regarded his father evenly. "Is that so?"

"No point in having him haul stuff back and forth. He might as well feel at home when he's there."

"Just don't get carried away," he warned his father. He wouldn't put it past the old man to try to convince Jake to move in.

"I have no idea what you mean," Frank retorted, heading for the door at a brisker pace than usual, clearly eager to avoid a drawn-out explanation.

Cole let him leave, then sat back with a sigh and braced himself for Cassie's return from work. He had a decision to make between now and then. He could agree to her terms or go to war. With his body already squarely on her side, in fact eager to join her in bed, the decision was all but made.

He just had to figure out if he could live with it.

Cassie wiped the counter at Stella's with slow, distracted strokes.

"I think it's clean now," Karen commented.

Cassie's gaze shot up. "What?"

She had almost forgotten her friend was there. Karen had come in right at closing, claiming that she'd had a sudden yearning for a piece of Stella's apple pie. Since Karen's pies had been winning ribbons at the local fair for years now, the explanation hadn't rung true.

Karen placed her hand over Cassie's to still the idle motion. "I said that the counter is clean." Her gaze narrowed. "What's on your mind? Did you and Cole have a fight?"

"We don't exactly fight," Cassie said. "Though yesterday we came as close as we ever have." She sighed. "He's so cool. Even when he's furious with me, he refuses to let down his guard. He just makes some sarcastic comment that's designed to put distance between us."

"Don't let him get away with it," Karen advised. "Call him on it."

"I do. Last night I told him he had to make a decision. We either work at a real marriage or I walk and I take Jake with me."

Karen's eyes widened. "You didn't?"

"What choice did I have? Things are impossible the way they are now. And after yesterday…"

"What happened?"

"We made love," she said, feeling the heat climb into her cheeks at the memory. "And it was the way it used to be—better, in fact."

"That's wonderful. And it's progress." She studied Cassie intently. "So why did you issue an ultimatum after that?"

"Because he would have gone right back to the way things used to be. He was already pulling back even while I was right there next to him."

"He's scared," Karen concluded.

The comment was so ludicrous that Cassie laughed. "Cole Davis isn't scared of anything."

"Sure he is," Karen said. "He's scared of the same thing all men are scared of, letting down their guard and getting hurt. Frankly, I think that's very positive."

"Pardon me if I have a little trouble following your logic. Why is that a good thing?"

"It means he loves you. You still have the power to hurt him and he knows it. It terrifies him. So what does he do? He puts those walls up to protect himself."

Cassie considered the explanation thoughtfully. It made a lot of sense. Unfortunately she wasn't sure how much longer she could fight to try to tear those walls back down. A lot depended on what Cole said when she got back to the hotel today. If he agreed to her terms for staying, they had a chance. If not…

"I don't know what to do anymore," she admitted.

"I've tried everything I can think of, including threatening to leave."

"Which would only prove to him that's he's been right all along not to trust you," Karen pointed out.

Well, hell. She was right about that, too. "I can't talk about this anymore. My head is spinning. Let's talk about you. How are you doing?"

"I'm getting through one day at a time," Karen said. "Lauren's been a huge help. She refuses to go away. I feel as if I am totally disrupting her life, but the truth is I'm glad of the company. And she's working as if she's obsessed. She's always had a magic touch with horses, but she's turning into an all-around rancher. I dread the day she goes back to her own life."

Her shoulders slumped and a weary expression settled on her face. "I don't know what I'd do without her. I thought I could do it all, but I can't, and I can't pay for extra help. If I lose the ranch, I'll feel as if I failed Caleb."

"You're not going to lose the ranch," Cassie said fiercely. "We'll all do whatever it takes to see to that." She studied her friend's face. "Unless, one of these days, you decide there's something you'd rather be doing. If you decide you want to sell, it will be okay, Karen. Caleb would understand."

"I'm not so sure of that," Karen said, then sighed.

"He would," Cassie insisted, then gave her friend's hand a squeeze. "You have to do what's best for you now. And you don't have to decide what that is today or even tomorrow. You take your time. And if you need extra help, call me. I might not be experienced, but I'm willing. And Jake's been learning to do chores at the Double D. He could just as easily do them for you. In fact, I'd prefer it."

Karen forced a smile. "Thanks. Now go home to your husband. Your work with me is done." Her grin spread. "And that counter hasn't been that spotless in years, so you're off the hook with Stella, too."

They walked out of the diner together, then went their separate ways. It wasn't lost on Cassie that both of them were heading home with unmistakable reluctance. There was a difference, though. Karen could never get her husband back, while Cassie still had a fighting chance with hers. Watching her friend climb dejectedly into the battered pickup that had been Caleb's, Cassie resolved to make the most of the chance she had.

Cole looked up when he heard Cassie's key turn in the lock. His pulse ricocheted wildly. This was it, the moment of truth. Do or die. A few more clichés rattled around in his head as he dared to face her, still trying to decide what to say.

"You're home," he said. Now there was a brilliant beginning, he thought, cursing his stupidity. He tried to salvage the moment. "Rough day?"

That was better, he concluded. It sounded like the start of a perfectly normal conversation between husband and wife. Unfortunately, there was nothing normal about any of this. It was awkward as hell.

"It was okay, at least until Karen came in." Her expression turned sad. "I'm worried about her. She's not handling Caleb's death well at all."

"How could she? He's only been gone a few months. It must be a terrible adjustment to make."

"She ought to sell the ranch before it kills her, too," Cassie said. "But right now she won't hear of it. She thinks she owes it to Caleb to stay."

"And as long as she thinks that, then that's what she needs to do," Cole said. "You can't push her. That ranch is her connection to him. It's little wonder she doesn't want to lose that."

Cassie sighed. "I know. Some things can't be rushed."

Her gaze locked with his, and they both knew that she wasn't talking only about Karen. "I'm sorry if I pushed too hard yesterday. I just want…I want things to be okay, to be good between us."

Cole nodded. Here it was, the moment of truth. "I want that, too," he said quietly. "I really do. I'm not saying it can happen overnight, but it is what I want. You need to know that. You need to believe it, even when I'm shutting you out."

"I'll try."

"And sleeping in the same bed will be a start," he added quietly. "If that's something you still want."

Hope lit her eyes. "I do," she said at once. "With all my heart."

"Good."

They stared at each other, neither of them moving, neither of them knowing what else to say, until finally Cole could bear it no longer.

"Come here," he said, beckoning her.

She hesitated.

"Cassie, you're not changing your mind already, are you?"

"No, but—"

"Come here," he commanded.

She took one step toward him, then eventually another, until their knees were touching. He reached up and touched her cheek, surprised to find it was damp with tears he hadn't noticed in the room's shadows.

"Oh, baby," he murmured, drawing her into his lap. "It's going to be okay."

"Is it?" she whispered, sounding more uncertain than he'd ever heard her.

"It is," he said confidently.

Given time, given commitment, given love, it would definitely be okay. Hopefully, he had just bought them the time they needed.

16

It wasn't okay, not by a long shot. Oh, Cole was trying. They were sharing a bed, but the gap between them hadn't been closed, not all the way.

Cassie had had high hopes for the move into the new house. Surely then, when they were in the home they'd designed together, the last pieces of their relationship would fall into place. But it wasn't working out that way.

The new house was still not the home she had envisioned. It was bright and airy. Her kitchen was amazing. The fireplaces turned even the spacious rooms into cozy refuges from the increasingly bitter weather of fall. They had already had one blizzard, and another was predicted before the end of the week. The snow was deep at the higher elevations, but here in Winding River it had melted rapidly, leaving mud and gloom in its wake. It was only the beginning of November, and already she was dreading being closed up indoors with a man who retreated into moody silences more nights than not.

But Cole, despite the fact that he was reluctantly sharing her bed, still kept a part of himself distant. They made love—sometimes sweet, tender love, sometimes wild, passionate love—but there was little joy in it.

Still, Cassie couldn't deny herself the one form of communication that Cole allowed. Nor could she regret what had happened because of it. They were going to have a baby. She'd planned to tell him when he got back from his business trip, though she had no idea how he would take the news.

Once in a long while she caught a glimmer of the old Cole, the man who had shared everything with her, the man who had trusted her with his most private thoughts. Other times it was like living with a stranger. Which, she wondered, would surface when she made her announcement?

A lot depended on that, because slowly but surely their current circumstances were draining the life out of her. She had to do something to fix it, but she was out of ideas. It wasn't possible to force someone to forgive, much less forget. Time, the great healer, wasn't working. And a baby couldn't be expected to save a faltering marriage.

Cole's father was no help at all. He reserved most of his snide comments for the times when the two of them were alone. Cassie usually managed to let them roll off her back. Fighting with Frank Davis was a waste of energy, at least over something as inconsequential as a few pointed remarks.

His attempts to turn Jake against her were something else entirely. She wasn't sure when she'd first realized that was what he was doing, but lately he'd stepped up the campaign.

Today Frank dropped Jake off at the end of the drive after a riding lesson at the Double D. Jake came into the kitchen with a sullen expression, uttered no greeting at all and started to walk straight past her. The show of belligerence, more and more frequent after he'd been with his grandfather, was the final straw.

"Hey, what's with the long face?" Cassie asked.

His reply was mumbled. He kept right on walking.

"Jake Collins, get back here."

He faced her with a dark look. "I'm not a Collins. I'm a Davis. Someday I'm going to own Grandpa's ranch."

He said it as if he expected her to challenge the claim. "I imagine that's true, if it turns out to be what you want. As for whether you're a Collins or a Davis, you were born with my name. If you'd like to think about legally changing that to Davis, I'll speak to your father."

Having Cole legally acknowledge Jake as his son was something they should have discussed, she realized. In fact, she was somewhat surprised that Cole hadn't insisted on it. Obviously, his failure to do so was grating on his father's nerves. Frank had clearly started planting the seeds in Jake's head to get the ball rolling.

Right or wrong, he was manipulating her son, just as he'd tried to do with Cole for years. She didn't like it.

Jake stared at her, clearly surprised by her offer. "You will?"

"Of course."

"Grandpa said you wouldn't. He said you were probably trying to keep me from being a Davis."

Cassie barely resisted the urge to tell Jake precisely what she thought of his grandfather. "That's not true," she said instead, keeping her tone mild. "To be honest, your father and I simply haven't talked about it, but we will. I promise."

Jake studied her intently for a long moment, his expression troubled. "Can I ask you something?"

"Of course."

"Are you and Dad gonna get a divorce?"

Cassie was stunned by the question. "No. Why would you think that?"

"Grandpa said you probably would and then I would live with Dad."

"Oh, he did, did he?" Her temper shot into the stratosphere. If Frank had been around, she might very well have clobbered him over the head with a cast-iron skillet. "Sweetie, your dad and I are working very hard to make us a family. That takes time, but it's what I want. It's what we both want."

"Promise?"

She hugged him tightly. "I promise. Now go on upstairs and do your homework. I need to run out for a little while."

The minute Jake had grabbed a handful of cookies

and a glass of milk, she snatched her jacket off a hook by the kitchen door and went to the barn. She saddled up a horse, because it was much faster to get to the Double D by cutting across their adjoining fields than it was to drive clear out to the highway and around.

She had never been quite so furious. Even after learning of the role that Frank and her own mother had played all those years ago in keeping her and Cole apart, she had struggled to understand their perspective, but this was too much. This was an attempt to scare her son, to make it seem as if his family was about to fall apart and that the only person he could rely on was his grandfather.

Her breath turned to steam as she urged the horse into a gallop that ate up the distance to the Double D ranch house. All she could think about was shaking Frank until his teeth rattled. Not that she could do it, given their difference in sizes, but she was darn well willing to give it a try. At the very least, she intended to give him a tongue-lashing that he wouldn't soon forget.

Oblivious to the fact that there were still lingering patches of ice on the ground, that snow had started falling again, she rode harder, her temper climbing.

When the horse lost its footing, she wasn't prepared for the sudden skid, the frantic attempt by her mount to stay afoot. The next thing she knew she was flying through the air, trying desperately to curl her body to protect the baby as the ground rose up to meet her.

But she misjudged. When she slammed into the rocky ground, she broke the fall with her hand and felt the bone snap. The pain was excruciating. And for the first time in her life she fainted.

Cole hated himself for falling in love with Cassie all over again. How could he be so weak that a woman who'd betrayed him not once, but twice, could still manage to steal his heart? He wanted so badly to accept the love she was offering, to move on, but a part of him insisted on fighting her every step of the way.

It had to stop. They couldn't go on like this. It wasn't fair to either of them, nor to Jake.

Cole came home after a two-day business trip to California prepared to let her go so they could both find some peace. He walked into the house to find the kitchen empty with no sign of dinner on the stove. He heard music from upstairs and gathered Jake was in his room doing his homework, though how the kid could think with that sound blaring in his ears was beyond Cole.

He climbed the stairs two at a time, knocked on Jake's door, then opened it without waiting for a response. He doubted his son could hear him over the music, anyway.

Sure enough, Jake didn't even look up from his books. Cole crossed the room and switched off the CD player. Jake blinked and stared at him, his expression brightening.

"You're home. When did you get here?"

"A few minutes ago. Where's your mom?"

"Isn't she downstairs?"

"No."

The response seemed to make Jake vaguely uneasy.

"Jake, what's going on?"

"I'm not sure."

"Did you two fight?"

"Not exactly. I just asked her about some stuff Grandpa said. I think maybe it made her mad. Maybe she went to see him."

"What did Grandpa say?"

"That you guys were gonna get a divorce and I was gonna stay with you. She said he was wrong." Worry puckered his brow. "He was wrong, wasn't he?"

Cole bit back a curse. Given what he'd been thinking when he walked in the door, his father hadn't been that far off—though only about the divorce. Cole didn't intend to try to keep Jake. Now was not the time to get into that, though.

"When was that?" he asked instead.

Jake shrugged. "I don't know. What time is it now?"

"After seven. It's already dark out."

"I guess it was about four. I went by Grandpa's after school for a riding lesson, then he brought me home."

Three hours? Cole thought, his stomach churning. Why on earth wasn't she back by now? He grabbed Jake's phone and called his father.

"Is Cassie there?" he demanded when his father answered.

"Cassie? Why would she be here?"

"Jake thought she might be heading over there."

"Maybe she just wised up and left you."

Cole let that pass. The most important thing right now was finding Cassie.

"I'm going out to look for her," he told his father. "If you give a damn about me or my son, you'll help."

"Well, of course I will," his father said defensively. "The snow's been coming down awhile now. No telling where she might be. Car could have run off the road."

But when Cole went outside, Cassie's car was parked behind the house where it always was. He checked the barn and saw that one of their horses was missing.

He looked up and realized Jake had followed him outside. He was shivering just inside the door of the barn.

"Is she gone?" Jake asked, looking as scared as Cole felt.

"She took one of the horses," he said. "I'm sure she's fine. She probably took shelter somewhere when the snow started."

"Why wouldn't she have turned around and come back?" Jake asked reasonably. "Or gone on to Grandpa's?"

He hunkered down in front of Jake. "I don't know, pal. I need you to do something for me, though. I want you to go inside and call nine-one-one. Tell the sheriff we need some help looking for your mom, okay? Can you do that?"

Jake nodded, his eyes wide.

"Then call your grandmother and ask her to come out here and stay with you."

"I want to come with you," Jake protested.

"No, this is more important. You can be the biggest help to your mom by calling the sheriff. Now scoot."

With one last backward glance, Jake took off for

the house. Cole saddled their second horse and rode off in the direction of the Double D. If it had had to snow today, why couldn't it have been earlier so there would be clear hoofprints for him to follow? Instead he was forced to slow down and guess which way she might have gone.

The temperature had dropped dramatically just since he'd gotten home. If Cassie was out here, injured, she wouldn't be able to last long. The sense of urgency doubled, even as his progress slowed.

"Come on, Cassie. Where are you? Help me. Give me some sign."

The distant, distressed whinny of a horse finally drew his attention. His own mount's ears pricked up.

"Is that Harley?" he murmured, and got a shake of a head and an answering whinny as a response. "Find him then. Let's find Harley."

The terrain had grown rockier and slicker. His frustration mounted right along with his anxiety. He had to find Cassie. He damn well didn't intend to lose her like this.

With a sudden rush of understanding, he realized that he couldn't lose her at all. What did the decision of a scared eighteen-year-old girl matter? If the decision of a twenty-eight-year-old woman was less understandable, even he could see that it had been driven by a fear just as deep-seated as the one she'd felt years before. Who was he to judge that?

All that mattered, all that had ever mattered, was that he loved her and she loved him. Nothing had ever changed that. They'd just lost their way for a while.

Now he had to find her and tell her that.

A heart-wrenching whinny of an animal in pain cut through the air, closer now, just over the rise, if he wasn't mistaken. He crested the hill and spotted them, horse and woman, both down, both way too still.

"Don't die, Cassie," Cole pleaded as he leaped to the ground and knelt beside her. In its own show of concern his horse edged closer to its disabled stablemate. "Dear God, please don't let her die."

He checked her carefully for injuries. The only obvious one was her broken arm, but she'd been here a long time. Could it be there was a more serious problem? He debated the wisdom of moving her, but the chances of anyone else coming upon them here were slim and time was essential. She'd already been out in the bitter cold for way too long.

He bundled her in his jacket, then checked the injured horse. "I'll get someone in here for you in no time," he vowed, running his hand over the horse's trembling flank. "You saved her life, you know. You told me how to find her. I'll do everything in my power to save yours, too."

Then he gathered Cassie into his arms and mounted his own horse, heading for home as quickly as the weather permitted. She moaned softly while he rode. She was obviously in pain, but she was alive, and for the moment that was all that mattered. Once he got her to a hospital, he would will her back to life.

The next hour was the longest of his entire life as Cassie fought her way back to him. When her eyes finally blinked open, her gaze wandered around until it locked on his.

"I knew you'd find me," she whispered hoarsely and then closed her eyes again.

The next time she awoke, Cole was asleep in the chair beside her bed. His eyes snapped open when he felt her fingers against his cheek. Her color was better, her eyes clear.

"How do you feel?"

"Alive," she said. "And grateful. Every time I tried to move, my arm hurt. I kept fainting."

He sighed when he met her gaze, then did what he'd vowed to do when he thought she might be lost to him forever.

"Good, because I have something to tell you, and I need to do it now, before I lose my courage. If you want your freedom, Cassie, I'll give it to you. Jake will stay with you."

She stared at him with an expression he couldn't read, so he plunged on.

"I didn't give you a choice about marrying me before, so I'm giving you one now. I love you. I want you to stay, but if you want to go, there will be no custody battle."

There was no mistaking the sheen of tears in her eyes then, and for an instant he was terrified that his gamble wasn't going to pay off, that she would go.

"You love me?" she said, and there was a note of wonder in her voice.

He shrugged. "Always have. I guess I always will. I just lost sight of that for a time." He studied her intently. "So, Cassie, will you go or stay? You can have some time to think about it."

"I don't need to think about it, not even for a second." A smile blossomed on her face, then spread. "Since I think we're about to have another baby, it looks like I'd better stay." She rested her hand protectively on her stomach. "Now I can't wait to know for sure."

"And if you aren't pregnant, will you still stay?"

"Yes, of course, because I love you and this family of ours. I was just beginning to wonder if you were ever going to figure out that we all belong together. I'd pretty much concluded that the media had gotten it all wrong all these years, that you weren't half as smart as they were always writing."

"I was smart enough to marry you," he said. "And to keep you."

She touched his cheek, her eyes shining. "Love me, Cole. Right here, right now."

He laughed at the urgency in her voice. "Sweetheart, you have a broken arm, bruised ribs. You were half-frozen when I found you."

"Then you can warm me up," she said.

Cole couldn't resist the invitation. He closed the door to the room, then deliberately turned the lock. Then he nudged her over in the hospital bed until he could sneak in beside her and love her the way she was meant to be loved, with total concentration and finally, at long last, with his whole heart.

Epilogue

"Jennifer Davis, what have you been doing? Rolling around in the mud?"

Cassie stared at her four-year-old daughter with dismay. They were having a party in twenty minutes, and Jenny was covered from head to toe in dirt. It was all over her clothes, even in her hair.

"I've been baking cakes," she announced happily. "For Grandma. See."

Cassie followed the direction of her daughter's gesture and groaned. There were, indeed, a half dozen "cakes" on the backyard table, each with a candle stuck crookedly into the mud. The vinyl tablecloth was a mess.

"I'm sure Grandma will be thrilled," she said. "Now get in here and let's see if we can clean you up."

Jennifer darted through the door and straight into her daddy's arms. Cole scooped her up before he realized the condition she and her clothes were in.

"Sweet heaven, now you need a bath, too," Cassie said. "What am I going to do? The guests should be here any minute. Mother will be mortified if Dr. Foster finds half of her family looking totally disreputable."

"I don't think your mother's going to be all that worried about a little mud. We're celebrating the fact that she's just gotten a clean bill of health after five years. She's a survivor, Cassie. Nothing else matters." His grin turned wicked. "Besides, I think the doctor is long past being shocked by anything we do. He's been asking her to marry him for the past four years. Clearly he's accepted the whole package."

Cassie still couldn't get over her mother's long-distance courtship with the surgeon in Denver who'd saved her life. It was the happiest she'd seen her mom in years.

Of course, she was still declining his proposal for reasons that eluded all of them. Cassie feared it had something to do with her, though her mother flatly refused to talk about it.

"Take your daughter and get cleaned up," she ordered Cole. "I'll try to scrub up the picnic table. And if you can pry Jake away from his computer, I'd appreciate it."

"Don't spoil my cakes, Mommy," Jenny pleaded, eyes bright with tears. "They're for Grandma."

Cassie sighed and went outside. A few minutes later her mother and Dr. Foster arrived, followed shortly by Frank Davis and the Calamity Janes. No one seemed the slightest bit dismayed by Jenny's contribution to the food, least of all Cassie's mother, who seldom took her gaze away from the doctor, anyway.

"They look blissfully happy, don't they?" Cassie whispered to Cole.

He grinned. "Not as happy as the two of us, but yes, they do look as if they're in love."

"Maybe I should give her a nudge, tell her to marry him."

"She's a grown woman. I'm sure she knows her own mind. Maybe our news will help."

She touched his cheek. "It will certainly reassure her that there are no more bumps in the road for us."

A few minutes later Cole stood and announced a toast. "First to our mom," he said. "You've proved just what a survivor you are."

He turned to Cassie. "And to my wife, who is about to make me a father again. Family and friends are what life is all about, and I can't tell you how grateful we all are to be here together today."

To Cassie's dismay her mother looked shaken by the news of the new baby. And Dr. Foster's expression turned resigned. Cassie crossed the yard and confronted her mother.

"Okay, what is it? You're not sick again, are you?"

"No, of course not," her mother said at once. She glanced at the man beside her. "It's just that we were considering getting married."

"Mom, that's fantastic. I couldn't be happier."

Her mother shook her head. "No, it's not possible. You're having another baby. I have to stay. And what Cole said about family. He's right. We need to be together."

"Now, Edna—" the surgeon began.

YOUR PARTICIPATION IS REQUESTED!

Dear Sherryl Woods Fan,

Since you are a lover of our books – we would like to get to know you!

Inside you will find a short Reader's Survey. Sharing your answers with us will help our editorial staff understand who you are and what activities you enjoy.

To thank you for your participation, we would like to send you 2 books and 2 gifts – **ABSOLUTELY FREE!**

Enjoy your gifts with our appreciation,

Pam Powers

SEE INSIDE FOR READER'S SURVEY

For Your Reading Pleasure...

We'll send you 2 books and 2 gifts
ABSOLUTELY FREE
just for completing our Reader's Survey!

YOUR READER'S SURVEY
"THANK YOU" FREE GIFTS INCLUDE:
▶ **2 FREE books**
▶ **2 lovely surprise gifts**

PLEASE FILL IN THE CIRCLES COMPLETELY TO RESPOND

1) What type of fiction books do you enjoy reading? (Check all that apply)
○ Suspense/Thrillers   ○ Action/Adventure   ○ Modern-day Romances
○ Historical Romance   ○ Humour   ○ Paranormal Romance

2) What attracted you most to the last fiction book you purchased on impulse?
○ The Title   ○ The Cover   ○ The Author   ○ The Story

3) What is usually the greatest influencer when you <u>plan</u> to buy a book?
○ Advertising   ○ Referral   ○ Book Review

4) How often do you access the internet?
○ Daily   ○ Weekly   ○ Monthly   ○ Rarely or never.

5) How many NEW paperback fiction novels have you purchased in the past 3 months?
○ 0 - 2   ○ 3 - 6   ○ 7 or more

YES! I have completed the Reader's Survey. Please send me the 2 FREE books and 2 FREE gifts (gifts are worth about $10) for which I qualify. I understand that I am under no obligation to purchase any books, as explained on the back of this card.

194/394 MDL GH9A

FIRST NAME	LAST NAME

ADDRESS

APT.#	CITY

STATE/PROV.	ZIP/POSTAL CODE

SW-515-SUR15

◆ HARLEQUIN™ READER SERVICE—Here's How It Works:

Accepting your 2 free Romance books and 2 free gifts (gifts valued at approximately $10.00) places you under no obligation to buy anything. You may keep the books and gifts and return the shipping statement marked "cancel." If you do not cancel, about a month later we'll send you 4 additional books and bill you just $6.49 each in the U.S. or $6.99 each in Canada. That is a savings of at least 19% off the cover price. It's quite a bargain! Shipping and handling is just 50¢ per book in the U.S. and 75¢ per book in Canada.* You may cancel at any time, but if you choose to continue, every month we'll send you 4 more books, which you may either purchase at the discount price or return to us and cancel your subscription. *Terms and prices subject to change without notice. Prices do not include applicable taxes. Sales tax applicable in N.Y. Canadian residents will be charged applicable taxes. Offer not valid in Quebec. Books received may not be as shown. All orders subject to credit approval. Credit or debit balances in a customer's account(s) may be offset by any other outstanding balance owed by or to the customer. Please allow 4 to 6 weeks for delivery. Offer available while quantities last.

BUSINESS REPLY MAIL
FIRST-CLASS MAIL   PERMIT NO. 717   BUFFALO, NY

POSTAGE WILL BE PAID BY ADDRESSEE

HARLEQUIN READER SERVICE
PO BOX 1867
BUFFALO NY 14240-9952

NO POSTAGE
NECESSARY
IF MAILED
IN THE
UNITED STATES

"Don't," her mother said sharply, cutting him off. "This is the way it has to be."

Cassie exchanged a look with the doctor.

"Okay," he said finally. "Then I guess we'll just have to go about this another way. I've talked to a few people. I can move my practice to Laramie. I'll be retiring in a few years, anyway, and this will be a good transition. If need be I can go to Denver and consult if something comes up with one of my patients there."

Cassie watched her mother's eyes begin to sparkle.

"You would do that?" Edna said to him. "You would give up your life in Denver?"

He nodded. "I'm a lot like your son-in-law. I know a good woman when I find her, and I'll do whatever it takes to hang on to her."

Cole joined them then, his gaze questioning. "A happy ending?"

Cassie looked up at him and nodded. "For all of us," she whispered. "Definitely a happy ending."

* * * * *

COURTING THE ENEMY

Prologue

Soul-deep weary, Karen walked into the kitchen at midnight, made herself a cup of tea and sat down at the kitchen table to face the mail. She mentally weighed the usual stack of bills against the intriguing envelope with its fancy calligraphy.

Even if she hadn't desperately needed a pick-me-up, she would have opted for setting the bills aside. There were always too many of them at the end of the month and not enough money in the bank. It seemed as if she and Caleb might never get their ranch in the black, might never be in a position to hire the extra help that would save them from doing all of the endless, backbreaking work themselves with only two seasonal men to pitch in.

As late as it was, she had just come in from the barn. Caleb was still out there, trying to save a sick calf. Always at the edge of bankruptcy, they couldn't afford to lose a single animal. She had seen the stress in his face, heard it in the terse, angry words from a man who'd always been quietly thoughtful and even-tempered.

She pushed all of that aside as she opened the thick vellum envelope, and removed what turned out to be an invitation to her high school reunion in Winding River, Wyoming, a hundred miles away. Immediately the cares of the day slipped aside. She thought of her lifelong friends, the women who had called themselves the Calamity Janes, thanks to their penchant for heartbreak and mischief gone awry.

This was perfect. A few days with her best friends would give her marriage exactly the boost it needed. It would bring some fun back into their lives. Though Caleb was older and hadn't gone to school with them, he had grown to enjoy their company as much as she did. And because he was the only husband who'd displayed staying power, they fussed over him in a way that both embarrassed and pleased him.

She was still thinking about catching up with Cassie, Gina, Lauren and Emma, when Caleb finally came in. She studied his face and tried to gauge his mood. Wordlessly he opened the refrigerator and took out a beer, slugging it back as if his throat were parched. Finally he glanced at her, then at the envelope she was holding.

"What's that?"

"An invitation. My high school class is having its reunion in July." She beamed at him. "Oh, Caleb, it's going to be such fun. I'm sure Gina, Lauren and the others will come back. There are going to be all sorts of events, a picnic, a dance, plus the town's annual fireworks on the Fourth."

"And how much is all of this going to cost? An arm and a leg, I imagine."

His tone dulled her enthusiasm. "Not so much. We can manage it."

He gestured toward the stack of bills. "We can't pay the electric bill. The feed and grain bill is two months overdue—and you want to go to a bunch of fool parties? And where exactly would we stay now that your parents have moved? You planning on driving a hundred miles each way every single day? Motels are expensive."

"We need this," she insisted stubbornly. "I'll find us a place to stay."

"We need to hang on to every single dollar we can get our hands on, or this time next year we're going to be worrying about a place to live."

It was a familiar refrain, and it was Caleb's greatest fear. Karen knew that and she didn't take it lightly. It wasn't just a matter of holding on to the ranch he loved, the ranch that had been in his family for three generations. It wasn't even a matter of pride. It was a matter of keeping the ranch out of the hands of the man he considered his family's worst enemy.

Grady Blackhawk had been after the Hanson ranch for years, the entire time Karen had been with Caleb. She couldn't recall a week that there hadn't been some communication from him, some sense that he was circling like a vulture waiting for the ranch to collapse under Caleb's ineptitude. She didn't fully understand Grady's motivation, because Caleb had flatly refused to discuss it. He'd just painted him as the devil incarnate and warned Karen time and again against him.

"Caleb, we're not going to lose the ranch," she said, clinging to her patience by a thread. "Not to Grady Blackhawk, not to anyone."

"I wish to hell I were as sure of that as you are. You want to go to your reunion, go, but leave me out of it. I have more important things to do with my time—like keeping a roof over our heads."

With that he had stormed out of the house, and she hadn't seen him again until morning.

She let the subject of the reunion drop, and a few days later, looking sheepish, Caleb apologized and handed her a check to pay for all of the events.

"You're right. We need this. We'll see all of your friends, maybe dance a little," he said, giving her a tired but suggestive wink that reminded her that they had fallen in love on a dance floor.

Karen pressed a kiss to his cheek. "Thank you. It's going to be wonderful. You'll see."

Instead, making up for time lost at the reunion turned out to be more than Caleb's heart could take. Only days after it was over, he collapsed.

She should have seen it coming, Karen berated herself en route to the hospital, should have known that no man could survive under so much self-imposed pressure.

Maybe if she hadn't been caught up with all of the Calamity Janes, she would have. Instead, though, she had stolen every spare minute to spend time with her best friends, time away from the ranch she could ill afford.

But with Emma working as a hotshot attorney in Denver at the time, Lauren lighting up the silver screen in Hollywood, with Gina running her exclusive Italian restaurant in Manhattan, and even Cassie living a few hundred miles away, Karen was determined to take advantage of every single second they were home. Seeing them rejuvenated her.

She was in Denver with Cassie, awaiting the results of her mother's breast cancer surgery, when the call came that Caleb was being taken to the hospital. A million and one thoughts raced through her mind on the flight to Laramie. Nothing her friends did or said could distract or reassure her. Guilt crowded in.

She had pressed Caleb to attend the reunion. She had left him alone to keep up with all of the ranch chores even after the events ended. It was little wonder that he had broken under the stress, and it was her fault. All of it. She would live with that forever.

But he would be all right, she told herself over and over. And she would make it up to him, work twice as hard from now on.

At the hospital, the doctor greeted her, his expression grim. "It was too late, Mrs. Hanson. There was nothing we could do."

Karen stared at him, not understanding, not wanting to believe what he seemed to be saying. "Too late?" she whispered as the Calamity Janes moved in close to offer support. "He's…" She couldn't even say the word.

Neither could the doctor, it seemed. He nodded, his

tone conveying what his words merely hinted. "Yes. I'm sorry. The heart attack was massive."

Sorry, she thought wildly. There was plenty of regret to go around. She was sorry, too. She would spend a lifetime being sorry.

But being sorry wouldn't bring Caleb back. It wouldn't save the ranch from Grady Blackhawk. It was up to her to do that.

And she would, too, no matter what it took, no matter what sacrifices she had to make. After all, her husband had paid for that damnable ranch with his life.

1

The kitchen table was littered with travel brochures, all provided by Karen's well-meaning best friends. She sat at the table with her cup of tea and a homemade cranberry scone baked just that morning and dropped off by Gina, and studied the pictures without touching them. She was almost afraid to pick up the brochures, afraid to admit just how tempted she was to toss aside all of her responsibilities and run away.

The Calamity Janes had known just how to get to her, selecting all the places she had talked about back in high school. London, of course. Always her first choice since so much of her favorite literature had been written there. And Italy because of the art in Florence, because of the history in Rome and the canals of Venice. Paris for the sidewalk bistros on shady streets and for the Louvre and Notre Dame. They had thrown in a cruise through the Greek isles and a relaxing resort in Hawaii for good measure.

Once the images would have stirred her imagination, the prospect of actually being able to choose one would have filled her with excitement, but today all she felt was sadness. Finally, after all these years, she could make her dream come true, but only because her husband was dead, only if she turned her back on everything that had mattered to him…to them.

Caleb was dead. The words still had the power to shock her, even now, six months after his funeral. How could a man not yet forty be dead? He had always appeared so healthy, so strong. Though he'd been ten years older, she had been drawn to him from the moment they met because of his vitality, his zest for living. Who would have guessed that his heart was weak… a heart that had been capable of such love, such tenderness?

Tears welled up, spilled down her cheeks, splattered on the glossy brochures for places she had put off seeing to marry the man of her dreams.

Not a day went by that Karen didn't blame the ranch for killing him. That and her stubborn determination to take time off for her high school reunion. Six months hadn't changed her mind about where the blame lay.

Nor had it dulled her grief. Her friends were worried about her, which explained the arrival this morning of all the brochures. They had remembered how she had once talked of leaving Wyoming behind, of becoming a flight attendant or a travel agent or a cruise director, anything that would allow her to see the world. They were using all of those old dreams in an effort to tempt her into taking a break.

A break, she thought derisively. Her so-called break

for that reunion was the reason Caleb was dead. Running a ranch didn't allow for breaks, not a ranch the size of hers anyway. It was a full-time, never-ending, backbreaking job, with often pitiful rewards.

Once she and Caleb had envisioned taking trips together, traveling to all the exciting, faraway places she had dreamed about before she'd met him and fallen in love. He had understood her dreams even if he hadn't shared them. This ranch had been his only obsession.

There had been other dreams, of course, ones they *had* shared. They had dreamed of filling the house with children, but they'd put it off. Just until finances took a turn for the better, he'd promised her.

Now there would be no children, she thought bitterly. No vacations to exotic locales. Not with Caleb, anyway. They'd never gone farther away from home than Cheyenne, where they'd spent their three-day honeymoon.

The Calamity Janes had obviously anticipated her protests that there was no money for a frivolous vacation, no time to indulge a fantasy. Her friends had prepaid a trip to anywhere in the world she wanted to go. It was Lauren's extravagant gift, most likely, Karen surmised. Lauren's and Emma's. Of Karen's high school classmates, the actress and lawyer were the only ones with any cash to spare right now.

Cassie had recently married a successful technology whiz, but their road was still rocky as Cole struggled to accept the fact that Cassie had kept his son a secret from him for years. Cassie wouldn't ask Cole for money, though Karen didn't doubt he would have offered if he'd known about the plan. Cole had been a rock since Caleb's death, pitching in to handle a hundred little details, things she would never have thought of. He'd wanted to do more, offered to send over extra help, but she had turned him down. Taking on the burden of running the ranch was her penance.

As for Gina, she had been in some sort of financial scrape with her New York restaurant that she flatly refused to discuss, but it was serious enough to have driven her out of New York and back to Winding River to stay. She spent her days in a frenzy of baking and her nights working in the local Italian restaurant where she'd first developed the desire to become a chef. There had been a handsome man hovering around ever since the reunion, but Gina steadfastly refused to introduce him or to explain his presence.

Karen loved them all for their support and their generosity. Her friends' hearts were in the right place, but she couldn't see how she could go to Cheyenne for a day trip right now, much less on some dream vacation. The work on the ranch hadn't died with her husband. Hank and Dooley were pitching in to take up the slack, but they were beginning to get nervous about how they'd be paid or whether the ranch would even survive. They were right to worry, too. Karen didn't have any answers for them. She knew, though, that Dooley, who'd worked with the Hansons for three decades, had persuaded the younger, more impulsive Hank to give her time to figure things out.

It was January now. She could tell them to find other work and manage for a while, but when spring came, she would have to have help once more. Better to scrape by and rehire these two, whose loyalty she was sure of, than risk finding no one she could trust come April.

She groaned even as the thought crossed her mind. She was beginning to think like Caleb, seeing betrayal and enemies around every corner. He had been totally paranoid about Grady Blackhawk's designs on their ranch. It was true that Grady wanted it. He'd made no secret of the fact, especially since Caleb's death, but it was unlikely that he'd try to get it by planting a spy on her payroll.

Apparently she needed this break more than she wanted to admit. She finally dared to reach for the brochure on London and studied the photos of Buckingham Palace, the Old Vic, Harrods, the cathedrals.

She tried to imagine what London would be like in winter, with snow dusting the streets. Currier and Ives-style images from her favorite authors came to mind. It would be magical. It would be everything she'd ever dreamed of.

It was impossible.

She sighed heavily and reluctantly put the brochure down again, just as someone knocked at the kitchen door.

When she opened it, her heart thumped unsteadily at the sight of Grady Blackhawk. He'd been at the funeral, too. And he'd called a half-dozen times in the weeks and months since. She'd tried her best to ignore him, but he'd clearly lost patience. Now here he was on her doorstep.

"Mrs. Hanson," he said with a polite nod and a finger touched to the rim of his black Stetson.

She had the whimsical thought that he was deliberately dressing the part of the bad guy, all in black, but the idea fled at once. There was nothing the least bit whimsical about Grady. He was quiet and intense and mysterious.

The latter was a bit more of a problem than she'd anticipated when he first came to pay his respects after Caleb's death. Karen had always liked unraveling puzzles, and Grady was the most complicated one she'd ever run across. Unfortunately, sifting through clues, ferreting out motives took time, time she didn't dare spend with her husband's longtime enemy.

She could just imagine the disapproval of Caleb's parents, if they heard she was spending time with Grady Blackhawk. Word would reach them, too. She had no doubts about that. Most of the people in the area were far closer to the Hansons, who'd lived here for decades, than they were to Karen, who was still regarded as a newcomer even after ten years as Caleb's wife. The phone lines between here and Tucson would be burning up as the gossip spread.

"I thought I had made it clear that I have nothing to say to you," she told Grady stiffly, refusing to step aside to admit him. Better to allow the icy air into the house than this man who could disconcert her with a look.

This man, with his jet-black hair and fierce black eyes, was now her enemy, too. It was something she'd inherited, right along with a failing ranch.

She wished she understood why Grady was so desperate to get his hands on this particular ranch. He had land of his own in a neighboring county—plenty of it from what she'd heard. But there was something about Hanson land that obsessed him.

Over the years he—and his father before him—had done all he could to steal the Hanson land. Not that he wasn't willing to pay. He was. But, bottom line, he wanted something that wasn't rightfully his, and he intended to get it by fair means or foul.

According to Caleb, Grady had no scruples, just a single-minded determination. He'd tried to buy up their note at the bank, but fortunately, the bank president was an old family friend of Caleb's father. He had seen the paperwork, foiled the attempt, then dutifully rushed to report everything to the Hansons. That much was fact.

In addition—and far more damning—Caleb had been all but certain Grady was behind a virus that had infected half their herd the previous year. He had also blamed Grady for a fire that had swept through pastureland the year before that, destroying feed and putting the entire herd at risk.

There had been no proof, of course, just suspicions, which Karen had never entirely bought. After all, Grady had been waiting in the wings, checkbook in hand, after each incident. Would he have been foolish enough to do that if he'd been behind the acts in the first place? Wouldn't he know that he'd be the first person to fall under suspicion? Or hadn't he cared, as long as he got his way?

"I think it would be in both our interests to talk," he said, regarding her with the intense gaze that always disquieted her.

"I doubt that."

He ignored her words and her pointed refusal to back away from the door. "I've made no secret over the years of the fact that I want this land."

"That's true enough." She regarded him curiously. "Why *this* land? What is it about this particular ranch that made your father and now you hound the Hansons for years?"

"If you'll allow me to come inside, I'll explain. Perhaps then you won't be so determined to fight me on this."

Karen's sense of fair play and curiosity warred with her ingrained animosity. Curiosity won. She stepped aside and let him enter. He removed his hat and hung it on a peg, then took a seat at the table. She took comfort in the fact that he didn't remove his coat. He clearly wouldn't be staying long.

His intense gaze swept the room, as if taking stock, then landed on the scattered brochures.

"Going somewhere?" he asked, studying her with surprise. "I didn't think you had the money to be taking off for Europe."

"I don't," she said tightly, wondering how he knew so much about her finances. Then again, just about everyone knew that she and Caleb had been struggling. "My friends do. They're encouraging me to take a vacation."

"Are you considering it?"

"Not with you circling around waiting for me to make a misstep that will cost me the ranch."

He winced at that. "I know how your husband felt about me, but I'm not your enemy, Mrs. Hanson. I'm trying to make a fair deal. You have something I want. I have the cash to make your life a whole lot easier. It's as simple as that."

"There is nothing simple about this, Mr. Blackhawk. My husband loved this ranch. I don't intend to lose it, especially not to the man he considered to be little better than a conniving thief."

"A harsh assessment of a man you don't know," he said mildly.

"It was his assessment, not mine. Caleb was not prone to making quick judgments. If he distrusted you, he had his reasons."

"Which you intend to accept blindly?"

It was her turn to wince. Loyalty was one thing, but her sense of fair play balked at blindly accepting anything.

"Persuade me otherwise," she challenged. "Convince me you had nothing to do with the attempts to destroy our herd, that your intentions were honorable when you tried to buy up the note on the land."

He didn't seem surprised by the accusations. He merely asked, "And then you'll sell?"

"I didn't say that, but I will stop labeling you as a thief if you don't deserve it."

He grinned at that, and it changed him from somber menace to charming rogue in a heartbeat. Karen nearly gasped at the transformation, but she wouldn't allow herself to fall prey to it. He hadn't proved anything yet. She doubted he could.

"If I tell you that none of that is true, not even the part about the mortgage, would you believe me?" Grady asked.

"No."

"What would it take?"

"Find the person responsible."

He nodded. "Maybe I will. In the meantime, I'm going to tell you a story," he said in a low, easy, seductive tone.

His voice washed over Karen, lulling her as if it were the start of a bedtime story. She was tired enough to fall asleep listening to it, but she sat up rigidly, determined not to display any sign of weakness in front of this man.

"Generations ago this land belonged to my ancestors," Grady began. "It was stolen from them."

"Not by me," she said heatedly, responding not just to the accusation but to the fact that she'd dared to let down her guard for even a split second. "Nor my husband."

He seemed amused by her quick retort. "Did I say it had been? No, this was years and years ago, before your time or mine. It was taken by the government, turned over to homesteaders. White homesteaders," he said pointedly. "My ancestors were driven onto reservations, while people like the Hansons took over their land."

Karen was aware that much had been done to the Native Americans that was both heartless and wrong.

She sympathized with Grady Blackhawk's desire to right an old wrong, but she and Caleb—or, for that matter, Caleb's parents and grandparents—weren't the ones to blame. They had bought the land from others, who, in turn, had simply taken advantage of a federal policy.

"You're asking me to make amends for something I had no part in," she told him.

"It's not a matter of paying an old debt that isn't yours. It's a matter of doing what's right because you're in a position to do so. And I certainly don't expect you just to give the land to me because I say it rightfully belongs to my family. I'll pay you a fair price for it, same as anyone else would. I guarantee it will be far more than what was paid for it all those years ago."

Before she could stop him, he named an amount that stunned her. It would be enough to pay off all their debts and leave plenty for her to start life over again back in Winding River, where she'd be with friends. It was tempting, more tempting than she'd imagined. Only an image of Caleb's dismay steadied her resolve. Keeping this ranch was the debt she owed to him. She could never turn her back on that.

"I'm not interested in selling," she said with finality.

"Not to me or not to anyone?" Grady asked with an edge to his voice.

"It hardly matters, does it? I won't sell this ranch."

"Because you love it so much?" he asked with a note of total disbelief in his voice.

"Because I can't," she responded quietly.

He seemed startled by the response. "It's not yours to sell?"

"Technically, yes. But I owe it to my husband to stay here, to do what he would have done, if he hadn't died so prematurely. This ranch will stay in Hanson hands as long as I have any control over it."

For a moment, he looked taken aback, but not for long. His gaze locked with hers, he said, "I'll keep coming back, Mrs. Hanson, again and again, until you change your mind or until circumstances force your hand. This place is wearing you down. I can see it." He gestured toward the brochures. "Obviously so can your friends. Make no mistake, I'll own the land…no doubt before the year is out."

His arrogant confidence stirred her temper. "Only if hell freezes over," she said, snatching the back door open and allowing a blast of wintry air into the room as she waited pointedly for him to take the hint and leave.

His gaze never wavered as he plucked his hat off the hook and moved past her. He paused just outside and a smile tugged at his lips. "Keep a close eye on the weather, Mrs. Hanson. Anything's possible."

2

Grady hadn't expected Karen Hanson to be as stubborn or as foolish as her husband. After the funeral he'd made a few calls to test the waters, but he had deliberately waited six months before going to see her. He'd wanted to give her time to see just how difficult her life was going to be. He'd guessed that by now she would be eager to get rid of a ranch that was clearly draining whatever reserves of cash she had. Obviously he'd misjudged her. He wouldn't make that mistake again.

More disconcerting than the discovery that she wasn't going to be a pushover was the realization that she got to him. Those big blue eyes of hers had been swimming with tears when she'd opened the door. Her flushed cheeks had been streaked with them. Her lips had looked soft...and disturbingly kissable. He'd had an almost irresistible urge to gather her in his arms and offer comfort. For a hard man with little sympathy for anyone, it had been an uncharacteristic reaction that made him uneasy.

He grinned as he imagined her reaction to that. If he'd even tried to touch her, no matter how innocently, she probably would have grabbed an umbrella from the stand by the door and clobbered him with it.

Even so, he hadn't been able to shake that image of lost vulnerability. A lot of women who worked ranches side by side with their husbands grew hard, their muscles well formed, their skin burnished bronze by the sun. By contrast, Karen Hanson's body was soft and feminine, her skin as pale as milk. The thought of that changing because she had to struggle to keep her ranch afloat bothered him for reasons that went beyond her refusal to give in and sell out to him.

He couldn't help wondering what drove a woman like Karen Hanson. Well...loyalty to her husband, for one thing. There was no question about that. Pride. Stubbornness. He sighed. He was back to that again. It was hard to fight with someone who'd dug in her heels in defiance of logic.

But what did she long for beyond the travel that those brochures implied? In his experience most women wanted love, a family, the things he hadn't had time for in his own life. Some wanted a meal ticket. Some had a mile-wide independent streak, needing little more than the occasional companionship of a man to make them content. Those were the ones who appealed to Grady. He had so many family obligations to the past, he didn't have time to think about the future.

He tried to fit Karen Hanson into a tidy little niche, but she wouldn't stay put. She was independent, no doubt about it, but her determination to fight her husband's old battles said a lot about how she felt about family. Ironically, that very loyalty, every bit as strong as his own commitment to his ancestors, was likely to stand in his way.

He had derided himself on the trip home for trying to analyze the woman based on a half-hour meeting that had been rife with tension. He knew better. His grandfather—the single greatest influence in his life—believed in the necessity for walking a mile in another man's moccasins before reaching conclusions about the choices they made. Thomas Blackhawk had tried to instill that same wisdom in Grady.

Unfortunately, Grady wasn't usually capable of the patience required. He tended to make snap judgments. He asked straight questions, liked straight answers.

"And look where that got you today," he muttered wryly. His grandfather would have been appalled, especially by the unveiled threat he had uttered on his way out the door.

He spent the evening taking stock, both of his own behavior and Karen Hanson's responses to it. Unfortunately, there was little definitive information to go on. She was beautiful, stubborn, hardworking and loyal. He'd gotten that, but not much more, certainly nothing about the best way to handle her.

There was only one way to remedy that. He needed to spend more time with her. He had to discover what made the woman tick, what her hopes and dreams were now that her husband was gone.

And how he could use it to his own advantage, he reminded himself sharply, when the image of her in his bed stole over him. He was going to have to keep that image at bay, he warned himself.

He'd spent his whole life working toward a single goal—getting that land back for his family. His great-grandfather had instilled a desire for retribution in his son, Grady's grandfather. The mission had been passed down to the next generation, and finally to Grady himself.

That land, part of his Native American heritage, part of a time when his ancestors had had no rights at all, was Blackhawk land. He couldn't let anything—not even a woman as desirable as Karen Hanson—distract him from getting it back while his grandfather was still alive to savor the triumph.

He chuckled dryly as he imagined how she was going to react to any attempt on his part to get to know her. She'd probably shoot him on sight if he showed up at the ranch again, especially if she guessed that his mission was to find her weaknesses and exploit them.

For once he was going to have to follow his grandfather's advice and rely on patience and maybe a little subterfuge to get what he wanted. There were a lot of chores around that ranch that needed doing. Karen struck him as a pragmatic woman. If he simply appeared one day and went to work, steering clear of her for the most part, would she run him off or accept the help because she knew she needed it? He was counting on the latter. Maybe over time, she would get used to his presence, come to accept it and allow him a little insight into her soul.

Grady lifted his beer in a silent toast to the ingenuity of his plan. By this time tomorrow he intended to have taken his first steps in Karen Hanson's shoes.

Of course, he admitted ruefully, it remained to be seen if he'd live to tell about it.

"Why not sell to him?" Gina asked as the Calamity Janes sat in the ranch kitchen eating pasta that she had prepared. The room was filled with the rich scent of garlic and tomato and basil. A plate of garlic bread had been all but demolished and there were only a few strands of spaghetti left in the huge bowl she had prepared for the five old friends.

Karen had put out an urgent call for their help within minutes of Grady Blackhawk's departure. She was counting on the Calamity Janes to give her advice and to keep her mind off the disconcerting effect his visit had had on her. Selling to Grady was not the advice she'd been expecting. She'd been hoping for some clever way to sidestep his determination permanently. That warning of his was still ringing in her ears.

"How can I sell to Grady?" Karen asked. "Caleb hated him. It would be the worst kind of a betrayal. And it would break his parents' hearts. Even though they've moved, they still think of this ranch as home."

"Do you want to spend the rest of your life struggling to keep the ranch afloat for two people who will never come back here? This place is a nostalgic memory for the Hansons. For you, it's nothing but back-breaking work," Cassie pointed out. "Don't forget, you were relieved when your own parents sold out and moved to Arizona. You said you'd never set foot on a ranch again." She grinned. "Of course, that was five minutes before you met Caleb, and from that moment on, all bets were off. You claimed to each and every one of us that you had always wanted to be a rancher's wife."

Karen frowned at the well-meant reminder. "No, to be perfectly honest, you're right. I don't want to be a rancher. I never did," she admitted. "But—"

Cassie cut her off. "Then consider Grady's offer if it's a fair one. Caleb would understand."

But Karen knew he wouldn't. The kind of enmity he had felt for Grady Blackhawk was deep and eternal. It was an emotional, gut-deep hatred that couldn't be abandoned in favor of practicality or sound business reasons or even sheer exhaustion, which was what she was beginning to feel as the endless days wore on.

"Okay, if the issue really comes down to keeping this place away from Grady Blackhawk, then *I'll* buy the ranch," Lauren said, drawing laughter.

"And what would you do with a ranch?" Karen asked, trying to imagine the big-screen superstar mucking out stalls or castrating bulls or any of the other backbreaking tasks required by ranching.

"You seem to forget that I grew up on a ranch, same as you," Lauren replied with a touch of indignation. "In fact, nobody around here had a better way with horses than I did."

"That was a long time ago. Somehow it's hard to picture now. It doesn't quite work with the glamorous image you've created in Hollywood," Cassie said.

Lauren scowled. "It could work if I wanted to make it work. This glamour stuff is highly overrated."

Karen thought she heard an increasingly familiar note of dissatisfaction in her friend's voice. She'd heard it when Lauren was home for the reunion, and it had continued to pop out from time to time on her return visits.

The fact that those return visits, even under the guise of checking up on Karen, were happening more and more frequently was telling. Lauren had done only one film in the past six months and turned down half a dozen offers. Compared to the pace of her career in the past, that was darned close to retirement.

"Okay, Lauren, spill it," Karen ordered. "What are you not telling us? Are you getting tired of being the multimillion-dollar superstar?"

"As a matter of fact, I am," Lauren said with a touch of defiance. "And you needn't look so shocked. I never intended to be an actress. I certainly never thought I'd be famous for my looks. I was the brainy one, remember? I wore glasses and had freckles and hair that wouldn't quite do what I wanted it to. I still do. Do you know that without my contacts and makeup and with my hair air-dried instead of styled, I can actually walk into a supermarket and no one looks twice at me?"

"Isn't that a good thing?" Karen asked. She had never been able to grasp how a woman as private and shy as Lauren had always been had learned to cope with fame.

"Yes, but it just proves how shallow the rest of my

life is," Lauren said. "It's all built on lies. Don't get me wrong, I'm not whining."

"Yes, you are," they all said in a chorus, followed by laughter.

"Okay, maybe a little. I just want something more."

"A ranch?" Karen asked skeptically.

Lauren's expression set stubbornly. "Maybe."

Karen shook her head. "Let me know when you make up your mind for sure. Until then, I think I'll just hang on to this place."

"You know what I think?" Emma said, her too-perceptive gaze studying Karen intently. "I think Karen's just holding out so she can keep this Grady Blackhawk coming around." A grin spread across her face. "Have you seen this man? I remember him from the funeral. He is seriously gorgeous. All dark and brooding, with trouble brewing in his eyes."

"I hadn't noticed," Karen insisted, but she had. God help her, she had.

"Liar," Emma accused. "You'd have to be blind not to notice."

"It was my husband's funeral," Karen snapped. "I wasn't taking note of the sex appeal of his worst enemy."

"What about today?" Emma persisted. "Did you notice today?"

Since in typical attorney fashion, Emma wasn't going to let up until she got the confession she was after, Karen conceded, "Okay, he's a good-looking man. That doesn't make him any less of a scoundrel."

"Have you figured out just why Caleb hated the man

so much?" Gina asked as she absentmindedly shredded the last piece of garlic bread into a little pile of crumbs.

"Because of the land, of course," Karen said. "Isn't that what we've been talking about?"

Gina was already shaking her head before Karen finished speaking. "I don't think so. There had to be more to it. I think this was personal."

"It's fairly personal when a man tries to buy up your mortgage so he has the leverage to take your land," Karen said. "It's even more personal when you suspect him of trying to sabotage your herd of cattle."

"I think there's more," Gina said stubbornly. "Caleb was the nicest guy in the world. He loved everybody. He trusted everybody. He even liked Emma's ex-husband well enough, though heaven knows why. He got along with everybody—except Grady Blackhawk."

"The bad blood between the Hansons and Blackhawks went back a lot of years," Karen reminded her. "It was always over the land."

"Maybe that's just what they said, maybe that was a cover for the real reason for the animosity," Gina said.

Karen sighed at her persistence. "Okay, Gina, what do you think it was about?"

"I think there was a woman involved," Gina said at once. "And a broken promise."

The rest of them groaned.

"If you ever decide to give up the restaurant business, maybe you could write romance novels," Emma said. "In this instance, it sounds to me as if you're reaching a bit."

"More than a bit," Karen said. "Can we change the subject?"

"You got us over here to talk about Grady," Emma reminded her. "You said you wanted advice. I could always have a restraining order drawn up to keep him out of your hair."

"Typical lawyer," Gina said with an undeniable trace of bitterness that ran awfully deep under the circumstances. "Turn a simple situation into a legal brawl. All Karen has to do is tell the man she's not interested in his offer. Period."

"Which I've done," Karen said.

"And you think that's the end of it?" Emma scoffed.

Karen thought of Grady's taunt as he'd walked out. No, unfortunately, she didn't believe it was over. He would be back. The only questions were when and what his tactics might be.

"He's not through," she admitted reluctantly. "He's not the kind of man who will give up easily. He's been after this land as long as I've known Caleb. And his father was after it before that. I doubt he took my refusal to sell all that seriously. In fact, it seemed to amuse him."

"All the more reason to sell to me," Lauren said. "I know how to deal with men like that. Hollywood is crawling with creeps who don't know how to take no for an answer."

"I'd love to hear how you handle them," Gina said, looking surprisingly despondent. "I've got one I'd like to shake."

Emma's gaze sharpened. "Care to explain that?"

"No," Gina said flatly. "But if Lauren has any techniques that are both legal and effective, I'd like to hear them."

"I can't talk with a lawyer present," Lauren joked. "She'd be duty-bound to turn me in."

"Illegal, then," Gina surmised. "I'll keep that in mind, if it comes to that."

Karen was about to jump all over the remark and demand answers, but a warning glance from Cassie silenced her. Maybe Cassie knew more of the story than the rest of them. She and Gina had always had a special bond, perhaps because they'd worked together so often when they were teens, both as waitresses, but with Gina always snooping around the kitchen, testing recipes of her own whenever she was given the chance.

"We're getting pretty far afield, anyway," Cassie said. "We need to help Karen decide what to do about Mr. Blackhawk if he comes around again. Since she won't let Emma file for a restraining order, does anybody have any other ideas?"

"Like I said earlier, speaking personally, that man gives me plenty of ideas," Emma said. "He's a hottie."

They all stared at her.

"A *hottie?*" Karen echoed incredulously.

"Are you denying it?" Emma asked.

"No, I'm trying to figure out how such a term became part of your Harvard-educated vernacular."

"Lauren," Emma said succinctly. "She spent all last night telling me which Hollywood leading men were really hotties and which ones weren't. It was quite an illuminating conversation. It set my heart aflutter, I'll tell you that."

"Oh, really?" Karen said. "Do you think maybe you've been single and celibate a little too long now? Maybe it's time to start looking for a replacement for your despicable ex-husband—or at least a hot date for Saturday night."

"I'm a single mom," Emma reminded her. "I don't have 'hot dates.'"

"Then look for something more serious," Karen advised. "I'm sure Caitlyn would be delighted to have a stepdaddy around, especially one who actually pays some attention to her."

"I think our friend here already found somebody," Cassie said, giving Emma a sly look.

"Don't be ridiculous. I have not," Emma protested.

"I don't know," Cassie countered. "I've seen you and the local newspaper editor with your heads together an awful lot lately. The two of you are in Stella's almost as much as I am, and I work there."

"And you know why that is," Emma said tightly. "It's about the case I'm working on. That's it. There is nothing personal involved."

"Protesting too much?" Cassie said, gazing around at the rest of them.

"Definitely," they chorused.

"Well, get over it," Emma snapped, gathering up her purse, her coat and her briefcase in a sudden rush. "I have to go."

She took a few steps across the room, then came back for the cell phone that was never more than an arm's length away. Then she swept out before any of them could react.

"Was it something we said?" Karen asked, staring after her.

"I think we hit the nail on the head," Cassie said, her expression thoughtful. "Wouldn't it be great if Emma did fall madly in love with Ford Hamilton or someone else in Winding River?"

"Just because you're married now doesn't mean that the rest of us have to jump into relationships," Gina pointed out.

"This isn't about having a relationship, though I think it would be great if she did," Cassie said. "It's just that I dread seeing Emma go back to Denver when this case here is over. She's been more relaxed the last few months, despite all of the commuting back and forth to Denver and the pressure of the trial coming up."

"That's true," Lauren agreed. "She almost forgot her cell phone tonight. For a while last summer I thought it was attached to her hand."

They all fell silent as they considered Emma's welfare. It would be nice if she stayed, Karen thought. In fact, about the only thing good to come out of their high school reunion was that the five of them were spending more time in Wyoming again. She had missed having a tight-knit circle of friends more than she'd realized. And now, with Caleb gone, she treasured the friendships more than ever.

"Thank you for coming all the way over here tonight," she told them. "I don't know what I would have done without you these past few months. Every time I've been ready to come unglued, you've been here."

"And we'll continue to be here whenever you need us," Lauren said. "You can count on it."

That made two things today she could count on, Karen thought—her friends, and Grady Blackhawk's threat that he would be back time and again until she gave up and sold him the land he wanted.

Maybe it was all of Emma's talk about Grady's undeniable sex appeal, but that threat wasn't striking fear into her the way it should have, not the way it had just this afternoon. In fact, to her very deep regret, she was beginning to feel just the slightest hint of anticipation.

3

Without even setting foot out of bed in the morning, Karen knew she was going to get up on the wrong side of it. Thanks to Emma, she had spent the whole night trying unsuccessfully to chase Grady Blackhawk out of her dreams. She'd awakened hot and restless, amid a tangle of sheets. She'd been feeling guilty to boot, all over sins her subconscious had committed in her sleep.

"I can't be blamed for that," she muttered as she shivered in the icy air and hastily pulled on jeans and an old flannel shirt of Caleb's. She hugged the shirt tighter around herself as a reminder of the man who'd really counted for something in her life.

She'd been doing that a lot lately, wearing shirts left hanging in Caleb's closet. Not all of them still held his scent, but the feel of the soft, faded flannel comforted her. It reminded her of evenings spent snuggled in his lap in front of a fire. It was a secret she'd shared with no one, fearful that her friends would chastise her for not moving on, for not letting go. She knew she had to, and she would when the time was right.

Just not yet, she thought with a sigh.

Once she'd tugged on thick socks and her boots, she went downstairs and turned up the thermostat to take the chill out of the air while she made a pot of coffee. To save on fuel costs, she would turn it back down again when she went outside to do the chores. Maybe it would only save pennies, but pennies counted these days.

She poured herself a cup of coffee, then took a sip. She cupped the mug in her hands to savor the warmth, then gazed out the window over the sink, hoping to catch a glimpse of the sunrise, rather than the more typical gray winter mornings they'd been having lately.

Instead, what she saw was Grady, unloading things from the back of his truck, looking perfectly at home. The sight of the man, after all those disturbing dreams, struck Karen as an omen. And not for anything good, either. No, indeed. His arrival definitely meant trouble. In fact, it looked almost as if he'd come to stay, as if he'd decided to claim this place whether she agreed to it or not.

She snatched a heavy jacket off the hook by the door and stormed outside, determined to put a stop to whatever he was up to. She was so infuriated by his presumption that he could just waltz in here and take over, she was surprised steam didn't rise from her as she crossed the yard.

"Why are you here again?" she demanded, her tone deliberately unfriendly. The time for politeness and feigned hospitality was past. "I thought I'd made myself clear yesterday. You're not welcome."

He barely stopped what he was doing long enough to glance at her. His gaze skimmed her over from head to toe, his lips curved into the beginnings of a smile, then his attention went right back to a stack of lumber he was pulling from the back of the fancy new four-by-four.

That truck, parked next to her dilapidated pickup, which was in serious need of a paint job and a tune-up, grated on her nerves almost as much as his attitude. The man seemed to be mocking her in every way he knew.

"I asked you a question," she snapped.

"I didn't mean to disturb you," he said without any real hint of regret. "Figured you'd be out checking on your stock by now. Saw a couple of fence posts down on my way in. I can get to those tomorrow."

She bristled at the thinly veiled criticism, as well as the suggestion that he'd be back again. In fact, it sounded suspiciously as if he intended to pretty much take over.

"The hands will be fixing the fence today," she said, wanting him to believe that she had all the help she required. "There's no need for you to trouble yourself."

He grinned. "It's no trouble. In fact, I have some spare time. I thought I'd help out with a few things around here," he said mildly. "I noticed your barn could use a little work."

In her opinion, he noticed too blasted much. It was annoying. "My barn is *my* problem. I don't want you anywhere near it."

"The work needs doing, right?"

"Yes, but—"

"And I have the time."

"I don't want you here."

"Never throw a friendly offer back in a man's face. He might think you don't appreciate a neighborly gesture."

Karen knew there was nothing friendly about Grady's intentions. He was up to something. She could see it in his eyes. And it wasn't as if he lived right down the road. He lived in the next county, too far away for there to be anything the least bit neighborly about this gesture.

Before she could respond to his taunt, he'd turned his back on her and headed for the barn, where paint she hadn't bought and tools she'd never seen before waited. He stripped off his jacket as if the temperature were seventy, instead of thirty-seven, and went to work, leaving her to struggle with her indignation and her desire to touch those broad shoulders he'd put on display in side yard. His flannel shirt was stretched taut over well-developed muscles, not hanging as Caleb's was on her.

"I can't afford to pay for all of this," she hollered after him.

He heaved what sounded like a resigned sigh and faced her. "Did I ask for money?"

"No, but I feel obligated to pay for any fixing up that goes on around here."

"Then you'll pay me something when you have it," he said as if it was of no concern to him when—or even if—she did. "This barn can't take another winter in the state it's in. It'll cost you a lot more to replace it if it falls apart than it will if I take care of a few simple repairs now."

His gaze locked with hers. "You know I'm right, Karen."

Hearing him say her name startled her. The day before and in their one prior meeting, he'd been careful to be formally polite, referring to her as "Mrs. Hanson" when he used any name at all. Today, using her first name, he made it sound as if he'd forgotten all about her relationship with Caleb, as if they were about to become friends. She shuddered at the prospect. She didn't need a friend who made her feel all quivery inside, a man who'd already stated quite clearly that he wanted things from her that she didn't intend to give. Sure, it was land he was after, not her body, but her erratically beating pulse didn't seem to know the difference.

"What I know is that you are presuming to intrude in my life, to take over and do things I haven't asked you to do. Why? So I'll be in your debt?"

"It's a gesture, nothing more," he insisted. "I just want you to see that I'm not the bad guy your husband made me out to be."

"If you're such a nice guy, then why won't you listen when I tell you that I don't want you here?"

"Because you don't really mean it. That's just your pride talking."

She scowled, because he was at least partially right. Her pride—along with some very sensible suspicions about Grady's motives—was forcing her to look a much-needed gift horse in the mouth.

"Oh, forget it," she mumbled. She clearly wasn't going to get rid of him, so she might as well let him do whatever he intended to do and get it over with. She'd just ignore him, pretend he wasn't there. She certainly had plenty of her own chores to do.

She stalked past him into the barn, fed and watered the horses, mucked out stalls, then saddled up Ginger, the horse she'd owned since she was a teenager.

"We're getting out of here, girl."

"Running away?" Grady inquired from just behind her, amusement threading through his voice.

"No, I'm going out to see if Dooley and Hank need any help."

"Lucky Dooley and Hank."

She frowned at the teasing. "What is that supposed to mean?"

"Just that I'd welcome your help, if you were to offer."

"This is *your* project, Mr. Blackhawk. You'll have to finish it on your own. If there's something you can't cope with, you can always leave."

His gaze locked with hers. "It's not a matter of coping. I'd just be glad of the company."

Goose bumps that had nothing to do with the chilly air rose on her skin. She turned away and concentrated on tightening the cinch on Ginger's saddle.

"I seem to make you nervous, Karen. Why is that?"

She frowned as she faced him. "You don't make me nervous, Mr. Blackhawk. You make me *mad.*"

He chuckled at that.

"You find that amusing?" she asked indignantly.

His gaze settled on her mouth. "No," he said softly. "I find it promising. A woman with a temper is always more fascinating than one who's docile."

"I'm not doing any of this to provide you with entertainment," she snapped, trying not to acknowledge that his words sent an unaccustomed thrill shivering down her spine and set her pulse to racing.

"I know," he said, his grin spreading. "That's what makes it so enjoyable."

Karen bit back a retort that would only have escalated the ridiculous debate and mounted Ginger. Stepping back, Grady touched a finger to the brim of his hat in a polite salute.

"Enjoy your ride."

"I intend to," she lied. She doubted she would enjoy anything as long as this impossible man was underfoot.

An hour later, though, after riding hard, then meeting up with Hank and Dooley to check their progress on the fence repairs, she was feeling more at ease. She expected that to change the minute she reached the barn, but to her surprise Grady was nowhere in sight. His truck was gone, too. The sigh that eased through her was tinged with something she couldn't identify. Surely not regret, she thought with exasperation. No, it was relief, nothing more.

Unfortunately, though, her relief didn't last long. The evidence of Grady's presence and of his anticipated return was everywhere. The tools, paint cans and lumber were right where he'd left them. The ladder was still propped against the side of the barn, and the paint had been scraped only from the highest boards, with plenty left untouched.

She had barely cooled Ginger down and started for the house when his truck appeared in the distance, an unmistakable splash of red against the dull winter landscape. Karen hurried inside to avoid another pointless confrontation.

But as the afternoon wore on and her gaze kept straying to the man who was diligently and methodically stripping the old paint off her barn, she sighed and accepted the fact that he wasn't going to go away. She had to find some way to make peace with him.

In her experience, home-baked cookies were generally an excellent peace offering. With nobody around to appreciate the results, she hadn't had the urge to bake for some time now. Still, as a gesture of loyalty to her late husband, she made a deliberate choice to bake oatmeal-raisin cookies, her father's favorites, rather than the chocolate chip that Caleb had loved.

When the first batch was still warm from the oven, she put some of the cookies on a plate, poured a mug of coffee and carried it all across the yard. As she walked toward Grady, she could feel his speculative gaze burning into her.

The gesture had been a mistake, she concluded as she met his eyes. He was going to make too much of it, twist it somehow and use it as an opening. Impatient with herself for allowing room for him to jump to a conclusion that a truce was in the offing, she plunked coffee and plate down ungraciously and scurried back to the house.

She was all too aware that Grady's intent gaze followed her every step.

"You are such a ninny, Karen Hanson," she chided herself as she slammed the door behind her. "Taking the man a few cookies was polite. It wasn't an overture that he could misinterpret."

But despite the reassuring words, she was very much afraid that he had. And who knew where that would lead?

Grady was satisfied with the way the day had gone. He'd made progress. At least Karen hadn't thrown him off the property. In fact, she'd baked him cookies, as if he were a schoolboy who deserved nourishment for doing a chore.

She'd regretted it, too. He'd seen that in her eyes and in the way she'd retreated to the house with such haste that he hadn't even had time to thank her.

One of these days they might actually sit down and have a real conversation, he mused. After that, who knew what might be accomplished? Maybe she would listen to reason.

Of course, in his experience, women were emotional creatures. Reason didn't matter half as much to them as it did to men. Which meant he would just have to appeal to Karen's heart. How he was supposed to do that when it was her heart that was telling her to throw his offer back in his face was beyond him, but he would figure it out. He was too close to his goal now to let anything stand in his way.

Grady figured he had another week's work on the

barn. Then he'd move on to something else. And something else after that, if need be. He considered the time and money an investment. After all, the work needed to be done anyway and the property would be his some-day soon.

Grady leaned against the rung of the ladder and munched on the last cookie. He hadn't had a decent oat-meal-raisin cookie in years, not since one of his class-mates had moved away in sixth grade. Luke's mama had baked the best oatmeal-raisin cookies ever. None he'd tried in all the years since had lived up to them… until now.

He stared toward the house, saw a light come on in the kitchen and knew she was in there fixing supper. Did she cook for herself now that Caleb was gone? Or did she put together a careless snack, a sandwich maybe, or even nothing more than a bowl of cold cereal and milk? That's what he found himself doing more nights than not. It didn't seem worth the effort to fix a hearty meal. When his body demanded something substantial, he drove into town and ate out. He'd be-come a regular at Stella's, ignoring the fact that Cassie Davis tended to regard him with suspicion much of the time. If she should consider the entrée he'd gained into Karen's life an intrusion, he might have to check his supper for arsenic.

Staring over at the house, he felt nagged by curios-ity until he convinced himself that going to the door to return his mug and give Karen a proper thanks for those cookies was the gentlemanly thing to do.

As he tapped on the glass, he could see her shadowy movements inside, saw her go still, hesitate, then finally move toward the door. He could imagine her sigh of resignation as she crossed the kitchen.

"Yes?" she said, her tone surly, her expression forbidding.

Grady saw past that, though, to the hint of loneliness in her eyes. Of course, her irritation was doing a mighty fine job of covering it up, but he'd caught a glimpse of it just the same. Or maybe that was just an excuse to prolong the encounter.

He held out the mug and the plate. "Just wanted to thank you for the coffee and the cookies."

"You're welcome," she said, taking the dishes and already starting to shut the door in his face.

He blocked it with the toe of his boot. He was about to do something he was likely to regret, but he couldn't seem to stop himself.

"What are you doing for supper, Karen?"

Her gaze narrowed. "Why? Are you inviting yourself?"

He grinned. "Not at all. My mama taught me better manners than that. I was going to invite you to join me over in Winding River. I'm partial to Stella's meat loaf, and that's the special tonight. I hate to eat alone."

She was shaking her head before the words were out of his mouth. "I couldn't."

"Don't want to be seen with me?" he challenged.

"That's not it," she said with a touch of impatience. "I've already started fixing my own supper. It would go to waste."

"I don't suppose there's enough for two?" he asked hopefully.

A smile tugged at the corners of her mouth. "Have you forgotten your manners so soon, Mr. Blackhawk?"

"Like I said, I hate to eat alone. I think my mama would forgive me just this once for being pushy. How about you? Can you forgive me? Maybe take pity on a poor bachelor who rarely gets a home-cooked meal?"

"Oh, for heaven's sakes, come on in," she said with a shake of her head. "You're impossible, Mr. Black-hawk."

Grady hid a grin as he entered. He hung his hat and jacket on a peg by the door, then sniffed the air. "Why, I do believe you're making meat loaf."

"Which I'm sure you knew before you made that outrageous claim about it being one of your favorites."

Grady didn't deny it. Instead, he looked around and asked, "What can I do? Want me to set the table, or are you afraid I'll steal the silver?"

"No silver," she said. "I think I can trust you with the stainless-steel utensils and the everyday dishes. You don't strike me as a clumsy man."

"I try not to be…especially when there's a beautiful woman watching."

She flushed at that, but in less than a heartbeat, her eyes flashed sparks. "Don't try flattering me, Mr. Blackhawk."

He frowned. "Can we get past the formalities? I've been calling you Karen all day long. Can't you call me Grady?"

He saw her struggle reflected on her face, knew

that she considered it one step closer to an intimacy she didn't want. She was too polite to tell him that, though. She merely nodded curtly.

"Grady, then."

"Thank you," he said, keeping his expression and his tone deliberately solemn.

"Are you mocking me?"

"Not mocking," he said. "Just teasing a little."

"Well, I don't like it," she said sharply.

"Oh, really? When was the last time a man teased you, Karen?"

"I'm sure you know the answer to that."

"When Caleb was still alive," he suggested. "Tell me about him."

She stared at him with surprise written all over her face. "Why?"

"Because I'd like to know how you saw him. I imagine it was quite a bit different from the way *I* viewed him."

"Yes, I imagine it was," she replied wryly. "He was my husband and I loved him."

"Needless to say, I didn't. He always struck me as an unreasonable man, one who twisted the facts to suit himself," Grady said, deliberately baiting her just to see the flash of fire in her eyes, the color blooming in her cheeks. He liked seeing her come alive, instead of wearing the defeated air he'd seen on his arrival the day before.

"Caleb was the fairest men I ever knew," she retorted, her voice as prickly as a desert cactus. "Which is why I owe it to him to think twice before I believe a word you say. You tell me you weren't responsible for any of those incidents that almost cost us our herd, but words aren't evidence. Where's your proof?"

He leveled a look straight into her soft blue eyes. "Where's yours?"

She swallowed hard at that and turned away, dishing up mashed potatoes, gravy and meat loaf with quick, impatient gestures that told him his barb had gotten to her.

Silently she slapped a fresh loaf of country sourdough bread on the table, along with home-churned butter, then took a seat opposite him.

"Shall we call a truce, Karen?" he suggested mildly. "Otherwise, we're going to ruin a perfectly fine meal, and we'll both end up with indigestion."

"Calling a truce with you is a risk," she said candidly. "You tend to take advantage every chance you get."

"I'm highly motivated. Is there anything wrong with that?"

"I suppose that depends on your motivation and your goal."

"You know mine. I've laid all my cards on the table. What about you? What motivates you?" He noticed that the travel brochures had been gathered up and tossed into a basket on the counter. "Dreams of faraway places?"

"Dreams can be a motivation," she conceded, though it wasn't a direct answer to his question. Her gaze met his. "Or merely a fantasy."

"Which are they for you?"

"Fantasy at the moment, nothing more."

She was fibbing, he decided, noting that the brochure for London was already dog-eared from handling.

"If you could go anywhere in the world you wanted, where would you choose?"

"London," she said at once, then seemed to regret it.

"Any particular reason?"

"Lots of them, but I'm sure you'd find then all boring."

"I wouldn't have asked if I didn't want to know."

She hesitated, then shrugged as if to concede his point. "I studied literature the one year I went away to college. I love Jane Austen and Charles Dickens and Thackery. I love Shakespeare's sonnets. And for me, London is permeated with the spirit of all the great British authors. Some of them are even buried in Westminster Abbey."

"You're a romantic," Grady concluded.

"You say that as if it's a crime."

"No, just a surprise. Romantics don't always do well in the real world. Ranching can be a hard life. There's very little romantic about it."

She gave him a pitying look. "Then you've been doing it with the wrong person. I found my share of romance right here."

"Is that why you don't want to leave? Nostalgia?"

"You already know why I won't sell this ranch—at least not to you."

Rather than heading down that particular dead-end road again right now, Grady concentrated on his meal for a moment. "You're a fine cook," he said as he ate the last bite of meat loaf on his plate.

"Thank you."

"You'll have to let me return the favor sometime. Not that I'll cook, but I'd be happy to take you out for supper."

"I don't think so, but thank you for offering."

That stiff, polite tone was back in her voice. Grady couldn't help wondering what it would be like to see her defenses slip, to hear her laugh.

Whether that ever happened or not wasn't important, he chided himself. He only needed her to trust him just a little, to persuade her that she wasn't cut out for the life of a rancher. And then to coax her into selling this land to him and not someone else.

He shoved his chair back and stood up. "Thanks for the meal. I'll see you in the morning."

She seemed startled. "No angling for dessert?"

"Not tonight," he said, then hesitated. "Unless you've got an apple pie warming in the oven."

She shook her head, amusement brightening her eyes. "No, just more oatmeal cookies."

He considered that but concluded, good as they were, he didn't dare risk staying. Sitting here with lovely Karen Hanson in her kitchen was entirely too cozy.

"I wouldn't mind taking one or two along for the drive," he said.

"After my cookies, then, and not my company? Should I be insulted?" she asked, but she put a few into a bag for him.

"I'll leave that to you," he said, giving her a wink that clearly disconcerted her. "See you in the morning."

"Yes," she said with what sounded like resignation. "I imagine you will."

Grady closed the door quietly, then stood on the other side feeling a bit disconcerted himself. He was already looking forward to morning, and that wasn't good. It wasn't good at all, because he knew that this time it had less to do with the land and more to do with the woman who was keeping it from him. And that hadn't been part of his plan at all.

4

Karen woke before dawn, did the necessary chores, left a note in the barn for Hank and Dooley and high-tailed it away from the ranch. She headed straight for Winding River, though she didn't have a specific destination in mind.

Okay, so what if she was running away? She had a right to, didn't she? Her home wasn't her own anymore, not with Grady evidently intending to pop up like a stubborn weed every time she turned around.

Sitting across the kitchen table from him the night before had rattled her more than she liked. Other than inflicting his presence on her in the sneakiest way possible, he hadn't been the least bit pushy. The subject of the ranch had hardly arisen at all.

Instead, he had been attentive and lighthearted. The conversation had been intelligent. All in all, he had been very good company. He'd flattered her some, reminding her that it was nice to receive a compliment from a man every now and again.

Just not from *this* man, she scolded herself. Nothing out of Grady's mouth could be trusted. It was all a means to an end, and that end was taking the Hanson ranch away from her, whether he actually mentioned his desire to buy the place or not.

Funny, that was how she thought of the ranch, not so much as her own but as still belonging to the Hansons, with her merely its guardian. These days the duty was weighing heavily on her shoulders.

A pale, shimmery sun was trying to sneak over the horizon as she drove onto Main Street in Winding River and headed straight for Stella's. Not only would the coffee be hot, but Cassie was likely to be working. Cole had chafed at her decision to stay on after the wedding, but Cassie had been insistent. In Karen's opinion, even now, with things between Cassie and Cole improving and Jake thrilled to be living with his long-lost dad, her old friend didn't trust that the marriage was going to last. Cassie wanted the security of her own money and a familiar job. Since Cole worked at home, he was there when nine-year-old Jake got home each day, but even if he hadn't been, Cassie would have found a way to remain independent.

"My gracious, you must have been up with the birds," Stella greeted her when Karen walked through the door.

"Before most of them," Karen said.

"Something on your mind?" the woman asked as she poured coffee and set the cup in front of her. "Won't be anybody else in here for a few minutes yet. I could listen."

Karen hesitated, then nodded. "If you wouldn't mind."

Stella sat down across from her. She had known all five of the Calamity Janes since they were in grade school, which was when she'd first opened the restaurant. With her ready smile, huge heart and nonjudgmental demeanor, Stella had been mother and friend and mentor to all of them at one time or another. She was playing the same role for another generation now.

"Okay, what is it?" Stella probed. "You still grieving over Caleb?"

"Yes, of course," Karen said a little too hastily, as if she had something to prove. "He's only been gone a little over half a year."

Stella's gaze narrowed. "The way you said that, all defensive when I just asked a simple question…it's another man, isn't it? You're attracted to someone and you're feeling guilty?"

"No," Karen denied heatedly, then flinched under Stella's steady gaze. "Okay, maybe. It's just that there's this man who wants the ranch. He's been pestering me."

"Grady Blackhawk," Stella said at once. "I've heard all about it."

"From Cassie, I imagine."

"From her and from Grady himself. He comes in here from time to time."

Karen thought of their conversation the night before. "For the meat loaf?"

Stella grinned. "That man does love my meat loaf. Of course, he's also partial to chicken-fried steak and pot roast. Any man who drives as far as he does for my food is either close to starving or he genuinely likes it."

"You sound as if you approve of him."

"I do," Stella said, regarding Karen closely. "Why does that surprise you?" She held up a hand. "Never mind. I know. It's because there was bad blood between him and Caleb."

"Can you think of a better reason?"

"Sure. One that you came up with on your own after giving the man a chance." She studied Karen gravely. "I think maybe that's what's bothering you. You're kind by nature. You give most people a fair chance to prove themselves. A second chance when it's called for. You're not doing that with Grady, and it doesn't sit well with you."

"Maybe that's right," Karen admitted. It was true that she liked to form her own opinions about people. And she'd never taken the view that a husband and wife had to have the exact same friends—so why was she so determined to make Caleb's enemy into her own?

Because Caleb was dead, of course. Who would stand up to Grady if she didn't do it? And it wasn't about personalities, anyway. It was about the ranch.

"Are you going to sell the ranch to Grady?" Stella asked, getting to the point.

"No," Karen said.

"Then what's the problem? Sounds to me as if your decision is made and it's final."

"He..." She regarded Stella with the helpless feeling of a teenager admitting to a crush. After a minute, she gathered her courage and said it. "Grady bothers me."

It felt surprisingly good to get the words out, words she hadn't been able to manage to her oldest friends, even when they'd given her ample opportunity to say them.

A grin tugged at Stella's lips. She didn't look the least bit shocked. "Is that so? Now, if you ask me, you've just admitted to being a full-fledged, red-blooded female. That man is something to look at. Ain't a woman living who would deny feeling her senses go into overdrive when he walks into a room."

"Really?" Karen asked hopefully. "Then I'm not being disloyal to Caleb's memory?"

"Sweetie, I would tell you the same thing if Caleb were still alive and sitting right here across from you. There's not a thing wrong with looking at a fine specimen of a man. Now *doing something about it* is a whole other story." Her gaze narrowed. "You thinking of getting involved with Grady? Is that the way things are moving?"

"Absolutely not," Karen said fiercely. She had never allowed her thoughts to stray beyond admitting to an attraction. And she wouldn't permit herself to go any further.

Stella chuckled. "Then you might want to temper that protest just a little. Sounds a little too emphatic, if you know what I mean."

Unfortunately, Karen knew exactly what she meant. "I'm in trouble, aren't I?"

"Not yet, but you could be looking at it," the older woman said. She reached across the table and patted Karen's hand. "And to tell the truth, I don't think that would be such a bad thing. There's no set timetable for grieving, not like in the old days, when people were expected to put everything on hold for a full year of mourning. Life goes on, Karen. It's meant for living. Caleb wouldn't begrudge you happiness. Just be sure the timing is right for *you,* not Grady."

"It's wrong," she said, as much to herself as to Stella. "Caleb hated him."

Stella gave her a serious look. "Meaning no disrespect to your husband—he was a good boy and a fine man—but he held on to grudges that weren't his. Don't you do the same."

Before Karen could ask what Stella had meant by grudges that weren't Caleb's, the door opened and the first rush of morning customers came in, bringing cold air and shouted pleas for hot coffee with them.

"Just think about what I've said," Stella said as she stood up. "I'll bring you your breakfast in a minute. Let me get these heathens settled down first."

"I haven't ordered," Karen pointed out.

"No need. You have the same thing every time, the number three with the egg scrambled."

As Stella walked away, Karen thought about that, thought about everything going on in her life. "I'm in a rut," she muttered, just as Cassie slid into the booth opposite her.

"Talking to yourself is not a good sign," she advised Karen. "I only have a second before it gets crazy in here. Are you okay? Need somebody to talk to?"

"I did, but Stella filled in."

Cassie grinned. "She always has. Now sit tight. I imagine Emma will be in shortly to keep you company.

Of course, Ford may be right behind her. The man's been like her shadow lately. She still says it's wearing on her nerves, but she hasn't chased him off yet. What about you? Did you chase Grady Blackhawk off permanently the other day?"

"Afraid not," Karen admitted ruefully. "In fact, that's why I'm here. He was at the ranch all day yesterday and said he'd be back today."

Cassie's expression turned indignant. "All day? What is wrong with that man? He wasn't pressuring you again, was he? Maybe Emma was right about getting a restraining order."

"No, he wasn't pressuring me, not the way you mean. In fact, just the opposite. He showed up and went straight to work without a word to me. When I caught sight of him, he was stripping the paint off the barn."

Cassie looked as stunned as Karen had felt when she'd first seen him outside. "What? Why would he do a thing like that?"

"Your guess is as good as mine," she said wearily. "He seems to have a list of projects he intends to help me with. Did I ask for that help? No. Do I want it? No. Does he listen to a word I say? No."

Her friend chuckled. "Interesting. A man who can't take no for an answer. I have one at home just like that."

"Don't even go there," Karen said.

Before the morning was out, she had advice from Emma and Gina and Lauren, all of whom had popped in and out of Stella's just long enough to grab some food before getting on with their days. Unfortunately, the only way Karen could get on with her day or her life would be to go home…where Grady would be waiting.

Since she was not prepared to deal with the man—or her own tangled emotions—again so soon, she headed for Laramie instead. Maybe a movie and some wistful window-shopping—the only kind of shopping she could afford right now—would get her mind off him. At the very least, it would mean she could delay dealing with Grady until tomorrow.

Unfortunately, the lead in the movie she chose looked a lot like Grady. And the actor who resembled her sexy nemesis was the romantic hero, not the villain. It seemed that everything was conspiring to change her opinion of Grady, which meant she was just going to have to cling more tightly to all the warnings Caleb had uttered over the years. Maybe, if she repeated them like a mantra, this uneasy weakening of her resolve would end, and she could go on with her life as before.

True, these days everything seemed a bit rocky and difficult, but she'd take that anytime over dealing with Grady and the unlikely, inappropriate feelings he'd begun to stir in her.

Grady didn't bother going to the door when he arrived the next day. He just started to work, counting on Karen to spot him sooner or later as she had the day before. He couldn't seem to stop his gaze from drifting to the house now and again, though, as he tried to imagine what Karen was up to inside.

Was she baking again? Those cookies had been the best he'd had in a long time. He couldn't help wonder-

ing if there were any left or when she might appear
with a few. Or maybe she'd taken the hint about an
apple pie. Maybe one was cooling on top of the stove
right now. He'd been on his own so long that the mere
thought of home-baked treats made his mouth water.

Fortunately, he'd learned never to rely on wishful
thinking when it came to food or drink. He'd brought a
thermos filled with coffee and a cooler with him. The
latter was filled with sandwiches and sodas, enough
to share in that warm, cozy kitchen if the opportunity
arose. He didn't like the stirring of disappointment
he felt when noon came and went with no sign of the
woman with whom he'd meant to enjoy his meal.

So far the only company he'd had were the two part-
time hands, who regarded him with suspicion when
they found him atop a ladder scraping the last of the
paint off the side of the barn.

"Who're you?" the grizzled older man had demanded within a few minutes of Grady's arrival.

"Grady Blackhawk," he replied, keeping his temper in check at their obviously dismayed reaction to
his name. "And you?"

"Ain't none of your business who we are. We belong
here and you don't. What are you doing on Hanson
property and makin' yourself right at home, at that?"

"Isn't that obvious?"

"Not to me it ain't," the old man said. "No way
Mrs. Hanson would let you come sniffin' around here,
much less approve of you bein' out here messin' with
her barn."

"And why is that?" he asked, curious to see what Karen might have said about him.

"Because now that her husband's dead and buried, you're trying to steal this place right out from under her," the younger man said. He gestured toward the paint cans stacked nearby in readiness for the next step in Grady's project. "You trying to work up a debt she won't be able to pay off?"

"Absolutely not," Grady insisted. "I'm just doing her a favor."

"Now why would you do that, unless you had somethin' up your sleeve?" the old man asked. "Nobody does somethin' for nothin'."

"Is that a fact?" Grady asked mildly. "Well, in this case, you're wrong. I'm just being neighborly."

"Humph!" the old man said with a snort of disbelief. "Good thing she ain't around to see this. Woman has enough on her mind without seein' you out here makin' like you have a right to be here."

"Karen's not home?" he said, barely concealing his disappointment.

"That's Mrs. Hanson to you," the old man retorted. "And no, she ain't here. So if you were hopin' to annoy her, you're plumb out of luck. She's gone for the day. Maybe longer, for all I know. Could be gone weeks. Maybe she finally went off on that fancy vacation her friends have been urgin' her to take."

Grady concluded the exaggeration was meant for his benefit. He should have seen for himself that she wasn't around. That heap of hers was gone. Maybe he'd just been hoping someone had come and towed it off to the junkyard where it belonged.

"Seriously," he said, "did she say when she'll be back?"

The two men exchanged a look, then the older one shook his head with obvious reluctance. "Not to me, she didn't."

"Me, either," the younger one said.

"I imagine she did leave you with chores to do, though, didn't she?" Grady said pointedly.

"That she did," the old man agreed.

Even so, for a minute Grady thought they might stand right there for the rest of the day to keep an eye on him. But eventually their sense of duty overcame their suspicions and they wandered away, the old man still muttering under his breath about the nerve of some people.

Ironically, Grady was actually relieved by their reaction. It meant there were people looking out for Karen, people who had her best interests at heart, even if they were sadly misguided where he was concerned.

Or maybe not, he thought wryly. Maybe they had it just right. His intentions weren't quite as honorable as he'd made them out to be. It would be wise if all of them remembered that, himself included.

He went back to work, contenting himself with the progress he was making in scraping off the old paint. That was why he'd come, after all. He wasn't here to see Karen Hanson with her big blue, vulnerable eyes and kissable lips.

And pigs flew, he thought with a sigh as his gaze

strayed time and again toward the driveway where he hoped to catch a glimpse of her beat-up old truck kicking up a plume of dust.

But as night fell, there was still no sign of Karen. Even though the two men had told him she'd gone out, Grady knocked on the door in case they'd merely been trying to throw him off, but there was no answer. No welcoming lights came on in the kitchen as it grew darker.

He poured himself a last cup of coffee from his thermos and settled into the shadows of the front porch to wait for her return. He was grateful for his sheepskin-lined jacket as the air turned cold. There was the scent of snow in it, though a blizzard hadn't been predicted before the following week.

As the minutes ticked by, he was tempted to throw in the towel and leave, but he stayed right where he was. He couldn't explain why he was so determined to hang around until Karen's return. He felt sure he wouldn't like the answer if he tried.

When Karen drove up at last, the headlights cut through the darkness, clearly outlining him in the rocker. She turned off the pickup's engine, but she didn't emerge. He could just imagine her sitting there, battling irritation…or maybe even temptation. Was she struggling with it the same way he was?

When she finally stepped from the car, slammed the door and headed his way with a brisk stride, he concluded irritation had won. He stood to meet her, eager for a battle that was bound to warm the air by several degrees.

"What are you doing here at this hour?" she asked mildly enough. "You're too far away from the barn to claim you're painting."

"I was waiting for you. You were out late for a woman with so much work to do around here," he said mildly.

"I thought *you'd* taken over all the hard chores," she tossed back. "So I figured I could take a day off," she added cheerfully.

"Is that it? My guess is you were hiding out. Surely, I don't scare you, do I?"

"Don't be ridiculous. You annoy me, you don't scare me. On top of that, my comings and goings are no concern of yours," she declared with an expected flash of temper that virtually heated the chilly night air.

He concluded that he'd hit the nail on the head. She'd stayed away today to avoid him and was thoroughly exasperated that the tactic had failed.

"A lady can never have too many people worrying about her," he said. "Not in this day and age."

She stuffed her hands into her pockets and met his gaze evenly. "Would it surprise you to know that the only thing in my life my friends are concerned about is *you?*"

Grady felt his lips twitch. "Not a bit. I imagine you've painted a pretty dark picture of me. Your two hands certainly seemed suspicious enough when they found me here."

"I imagine they were. Dooley and Hank were very loyal to Caleb. They look out for me."

"There's no need to worry about me. I'm not such a bad guy," he asserted.

"Couldn't prove it by me."

"You realize, of course, that you don't know me at all," he reminded her yet again.

"I know enough."

He took a step closer, admiring the fact that she didn't back away. "Such as?"

"You're a scoundrel and a thief," she said flatly, dredging up old news.

Even though they'd been over this ground before, it was evident she intended to cling to that description. Maybe it was what she used to battle the undeniable sparks of attraction zinging between them even now.

He stepped closer, deliberately crowding her. She continued to stand her ground, though there was an unmistakable flash of alarm in her eyes. "Really?" he said softly. "You know that for a fact?"

"My husband said—"

He lifted his hand and brushed a wayward strand of hair away from her cheek, felt her skin heat. "Yes, you've quoted him before," he said, pulling away before the gesture could turn into a caress. "But what do you know, Karen? Not rumor. Not innuendo. Pure fact."

In the light of a pale half-moon, he could see her throat work as she struggled with the possibility that she had judged him unfairly. It was clear she didn't have an answer for him, and just as clear that she didn't like that about herself.

"I'll make you a deal," he said in the same coaxing tone he'd use to gentle a wild horse. "You get to know me. Spend time with me. If you still think I'm a scoundrel and a thief, I'll walk away and not bother you about the land again. If I prove otherwise, you'll sell the ranch to me and get on with that traveling you've always dreamed about."

"I can't," she said, her voice a little breathless.

"Why not? Don't you trust your own judgment?"

"Of course, but—"

"It's a fair deal, Karen. You know it is."

"I still can't do it," she said.

She said it flatly, but Grady thought there was a slightly wistful note in her voice for the first time.

"Suit yourself. I'll just come up with some other way to go about this," he said with an indifferent shrug, and started to walk away. He didn't get far.

"This experiment of yours," she called after him, sounding resigned. "How long would it last and what would it entail?"

He turned back to face her. "As long as it takes and whatever's necessary."

She shook her head. "Absolutely not. It'll only work if there are rules and we both agree to them."

"Okay, then," he relented. "A month and we'll only share a few meals, a little conversation. Nothing more. What's the harm in that? We got through dinner last night without the world coming to an end, didn't we?"

"I suppose."

"So, what do you say? Is it a deal?"

"Two weeks," she countered, her defiant gaze locked with his.

"Two weeks," he agreed, seizing it. He bit back his desire to utter a whoop of triumph. "Lunch and dinner."

"You'll be satisfied with that?" she asked, gaze narrowed as she studied him. "Whatever my decision at the end of two weeks, you'll live with it? You'll accept it if I say you haven't convinced me of anything?"

"That's the agreement."

She held out her hand. Grady clasped it, felt her tremble, and knew he'd just made the smartest deal of his life.

As he walked away, he murmured under his breath, "Two weeks is a start, darlin'. That's a real good start."

5

*W*hat had she done? Karen rested her head on her arms and groaned as she considered Grady's trap and the way she'd neatly stepped into it with virtually no hesitation at all. She had invited the enemy into the camp and promised to break bread with him. She had to be out of her mind.

But somehow, in the quiet stillness of the night, she hadn't been able to resist what he was offering—a chance to end this battle once and for all.

More, it was a chance to unravel a puzzle that was increasingly complex. Why she cared so much about that didn't bear thinking about. She feared it went beyond fair play, beyond curiosity. In fact, she had a terrible sense that it had to do with a yearning that had started in the pit of her stomach and hadn't let up since the day he'd appeared in her kitchen.

It could be as simple as a yearning for companionship, something she'd missed desperately in the weeks and months since Caleb's death. A worrisome voice in the back of her mind told her it was something more, something specific to Grady, the allure of the forbidden.

She hadn't been the rule-breaker all those years ago. That had been Cassie. But, oh, how Karen had longed to be just like her, to shake things up, defy convention. Spending time with Grady would certainly qualify. There would be talk. Her in-laws were likely to be outraged. Deep down, even she disapproved of the choice she had made.

But it was done now. She couldn't go back on her word. It was only a few meals, she reminded herself. How difficult could that be? How much trouble could she get into by spending an occasional hour in Grady's company?

She found out when lunch turned out to be a daily ritual and dinner slipped into the schedule six nights out of seven. By the end of the first week of their agreement, she'd almost grown comfortable having Grady around. She'd almost forgotten why he was there. The wicked danger of it all faded when he continued to behave like a perfect gentleman.

Then came the Saturday night that snow started falling while they were sharing a meal of beef stew and homemade bread. Karen wasn't aware that the weather had changed outside as Grady beguiled her with stories of his grandfather.

As the tales unfolded, it became evident that Thomas Blackhawk was an amazing man, one who fought to preserve his Native American heritage while getting

along quite well in a white man's world. He was mayor
of his town in the northwest part of the state and there
was some talk that he might run for a position as delegate from the region to the state legislature.

"The first time I ever saw him dressed in a suit and
tie, I couldn't believe it was him," Grady said, his eyes
twinkling. "I'd seen him most often in jeans and flannel, but there he was speaking to a crowd at a town
meeting, wearing this fancy black suit, his lined face
filled with pride. It was quite a transformation. When
I commented on it afterward, do you know what he
said?"

"What?" Karen asked, fascinated.

"That all the fancy clothes in the world couldn't
make a man respect you. It was actions that did that."

"You love him a lot, don't you?"

"It's more than that," Grady said. "I love him and I
admire him. He lives a very simple life in the middle of
nowhere, in a house he built himself. As a kid I spent
a lot of time with him, listening to him talk about nature, about our place in the universe. He taught me all
of the old legends and practices, but those weren't the
most important lessons, by far."

"What were the really important ones?" Karen
asked.

"He taught me about self-respect and loyalty, about
family and duty."

She thought she saw where this was going. "Was he
the one who taught you to hate the Hansons?"

"Not to hate them," Grady denied. "My grandfather has never hated anyone. He just made me aware

that this land should have belonged to his father, that
it should have been Blackhawk land."

"In other words, he planted a seed in your head, watered it regularly and now it's grown into this obsession," she said, derision cutting into the admiration she
had begun to feel for Thomas Blackhawk.

"It's not an obsession, Karen. It's a commitment. I
want my grandfather to stand on this land someday,
look around and know that it's back with its rightful
owners, that it's Blackhawk land again."

"Would he be happy about that if he knew the price
you'd paid?" she asked.

"Dollars aren't the issue," he told her.

"No," she agreed. "And I wasn't talking about the
amount of money you say you're willing to put on the
table. I was talking about the rest, the attempts you've
made to force Caleb, and now me, to sell."

He regarded her with obvious impatience. "Dammit, I've told you I had nothing to do with trying to
sabotage your herd."

"If not you, who?"

"Both things could have been accidents. Cattle get
ill. Pastures catch on fire during a dry summer."

She regarded him evenly. "Do you honestly believe
that's what happened? Isn't it a little too coincidental
that both the outbreak of disease and the fire happened
to our herd and no one else's?"

"I'll admit it looks suspicious, but I had nothing to
do with any of it."

"So you say."

"In a lot of very powerful circles, my word is good enough."

"All that tells me is that the world is filled with foolish people," she said, stubbornly clinging to her—no, Caleb's—conviction that Grady couldn't be trusted. She needed these reminders from time to time. Otherwise, it would be too easy to start to like him a little too much, to begin to believe the pretty words that tripped so easily off his tongue.

He gave her a steady look, one clearly designed to rattle her. "Can you honestly sit there and look me in the eye and tell me that you think I'm capable of trying to destroy your herd just to get what I want? Have I done anything in the last week that was the least bit underhanded? Have I pressured you in any way?"

"No," she was forced to admit. Not unless the fact that he was here in the first place counted as a crime. The truth was he'd been helpful and considerate. He'd done everything in his power to ingratiate himself with her, tackling odd jobs too long ignored. The ranch buildings had never been in better condition.

"Well, then, shouldn't you be starting to trust me just a little?" he asked.

"I do," she conceded with a sigh, then met his gaze. "A little."

He grinned. "Another good start, darlin'. We're making progress."

Karen wasn't sure they were making the right kind of progress. She was absolutely certain Caleb wouldn't approve of it. She pushed away from the table, because it was becoming too tempting to linger, to share a second cup of coffee and a little more conversation each time they were together.

"I'd better get these dishes washed," she said, turning her back on him.

Grady was on his feet at once. "Let me help."

"No need," she insisted. "I'm sure you want to be heading home."

He grinned at that. "Not especially. The company's better right here. And it's Saturday night, a time to settle back and relax a little. I brought a video. I thought maybe we could make some popcorn and watch it together."

The prospect was more alluring than she cared to admit. "Sorry," she said edgily. "No popcorn in the house."

"I brought that, too."

"You do think of everything, don't you?" she said in a way not meant to be complimentary.

"I try to," he agreed, not taking offense. "Shall I get the movie, or are you going to turn me down?"

She hesitated, then asked, "What movie is it?"

"One of Lauren's," he said with a smug expression. "It just came out on video."

She frowned at him. "You knew I wouldn't be able to resist that, didn't you?"

"No, but I was hoping."

The chances to get to Laramie for a movie had been too few and far between. The one she'd seen a week ago had been the first one since before Caleb's death. The last one of Lauren's she'd viewed in a theater had been a year ago. She told herself she was merely eager to catch up on her friend's career, not for the lingering company of the disconcerting man who'd brought the video.

"Get it," she told him. "I'll finish up here."

Grady grabbed his jacket and opened the back door, allowing a blast of frigid air into the kitchen. When he shut it again without taking a step outside, Karen regarded him with curiosity.

"Anything wrong?" she asked.

"I suppose that depends on your point of view," he said with a wry note in his voice.

She crossed the room and opened the door to see for herself. Great white flakes of snow were swirling around in blinding sheets. She could barely see the lighted outline of the barn in the distance. The ground had already been blanketed with a layer several inches thick. At this rate, the roads would be impassable in no time, if they weren't already.

Even as the implications of the blizzard sank in, she couldn't help being awed by the beauty of the snow-covered landscape. Rugged terrain softened and glistened.

She had learned long ago how to weather a storm. There were supplies on hand, a generator to keep the most basic electricity functioning and a well-stocked woodpile by the back door.

The only problem, of course, was the fact that she was going to be stuck here for who-knew-how-long with Grady. She couldn't send him out in this, not with the distance he'd have to drive. Maybe if he lived just up the road, they could have risked it, but he was miles from home.

The prospect of allowing him to stay under her roof didn't disconcert her nearly as much as it should have. This was an emergency. Who could make anything of it if he stayed? Who would even know?

She closed the door carefully, then announced briskly, "You'll stay here, of course. I'll go check the guest room and make sure you'll have everything you need."

"Karen," he said softly, drawing her attention.

"Yes?"

"I didn't plan this."

She allowed herself a brief smile at that. "No, I imagine not even *you* can control the weather."

"I didn't know it was predicted," he amended.

"Grady, I know enough about storms to know that they can come up unexpectedly, be worse than anticipated, any of that. I'm not thinking that you somehow conspired to find a way to spend the night here."

He nodded. "Okay, just so we're clear."

"We are," she said, amused despite herself. "Why don't you go ahead and get that movie and the popcorn?"

"If you're sure. I could still try to make it home."

"And wind up stranded in a snowdrift? I don't think so. I don't want that on my conscience."

"And we both know how worrisome you find that conscience of yours," he said lightly. "I'll get the movie. And I'll check on the stock in the barn to make sure there's plenty of feed."

"Thank you. Now go, before it gets any worse."

Only after he had gone outside did she sag against the kitchen counter. She had just invited Grady Blackhawk to stay in her home. The only thing the Hansons would consider a worse betrayal was if she'd invited him into her bed.

Grady trudged through the deepening snow to the barn and checked on the horses. It took no more than a few minutes, but by the time he went back outside, the house was lost behind a seemingly impenetrable wall of white. He found the guideline installed for occasions just like this and made his way slowly through drifts that were now knee-high and growing.

Thankfully his truck was parked close to the house. It took him several minutes to wipe the layer of snow from the door. The lock was frozen, but he always kept a de-icing tool in his pocket this time of year. Shivering, he got the door open, grabbed the video and popcorn, then closed the truck up and headed inside. He stomped the snow from his boots on the back steps, then removed his jacket and shook it off before stepping into the kitchen.

The heat felt like heaven to his stiff fingers. Not even gloves had been much protection against the falling temperature and wind. He was rubbing his hands together when Karen came back into the kitchen. She took one look at him and grinned.

"My, my, an honest-to-goodness snowman in my kitchen," she teased.

"I shook my coat off," he protested. "And knocked most of it off my boots."

"But you should see your hair," she said, stepping closer to brush away the lingering snow. "Even your eyelashes are covered."

As her fingers grazed his cheek, Grady felt his breath catch in his throat. The temptation to kiss her was so powerful it was almost impossible to resist. Her sweet, warm breath was fanning against his skin. Her lips looked warm and inviting. In fact, they promised the kind of heat that could chase away that last of his chill.

No, he told himself firmly. He couldn't do it. It would ruin everything. Certainly, it would destroy her fragile trust in him.

He forced himself to take a step back, to capture her hand in his and hold it away from his face.

"Thanks," he said a little too curtly. "I can finish up if you'll get me a towel."

There was a startled flash of hurt in her eyes before understanding dawned. Then, cheeks flaming, she nodded and quickly ran from the room. When she returned, they had both regained their composure.

Grady toweled his hair dry as Karen made hot chocolate. His gaze kept straying to her rigid spine, to the soft curve of her hips, to the bare nape of her neck. He wanted to trail his hand down her spine until she relaxed, to rest his palm against that very feminine backside. He wanted to press a kiss to her neck, feel the shudder ripple through her.

He wanted things he had no business wanting, he

chided himself, turning away. Staying here might be a
necessity tonight, but it was a bad idea. He'd honed his
willpower over the years, resisted more than his share
of temptation, but this…this was torment. Karen Hanson was the kind of woman made for loving—not just
physically, though that was the strongest temptation at
the moment—but through and through.

Was that how Caleb had seen her, Grady wondered,
as a woman who deserved a carefree world? Was that
why he had struggled so hard to keep this ranch afloat,
to give her a home? It was funny how the last week or
so had taught him a thing or two about Caleb Hanson,
when his goal had been getting to know the man's wife.
He found himself walking in the man's shoes, understanding his stubborn determination in a way he never
had before, even admiring it.

"The hot chocolate's ready," Karen said, breaking
into his thoughts. "You'd better get started on that popcorn, or the drinks will be cold before it's done."

"I just need a couple of minutes," Grady said.
"Where's your microwave?"

She grinned at him. "I don't have one. You're going
to have to pull this off the old-fashioned way."

His gaze narrowed at her amusement. "You don't
think I can do it?"

"It will be interesting to see, won't it?" she challenged him.

He shook his head with exaggerated pity. "You've
forgotten already about the bare-bones lifestyle my
grandfather lives. I'm used to roughing it," he said as
he reached for a covered pan. He set it on the stove,

turned on the heat, then dumped the contents of the bag into the pan and covered it. "Piece of cake. You'll see."

Grady's gaze clashed with hers and held. She didn't seem to be impressed yet.

Her gaze never wavered. Time fell away as he listened to the beating of his heart, and watched the flicker of some unreadable emotion in her eyes.

"Smells like it's burning," she said cheerfully, breaking the mood and the eye contact after several minutes.

He tore his gaze away, saw smoke billowing from the pan, and muttered a soft curse. He grabbed the pan off the stove and dumped it into the sink. He could hear the few last kernels popping even as he scowled at the offending pot. He'd been oblivious when they started to pop, oblivious to everything but Karen.

Her low chuckle drew his gaze. He studied her for a second, and saw the twinkling satisfaction in her eyes.

"You did that on purpose, didn't you?" he accused.

"What?" she asked, all innocence.

"Distracted me."

"Did I? How?"

"You kept my attention so I wouldn't notice what was happening on the stove."

"Why would I do that?"

"To prove a point."

She grinned broadly. "Well, you have to admit, you were awfully sure of yourself."

"And you were willing to sacrifice the popcorn just to take me down a peg or two?"

"It seemed like a fair trade to me," she said without the least bit of remorse.

Grady sighed. "I really, really like popcorn when I watch a movie."

"We don't have to watch it," she said. "The power could go any minute, anyway, and the generator doesn't keep anything going except the furnace and the hot water heater."

He deliberately locked gazes with her, just as she'd done with him. "If we don't watch the movie, what did you have in mind?"

"We could go to bed," she said with a perfectly straight face.

A smile tugged at his lips. "Somehow I don't think you mean the same thing by that as I would."

Her gaze faltered then. She swallowed hard. "No, I imagine I don't."

"Then let's watch the movie. It's the safest thing that comes to mind at the moment."

They took their hot chocolate into the living room. Grady turned on the TV, popped the video into the player, then deliberately sat right smack in the middle of the sofa opposite it. Karen regarded him with narrowed eyes for a heartbeat, then sat next to him, albeit a careful few inches away. He barely hid a grin.

He pressed the start button on the remote, and Lauren's gorgeous face filled the screen. She was a beautiful woman, but she had nothing on the woman beside him, Grady reflected. As the images on the screen flickered, it wasn't the story, or even Lauren, that captured his attention. It was Karen.

She was totally absorbed in the romantic comedy, her eyes alternately shining with pleasure or misty with unshed tears. From time to time her lips curved into a smile.

When the movie ended, Grady couldn't have said what it was about, but he knew every nuance that had registered on Karen's face.

"That was wonderful," she said, her eyes sparkling.

"Yes, it was," Grady said, though he was talking about something else entirely. Watching her when her guard was down had been a revelation. The laughter had been close to the surface, completely uncensored. The flow of tears had been uninhibited.

He lifted his hand and touched her cheek, then brushed away the last traces of happy tears. She trembled, but she didn't move away.

Once again, it was up to him to stop, up to him to be rational. The tests were getting harder and harder... the results more and more uncertain.

"I still can't believe that glamorous woman on the screen is my friend," she said, her voice a shaky whisper. "She used to steal the Twinkies out of my lunch box."

"Did she ever steal your boyfriends? That would be a far more serious crime."

"Never," she said fiercely. "Despite her reputation for having romances with her leading men, despite the two well-publicized marriages and divorces, the Lauren I knew was a shy girl. Most of the dates she had in high school were ones we set up for her. But even if she'd been some junior femme fatale, she would never have stolen our boyfriends. It would have gone against everything she believed about friendship."

She looked at him. "What about you? Were you a love-'em-and-leave-'em kind of guy?"

"Nope," he said, responding to the question as solemnly as she'd asked it. "Only one girl ever stole my heart, and then she broke it. I haven't been anxious to repeat the experience. Haven't had time, either, for that matter."

"You seem to have a lot of time on your hands now," she pointed out lightly. "Or do you justify all your time here as work? Part of your self-declared mission in life?"

He bit back his irritation that they were once again on the subject of her distrust of him and his motives.

"I'm here because I want to be," he said, choosing his words carefully. "You need some help, and I can provide it."

"And?" she prodded.

"That's it," he insisted, getting to his feet and heading upstairs before he did something to prove just how badly he wanted to stick around.

"Grady?"

He stilled, commanding himself not to turn back, fearful of what might happen if he did.

"There are towels in the bathroom, the blue ones," she said. "And your room's at the top of the stairs on the left."

"And yours?" he asked, unable to stop the question.

"Down the hall," she said

"I'll keep that in mind," he said quietly.

And in the meantime, he'd say a little prayer that it was a very long hall.

6

Karen snapped awake in the morning to the scent of coffee brewing.

Caleb, she thought for a heartbeat, before she remembered and her mood shattered.

No, not her husband, but his worst enemy, she realized, sinking back against the pillows and drawing the covers up. The gesture was partly because it was cold, but also a halfhearted attempt to hide, to pretend that just outside her door nothing was different. Burrowing under the covers had been her way of trying to escape notice since childhood, when she hadn't wanted to leave the warmth and safety of home to go to school.

Of course, that had all changed once she had had the Calamity Janes in her life. From then on there had been no hiding. She had been anxious to get to school each morning to see what adventure Cassie had dreamed up overnight, or what treat Gina had baked in her ongoing experiments with recipes.

But that was then. Things were a whole lot more

complicated in her life now. She had plenty of reasons to hide, and the most disturbing one was currently in her kitchen.

She snuggled under the quilt her mother had made for her as a wedding present and tried to imagine what it must be like outside this morning. The sun was already up, its brilliance pouring through the windows, casting fingers of warmth and light across the room. The wind had died down. In fact, it was perfectly still, as if the snow were absorbing sound.

When the scent of coffee was joined by that of bacon sizzling, Karen could no longer resist. She couldn't think of the last time someone had had breakfast on the table for her. That had always been her task, while Caleb was out tending to the animals. This time of year she had made oatmeal with raisins and warm milk to go along with the eggs and bacon Caleb had insisted on.

She pulled on thermal underwear and jeans, then deliberately chose another of Caleb's flannel shirts.

After she'd brushed her teeth, washed her face and combed her hair, she caught sight of a seldom-used bottle of perfume on the counter. What harm could there be in a little spritz? It wasn't vanity, she assured herself. Or an attempt to be alluring for Grady. It was just a little scent of lilacs to remind her of spring.

She added heavy socks, then did a haphazard job of making her bed before bracing herself and heading downstairs to find her boots…and whatever else awaited.

As she approached the kitchen, she felt amazingly ill at ease, as uncertain as if the night had been far more intimate and this was the uncomfortable morning after. In some ways it was worse, because the desire had been there, shimmering between them, but they had carefully ignored it.

Hovering just outside the kitchen door, her boots in hand, she watched Grady at work at the stove, his movements efficient and confident. It was a revelation to her after a father and a husband who'd never shared in household chores. Seeing Grady deftly flip a pancake only added to his masculinity. It certainly didn't diminish it as her father and Caleb believed it might if they lowered themselves to help in the kitchen.

"You might as well come on in," Grady said without turning around, amusement threading through his voice.

"Do you have eyes in the back of your head?" she grumbled, stepping into the kitchen, dropping her boots onto the floor and reaching for a mug. "I know you didn't hear me. The floor didn't creak once."

"Nope. I smelled the scent of lilacs. Given the time of year and the weather, it had to be you."

He turned, coffeepot in hand, to fill her cup. His warm gaze rested on her in a way that left her feeling oddly breathless. He was so at home in her kitchen, so at ease, for an instant she almost felt as if this were his house and she was the guest.

"Did you sleep well?" he asked.

Karen smiled at the question.

"You find that amusing?"

She nodded. "I was just thinking that you look as if

you've made yourself at home. Now you're inquiring about my night as a good host would."

He grinned. "I notice you're not inquiring about mine, so I'll tell you. I slept very well. Had some fascinating dreams, too."

Her breath snagged. "Oh?"

"Shall I tell you about them?" he inquired, a wicked twinkle in his eyes.

"Why don't we leave them to my imagination," she said.

He shrugged. "It's up to you, but they certainly kept me warm."

"Grady!"

He chuckled. "Okay, I won't tease. How many pancakes can you eat?"

She eyed the size of them. They were twice as big around as the ones she made. "Two," she decided.

"Bacon?"

She glanced at the plate and saw that he'd fried half a dozen strips. "Two strips."

He studied her. "Two eggs also?"

"Nope. Only one."

"Good. I was worried you were getting into a rut."

"I probably am," she admitted, thinking about the sameness of her life the last ten years. "But food's the least of it."

Grady fixed his own plate and sat down opposite her. "Can I ask you a question?"

She feigned shock. "You're asking permission? It must be a doozy."

"It is personal," he conceded. "And you may not want to talk about it, not to me, anyway."

Now he'd stirred her curiosity. "Ask," she said.

"Do you regret marrying Caleb?" When she started to react with indignation, he held up his hand. "No, wait. I don't mean Caleb specifically, I guess. I know you loved him. I mean do you regret sacrificing all those things you'd hoped to do by marrying a rancher?"

There was less to offend in the way he'd rephrased the question. She took a sip of her coffee and considered it thoughtfully.

"You're right. I did give up a lot," she conceded eventually. "I had so many ambitious dreams."

"About traveling?"

"Travel, adventure, education. Not education as in school, but the kind of learning that comes with seeing places and meeting people. I wanted to feel history by standing in the middle of Westminster Abbey or Trafalgar Square, or standing on the steps of Parliament in London. I wanted to visit the Colosseum and the Vatican. I wanted to learn about artists like van Gogh and Monet and Rembrandt by standing in front of their works in the Louvre and other famous museums."

"Yet you gave all of that up to marry Caleb," he said.

She met his gaze. "Yes. Because, in the end, he mattered more," she said simply. "The rest…we would have done it one day, together if…" She sighed, battled against the familiar threat of tears, steadied her voice. "If things had been different."

"You never resented him?"

"Not once," she said honestly. "And don't forget, I

knew what I was getting into. I was raised on a ranch. This life wasn't new to me, and it has its good points." She glanced toward the window where tree branches were covered with blankets of sparkling snow. "Mornings like this are among them."

"They are, aren't they?" he said quietly, following her gaze to the pristine white scene outside.

When he turned back to her, there was a twinkle back in his eyes. "Do you know what I like about a day like today?"

"What?"

"It gives you permission to play hooky. The roads will be impassable for hours yet. Once you've checked to make sure the horses have fresh water and feed, the day is yours."

She grinned at the boyish enthusiasm on his face and in his voice. "So, what do you do when you play hooky?"

"Well, now, that depends. When I'm all alone, I build a roaring fire, pick a book I haven't had time to read and settle down in a comfortable chair." His gaze sought hers and turned warm. "When I have a lovely companion trapped inside with me, there are all sorts of interesting possibilities."

Heat shot through her. Anticipation made her feel all quivery inside. She swallowed hard. "Such as?"

"Now don't go getting ideas," he teased. "I'm not easy. I won't be taken advantage of, just because we're locked away here all alone."

She chuckled and the tension was broken. "You're outrageous, you know that, don't you?"

"I do try. Now, seriously, what are our options? Scrabble? Cards?"

"I have a shelf filled with good books," she offered.

"Oh, no, that would be fine if we didn't have each other. Since we do, we need something we can do together." His gaze locked on hers. "Now, there you go again, getting ideas."

"I am not," she insisted, but she could feel a blush creeping up her cheeks. How could he joke so easily about an attraction that she was desperate to ignore? Perhaps because he'd had more practice at casual flirtations, while she'd had none.

"Okay, then, how about…" He paused, then said, "A jigsaw puzzle?"

She stared at him, astounded. How could he have known that she had a dozen of them stacked in a cupboard for days just like this one? Had he guessed? Or had he been snooping? Surely she hadn't mentioned it.

"Does that appeal to you at all?" he asked, his expression totally innocent. "Do you have any around?"

"Quite a few," she admitted. "But are you sure you want to do that? It seems, I don't know…a little tame, maybe?" Caleb had certainly never been interested in doing one with her. He'd considered it a waste of time to put something together, only to take it apart again. He was too practical for that.

Grady winked. "You've never done a puzzle with me. How about this? I'll go check on the horses. You clear things up in here and get us set up with the most complicated, challenging puzzle you have. I'll bring in some more wood for the fire when I come back."

She nodded. "Sounds like a plan," she agreed, already anticipating the lazy morning ahead. Even the company was surprisingly appealing. Grady continued to startle her with his unexpected insight into her personality and what would make her happy. Was that because he was incredibly sensitive and intuitive, or because he was devious and clever? For the next few hours, maybe it didn't even matter.

An hour later they were in front of a blazing fire. The damp wood was popping and snapping as it caught. Karen had chosen two puzzles, one a detailed country scene with only five hundred pieces, the other a wickedly difficult thousand-piece image of hundreds of tropical fish. She left it to Grady to decide.

"The fish," he said at once. He brought paper and pen to the table.

"What are those for?"

"To keep score, of course."

"You keep score when you put a puzzle together?"

"I told you it was more of a challenge when I did it. Are you game?"

Her competitive spirit kicked in. "Absolutely." She'd put this puzzle together once before. She knew exactly where some of the trickiest sections were and what to watch for. "How are you scoring? Total number of pieces we each put together?"

"Exactly. We have one hour."

She looked up from her assessment of the pieces spread across the table. "An hour?"

He grinned. "After that, if it's necessary, we work together to finish it. Agreed?"

"Agreed," she said, and solemnly held out her hand.

Grady's clasp was warm and brief—his attention was already totally focused on the puzzle. Before she'd even had a chance to catch her breath, he'd snapped his first two pieces together.

Karen forced her concentration back to the puzzle. She found two linking pieces of her own, then a third. Within a few minutes she had the bottom right corner of the puzzle coming together nicely.

She glanced across the table and saw that Grady was at work on the top left section, his brow furrowed, his gaze intent. His total absorption was endearing somehow. It made her wonder if he would be that totally absorbed when he was making love.

As soon as the thought crossed her mind, her cheeks burned. No more of that, she chided herself, forcing her gaze back to the puzzle. It would play havoc with her concentration.

As it turned out, it already had. Though she tried to get back into it, all the pieces began to look the same. She tried to fit together several that were wildly mismatched…as she and Grady were, she reminded herself.

Stop that! she ordered herself as his knee bumped up against hers, sending an electric current racing down her leg. Her thoughts turned chaotic again. Suspicious, she stared at him. Had the grazing of his knee been intentional? Was he deliberately trying to distract her? Was this payback for her game to ruin his popcorn the night before? If so, she couldn't tell it from his expression. He appeared completely focused, completely oblivious to her presence, and his section of the puzzle was growing by leaps and bounds.

She shifted her foot under the table until it found his leg. To justify her uncharacteristic actions, she told herself this was war as she began a slow, upward slide, her gaze locked intently on the table as if she had no idea what was happening beneath it. Grady jolted as if she'd prodded him with a hot poker from the fireplace. She bit back a grin, delighted that she had his full attention.

That bit of distraction allowed her to quickly assemble several more puzzle pieces, and she grinned as she saw she had completed the full outline of the right side.

The next time Grady reached for a piece, she made sure she reached for it at the same time, her hand covering his.

"Oh, sorry," she said sweetly, as she withdrew.

He watched her, his gaze narrowed. "What are you up to, Karen?"

"Up to?" she said innocently. "I just thought that piece was the one I needed."

"Did you now?" he asked suspiciously. "Where did you think it went? Show me."

She took it and tried it in the bottom corner. Of course, it didn't fit. "Guess not," she said with a shrug. She handed it back to him.

"You're dangerous," he said huskily. "You know that, don't you, Karen?"

No man had ever suggested she was dangerous, and Karen discovered she liked it that Grady had. "Remember that," she advised as she went back to work on the puzzle, deliberately ignoring him.

Naturally Grady wasn't satisfied to leave it at that. Feeling his gaze on her, she glanced up to find his dark eyes studying her intently.

"Shouldn't you be concentrating on the puzzle?" she inquired.

"You're more fascinating," he said.

Truthfully, *he* was more intriguing than the puzzle, too, but Karen didn't dare mention that. The teasing actions she had meant to distract him had affected her as well. The deliberate flirting had made her a little too aware of him as a flesh-and-blood man, instead of an abstract enemy. She was losing her grip on that negative image of him, letting the barriers crumble.

When she realized that he was no longer staring at her but at the puzzle, that he'd used these few minutes to complete another big chunk, she recognized that letting her guard down, even for a second, was a mistake. It was a lesson she needed to keep in mind.

Glancing at the clock, she saw that there were fifteen minutes left in their competition. Grady had a serious lead. She couldn't let him win. Not at this. Not at any of his games. The stakes were too high and, for one terrifying minute, she had lost sight of that.

It wouldn't happen again, Karen vowed, as she went back to work on the puzzle with total concentration. This might be just a silly contest, but Grady was clearly playing as he did everything, with a winner-take-all attitude. It would be wise to remember that, because the next time she might lose more than a game.

* * *

Grady had never expected to get turned on by doing a jigsaw puzzle. Oh, he'd always found competition to be invigorating, but arousing? Never. Which meant this had to do with his opponent.

He glanced at Karen, amused by her flushed cheeks, by the tip of her tongue caught between her teeth, as she focused totally on the puzzle. She was a feisty, sneaky competitor, far more devious than he'd ever envisioned. She had taken him totally by surprise when she'd flirted outrageously in a very successful attempt to distract him.

Not only was he distracted from the game, he was totally absorbed by the female puzzle sitting opposite him. He realized that he was no closer to his goal of understanding Karen than he had been on the day he'd decided to start spending time with her. There were too many layers, too many contradictions.

Her blind loyalty to her husband's memory bumped up against her sense of fair play. Her wistful dreams clashed with the harsh reality of her life. She was stubborn and hardheaded, yet vulnerable. Her eyes could flash with defiance and anger one minute, with heat and desire the next. And heat and desire were what she aroused in him, on a more continual basis.

Something was happening between the two of them, but Grady was at a loss to understand it or to predict where it might lead. Nor did he dare jump to any conclusions, because one misstep could ruin everything.

The ringing of a phone jarred the peaceful ambiance. Karen looked up, startled, and maybe even a little bit afraid. Or was it guilt that caused the color in her cheeks to heighten again? Guilt that she was sharing the day with him?

It took her a minute to react, but then she bolted for the kitchen. He heard her answer the phone with a terse greeting, then her voice dropped and he could hear nothing at all.

Knowing it would infuriate her, he used the time to add another dozen pieces to his section of the puzzle. He studied her work and his own and concluded that he had the game easily won.

When she came back into the room, she looked shaken.

"Everything okay?" he asked.

She nodded, but her expression remained troubled and she stood several feet from the table, as if she didn't dare sit down and join him.

"I don't believe you," he said bluntly. "Who was on the phone?"

"Just Gina, making sure that everything was okay out here."

So far, he didn't see the problem. "And?"

Worried blue eyes finally met his. "She'd heard you were here."

"How would she hear a thing like that?" he asked.

"One of the neighbors apparently saw you turning in here earlier in the day yesterday. Somebody asked Hank about it, and he told 'em to mind their own business. Dooley apparently wasn't so circumspect."

Grady was indignant. "Seems like a lot of commotion over you having a visitor."

"Not just any visitor," she reminded him. *"You."*

"So what?"

"Grady, don't play dumb. You know how the Hansons will feel when they hear about this. It's bad enough that people are probably calling every ten seconds to report that you've been stopping by to help out. When they hear you were here overnight, they're going to go ballistic."

He reached for her hand, but she snatched it away. "Karen, nothing happened last night."

She scowled at him. "Don't you think *I* know that? But it's appearances that matter."

"Really?"

"With Caleb's parents, it is."

"And their opinion matters to you?"

"Of course it does. He was their son. This was their home. I have a duty..."

He found himself battling exasperation. "The only duty you have is to yourself."

She shook her head. "You're wrong. People don't live just for themselves. You have to consider the impact your actions could have on everyone you care about." Her gaze challenged him. "Isn't that what you're doing?"

He regarded her with confusion. "I don't know what you mean."

"Don't you? You told me you want to buy this ranch because of your grandfather," she reminded him. "It's never been about you, has it? It's been about your sense of duty toward a man you admire and love and to those who came before him, people you never knew at all."

The accuracy of her assessment made him pause. "Okay, you're right."

"So you have your obligations and I have mine. I don't want to hurt the Hansons, Grady. I really don't."

"And my being here will hurt them."

She nodded.

Because he hated seeing her so unhappy, he stood up. "I'm sure the highway has been plowed by now. My truck will make it down your driveway. I'll go." His gaze locked with hers. "If that's what you want."

"I do," she said, but there was little conviction in her voice. Clearly she was struggling with herself.

Again Grady took pity on her. He would go, but not before he stepped closer, trailed a finger along her cheek. Unable to resist, he rubbed the pad of his thumb across her lower lip, needing to know if it was a soft as it looked. It was, and it quivered beneath his touch.

"It's okay, Karen," he told her quietly.

"It's not," she said. "I shouldn't be insisting that you go. If something happens—"

"Nothing is going to happen. I'll call you when I get to my place, if it'll make you feel any better." He forced a grin. "Though I'd think you might actually feel better if I slid into a ditch."

She stared at him, clearly aghast at the suggestion. "How can you say a thing like that?"

"I am a thorn in your side, aren't I?"

"True," she admitted with her unfailing candor. Then she sighed. "But I'm starting to get used to it."

Another tiny triumph, Grady concluded. He would savor that on the long, cold, risky ride home.

7

Grady stayed away for two weeks. Even though it was something she'd once hoped for, Karen found herself watching the driveway day after day, regretting the attack of conscience that had had her sending him off after the snowstorm.

She knew he'd gotten home safely, not because *he'd* called, but because his housekeeper had. It was as if he'd taken her cue and decided to go one step further, cutting off all contact. The disappointment she had felt the second he had left had only grown in the days since that afternoon.

"You certainly look miserable," Gina declared when Karen drove into Winding River to have a spaghetti dinner at the restaurant where her friend was filling in as cook. Tony had used Gina's willingness to step in for him as the perfect excuse to take his wife on a long-promised trip to Italy.

"Just what every woman wants to hear," Karen said.

"Maybe I should have stayed home. I can probably boil pasta as well as you can."

"Ouch," Gina protested.

"Well, I can."

"But your pasta isn't homemade. Mine is."

"You've got me there, though I doubt I'd notice the difference."

"Which brings us back to miserable," Gina said, sitting down opposite her. "I've got some time to talk. We're not that busy. What's going on?"

"Nothing," Karen said honestly. There was nothing good or bad going on in her life. Every day it was just more of the same exhausting work and loneliness. She'd had a brief respite, thanks to Grady...which made it seem even more depressing now.

"Hey, this is *me* you're talking to, not those nosy in-laws of yours," Gina said. "Tell the truth. Is this about Grady Blackhawk?"

Karen's gaze shot up. "Why would you think that?"

"Just hazarding a guess. You two were spending a lot of time together until I told you I'd heard rumors floating around town about him being at the ranch the night of the snowstorm. Is he still coming by?"

"No."

"Did you two have a fight?"

"Not exactly."

Gina regarded her with exasperation. "This is like trying to get information out of the CIA."

Karen grinned despite herself. "Sorry. I'm not being deliberately tight-lipped. I just don't know what to say. After you called, I explained what you had said, and I told him it would be best if he left. He seemed to understand."

"But he hasn't been back," Gina concluded. "Hasn't called, either?"

"Nope."

Her gaze narrowed. "And that really bothers you, doesn't it? Were you starting to trust him, Karen? Maybe even like him? Was this turning into something for you?"

Karen felt compelled to deny it, even though the truth was that Gina had hit on the problem. "It was a pain in the neck at the outset," she said. "It's a pain in the neck now. Nothing's changed."

"Except that you've realized that the pain is actually a gorgeous, sexy man," Gina guessed, clearly not buying her disclaimer.

Karen sighed. "Yes, well, there is that."

"And that maybe you wouldn't mind getting to know him a lot better," Gina continued. "At least if there weren't all these obstacles in the way."

"But the obstacles are real," Karen said despondently. "Caleb, his parents, the ranch—how can I overlook any of that just because I've been feeling a little lonely and Grady has filled a void in my life?"

Gina stood up. "I'm getting you a glass of wine. No, a whole bottle of wine."

Karen regarded her with alarm. "I can't drink and drive all the way back to the ranch."

"You're not going to. You're going to drink and walk to my place and spend the night." Gina walked off toward the bar before Karen could protest.

While Gina was gone, the rest of her words sank in. When she returned, Karen studied her intently, then asked, "Since when do you have a place in Winding River?"

Gina winced. "You caught that, did you? Since I agreed to stick around and help Tony out. I couldn't keep crashing at my parents' place, so I rented an apartment here in town."

"For how long?"

Gina shrugged. "Yet to be determined," she said, casting a look across the dining room to a table by the window. The man who'd been hanging around off and on since the reunion was sitting there with an empty wineglass and a stack of paperwork. He looked as if he'd set up a permanent office right there. At the moment he was the only other customer.

"Do you want to tell me who he is and what's going on?" Karen asked, studying her friend's face with concern.

"Nope," Gina said.

Alarm rose as another thought occurred to her. "He's not stalking you, is he?"

"Not the way you mean," Gina said wryly. "Drink your wine. I'm going to fix your dinner. Forget spaghetti. This will make your mouth water. It will transport you straight to a trattoria in Rome."

Karen noticed that, on her way across the room, Gina paused to splash a little wine into the man's glass, though she carefully avoided his gaze, ignored whatever he said and kept right on going toward the kitchen, where the waitress was no doubt filing her nails.

Interesting, Karen thought. And troubling. Gina had never been known for her reticence. In fact, her bubbling enthusiasm and firsthand knowledge of Italian cuisine, combined with her innovative technique in the kitchen, had made her the perfect candidate for running a successful New York restaurant. She wasn't bubbling now, though. At least not with the mysterious stranger.

And in all these months there had been no mention of that New York bistro or who was running it in her absence. Direct questions had been ignored or evaded, which was very unlike the candid Gina of old.

Another mystery, Karen concluded with a sigh. Her life seemed filled with them lately. And Grady was the biggest one of all. Had he been insulted, even hurt, by her cavalier dismissal that day? Had he simply given up the fight? As incredible as that might be, it was a possibility.

Maybe he was simply away on a sudden trip. She knew he had a ranch, but he also had other business interests. Perhaps he'd had to go to Cheyenne or Denver or who knew where else he might have his finger in some corporate pie. Maybe this disappearing act had nothing to do with her at all.

She sighed at the thought. More troubling than his disappearance was her reaction to it. She missed him, dammit. As Gina had guessed, Karen had gotten used to Grady's company, exasperating as it was at times.

"It was just a habit," she muttered. Like anything else that was bad for her, it could be broken.

"Deep thoughts?" a familiar male voice inquired behind her.

Her head snapped around, her gaze clashed with Grady's, the wine she held with suddenly trembling fingers splashed on the table.

"Where have you been?" she asked before she could bite back the words. Even she recognized they were a stark contrast to her previous greetings demanding to know why he *was* there.

"Miss me?" he asked, a devilish twinkle in his eyes.

"No more than I would a swarm of bees," she retorted.

He slid into the seat opposite her, taking note of the second glass of wine. "Where's your date?"

"I'm here alone."

"Good. Then I'll join you," he said, taking a sip from the untouched extra glass Gina had left for herself.

Karen frowned, annoyed by his presumption and by her own eagerness to have him stay. "Grady, you can't just waltz in here and invite yourself to have dinner with me."

"Why not?"

"Just because."

"Because it's going to stir up more talk?" he asked, regarding her with a pointed look.

"That, too," she agreed.

"And what else?"

"Maybe I don't want to have dinner with you."

"Maybe?" he teased. "Let me know when you decide, then we'll discuss it. Until then, I'll just sit here and enjoy the wine and the vision of a beautiful woman sitting across the table from me."

"I don't want you here," she said with more conviction. "And you know perfectly well why it's a bad idea."

He studied her thoughtfully, then shook his head. "Yes, you do want me here. You just feel compelled to deny it. You're tough enough to stand up to a little idle gossip."

"If you believe that, then why did you leave the house when I asked you to?"

"Because my being there had clearly upset you and because I was way too tempted to kiss you senseless to make you forget that inconvenient conscience of yours."

"And now?"

"You're here. I happened by. I consider that fate." He smiled, then turned his attention to the menu. "What are you having?"

Because she knew from experience there was little point in arguing, she gave up. Besides, the truth was, she was so happy to see him, so happy to know that he wasn't furious with her, that her heart felt lighter than it had in days.

"I have no idea what I'm going to eat."

"You haven't ordered?"

"Gina wouldn't let me. She's fixing what suits her."

Grady nodded. "Maybe I'd better stick my head in the kitchen and make sure she fixes enough for two."

As he crossed the restaurant, Karen watched him intently. Her pulse had kicked into high gear the second she heard his voice and hadn't let up since. This wasn't good, she thought. Not good at all.

Gina came stalking out of the kitchen on Grady's

heels and followed him straight to the table. Her indignant gaze came to rest on Karen. "Are you okay with this?"

"He's not going away," Karen said with an air of resignation. "I guess I'll have to make the best of it."

"I can kick him out," Gina offered.

"You and who else?" Grady demanded, regarding Gina with amusement.

Gina's gaze strayed to her mysterious man. "I can muster up some help if I need it," she declared.

"No need," Karen said. "Grady will be on his good behavior." She looked at him. "Won't you?"

He winked. "The best. And I'm a really big tipper."

Gina grinned then, apparently satisfied that there would be no fireworks. "I'm counting on it."

After she'd gone, Grady looked at Karen. "She's very protective of you."

"As you've figured out by now, I'm sure, there are five of us who grew up together. We've been best friends ever since. There's nothing we wouldn't do if one of us needed something."

"And these are the friends who are willing to bankroll your vacation?"

"Some of them, yes."

"It must be nice to have a circle of friends you can count on."

Her gaze narrowed at that. "Don't you?"

"I have acquaintances," he said with no trace of self-pity. "And I have my grandfather. That's always been enough."

She thought she detected a rare note of wistfulness in his voice. "It has been? Not now?"

His gaze met hers. "No," he said quietly. "Not now."

Deep inside, she felt something give way. It was the last of her defenses crumbling...and for the life of her, she couldn't seem to regret it.

Even though she'd been anticipating—no, dreading—the call, hearing Anna Hanson's voice on the phone first thing the next morning would have been disconcerting enough for Karen under any conditions. But Grady had arrived not five minutes earlier. He was standing right next to her. That was enough to fill her with guilt. Added to the discovery she'd made the night before about just how vulnerable she was to this man and the guilt tripled.

"Anna," she said with forced enthusiasm. "How good to hear your voice."

"Is it?" Anna said in that dire tone that meant she had plenty to say to Karen, none of it good.

Anna Hanson hadn't entirely approved of her son's choice of a wife for reasons that had never been clear. Maybe she would have resented any woman chosen by her only son.

And when Caleb had died, Anna had all but said she believed Karen was responsible in some way. Had she known that Karen, in fact, blamed herself, she would have thrown it in her face at every opportunity. Even as it was, the tension between them had been thick ever since the funeral. Anna called only when she felt duty-bound to check in on the condition of the ranch, and seemed to have no concern about how Karen was managing with her grief.

"Of course it's good to hear from you," Karen said, scowling at Grady, who rolled his eyes, clearly aware of the reason for this call. "How's everything in Arizona? Is Carl doing okay?"

"He'd be much better if we hadn't been hearing certain things," Anna said, her tone grim.

Karen barely contained a sigh. At least the woman hadn't wasted any time getting to the point. "What things?"

"That you and that terrible Grady Blackhawk have been carrying on."

"Excuse me?" Karen said, though she was less stunned by the accusation than she would have been if Gina hadn't warned her that rumors were circulating about the night of the storm. She was only surprised that they'd taken so long to reach her in-laws.

"The first time I heard it, I dismissed it," Anna claimed, sounding self-righteous. "But we've had three calls this morning alone. Apparently everyone in the entire region knows that he's spending every single day at the ranch with you. That was bad enough, but then he was there overnight. Was he sleeping with you in my son's bed?"

Karen had always tried to ignore her mother-in-law's attitude for Caleb's sake. She had wanted a smooth coexistence, if a friendship was impossible. But Caleb was no longer a consideration. She no longer had to bite her tongue. Years of pent-up anger roared through her.

"How dare you," she said sharply, aware that Grady

had moved closer and laid a supportive hand on her shoulder. She shuddered at the contact, especially given the context of the conversation, but she didn't move away.

"I loved your son," she told Anna emphatically. "I never gave him or you any reason to doubt that. I certainly wouldn't do anything disrespectful of his memory under his roof."

"Then why is that man there every single day? Why did he spend the night? And how could you be seen in public with him last night, flaunting your affair in front of our friends?"

Karen wasn't exactly certain how to answer that. "He stayed the night because he was stranded by the storm. And whether you want to believe me or not, there is no affair."

"If you say so," Anna said skeptically. "But that doesn't explain what he's been doing there in the first place."

"He's been helping out."

"You surely don't need the help of the likes of Grady Blackhawk. Or are you running the ranch into the ground?" Anna asked bitterly.

Karen restrained her temper. Another outburst would solve nothing. "Anytime you and Carl would like to come back and take over running this place, you're more than welcome to. In fact, I'd be delighted to sell it back to you," she said to remind the woman of the fact that she and Caleb had taken out a mortgage of their own to pay his parents the money they needed to retire. It was the size of that mortgage that had kept them in debt, but Caleb had insisted it was only fair.

"Well, I never..." Anna said. "I'm going to put Carl on. Maybe he can get through to you."

Karen's relationship with Caleb's father had always been more cordial. He had been as hardworking as his son. In fact, if it had been up to Carl, he would have stayed on after the funeral to help out, but Anna had been insistent that they needed to get back to Arizona where she had a brisk social calendar lined up, now that she was happily ensconced in a fancy retirement village.

"Don't mind Anna," he said the minute he got on the line. "She just took Caleb's death real hard. She doesn't mean half of what she says."

"But the other half, she does," Karen pointed out wryly. "I've never known which half to listen to."

"Neither, would be my advice," he said. "You doing okay, Karen? Hank and Dooley giving you enough help?"

"We're managing."

"What about this Blackhawk fellow? Has he been hanging around, like Anna hears?"

Karen sighed, glancing over at the man in question. "He wants the ranch. He's made an incredible offer."

Maybe Carl would tell her to go ahead and sell. If she had his permission, maybe this wouldn't continue to eat away at her, and she could get away from the ranch and from Grady, finally escaping all the memories that haunted her here, good and bad.

"I don't want that ranch in Blackhawk hands," Carl

said flatly. "If you want to get out, I can understand
that. Nobody knows better than I do what a thankless
task it is trying to keep a small ranch running in the
black. Just promise me you'll sell to anybody but him.
Why should that man be rewarded after all the sneaky,
conniving things he and his family have done to us
through the years?"

Karen didn't have an argument for that. Grady had
been working hard to prove that she'd misjudged him,
but he hadn't offered any proof at all that he hadn't
been behind the sabotage of their herd. Someone had
infected those animals and set fire to that pasture. If
not Grady, then who? Until she knew for certain, Carl
was right. She couldn't sell to Grady.

"I won't do anything at all without talking it over
with you," she promised her father-in-law.

"That's good enough for me. You take care of yourself, Karen. I don't want you wearing yourself out at
your age out of some misguided sense of loyalty, you
hear me? If the time comes when you can't do it or even
if you just decide you want a different life, then you
grab your chance. I love that land, but it's just land. It's
not worth dying for, the way Caleb did."

"I love you," she said to him, tears stinging her eyes.

"You, too. You were a good wife to my boy and I
will always be grateful to you for that."

Karen slowly hung up the phone, not daring to look
at Grady.

"The Hansons, I presume," he said caustically. "Did
they manage to restore your sense of purpose?"

"I'm not going to discuss them with you," she said, already reaching for her coat. "I've got work to do."

"Where are you going?" he asked as she pushed past him.

"To the barn. Not all of us have time to fritter away."

He stopped her in her tracks. "Is that what you think I'm doing around here, frittering away my time?"

Her gaze clashed with his. "Isn't it? You have plenty of people working for you, I'm sure, people who do whatever needs doing on your ranch. I don't. If something needs to be done around here, I do it myself."

She jerked away from his grasp and ran outside, tears streaking down her face, all but turning to ice in the frigid February air. She headed straight for the barn and Ginger's stall, leaning against the horse for comfort, absorbing her body heat.

When her tears had dried and her nerves settled, she reached for a brush and began grooming the horse as a reward for her patience. The steady strokes were soothing to both of them. Eventually she was calm enough to think about what had just happened, not just on her phone, but in her kitchen.

She had taken Anna's attack out on Grady, no doubt about it. She'd figured he deserved it, since he was the cause of it. The plain truth was, Anna had ladled on guilt and Karen had accepted it because she was riddled with guilt already. Then she had lashed out at the cause.

She owed him an apology. She was the one who'd agreed weeks ago and again the night before to his visits. She had known there would be talk, known deep down that sooner or later it would reach Caleb's parents and that there would be a price to pay.

What was one more disagreement, one more disapproving lecture, from a woman who hadn't been any less critical when Caleb had been alive?

Finished in the barn, Karen walked slowly back to the house, where she overheard Grady on the phone.

"I want it taken care of today, do you understand me? This has dragged on long enough."

Her heart thudded wildly at the implication. Was he tired of trying to outwait her? Was he somehow going to force the issue?

She let the door slam behind her and stood in front of him, her pulse thundering. "What was that about?" she demanded. "What are you up to now?"

The dismay on his face seemed proof enough of his treachery.

"You will not get this ranch," she said, jabbing a finger in his chest. Because it felt so good, she did it again, and then again, until tears were streaming down her cheeks and she was pounding on him with her fists. "You won't, dammit! I won't let you."

Grady let her rant until she wound down. Then he gathered her close, murmuring soothing, nonsensical words. Slowly she relaxed against him. Every inch of her was suddenly awakened to the sensation of their bodies pressed together, of his arms tight around her, his breath fanning her cheek.

"It's okay, darlin'. It's okay," he reassured her. "That call wasn't about the ranch, I promise. It was about something else entirely."

She wanted to believe him, wanted to believe she had misunderstood, but how could she? She lifted her head from his chest to look into his eyes. What she saw there was even more troubling than the treachery she'd suspected. There was hunger and yearning and the kind of seething passion she'd almost forgotten existed.

His gaze locked with hers, he tenderly wiped the tears from her cheeks. His thumb caressed her mouth. The flash of heat in his eyes turned brighter. The air around them suddenly felt charged with electricity... and with anticipation.

And then, before Karen could guess his intentions, his mouth covered hers. The kiss was everything she'd ever imagined—and feared. It was devastating. It was pure temptation.

And Grady had stolen it.

If he could steal a kiss so cleverly when she'd been furious with him only moments before, would stealing the land she'd grown to despise be any challenge for him at all?

8

The first time Grady kissed her, Karen reacted with shock and dismay. How could she have let it happen? Why hadn't she stopped it, slapped him, done anything to show her displeasure?

A quick peck on the lips could be explained away as a hit-and-run gesture, hardly worthy of protest, but this had been more than that. It had gone on and on. There had been plenty of time for the act to register and draw an appropriate protest, rather than weak-kneed compliance.

The taste and feel of him was still on her lips as she took a step back and then another, trembling with what should have been outrage but wasn't.

"Why did you do that?" she demanded, her back braced against the sink as she finally—belatedly—put as much distance as possible between them.

"Because I've been wanting to forever," he said, not looking the least bit remorseful. In fact, he looked suspiciously as if he might intend to do it again.

And, God help her, Karen wanted him to. Her pulse was thundering like a summer storm. Her breasts ached. Any second the temptation to reach for him, to slip back into his embrace, would be too much for her.

There was no time to recite all the reasons why it was a terrible idea. Instead, she counted slowly to ten and back again, as if that alone would cool her yearning, as the same technique was used to temper anger.

She heard Grady's low chuckle and her gaze snapped to his to find amusement lurking in his eyes. "What?" she demanded.

"It's not going to work," he told her, clearly understanding the mental war she was waging. "I'm not going away and I *am* going to kiss you again. There's your fair warning. Never let it be said you didn't get one."

She swallowed hard, accepting the warning as pure truth. All that remained was the anticipation.

"When?" she asked, hoping that knowing that much would give her time to prepare, time to win the struggle with a desire that had caught her by surprise.

He tilted his head, studied her intently, then responded solemnly, "Now, I think. Before you work yourself into a frenzy worrying about it."

She gulped even as he claimed her mouth yet again with even more ingenuity, more wickedly clever passion. This time Karen wasn't simply an innocent bystander to the kiss, either. She kissed him back, responding to every persuasive nuance. All those protests and denials had been for nothing, because there was no mistaking that she was as caught up in the moment as he was.

Her head was spinning, her pulse racing. There was so much heat—too much. And the neediness, the overwhelming sense of urgency slammed through her with unexpected force, leaving her reeling. She had never expected to feel like this again, certainly never with Grady Blackhawk.

His name, his identity, finally snagged her attention, cutting through all the other commanding sensations. She was appalled and shaken that she was willingly in the arms of the enemy, though it was getting harder and harder to think of him that way.

Even so, it took her a long time to disengage from his embrace, longer still to take a faltering step back.

"This is my proof," she murmured, still dazed from the feel of his mouth on hers, but determined to inject a haughty note of disdain into her voice.

"Proof of what?" he said as he trailed more kisses down the side of her neck.

"That you're a scoundrel and a thief. You stole that kiss," she accused, managing to get the words out with a straight face, even though she knew it was a blatant lie. He had stolen nothing. She had given it to him willingly.

Laughter filled the air. Evidently he was no more convinced of the lie than she was.

"Maybe the first one, darlin'," he conceded. "But the second one you gave me of your own free will. You can't count that one against me, and I'd say it negates the implications of the first one. Once two people start to tango, so to speak, the blame pretty much falls by the wayside."

She frowned at him. "You would say that, wouldn't you? It serves your purpose."

"And what is my purpose?" he asked, studying her with mild curiosity.

"To get my land," she said at once, but she was no longer as certain as she had once been. A part of her was beginning to believe that he just might be after her, instead.

Grady went home that night and called his private detective, the one he'd had working for weeks to find out who might be behind the sabotage intended to take out the Hanson herd. Karen had walked in on him when he'd called Jarrod Wilcox earlier from her kitchen. He wanted to reemphasize to the man the urgency of the investigation. He needed results fast. He was growing less and less certain about why, though.

At first, he'd merely wanted Karen to know the truth so she could begin to trust him. He'd hoped that that would be the first step to getting her to sell the ranch to him. Now it was all tangled up in something personal. He wanted her trust, because he couldn't bear to see that condemning look in her eyes one more time.

"I told you this afternoon that this is all but impossible," Jarrod told him. "For one thing, the incidents took place a year ago or more. If there was any kind of physical evidence, it's long gone. Seems to me like you're throwing good money after bad by keeping me on your payroll."

"If that's your attitude, maybe I am," Grady snapped. "Maybe somebody else would approach this with a more positive attitude, maybe be a little more aggressive."

"Anybody legitimate would tell you what I'm telling you—forget about this."

"What about the mortgage? Surely there's paperwork about any attempt to buy up the Hanson note. The president of the bank didn't just make that up. He either had a letter or a face-to-face meeting."

"He claims the latter, and he claims it was with you," Jarrod said.

"Since I've never set foot in that bank, he's lying, then. Who's paying him to lie?"

"Have you considered asking him that yourself? It'll be a whole lot harder for him to pull off the lie if you're looking him in the eye."

Grady sighed. "You have a point. I'll get on that first thing in the morning. Meantime, I want you to look into every person who owns land adjacent to the Hanson ranch. Either somebody wants that land for themselves or they have a reason for keeping me from having it."

"Will do."

"By the end of the week," Grady added.

"It's Wednesday now."

"Then you'll just have to get your butt in gear, won't you?"

Jarrod sighed. "I'll be in touch."

Grady impatiently jammed the phone back in its cradle, only to realize that his grandfather was standing in the doorway, regarding him with curiosity. He crossed the room in three quick strides to embrace the man who meant more to him than anyone.

Even at seventy-five his grandfather was an impressive man. His thick black hair fell past his shoulders in braids that were streaked with gray. His tanned face was carved with deep lines, his black eyes intense, his bearing proud.

Thomas Blackhawk took a step back, his hands on Grady's shoulders, and studied his face. "You look troubled."

"Exasperated," Grady said.

"Perhaps you should spend some time with me up in the mountains," Thomas suggested. "It might give you some peace and some perspective."

"I imagine it would," Grady agreed. "But right now I don't have the time."

His grandfather's weathered face creased with a half smile. "All the more reason to come, don't you think?"

"I'll think about it," Grady promised. He gestured to a chair. "Can I get you something? Coffee? A drink? I have some of that disgusting orange soda you love so much."

"That would be good. And a man who lives on caffeine has no room to criticize my choice of beverage."

Grady brought his grandfather the bottle of soda. "What brings you all the way down here? Usually if I want to see you this time of year, I have to come to you."

"I have heard some troubling things."

Grady's gaze narrowed. "About?"

"You."

Uh-oh, Grady thought. The meddling Hansons were innocent babes in the wood compared to his grandfather. "Oh?" he said, keeping his expression neutral.

"You have been spending time with the Hanson widow, true?"

"Yes."

"Why? You are not pressuring her to sell you the land, are you?"

"We've discussed it," he said, choosing his words carefully. They had been over this ground before. But Grady believed that despite his grandfather's denials in recent years, he wanted that land returned to the Blackhawk family. He'd just tired of the futile battle.

His grandfather regarded him with resignation. "Why can't I make you see that this is unnecessary? For years I told your father to let it be, but he refused to listen. You are the same. That land means nothing to me."

"It is Blackhawk land," Grady said fiercely.

"It *was* Blackhawk land."

"It was stolen from our ancestors."

"At a troubling time in our history," his grandfather agreed. He peered at Grady intently. "Tell me something. Do you need this land for your ranch?"

"No, of course not. It's not even near here."

"Nor do I," his grandfather said. "So why are you stirring things up, if it is no longer of any importance to us?"

"It's a matter of principle," Grady said.

"Is this principle more important than the woman?"

So, Grady thought with a sigh, his grandfather had

heard that there was more between Grady and Karen than a battle over acres of ranch land.

"One thing has nothing to do with the other," Grady replied, mouthing the lie that was becoming second nature to him.

"Explain that to me," his grandfather said. "It seems to me the two are inevitably intertwined."

"I can keep them separate," Grady insisted.

"Can she?" Thomas Blackhawk rose stiffly to his feet. "Think long and hard before you choose unwisely and trade one thing for another. It would not be the first time one of our people made that mistake."

"Meaning?"

"That things are not always what they seem at first glance. And there are many ways to bring things full circle."

Grady regarded him with impatience. "And I suppose that your enigmatic response is all you intend to say?"

"For now," his grandfather agreed, his eyes twinkling.

"Riddles," Grady muttered. "I ask for advice, and all I get are riddles."

"You are the brightest of my grandsons. Use your intelligence to figure them out."

"And if I can't?"

"Then listen to your heart."

His grandfather's words lingered long after he had gone. Grady was up all night thinking, but he couldn't seem to convince himself to stray from his original course of action. For too many years he had lived with the need to see that land restored to the Blackhawks. The memory of his ancestors deserved that, even if those living no longer thought it mattered.

It was only after hours of tossing and turning that he understood the second part of what his grandfather had been trying to tell him. In effect, his grandfather had given his blessing to a relationship between Grady and Karen. But what was that nonsense about bringing things full circle?

Another riddle, he concluded with a sigh. His grandfather was a master of them. Unfortunately, Grady seldom had the patience to unravel them, not with the very real mystery of the sabotage to the Hanson herd standing between him and his goal.

Grady walked into the First National Bank of Winding River promptly at nine o'clock and headed straight for the president's office. Ignoring the secretary's indignant protests, he strolled into Nathaniel Grogan's office.

"Shall I call security, sir?" Miss Ames asked, casting a look of alarm in Grady's direction.

Grogan waved her off. "I can handle the gentleman."

"Could be you're being overly optimistic," Grady observed when the door had closed behind the indignant secretary.

"What's on your mind, Grady?"

Grady nodded at the acknowledgment of his identity. He'd known Nate for years, so it seemed highly unlikely that the man would have mistaken an impostor for him, which meant that face-to-face meeting he'd claimed had been a blatant lie.

"I'm sure you can figure that out," Grady told him.

"The mortgage on the Hanson land."

Grady gave him an exaggerated look of approval. "Bingo."

"What about it?"

"Apparently you told Caleb Hanson that I tried to buy up that mortgage. You told the same thing to Jarrod Wilcox. Yes or no?"

"I told them that, yes."

"Even though you know it's a blatant lie."

"I don't know that." Grogan reached into his desk drawer and pulled out a file. "Here's the paperwork, all filled out nice and proper. That's your signature at the bottom."

Grady's gaze narrowed as he studied the paper. "It's a damn fine forgery," he said at last.

"Are you telling me that's not your handwriting?" the man asked, clearly taken aback.

"That's what I'm telling you. I never filled out that paperwork. And whoever witnessed it and said I did is lying."

The old man seemed shaken by his vehemence. "Let me get Miss Ames in here. That's her notary seal on this."

He buzzed for his secretary. "In here now, Miss Ames."

The door opened at once, but the woman was slow to enter. "Yes, Mr. Grogan?"

"I want you to take a look at something."

She edged around Grady, then took the papers her boss held out.

"Is that your stamp on there?" Grogan asked.

She looked it over carefully, then nodded.

"And is this the man you saw sign those papers?" he demanded.

Another flicker of alarm flashed in her eyes as she glanced Grady's way. Her response was inaudible.

"What was that?" Grogan snapped. "Speak up, Miss Ames."

"I said no, sir. I've never met this gentleman."

"*This* is Grady Blackhawk," Nate told her. "Now my next question is, who in hell signed the papers?"

Miss Ames seemed to shrink inside her smart business suit. "I don't actually know," she said, then burst into tears.

Both men stared at her incredulously, but Grady was the first to speak. "Aren't you supposed to witness something before using your seal?"

Her head bobbed as the tears continued to fall. "Yes, but these were on my desk one morning with a note to put the seal on them and leave the file for Mr. Grogan. That's what I did. I thought it must be really urgent." She regarded her boss with dismay. "I thought it was what you wanted, that it wouldn't matter if I broke the rules since you were the one telling me to do it."

The bank president simply stared at her. "I know you've only been here a short time, but have I ever asked you to do anything dishonest?"

"No, sir. That's why I thought it must be very important."

"And you have no idea who put the papers there?"

"None. They were there when I arrived for work. You were in your office, so I was sure you'd left them, just like the note said."

"I don't suppose you kept the note," Nate said.

She shook her head. "No, sir."

Grogan sighed heavily. "You may go, Miss Ames."

"You're...you're not firing me?"

"Not at this time," he said. "Not until we get all of this sorted out, at any rate. But if I find you know more than you've told us just now, you *will* be out of here. Am I making myself perfectly clear?"

Her head bobbed. She left the room looking so terrified that Grady almost felt sorry for her.

"I apologize," Grogan said. "I don't know what she could have been thinking."

"That she was doing you a favor, I'm sure," Grady told him wryly. "Obviously she's very loyal to you."

"Or to someone else," Grogan said wearily. "I'll straighten this out. I promise you that. And I will call Mrs. Hanson and explain things to her."

Grady nodded. "I wish you would. And one more thing. Were you the one who warned Caleb Hanson about this so-called attempt on my part to buy up his mortgage?"

"Yes. I saw to it that the application was denied and then told him what was going on. He and his family have banked here for years. I thought he had a right to know."

"Who else could have left those papers on your

secretary's desk, especially before she arrived in the morning?"

"Anyone who works here. The other employees arrive here around eight. Miss Ames drops her son off at school. She doesn't arrive until closer to eight-thirty. It wouldn't take a minute to drop off the file. People leave papers on Miss Ames's desk all day long. No one would think a thing about it."

"But it couldn't have been an outsider, correct? It had to be someone working here?"

"So it seems." He looked Grady in the eye. "I'll get to the bottom of it. You have my word on that."

Grady nodded. He didn't doubt that Nathaniel Grogan's intentions were honorable, but as Jarrod Wilcox had already pointed out, this incident, like the others, had taken place long ago. Finding answers wasn't going to be simple. People's memories faded. Except, of course, for the person who'd done it. He or she wouldn't have forgotten. But could the wrongdoer be persuaded to tell the truth?

"I'll hold you to that," he said as Nate walked with him onto the main floor of the bank.

Just as they stepped into the marble-floored lobby, Karen walked through the front door, took one look at the two of them and turned pale. Then bright patches of color flared in her cheeks right before she turned and fled.

"Dammit," Grady muttered, and took off after her. He knew what she was thinking, knew she was adding up two and two and coming up with a hundred and ten or whatever number would be most damning.

He caught up with her halfway down the block and fell into step beside her. She didn't even glance over at him.

"Good morning," he said, being deliberately upbeat.

"I have nothing to say to you."

"That's fine, because I have quite a lot to say to you," he said, steering her into Stella's before she could protest. He knew her well enough to understand that she wouldn't make a scene, not here in front of her friend Cassie, who was staring at them, clearly ready to intercede.

"This looks like a nice quiet place to talk," Grady said tightly as he aimed for the booth in the back.

He stood there until she sank onto the seat with a resigned sigh, then he slid in next to her just to be sure she couldn't bolt before they had this out.

"Everything okay?" Cassie asked, her worried gaze on Karen.

"Fine," Grady said. "Bring us two cups of coffee." He glanced at Karen. "Have you had breakfast yet?"

"It's after ten. What do you think?"

He bit back a grin, then glanced up at Cassie. "I guess the coffee will do for now."

He noted that Karen's hands were folded primly on the table, that her gaze was everywhere but on him. Those angry patches of color in her cheeks hadn't faded. He warned himself to give it another couple of minutes before saying anything. Maybe once she'd had her coffee, her temper would die down and she'd be ready to listen to reason.

Cassie brought the steaming cups to the table, then

lingered, but when neither Karen or Grady looked up, she sighed and walked away.

"I suppose you were wondering what I was doing with Nate Grogan," he said finally.

"I don't think it takes much imagination to figure that out," she snapped. "Did he agree to let you buy up the mortgage this time?"

"I never tried to buy the blasted mortgage," Grady retorted. "Not today. Not two years ago."

"So you say."

"Ask Grogan. He intends to call you to explain what happened anyway."

"I'm sure he'll say whatever you want him to say," she said.

"He didn't before, did he? Wasn't he the one who called Caleb to tell him what I was supposedly up to?"

She hesitated at that. "Yes," she conceded.

"Well, today he found out that I was not the person who filled out that original paperwork. I'm sure he'll tell you that if you ask."

She turned to him at last, her blue eyes filled with confusion. "But the papers...?"

"They were forged by someone and later notarized by a loyal secretary who thought she was doing what Grogan wanted her to do."

Her gaze searched his and Grady thought he saw a faint flicker of hope in her eyes. "Honestly?"

"I won't lie to you, Karen. I haven't before and I won't start now. I want that land, but I have never done anything devious or underhanded to try to get it."

A sigh seemed to shudder through her at that. "I want to believe you," she admitted.

"Then do it," he pleaded. "Believe me. Trust me."

"If only it were that simple," she whispered.

She didn't have to say what she was really thinking. Grady knew. Caleb had labeled him the enemy. How could he possibly overcome the accusations of a dead man, especially a dead man that she had loved with all her heart?

At that moment, for the first time, Grady understood the true meaning of hatred and jealousy. He hated Caleb Hanson, not for all of the lies he had believed about Grady and shared with his wife in the past, but for his ability to rob them of a future even from the grave.

9

Something had changed in that split second when Grady had looked into Karen's eyes at Stella's. It was as if a light had gone off inside him, as if he'd been defeated. It wasn't long before he'd made his excuses and left, leaving her staring after him in confusion.

She had told herself then that it would pass, that things would return to normal, that he would pop up when she least expected him at the ranch, but it hadn't happened that way. Just as he'd disappeared before when she'd hurt him, he hadn't been around for days now. Even Hank and Dooley, who had regarded him with suspicion from the beginning, had commented on his absence.

"Thought he was becoming a permanent fixture around here," Dooley said, a hint of disapproval plain in his voice.

"Well, he wasn't," Karen said defensively. Hiding her confusion behind anger, she added, "And we don't have time to stand around gabbing about a man who had no business being here in the first place."

"Fine by me," Dooley said.

"And me," Hank said fervently. "The boss never did like him."

"I'm the boss now," Karen reminded him. "You need to worry about what *I* like."

Dooley's eyes widened. "Are you saying you trust a scoundrel like Grady Blackhawk?"

"He's not a scoundrel," she said. "And what I was saying is that you both have work to do. Didn't I ask you to finish checking that fence today? I saw another section down when I drove back here yesterday. We're going to be moving the herd in a few weeks and I don't want them wandering off our land. We can't afford to lose a single head."

"Yes, ma'am," Dooley said, his tone respectful, even if he was regarding her with a worried frown that suggested he wasn't entirely certain she was in command of things.

After both men had left, she sat down with a sigh. Who was she kidding? She might be in charge, but she was only holding on to this place by a thread. She knew well enough what needed to be done, but she didn't have the resources to make much of it happen. Lately it seemed she lacked the stamina as well. She simply wanted to crawl under the covers and sleep the winter away.

For a brief time Grady's presence had stirred her out of that depressing inertia, but now that he was no longer around, she couldn't seem to shake it.

The welcome ringing of the phone jarred her out of her misery.

"Hey, girl," Lauren said, her cheerful voice bringing a much needed smile to Karen's lips.

"Hey, yourself. What's up in Tinseltown? I need some hot Hollywood gossip to perk me up."

"Since when do you care about celebrity gossip?"

"It's the closest I'm likely to come to having any glamour in my life," Karen said. "Come on. Spill something absolutely titillating."

"Sorry. I've been holed up trying to learn my lines for this new movie. Brad Pitt could get married and I wouldn't know it."

"Brad Pitt *did* get married," Karen pointed out with a chuckle. "Ages ago, in fact."

"See what I mean? I'm oblivious."

"What good is it having a friend who's a superstar if you never know any hot secrets?"

"I do know one," Lauren retorted. "I know that a certain rancher has been seen hanging out with her mortal enemy. Quite an intense little tête-à-tête from what I heard."

"Cassie blabbed," Karen said with a resigned sigh. She should have known her friend would make way too much out of that public appearance she and Grady had made at Stella's. It had probably taken all of fifteen seconds for her to spread the word to the others.

"I never reveal a source," Lauren said loftily. "So, what's the scoop with the sexy Mr. Blackhawk? Are you two becoming an item after all?"

"Don't be ridiculous," Karen snapped, pushing back

the thought of those two steamy kisses. "Even if I was attracted to him, which I'm not, how could I get involved with Grady?"

"Because of Caleb," Lauren said flatly.

"Of course because of Caleb."

"You have to live your life for *you* now," Lauren reminded her, her tone gentle. "I'm not saying you shouldn't remember Caleb, but you can't take on his baggage, Karen. If you like Grady, if you want to spend time with him, that's your decision to make."

"Not according to the Hansons," Karen said dryly.

"Oh, what do they know?" Lauren said, dismissing the importance of the opinion of Karen's former in-laws. "Besides, they're in Arizona."

"With a direct hotline to the gossip in Wyoming," Karen reported.

"Ignore them," Lauren advised.

"How can I? They're Caleb's parents."

"So naturally they're going to be upset if you get involved with someone new. They'll get over it."

"Not if it's Grady," Karen said flatly.

"Then you *are* interested," Lauren said, seizing on her slip and obviously concluding that Karen regretted being unable to act on her fascination with the man.

Karen sighed. "I don't know how I feel about him."

"Is he pressuring you to decide that right this second?"

"No. Actually he hasn't been around much lately. Not since the morning Cassie saw us together. I think something I said or did upset him, but I can't imagine what. He's a very complex man."

"A break may be exactly what you need. Give it some time. You're a smart woman. You'll sort out your feelings when the time is right." Lauren hesitated, then asked, "Do you want me to come home? I'm a pretty good judge of character."

"Oh, really? I can list two lousy marriages that say otherwise."

"Ouch," Lauren said. "No one can see their own mistakes until it's too late. Everyone else's, however, are crystal clear. An outside opinion wouldn't hurt and I can be there tomorrow."

"No. You've put your career on hold enough for me as it is. I can't ask you to come running every time I get scared."

"Scared?" Lauren teased. "Of Grady or yourself?"

"Maybe both," Karen admitted.

"You listen to me, Karen Hanson. Nobody I know has a better head on her shoulders than you do. Trust your instincts. And anytime you want me there for backup, you call. I can drop everything and be there in a few hours. To tell the truth, I like feeling needed for a change. Say the word and I'll be back there mucking out stalls and working with the horses for as long as you need me."

Karen was so startled by the heartfelt sincerity of the offer that she was at a loss for words. It wasn't the first time the offer had been made, but something in her friend's voice suggested that she was truly hoping to be asked to rush home.

"Stunned into silence?" Lauren asked.

"Truthfully, yes. You've hinted around about wanting to come home for good, but that's the first time you've come right out and said it. What's wrong, Lauren? What haven't you been telling us?"

"There's nothing wrong," her friend assured her. "Nothing I can put my finger on anyway. I'm sure whatever it is, I'll get over it. But the offer stands, no matter what. If you need me, just say the word."

"Thank you," Karen said softly. "And…Lauren?"

"What?"

"If you need to be here, don't wait for an invitation. I've got a room waiting anytime you want to come. I mean that. And if it's hard physical work you're looking for, I can supply that, too."

"I know you mean it. and I love you for saying it. Take care, sweetie."

"You, too."

Karen had barely hung up when she realized she wasn't alone. She turned to find Grady standing just outside the screen door. Still troubled by her conversation with Lauren, she barely spared him a glance. And this time, she refused to get her hopes up. His habit of coming and going when she least expected it was too disconcerting.

"Anything wrong?" he asked, his expression concerned as he stepped inside without waiting to be invited.

"Not with me," she said, injecting a false note of cheer into her voice. She was not going to discuss Lauren's odd mood with a man she didn't entirely trust. If it wound up being splashed all over the tabloids, she would never forgive herself.

Even as the thought of Grady pitching such personal information to a tabloid ran through her mind, she scolded herself over the absurdity of it. Why would he do such a thing? He certainly didn't need the money. And he was trying to prove to her that he was trustworthy. Wouldn't such a deliberate act of betrayal be counterproductive? It just proved how deep her own distrust ran.

"I thought I'd stop in and let you know that I'll be out helping Hank and Dooley today. The fence along the highway is down."

"I know. I spotted it yesterday. They're out there now. They can handle it."

"I'm sure they'd be grateful for an extra pair of hands."

Her gaze narrowed. "Look, it's been obvious the past few days that you have a life of your own to live. You don't have to keep doing this."

"Doing what?"

"Pitching in around here. Stay home and take care of your own chores."

Amusement lurked in the depths of his eyes. "So you did miss me?"

"I never said that."

"You didn't have to."

She frowned at him. "Is that why you stayed away, so I'd miss you?"

"No," he said curtly. "Now let me make this clear for the last time. I don't mind helping out around here. I like the company."

She regarded him with skepticism. "Hank and Dooley's?"

"Hardly," he said, grinning at last. "But the boss lady has a certain way about her that I find intriguing."

Her heart fluttered at the compliment. "Is that so?"

He nodded. "Besides that, she owes me dinner. Our deal's not over."

"I thought you'd forgotten about that. Besides, the two weeks were up long ago."

"We missed a few nights," he reminded her.

"I never gave you a rain check."

"But you wouldn't renege on a deal, would you? Doesn't that go against that conscience of yours?"

"I suppose."

"That's settled, then. And just so you know, I have a real hankering for apple pie."

"Stella's is good," she told him.

"But I'll bet yours is better." His gaze caught hers. "Still warm from the oven with a big scoop of vanilla ice cream melting into all the little crevices."

Karen swallowed hard. Somehow he had managed to make a perfectly ordinary slice of pie sound like something wickedly sensual. Or was that just her state of mind?

"How about it?" he asked. "Pie for dessert?"

She gave him a resigned look. "I'll see what I can do."

He winked at her. "I'll be counting on it."

Don't, she thought to herself after he'd gone. *Don't count on me, Grady.*

Because the truth was, if push came to shove, she

had no idea which of the men in her life she'd choose…
a ghost or the flesh-and-blood man who was tempting
her more and more each day, despite his entirely too
unpredictable comings and goings.

Grady heard the argument long before he spotted
Hank and Dooley.

"I say we've got to tell her," Hank shouted fiercely.
"The woman has a right to know that someone deliberately cut this fence."

"Mrs. Hanson's got enough on her mind," Dooley
argued. "We're taking care of it, aren't we? There's no
harm done. Why get her all worked up about a problem
that won't exist after today?"

Grady crested the hill and spotted the two hands
squared off, a section of barbed wire in Hank's hands.

"I'm telling you she needs to know that somebody's
out to get her," Hank countered. "She ought to be calling the sheriff. This isn't right." His gaze narrowed as
he looked at Dooley. "Or is there some particular reason you don't want the sheriff involved?"

The old man drew back his fist and aimed a punch
straight for Hank's face. It landed solidly, snapping the
younger man's head back.

Grady leaped from the saddle and got between the
two men. "Okay, enough. What the hell's gotten into
you two?"

Whatever distrust they felt toward him was apparently less than they were feeling about each other at
the moment, because both men started hurling accusations so fast and furious, Grady could barely keep up.

"Hold it!" he commanded finally. "One at a time. Dooley, you first."

Hank glared at Grady as a look of satisfaction spread across the old man's face.

"Like I was trying to tell this pea-brain here, the boss already has too much on her mind," Dooley said. "There's no need to worry her with this latest incident, since we're taking care of it."

"The incident being that someone deliberately cut the barbed wire?" Grady concluded.

"Exactly," Hank said, holding out the section of wire. "Cut through, clean as a whistle. This is new fence, too. Put it in myself just last spring."

Grady didn't like the implication one bit. Once again, someone was trying to sabotage the Hanson operation. It didn't take a genius to figure out that the blame was going to fall on his shoulders sooner or later. That raised those same two interesting possibilities again. Either someone wanted to force Karen out of business for their own reasons, or they wanted to cast more doubt on his integrity simply to keep her from selling to him.

"Who owns the land on the other side of the highway?" he asked Dooley.

"Tate McDonald."

The name meant nothing to Grady. "Has he been around long?"

"Bought the place eight, maybe nine years ago," Hank said. "About the same time I came to work for the Hansons."

"Has he been looking to expand?" Grady asked.

Both men exchanged a look, then shook their heads.

"He's not here much," Dooley said. "Spends most of his time in California, from what I hear. His foreman runs the place. They keep a small herd over there, nothing like what Duke Walters had when he owned it."

That didn't mean that McDonald didn't aspire to having a much bigger operation in the future. Grady resolved to find out what he could about the man.

He already knew that the land to the west had been owned by the same family for sixty years—the Oldhams—and that the property due north belonged to Jack Fletcher, a cantankerous ex-rodeo star who trained horses and whose daughter, Maggie, had a difficult streak of her own. None of them struck him as the kind of people who'd try to force a neighbor out of business, but he'd have Jarrod Wilcox do some checking, just in case.

Grady took the piece of wire from Hank. "I'll hang on to this. For the time being, let's not say anything to Karen. Both of you keep your ears open when you go into town. See if anybody's bragging about being up to some mischief out this way. I'll check out this Tate McDonald."

Both men regarded him skeptically. "Isn't it to your advantage if somebody *is* stirring up trouble for Mrs. Hanson?" Hank asked. "If she goes under, you can buy this place for next to nothing."

"I've already made her an offer for a good deal more than the land is worth. I won't renege on that."

Dooley snorted. "Doesn't mean you wouldn't like to get it for less."

"You can believe me or not, but I'm not interested in ruining her," Grady said flatly. "She'll get a fair price if she decides to sell. And if she sells, it won't be because I've done something to make her desperate."

Dooley regarded him intently. "And you swear you're going to get to the bottom of this latest damage?" he asked.

"I swear it."

Once again, the two men exchanged a look, then seemed to reach a conclusion.

"All right, then," Dooley said. "But we're keeping an eye on you."

Grady bit back a grin at the warning. "I wouldn't have it any other way."

Karen was getting better at gauging Grady's moods. She didn't allow herself to consider what that meant. All that mattered was that he hadn't been himself since he'd returned from working on the downed fence. He was virtually silent all through dinner and as soon as he'd finished his serving of pot roast, he excused himself.

Karen scowled as he rose from his place at the table. "Okay, that's it. Sit back down, Grady Blackhawk."

Clearly startled by the command, he stared at her. "What?"

"I said to sit down." She frowned until he'd complied. "Now tell me what has you in such a foul mood."

"I'm not in a foul mood," he insisted, looking vaguely bewildered by the accusation.

"Okay, maybe that's the wrong word, but you certainly aren't yourself. You haven't been since you got back."

"I just have a few things on my mind."

"That's obvious enough. What things?"

"Nothing worth mentioning," he insisted.

"Or nothing you want to get into with me?" she challenged.

A guilty expression passed across his face. "Why would you say something like that?"

"Because you usually have plenty to say. Because you're the one who wanted to share these little getting-to-know-you meals, and you haven't said two words all evening. Because you all but begged me to bake you an apple pie, and now that I have, you're about to walk out the door without even tasting it. I'd say the evidence is overwhelming."

A grin tugged at his lips. "Is that so, Sherlock? Any other clues you'd care to mention?"

"No, I think that about does it," she said, arms folded across her chest. "I've said my piece. Now it's time for you to say yours."

"And if I don't?"

"Then you'll sit there until you think better of it."

This time he had the audacity to laugh. "Who's going to make me?"

"Me," she declared.

"Oh, really? Now that is a fascinating prospect. Care to share your tactics for keeping a man who's twice your size where you want him?"

"You don't want to know," she said. "Trust me, though. I can do it." She wasn't exactly sure how, but she would manage it, if it came to that. "Now, talk. What happened when you were with Hank and Dooley? Did the three of you get into it about something? I know they distrust you, but they're just being protective of me."

"I know that. And I respect the fact that they're loyal to you."

"Then you didn't have an argument?"

"No."

She regarded him with exasperation. "But something did happen?"

He beamed at her. "I'll take that pie now. Make it a big piece with lots of ice cream on top."

"Not a chance. It's too late for that. I want to know what went on out there today or that pie goes straight into the garbage."

Grady sighed heavily. "You're a very persistent woman, you know that?"

"Yes," she said proudly.

"It's a very annoying trait."

"I suppose that depends on your point of view," she countered.

"I imagine I could distract you, if I wanted to," he said, eyeing her thoughtfully.

"I doubt that."

"Are you challenging me to try?"

Karen spotted the spark of mischief in his eyes and realized that she'd just made a serious tactical error. Before she could correct it, he was on his feet and reaching for her.

With a look of grim determination, he slanted his

mouth across hers. Whatever his intention, though, whether to silence her or challenge her, it quickly became something else entirely. The coaxing kiss turned greedy. Gentle persuasion became breath-stealing hunger.

All thoughts about winners and losers in their battle of wits fled as they set a new, common goal: passion. Karen's head went spinning, her pulse ricocheted wildly, her blood heated and pooled low in her belly.

This is wrong, she thought. *Wrong, wrong, wrong.*

And yet she couldn't seem to stop, couldn't seem to pause even long enough to catch her breath. A frantic neediness was making her breasts ache and her body eager. Grady had moved beyond kisses now. His hands were everywhere, gentle, persuasive, provocative.

Karen felt the buttons on her dress give way, felt the cool air against her overheated skin, then the warmth of Grady's clever caresses as they streaked fire in their path. She wanted things she had never expected to feel again, wanted to feel gloriously alive and loved and irresistible. Grady was giving her all of that with his wicked kisses and increasingly intimate touches.

"Not here," she pleaded, when her dress was in a tangle around her feet and her bra was across the room.

"Tell me where," he said, scooping her into his arms.

"Upstairs."

At the top of the stairs, he hesitated, and so did she. Not in her room, not in the bed she'd shared with Caleb.

"Over there," she said, gesturing toward the guest room with its colorful quilt on an antique iron bed.

There were no memories in this room, no personal mementos of her years with Caleb.

The sheets were crisp and smelled of sunshine, not the lingering—or imagined—scent of a familiar after-shave. The mattress was firm, not shaped by years of accommodating two bodies that slept curved together in the middle.

She couldn't help thinking of the contrasts as Grady lowered her onto the bed, then slid in next to her, his gaze tender as he slowly stripped away her remaining clothes. The trip to the second floor had eased the tension, the frantic need, but with one glance, one touch, he was able to bring it back until she was lying there trembling and desperate for the feel of him deep in-side her.

She tugged at his shirt with impatient fingers, push-ing it up and over his head, then setting to work on the snap of his jeans with total concentration. She couldn't seem to manage it, though. Her fingers trembled and, next to the heat of his bare belly, they felt icy cold. He rested his hand atop hers, then met her gaze.

"It's okay. There's no rush," he reminded her.

"There is," she insisted, struggling to free herself from his grasp so that she could finish what they had begun.

She almost missed the flash of wariness in his eyes, it came and went so quickly. But it had been there and for an instant, she felt a flicker of shame.

"I'm sorry," she whispered, her voice ragged.

"Why?"

"I don't want you to think I'm using you, that I just want this to be over with."

His smile was tinged with unmistakable sadness. "Isn't that the truth, though? At least part of it?"

"Maybe," she finally confessed in a small voice. "I want you, Grady, but I'm scared."

"Of what?"

"That it's for all the wrong reasons, just like you said."

He rolled away from her, locked his hands behind his head and stared at the ceiling until his breathing steadied. Karen felt bereft, but she didn't pursue him, didn't dare touch him the way she desperately wanted to.

Finally, when she thought she wouldn't be able to bear the tension building inside her for another second, he reached for her hand, pressed it to his lips. "Another time," he said quietly and without rancor.

Tears stinging her eyes, she reached for the sheet, clutched it to her bare breasts. "Are you sure?"

His gaze met hers. "Oh, darlin', if I am sure of anything in this world, it's that. There will be another time for this, for the two of us. And when it happens, we'll both be sure it's the right thing for the right reasons."

A smile curved his lips. "Now come over here and cuddle up beside me."

Sheet firmly tucked in place, she slid closer until she could feel his heat warming her and the steady beating of his heart beneath her ear. And in that moment, her heart filled with gratitude and maybe something else, something that felt an awful lot like the first amazing moments of falling head over heels in love.

10

With Karen curved securely against him, Grady was having a hard time thinking straight, but he forced himself to concentrate on that severed barbed wire. It was about the only thing sufficiently fascinating to distract him from the warmth of her body curled next to his.

First chance he got, he was going to track down Tate McDonald and then get his private investigator doing checks on all of the neighboring property owners. One of them was holding a grudge against Karen, or against him. Since he'd never even met McDonald and barely knew the Fletchers or the Oldhams, it seemed likely the dispute was with Karen. Either way, it needed to be settled before things got ugly.

Karen sighed softly, her breath stealing across his bare chest and ruining his concentration. He thought he'd been rather clever at distracting her from all of her questions earlier, even if the outcome had been less than what he'd anticipated. He could wait until she was ready to make love, even if it was getting more and more difficult.

She moaned and snuggled more tightly against him. The sheet slipped away, revealing way too much of an alluring breast, a taut dusky nipple. His breath caught in his throat as he struggled yet again against temptation. He was more sinner than saint, and this was too much.

Gently he shook her awake, tugging the sheet back into place as her eyes blinked open, registering first surprise, then sleepy delight, then worry as she realized she had fallen asleep in his arms. The reactions pretty much summed up their relationship, a curious mix that had kept Grady off guard for weeks now. He'd tried staying away twice now, but it hadn't worked. He'd concluded he was going to have to see this through to whatever ending it was headed for.

"I must have fallen asleep," she said, gathering the sheet more securely around her. "I'm sorry."

"Don't be. There is nowhere I'd rather be."

"Really?" she asked skeptically. "You seemed to be in an awfully big hurry earlier. Don't think I've forgotten that."

He sighed. "I was hoping you had."

"Not that the distraction wasn't fascinating," she said, "but I have a very good memory."

"Apparently," he agreed, thinking of more than her interest in his earlier activities. She also had a very long memory when it came to her late husband's prejudices.

"So?" she prodded.

He regarded her with feigned innocence. "So?"

She nudged him sharply in the ribs with her elbow. "Don't play dumb, Grady. I want to know what had you so distracted over dinner. What happened when you were with Hank and Dooley? Did it have something to do with the fence?" Sudden understanding spread across her face. "Was it deliberately cut?"

The woman was too smart for her own good and Grady wasn't about to lie to her. "Yes," he said tersely.

"But who...?"

He noticed that she didn't immediately jump to the conclusion that he might be responsible. That was progress, he supposed.

"We're going to find out," he told her. "As soon as I get home, I'm going to start making calls."

"Which explains why you were so anxious to get out of here earlier," she concluded.

"Exactly."

"Make the calls from here," she said. "I want to know what you find out."

He nodded and reached for his jeans. When he was dressed, he glanced back at her tousled hair and the rumpled sheets. It looked as if much more had gone on in that bed, he thought with regret. Apparently Karen could read him even better than he'd realized. Her expression faltered.

"I'm sorry," she whispered.

He bent down and kissed her thoroughly. "You don't ever have to be sorry for not doing something you're not ready for. I can wait."

Her gaze searched his. "Can you?"

"For you? Absolutely."

She returned his gaze, her expression earnest, her brow puckered. "I can't promise I will ever be ready."

"You will be," he said with total confidence. He believed that as he hadn't believed in anything else in a very long time.

Karen took her time before following Grady downstairs. She needed to think about what had happened... and what hadn't. She also wanted to absorb Grady's easygoing acceptance of all of it. The lack of pressure—the willing restraint—had been a surprise. She'd always believed him to be a man who simply took what he wanted. In fact, hadn't she counted on it earlier, expecting him to ride roughshod over her doubts, leaving her no choice but to make love?

But, then, there had been a lot of things she'd thought about Grady that she was discovering to be untrue. He was kind and thoughtful and unfailingly decent, at least in his treatment of her. She was beginning to doubt that he had ever been the thief and scoundrel Caleb had accused him of being.

More surprising than Grady's behavior in the past few hours was her own. She had nearly made love with a man she'd been taught to distrust. More significant, she couldn't seem to make herself regret it. In fact, if she was feeling any regrets at all, it was that she had faltered along the way and still didn't know what sort of magic she might have found in Grady's arms.

She moaned and covered her face. What was happening to her? How had she let this happen? How had she allowed it to go so far? And why didn't she feel the least bit guilty about any of it?

Because she had no answers—and was fairly certain she wouldn't like any of them, anyway—she hopped out of bed, took a quick shower, then joined Grady downstairs just as he hung up the phone. His expression was grim.

"What?" she said at once. "Have you found something?"

"Only that Tate McDonald is a very wealthy absentee owner, that your other neighbors are in debt, but no more so than any other small rancher, and that if anyone has a vested interest in ruining you, it's me." He shrugged. "That's the consensus, anyway."

"Well, we both know that's not true," she said.

He gazed into her eyes. "Do *you* know that?" he asked, his expression intent.

Karen nodded slowly, her gaze never shifting from his. "I do," she assured him, startled to find that she meant it.

Satisfaction spread slowly across his face. He touched her cheek. "Thank you."

"Don't thank me. You've more than proved yourself to me." She reached for the pot of still-warm coffee and poured two cups. "Now we just have to determine who's out to destroy me and ruin your reputation at the same time."

He grinned. "Simple as that, huh?"

"I didn't say it was going to be easy," she said, getting a notebook and pen from a drawer by the refrigerator. "We just have to be systematic and logical."

"In that case, I need that pie you promised me," Grady declared. "I can only be logical on a full stomach."

When she started to stand, he waved her back to her chair. "I can do it. Do you want some?"

"Of course."

He cut two big slices, retrieved the ice cream from the freezer and added huge dollops on the pie. She grinned at the size of the portions.

"Obviously you're planning on a long night," she commented.

"A very long night," he agreed.

One they wouldn't be spending together in bed, she thought with more than a little twinge of regret. Oh, well, the die had been cast earlier in the evening, anyway, and it was for the best. They'd both decided that. At least for now.

She took a bite of pie, savoring the burst of apple and cinnamon and sugar on her tongue, then picked up her pen. "Let's start with this McDonald person, since he's a stranger. What have you found out about him?"

"Just what I told you, that he has a lot of money and he's dabbling in ranching."

"You've never had any dealings with him?" she asked.

"None at all."

"Then we can assume for the moment that there are no grudges."

"How about you? Have you had any run-ins with him?" Grady asked.

"Never met him."

"Okay, then, how about the Fletchers? They've been the Hansons' neighbors for years. Have they always gotten along?"

"Always," Karen said, but her expression turned thoughtful. "Of course, there might have been a problem when Caleb decided to marry me. I think Maggie Fletcher had her eye on him, and her father really wanted the match."

Grady nodded. "Jealousy. That's always a good motive for revenge, but Maggie doesn't strike me as the type of woman to go around poisoning cattle or cutting fences. How about you? What do you think of her?"

Karen considered the woman who'd made no secret of her infatuation with Caleb. Tall and slender, with a no-nonsense manner, Maggie had always been polite, if distant, with Karen. There had never been any question of them becoming close friends. Even if Caleb hadn't stood squarely between them, their personalities were unsuited. Maggie wore a perpetually dour expression, made worse by the realization that she would never have the man she loved.

"I feel sorry for her," Karen said. "I think she really did care for Caleb. I know she was distraught at the funeral."

"Would she have tried to ruin him for not marrying her?"

"No," Karen said slowly. "She might go after me, but never Caleb. I was the one she blamed for destroying her chances with him."

Grady's expression turned thoughtful. "Then she could be seeking revenge on you now," he suggested.

"But why? Caleb's gone. What does she have to gain?"

"She might still be hoping for some sense of satisfaction that she was right all along, that you were wrong for Caleb and that she would have been the better choice," Grady said.

"I suppose," Karen said, but it didn't ring true. "But that wouldn't explain the earlier incidents. Remember, those happened before Caleb died."

"What about Maggie's father? Would he have wanted to get even with Caleb for spoiling his plan for uniting the two families?"

"Possibly," Karen admitted, though she had a difficult time imagining either of the Fletchers deliberately trying to sabotage her cattle. "Let's think about the Oldhams for a minute. There was a feud between them and the Hansons a zillion years ago. Something about water rights, I think."

"Is it still going on?"

She shook her head. "It was settled ages ago. They have access to the creek that flows through our property. Caleb's grandfather wrote up the agreement himself."

"But if they had this land, the issue could never come up again, right?"

"True."

"I'll visit them tomorrow," Grady said. "Maybe they don't want to take a chance that you might renege on the agreement."

"If you go, I'm coming with you," Karen insisted. "This is my ranch that's being targeted."

"Fine. We'll go right after we get the chores done in the morning."

Once again, Grady's assumption that the chores were his to share took her aback. At the same time, it gave her a warm feeling in the pit of her stomach to know that she was no longer facing everything— not the daily grind, not the battle to keep the ranch afloat—alone.

Grady rubbed a hand across his face. "It's late. I'd better get out of here."

Karen considered offering to let him stay in the guest room, the room they had almost shared earlier, but thought better of it. Her resolve where Grady was concerned was weak enough. It wasn't fair to keep putting him in the position of having to hold back whenever their hormones got the better of them. She couldn't let him stay here until she was ready to let him share her bed.

"It's a long drive," she said eventually. "How about another cup of coffee before you head out?"

He shook his head. "I'll be fine, and the sooner I go, the more rest I'll get, and the sooner I can get back here in the morning."

She walked him to the door. He reached out and cupped the back of her head, then bent to kiss her gently on the forehead. "We're going to get to the bottom of this. I promise you."

But then what? she wondered when he had left. Was he only helping her to solve the puzzle, to tie up loose ends, so that the land would be free and clear of problems when he got his hands on it? That was possible, she told herself. Even likely. And yet, somehow she could no longer make herself believe it.

If discovering that she had feelings for Grady had surprised her, if the depth of her desire for him had startled her, then the discovery that she trusted him was the most shocking thing of all. Feelings—lust— had nothing to do with common sense or logic. They were matters of the heart.

But trust, especially when it involved an old enemy, required more. It meant that both her heart and her head had examined the facts and found Grady Black-hawk trustworthy.

But what if you're wrong? a tiny voice in her head demanded. *What if Grady is simply sneakier and more clever than you ever imagined?*

Then she would pay a terrible price in guilt and self-recriminations, she concluded. But it was her decision to make, not the Hansons', not even Caleb's.

And the bottom line was that she had learned to trust her instincts where Grady was concerned. He might want her ranch, but he was not the one out to hurt her.

Someone was, though, and she intended to find out who.

Though the prospect was very distasteful to her, Karen called Caleb's parents in Arizona first thing in the morning. They knew more about the old feud be-tween the Oldhams and the Hansons than she did. They also knew more about the high hopes Maggie Fletcher had had where Caleb was concerned.

When Caleb's father answered the phone, she couldn't hide her relief. He would give her straight, thoughtful answers, not a diatribe against Grady, which was all she could have expected from Mrs. Hanson.

"This is old news, but I assume you've got a reason for asking about it," Carl Hanson said.

"There's been another incident," Karen told him. "The fence along the highway was deliberately cut this week."

"That's a pretty obvious place for a person who wanted to do any real damage, don't you think? You were bound to spot the problem."

That hadn't occurred to Karen before, but he was right. Anyone hoping to cause a serious loss of her herd would have cut the fence in some place less likely to be discovered until it was too late.

"What do you think that means? Was it just a warning?"

"Or maybe some kids up to mischief," he suggested.

"If this was the only thing, maybe," she said thoughtfully. "But coupled with the incidents in the past, I don't think so."

"Could have been it was meant to throw suspicion on Grady, so they wanted you to find it right off," he said.

"That makes sense," she agreed. "But who would gain anything by that? Has anyone else ever expressed interest in buying the ranch? Are the Oldhams in any position to buy it to protect the water rights?"

"Not unless they've had a sudden windfall," he said.

"Besides, that agreement worked out years ago is airtight. They don't have anything to worry about."

"What about Maggie Fletcher?" Karen asked reluctantly.

Caleb's father sighed. "Ah, yes, Maggie. Now there's a sad situation. Her father was expecting her to pair up with Caleb. He wanted to see the two ranches joined. I don't know which of them was more disappointed when Caleb chose you. I know her father blamed her, told her she wasn't woman enough to catch Caleb. I always thought the way he treated her was downright cruel."

"Would she hate me enough to try to ruin the ranch?"

"*She* wouldn't, but that father of hers is another story. I wouldn't put anything past Jack Fletcher. I told Caleb to keep an eye on him when those last incidents took place, but you know my son. He didn't want to believe it. More likely, he just wanted to believe Grady was behind it."

This wasn't the first time that Karen had gotten the feeling that the animosity between Caleb and Grady ran deeper than one man's desire to own land belonging to the other.

"Was there more going on between Caleb and Grady than I know about?" she asked.

Mr. Hanson hesitated. "I don't know what you mean."

"The feelings and bitterness seemed to run awfully deep, at least on Caleb's part. Was it just about the ranch?"

"The ranch is the only thing I know about," Caleb's

father insisted, but something in his voice suggested he was holding back.

That false note lingered in her head long after she'd hung up the phone. When Grady arrived, she poured him a cup of coffee before he could protest, then gestured toward a chair.

"I need to get to the bottom of something," she said as he regarded her warily.

"Okay."

"How well did you and Caleb know each other?"

"We didn't," Grady said tersely.

"Oh, come on. You must have. I know you contacted him more than once about buying the ranch."

"That doesn't mean I knew him, just that I had my lawyer make repeated inquiries."

She regarded him skeptically. "You never even met?"

"Never."

"But he hated you," she said. "Hate that deep doesn't come from some intellectual dispute over a piece of land."

"Some people are passionate about what's theirs," Grady countered.

She studied him intently. "There's something you're not telling me, isn't there? You're as tight-lipped about this as Carl Hanson."

He regarded her with surprise but not dismay. "You asked him about this?"

"Just this morning. He wouldn't answer me, either."

"No, I imagine he wouldn't," Grady said, his expression wry.

"What's *that* supposed to mean?"

"Can't you drop this? It's not important. If Caleb had wanted you to know, he would have shared it with you. The same with Carl."

"Well, you're here and they're not," she said with a hint of exasperation. "Tell me, Grady. Why did my husband have it in for you? Why was he so determined that you not get this land?"

"That's easy," he said, though he didn't meet her gaze. "Because it was his and he was possessive."

"You're talking about the land, but it went beyond that. I can see it in your eyes."

"You're imagining things."

Karen lost patience. "Dammit, Grady, tell me. Was it about a woman? Did you and Caleb fight over some woman?"

Grady sighed heavily. "Not the way you mean," he said finally. "And it wasn't me."

"You're talking in riddles," she accused.

His lips curved slightly at that. "Apparently it's a family trait. My grandfather does that, too, when he doesn't want to answer a question."

"Well, I intend to keep coming back to this one until you give me a straight answer," she said. "So why not get it over with?"

"Okay," he said with obvious reluctance. "This was about my father and Anna Hanson."

Stunned, Karen stared at him. "Caleb's mother?"

He nodded.

"But how? When? Before she married Carl?"

"No, unfortunately, it was much later. They almost ran off together."

Karen couldn't seem to take it in. "Anna Hanson almost abandoned her family to run away with your father?"

"They would have left, if my father hadn't been killed in an accident on his way to get her. He was late because he had stopped to try to explain to me why he wouldn't be home. She blamed me for his death. It's irrational, I know, but she couldn't blame herself."

"My God," Karen whispered. "And Caleb knew?"

Grady nodded. "He knew. He'd seen them together, and he found her bags packed on the night of the accident."

"What about Carl?"

"He knew as well, but he acted as if nothing had happened. For the sake of his pride, I suppose, he pretended that Anna had never had any intention of going anywhere with my father. He and Anna just went along with their marriage."

Karen thought about her husband, about the occasional dark looks he had cast at his mother, about the tension that sometimes flared between him and his father. He'd never been able to bring himself to blame either of them for the choices they had made back then, and Charlie Blackhawk was dead, so he had blamed Grady, instead. All of that anger and hurt had been directed at the only person who'd been as innocent of blame as Caleb himself had been.

"What about your mother?" Karen asked Grady. "How did she take all of this?"

His expression turned grim. "She wasn't as good at pretending. She turned to alcohol. I don't think she had a sober minute for ten years before it finally caught up with her and she died."

"How old were you when she died?"

"Nineteen."

"Which means you were only nine when all of this happened?"

He nodded.

"And Caleb was thirteen?"

"An age when a boy is all caught up in his own raging hormones and doesn't want to think about his parents as sexual beings. He certainly doesn't want to think of his mother wanting to be with a man other than his father in that way."

"But to blame you," Karen said. "How could he?"

"It wasn't logical, unless you believe the sins of the fathers live on in their sons, though I doubt any of that was on Caleb's mind. I was just an easy target for all that pent-up rage he couldn't express to the people involved."

Pent-up rage, Karen thought, wondering if that had ultimately been the stress that had damaged Caleb's heart. Was it possible that even years later, he had quite literally died of a broken heart?

As saddened as she was by that, she couldn't help being glad that the secret was finally out. It helped her to see everything in a new light. It helped to know that Caleb's judgment of Grady had been so terribly misdirected. Wasn't that what Stella had hinted at so many weeks ago? Obviously she had known the whole story.

Perhaps if Caleb had ever gotten to know the man he considered an enemy, he would have seen that Grady was as much a victim as Caleb himself had been. And the fierce competitiveness and anger that only Caleb had felt might not have contributed to his death.

11

It was almost noon by the time Grady and Karen were able to drive over to see the Fletchers and Oldhams. They were about to leave when they heard a commotion outside. Grady opened the back door just in time to see Dooley thundering toward the house, his horse at a full gallop. The old man looked mad enough to break a few boards in two with his bare hands. He reined in his horse just a few feet from where Grady and Karen stood.

"Dooley, what is it?" Karen asked, regarding him with alarm. "Where's Hank?"

"I left him in the pasture," he said, casting a worried frown at Grady. "Could I have a word with you?"

"Hold it," Karen commanded. "If you speak to anybody around here, Dooley Jenkins, it'll be me. What's happened? Is Hank okay?"

Dooley's expression turned resigned. "He's fine, but that prize bull you just bought, he's not so good."

Grady saw the color drain out of Karen's face. He

put an arm around her waist, but she seemed oblivious to it. He could feel her trembling. This was just one more blow to a woman who'd faced too many of them.

"What happened? Is he sick?" she asked.

"Not sick," Dooley said. "Shot."

Karen gasped. "Shot? By whom? Was it an accident?"

"Not unless you believe people are taking target practice in your pasture and that bull just got in the way," Dooley said with disgust. "Looks to me like somebody took dead aim at him."

"Is he alive?" Grady asked.

"Barely."

"I'll call the vet," Karen said at once, and disappeared inside, her spine straight, her familiar resolve back in place.

When she'd gone, Grady regarded the old man intently. "Any chance he'll make it?"

"Not much of one, if you ask me. Whoever did this knew what he was doing. He got him good. Calling the vet's probably a waste of time and money."

"Still, she has to try or she'll never forgive herself," Grady concluded. "I'll saddle the horses and ride out with her. Can you wait and bring the vet out when he gets here?"

"Will do," Dooley agreed. "Then I want to help you find the son of a bitch who did this. The missus was counting on that bull for breeding. Paid an arm and a leg for him."

"Let's not worry about that now," Grady said grimly. "I can spare a couple of bulls. I imagine Frank Davis will offer to help out, too, once his son gets wind of this from Cassie." He met Dooley's gaze. "One more thing, from now on Karen doesn't go anywhere on this ranch without one of us with her."

"Got it," Dooley said, his expression somber. "When you're not around, me or Hank will stick close by, no matter how much she grumbles about it."

Grady grinned. "I imagine she'll grumble quite a lot."

Dooley's lips twitched. "Yes, indeed. The woman can't stand to have anybody coddling her. She's dead set on proving she can handle anything that's thrown her way. Been that way ever since Caleb died."

"I doubt she was counting on this, though," Grady said. "From what you say, whoever took aim at that bull was up to no good. I don't want to wait around to see what he has in mind next. I think it's time to get the sheriff involved."

"She won't thank you for that," Dooley said.

Grady figured that was probably an understatement, but he couldn't afford to worry about Karen's reaction. It was more important to keep her safe.

"Once we're gone, can you call and fill him in?" Grady asked.

Dooley chuckled. "If you think having me do the deed will save your hide, you're dead wrong, but I'll do it. Now get those horses saddled before she comes out here and wants to know why the two of us are lollygagging when there's a crisis."

Dooley seemed to be taking to his role as co-conspirator and self-appointed protector even better than Grady had anticipated. He grinned at the old man.

"You're a good person to have around, Dooley."

The old man nodded as if the compliment were his due. "Had my doubts about you, when you first started hanging around here, but you ain't so bad yourself."

"What is this, some kind of mutual admiration society?" Karen demanded when she found them both right where she'd left them. Evidently she'd heard the tail end of their conversation, too. "The vet's on the way. Come on, Grady. I want to get out to that field. Maybe there's something we can do till he gets here."

But there was nothing to be done. By the time they reached Hank, the bull was dead. The hand had tried to stanch the flow of blood with his own shirt, but the effort had been futile.

Her expression devastated, Karen fell to her knees beside the animal and ran her hand over his blood-soaked chest. "Damn whoever did this," she whispered, tears streaming down her cheeks. "I don't care if it was an accident."

The last was muttered as if she were clinging desperately to an explanation she could understand.

Grady glanced at Hank, who subtly shook his head, confirming Dooley's opinion as well. Grady studied the massive beast and saw what the two men had seen, three distinct wounds. One shot might have been an accident, but three? Not a chance.

Grady glanced up at the sound of hooves pounding across the field. Looked as if Dooley had been successful in getting the sheriff out here in record time, right along with the veterinarian, whose services were no longer needed.

Karen rose stiffly from the ground, her complexion pale, bright patches of color in her cheeks and a flash of anger in her eyes. Surprise streaked across her face when she spotted the sheriff.

"Michael, what are you doing here?" she asked as if it weren't perfectly obvious that someone had alerted him.

"Dooley called me. Said there was a problem."

"Some fool accidentally shot my new bull," she said.

"It wasn't an accident," Grady said quietly, ignoring the protest forming on Karen's lips.

"Oh?" Michael Dunn said, stepping close to examine the animal. "Three bullet wounds. You're right, Blackhawk. That's no accident."

He glanced at Karen. "Why don't you tell me what else has been going on out here? I understand there have been a few other incidents."

Karen scowled at Dooley, then turned back to the sheriff. "Nothing serious. Some fence was cut."

"And an unexpected outbreak of a virus in our herd," Dooley added pointedly. "That was about a year ago, along with another section of fence destroyed. And a fire that burned out most of the pasture."

"Any idea who's behind it?" Michael asked, his gaze subtly shifting toward Grady.

"Not me, if that's what you're thinking," Grady told him.

"It's no secret that you want this land."

"I imagine it's no secret that I've also offered to buy it, fair and square."

"That's true," Karen said.

"But you turned him down, am I right?" the sheriff persisted.

"Yes, but—"

Michael cut Karen's protest off in midsentence. "Which means he has an excellent motive for pulling a few stunts that might make you change your mind," he concluded.

"Don't you dare jump to such a ridiculous conclusion," Karen snapped. "Grady is not behind this. Besides, he was with me when the bull was shot."

"He could have paid someone to do that," the sheriff countered.

"Then why would he tell me to call you?" Dooley demanded, shrugging when Grady scowled at him. "Better to have her getting all worked up over you insisting on getting the sheriff than having you hauled off to jail, because the sheriff's got his facts wrong."

"Maybe, maybe not," Grady said, when Karen whirled on him.

"You're the one who got the sheriff out here?" she demanded.

"Not technically," Grady said, then conceded, "But it was my idea."

"And a really brilliant one, don't you think?" she snapped. "Couldn't you see that this was exactly what would happen?"

"Actually I thought the sheriff might be a bit more open-minded," he said with a pointed look at Michael.

"Oh, for goodness' sake, when has a law enforcement officer ever been open-minded? He wants to solve the case as quickly as possible, period."

Michael winced. "Usually we prefer to nail the right suspect," he corrected.

"Couldn't prove that by me," Karen said. "Not based on the last ten minutes, anyway."

Michael sighed. "Why don't we all go back to the house and talk this through rationally?"

"What an absolutely brilliant plan," Karen said sarcastically.

Grady grinned at her. "Darlin', I think you've won. You might want to be a bit more gracious about it."

She scowled at him. "I'm not feeling especially gracious at the moment. In fact, I'm mad enough to knock a few heads together."

"Any heads in particular?"

"Besides yours?" she inquired sweetly. "And Dooley's and Michael's?"

"I'd say that about covers it," Grady said, grinning at her.

"This is not the least bit amusing, Grady Blackhawk."

His expression sobered at once. "The situation? No, not at all. But you? You are something else."

Her frown deepened. "Don't even go there. One word about how cute I am when I'm angry, and you're going to be as dead as that poor old bull."

Dooley guffawed, then covered his mouth and looked away.

Karen whirled on him. "I'd watch it, if I were you. You're next on my list."

"Me? What did I do?" Dooley asked, looking hurt.

"You got the sheriff out here."

"Somebody had to," he said flatly. "Grady was right. It was time."

Grady touched her cheek. "You know it was," he said quietly.

She heaved a heartfelt sigh, then nodded. "Maybe so, but I don't have to like it."

"No, darlin'," he agreed sympathetically. "You definitely don't have to like it."

After the morning she'd had, she was pretty much entitled to hate the world.

Karen couldn't seem to hold on to anything. She dropped the coffee mugs on the floor, shattering one of them. When Grady brushed aside her attempts to clean it up and did it himself, she tried to get the coffee grinds into the coffeemaker, only to spill most of them on the counter.

Tears stung her eyes when Grady put his hand over hers.

"Sit down," he said. "I'll make the coffee. You need to get some food into you. It's way past lunchtime."

"I can't eat. I have to do something," she said, her voice catching. "If I don't, I'll fall apart. This was the final straw. I am never going to be able to keep this place now."

"Of course, you are, if that's what you want," he insisted.

"I can't afford to replace that bull."

"Insurance will cover the cost."

She shook her head. "I had to let it lapse."

"Then I'll bring over a couple of my bulls, or Frank Davis can bring over one of his. Cole will insist on it."

"I don't want Cassie dragging Cole or her father-in-law into this. And I don't want to rely on you any more than I have already."

"This is an emergency, and folks around here help each other out. You know that. You'd do the same for a neighbor if he needed help."

"Yes, of course, but—"

"No buts," he said. "Now I would suggest you cut the sheriff a piece of that apple pie you baked yesterday, but I'm not sure you ought to be handling a knife at the moment."

"Very amusing," she said, already reaching for a plate and a knife.

She managed that task with no further disasters, probably because she was going about it in slow motion just to prove Grady wrong. She put the pie in front of Michael, then began pacing.

"Sit down," the sheriff suggested.

"I can't. I'm too jumpy."

"Okay, then, why don't you begin at the beginning and tell me what's been going on out here."

Karen gave him the short version, leaving out all of her suspicions about the neighbors. Grady, unfortunately, wasn't so reticent. He laid out every piece of information they'd discussed about old grudges and recent jealousy. Michael nodded when he was finished.

"Okay, then, I'll see what I can find out." He regarded Grady with a pointed look. "You stay out of it. This is an official investigation now. I don't want a couple of amateurs nosing around."

"Whatever you say," Grady agreed.

Karen kept her mouth clamped shut, since she didn't want to lie straight to the sheriff's face. There was no way she was going to stay out of this. That was her bull lying dead out there, her ranch that was under attack.

"I didn't hear any agreement from you," Michael said, his gaze leveled on her.

"I understand what you're saying," she said.

Michael's gaze narrowed. "That's not quite the same thing as saying you'll leave this investigation to me, now, is it?"

"Not quite," she said cheerfully. "How clever of you to see that." Actually, she was surprised that he'd caught the subtle distinction.

"Karen, I'm warning you," he said, his expression grim. "Stay out of it."

"I hear you," she said again.

He sighed heavily, then turned to Grady. "Keep her from meddling in this. If she starts asking a lot of questions, whoever's behind this just might decide that she's a threat."

Grady nodded. "I'll do what I can. I won't let her out of my sight for a minute."

Michael seemed to conclude that that was the most satisfying answer he was likely to get. "I'll be in touch," he said.

The minute he was gone, Karen reached for her jacket.

"Where do you think you're going?" Grady demanded. "You heard what the sheriff said."

"And you heard what I said—or, rather, what I didn't say. I'm going to see Maggie Fletcher. And once I've had a chat with her, then I'm going to see the Oldhams, just the way we planned. Are you coming with me or not?"

"Is there any way I can talk you out of this?" Grady asked.

He reached out and caressed her cheek, his gaze intent. "Maybe persuade you to rethink your plan?"

His touch raised goose bumps, but she managed to shake her head. "No," she said flatly. "There's nothing you can say or do to stop me."

With a resigned sigh, he reached for his coat. "Let's go, then. I just hope we don't bump straight into the sheriff ten minutes after he warned us both to stay out of his way."

"He'll be going to the Oldhams. They're closest. That's why we're going to see Maggie."

"And you don't think we'll cross paths on the highway?"

"As long as we're on the highway and not in her driveway, he won't be able to prove a thing," she said airily.

Grady chuckled. "You have a much more devious mind than I'd ever imagined. I like it."

For the first time all morning, a grin tugged at her

lips. "I knew there was some reason you were sticking around."

"Oh, believe me, darlin', there are a lot of reasons I'm here," he said, his gaze locked with hers. "That's not even close to the top of the list."

Karen swallowed hard at that. She wanted desperately to ask about that list, but now wasn't the time. Later, though, she intended to find out what—besides her land—would keep a man like Grady interested in her.

Maggie Fletcher looked exhausted. Her normally ruddy complexion had a gray cast to it. Her short hair was mussed, as if she'd been running her fingers through it in a nervous gesture for hours, if not days. Her eyes, which Grady recalled as a vibrant, glowing amber color, were listless, though they sparked a bit brighter when she spotted Karen emerging from Grady's truck.

"What are you doing here?" she demanded ungraciously, ignoring Grady completely to focus on Karen.

"We need to talk," Karen said.

"Why?" Maggie asked, not bothering to hide her hostility.

"Because of Caleb."

Unmistakable pain darkened Maggie's eyes before the sparks came back livelier than ever. "I will not discuss Caleb with you. It's because of you he's dead."

Karen winced, but she didn't back down. "I'm sorry you feel that way."

"It's the truth," Maggie said.

Grady saw Karen's shoulders sag at Maggie's refusal to back down from the accusation, but again she stood her ground.

"I know you cared for him," she said gently.

"I loved him," Maggie said fiercely. "He and I would have been perfect for each other. That was the way it was meant to be." Years of bitterness came boiling out as she hurled hateful comment after hateful comment at Karen. "You killed him. Instead of helping him, you drove him into an early grave with your demands."

"I made no demands on Caleb," Karen said. "It was his choice to work as hard as he did to save the ranch. That land meant the world to him."

"But nothing to you," Maggie accused. "He told me you hated it, that you asked him to sell."

Karen reeled at that. She reached out for support, but there was nothing there. Grady took a step closer and she latched on to his arm.

"I didn't," she whispered. "I never asked him to sell. If he told you that, it was a lie."

"Oh, really?" Maggie shot back, her tone scathing. "Then why are you with *him?*" She glanced pointedly at Grady. "Everyone knows he wants that land. I'm sure you can't wait to take his money and go off on one of those trips you were always going on and on about. Do you know how guilty it made Caleb feel that he couldn't take you?"

Karen faltered. Her cheeks turned pale. "I...I need to sit down."

"Then get into your fancy truck and leave," Maggie said. "There's no place for you here."

For an instant, Grady thought Karen might argue, might insist on asking all of the questions she'd had no chance to direct at Maggie, but she didn't. Looking defeated, she turned toward the truck. He saw that she was safely tucked inside and that the heater was working, before walking back to Maggie himself.

"Just how much time were you and Caleb spending together while he was married to another woman?" Grady inquired. "Were you having an affair, the way you clearly want Karen to believe? Or is that just some spiteful suggestion you wanted to plant in her head to add to her grief?"

Maggie's expression faltered.

"I thought so," he said. "You're a cruel woman, Maggie Fletcher. It's little wonder that Caleb chose a woman like Karen over you."

He turned on his heel and headed for the truck.

"Damn you, Grady Blackhawk," Maggie shouted after him. "And you, too, Mrs. High-and-Mighty Hanson. I hope you wind up in the ground right next to Caleb, and the sooner the better!"

When Grady got into the truck, he took a deep breath before facing Karen. She was visibly trembling, her composure shattered.

"I had no idea," she whispered.

"It was all lies," Grady told her. "Caleb wasn't spending time with her, sharing secrets with her."

"I know that," Karen said dismissively, as if the notion had never crossed her mind. "I had no idea she was so angry, so bitter. I knew she resented me, but this…" She shuddered.

Grady reached for her icy hands, clasping them in his until he felt the warmth return.

"She could be the one, Grady. She's angry enough to do all of those things, even to have killed that bull."

"If we can see that, Michael will see it as well. Let him deal with her."

"Oh, you can be sure I won't be coming back here," Karen reassured him.

"Good, because she's just unstable enough to try to hurt you in some misguided attempt at seeking justice for Caleb's death."

"She wouldn't go that far," Karen said, but she didn't sound nearly as certain as she might have an hour ago.

"It's not a chance you can take," Grady insisted. "Steer clear of her. At the very least, she needs some help."

Karen sighed and turned to look out the window. She was huddled by the door, looking more dejected than she had since he'd first seen her at Caleb's funeral.

Making a sudden decision, Grady turned the truck toward Winding River. Karen barely seemed to notice, which only confirmed his opinion that she needed something drastic to cheer her up. And she needed food. There was one place where she could get both—Stella's.

Karen seemed oblivious to everything until they approached the outskirts of town. She blinked then, and turned to him.

"What are we doing here?"

"We're going out to dinner at Stella's. It's meat loaf night. Any objections?"

"No," she said dispiritedly.

As soon as they walked into the restaurant, he caught Cassie's eye. As Karen headed straight for the booth in the back, he called Cassie aside.

"Can you get Gina, Cole and anybody else you can think of in here for dinner? Karen's had a rough day. She needs some friendly faces and lively conversation."

Cassie nodded without the slightest hesitation. Nor did she ask a lot of unnecessary questions. It was apparently enough that her friend needed help.

"Emma's in town, too. I'll have them here in fifteen minutes and Stella can take over for me." She studied Grady intently. "You really care about her, don't you?"

Grady wasn't entirely comfortable discussing his feelings, not when he hadn't fully analyzed them himself yet. But the expression on Cassie's face showed none of the disapproval or suspicion he might have anticipated.

"Yeah," he admitted. "I care about her."

"Good," Cassie said with an approving nod. "That way the rest of us won't have to kill you."

He chuckled. "Well, there's a relief all the way around."

She grinned. "Isn't it, though. Now go on back. Reinforcements will be here soon."

"You're a good friend, you know," he said gratefully.

"Yes," she agreed. "But so are you. And isn't it nice that she has so many of us?"

Grady was surprised at just how comforting he found that fact. He'd always been pretty much a loner, and had always been able to convince himself that he didn't need anyone, except maybe his grandfather.

But as he watched first Gina, then Emma and finally Cole and Cassie slide into chairs around the big table at the back of Stella's, as he saw the beginnings of a smile tremble on Karen's lips, then finally heard the sound of her laughter, for the first time ever he regretted not being part of a larger circle of friends himself.

12

For a day that had begun so traumatically, it was moving toward an amazingly happy conclusion. Karen looked around the table at Stella's and felt a familiar warmth steal through her. She'd been surprised when first Gina and then Emma had shown up, even more startled when Cole and Cassie had joined them, then she had caught the conspiratorial wink between Cassie and Grady and known that he was responsible for gathering her friends together just when she needed them the most.

She reached for his hand. "Thank you," she whispered in his ear.

He faced her with an unbelievably innocent look. "For what?"

"For knowing exactly what I needed," she told him. "And for making it happen."

"I just spoke to Cassie," he said, shrugging it off as if it had been no big deal.

"And told her I'd had a lousy day," Karen added.

He looked embarrassed at being given credit for something so simple. "Something like that. She did the rest."

"You're an amazingly thoughtful man, Grady," she said, even though it was evident the praise was making him uncomfortable. "It couldn't have been easy. You had to wonder how they'd feel about you being here with me."

"Because they were all friends of Caleb's," he said flatly. "Yeah, well, I figured I could handle whatever cross-examinations they cared to dish out. So far, they've been fairly restrained."

"I imagine Cassie warned them off because she didn't want me any more upset than I was when I came in here. Now that my mood's improved, though, watch out." She glanced across the table, grinned and told him in a conspiratorial tone, "Emma's getting that gleam in her eyes, the one she gets right before she destroys a witness."

He followed the direction of her gaze to check out the attorney, who was indeed regarding him with a speculative expression and a worrisome hint of distrust.

"I think I'll go make a few calls," he said, clearly anxious to duck out.

"Oh, no, you don't," Karen said. "I don't want her thinking you're a coward."

"Not a coward, just cautious. I don't want to ruin the mood by telling your friend to mind her own business. She might take offense."

Karen chuckled. "If you think that's going to faze her, you're crazy. Emma thinks everything is her business, especially if it affects one of us. Now sit here and face the music. I'll protect you."

"So, Grady," Emma began, leaning toward him, "how did you happen to be at the ranch when Karen got the news about her bull being shot?"

"We had some plans," Karen said, hoping to waylay that part of the inevitable interrogation.

Of course, that was exactly the wrong thing to say. The glint in Emma's eyes brightened. "Oh, really? What sort of plans?"

Karen was about to respond, when Grady laid a hand over hers and shook his head.

"I can handle this," he said, then turned to Emma. "We were going to pay a few calls on Karen's neighbors."

That seemed to disconcert Emma completely. "Why?" she asked, her expression baffled.

"Just to chat," Grady said cheerfully. "Haven't you ever dropped by to pay a neighborly visit?"

"Well, of course, but the two of you, together…" Her gaze narrowed. "What's going on? Were you counting on Karen to smoothe the way for you so the neighbors would accept you once you've stolen her ranch from her?"

Grady sighed. "I'm not stealing anything. As an attorney, surely you know the inadvisability of making slanderous accusations."

Emma refused to back down, just as Karen had predicted. She merely leaned forward, her gaze intimidating, and said, "If the shoe fits, Mr. Blackhawk."

"It doesn't," he said mildly. "Which brings us back

to being careful about the words you choose to describe a legitimate business offer."

"Then you still want the ranch," Emma concluded.

"Of course. That hasn't changed."

She glanced at Karen. "And you're still refusing to sell?"

"So far," Karen said, determined to match Grady's light tone.

"Then it seems to me as if your continued presence at the ranch constitutes harassment," Emma said to Grady.

When a dull flush crept into Grady's cheeks, Karen concluded enough was enough. "Okay, that's it," Karen advised her friend. "Grady is not harassing me. He's helping me to figure out who's behind all of the attempts to ruin me."

Her announcement was greeted by a collective gasp.

"What attempts?" Gina demanded. "And why haven't you said anything about this to us?"

"I didn't think they amounted to anything, at least not until today."

Cole turned to Grady. "But you disagree? These are serious?" he asked.

Grady nodded. "Serious enough. Cut fence lines, an infection deliberately spread to her herd and today somebody shot the bull she was counting on for breeding."

"Damn," Cole muttered, then looked at Karen. "No need to worry about that. I'll speak to my father. He just bought a prize bull for stud. I'm sure he'll work something out with you."

"Thank you. Grady's already volunteered to bring over a couple of bulls from his herd."

Emma continued to regard Grady with suspicion. "Why would you do that?"

His gaze never wavered from hers. "Why wouldn't I?"

"I'm sure you'd rather see her go bankrupt," Emma accused.

"You're wrong," Grady said flatly. "At this point, the only thing I care about is keeping her safe."

Emma regarded him with shock. "You think Karen's in danger?"

"Whoever shot that bull was making a statement," Grady said. "So, yes, I think she could be in danger."

"Then you'll move in with us, Karen," Cassie said at once.

"Absolutely," Cole agreed.

Karen sighed at the rush of protectiveness. "Thank you, but I'm not going anywhere. I'll be just fine at the ranch. The whole purpose of this is to chase me away. I won't give in to that."

"Her hands and I will see that nothing happens to her," Grady added.

"The hands will be in the bunkhouse, and you'll be in the next county," Cassie pointed out.

Grady's gaze clashed with hers. "No," he said. "Until this is resolved, I'll be at the ranch."

Karen's mouth gaped at the unexpected declaration. This was a turn of events she definitely hadn't anticipated. "You will?"

"Oh, no," Emma said. "You're not using this to get your foot in the door out there."

"Oh, Emma, be quiet," Karen snapped. "This is between Grady and me."

"But—" Emma began.

"Emma, I said I would handle it," Karen said pointedly, ignoring the stunned expressions around the table. She touched Grady's cheek. "I appreciate what you're trying to do, I really do, but it's not necessary. Once we tell the sheriff about our conversation with Maggie, I'm sure it won't be long before he brings her in for questioning."

"There's no guarantee he'll arrest her," Grady argued. "Nor do we know for certain that she's behind this. We only know how deep her bitterness toward you runs."

Gina held up a hand. "Hold it. Are we talking about Maggie Fletcher?"

Karen nodded.

"You think she's behind all of this?" Gina asked, her expression incredulous.

"It's possible," Karen said cautiously. "She wasn't happy about me marrying Caleb. And this morning she made it abundantly clear that she still resents me."

Cole shook his head. "Maggie's not at fault here, not if you're including what happened to the bull," he said. "Maggie couldn't hit a barn at ten paces. She's terrified of guns, has been ever since her daddy got hit by a ricocheting bullet when he was trying to teach her to shoot. That's what ended his rodeo career."

"Oh, my God, I'd forgotten that," Karen said, recalling how the story had circulated through several counties, making Maggie the butt of a barrage of jokes. "You're right. Her aim was so bad that her father declared her a danger to herself and everyone around her. She hasn't picked up a gun since."

"That you know of," Grady said, clearly unwilling to give up their prime suspect so readily. "Maybe she's been practicing."

No one seemed to buy that, Karen included. "That brings us back to square one," she said. "We have no idea who's been behind these attacks."

Grady's grim expression turned determined. "All the more reason for me to move in with you until this is settled." He scowled at her. "Don't even waste your breath arguing with me."

Karen didn't intend to try. For once, Emma remained silent as well. And after intense scrutiny of Karen's face, even Cassie gave up trying to persuade her to move in with her and Cole.

Grady gave a nod of satisfaction. "I guess that's settled then."

It was settled, all right. What was less certain was why the decision had set off a surge of anticipation deep inside Karen. She was pretty sure it had absolutely nothing to do with her sense of security. In fact, quite the opposite. Having Grady move in represented a whole new kind of danger.

Grady couldn't pinpoint the precise moment when his mission had shifted, but there was undeniable proof that it had. He couldn't be in the same room with Karen without wanting her, without trying to seize whatever kisses she was willing to permit him. He wanted kisses and a whole lot more, which was just one reason he'd maneuvered his way into staying at the ranch.

The fact that she hadn't fought him harder suggested that she was accepting his presence, accepting that there was something incredible happening between them despite all the odds against it.

"I'll need to run out to my place and get a few things," he told her after they'd left Stella's.

She nodded, though her gaze seemed determinedly fixed on the passing scenery.

"You can come along. In fact, I'd feel better if you did. I don't want you alone at your house even for a couple of hours."

She turned a quick glance on him, then turned away again. "I'll be fine," she insisted. "I'll need to tidy up the guest room so it's ready for you."

He grinned at that. She clearly intended that as a message to him curbing any expectations he might have about moving into her room, rather than down the hall. She seemed to have forgotten that that guest room had already been the scene of an incredibly intimate encounter.

"You had any company since we were in there the other day?" he inquired wryly.

A blush bloomed on her cheeks. "No, of course not, but…" Her voice faltered.

"Then I'd say any tidying up can wait. We barely rumpled the sheets."

She frowned at his teasing. "Whose fault was that?"

"I'd have to say it was a mutual decision," he said, grinning at her.

"You'd be wrong," she countered. "You made the decision all on your own, thinking you knew best, just the way you're doing now."

He turned to meet her gaze. "Are you saying you have regrets about the way things turned out?"

"Well, of course, I do, don't you?"

"Speaking from a purely personal perspective, I'd have to say that night's been on my mind a lot."

"Would you have changed the outcome?" she persisted, her gaze now clashing with his.

Grady thought about it, thought about how he'd been aching to make love to her for a long time now, but eventually he shook his head. "No, I can't say that I would."

Her eyes widened in obvious surprise. "You wouldn't?"

"Despite all these claims you're uttering now, you weren't ready to accept me into your life, much less into your bed. We made the right decision." He reached for her hand, lifted it to his lips. "But we can certainly reconsider it."

She gave a little nod at that. "I think we should." Her heated gaze locked with his. "In fact, why don't you forget that trip out to your place, so we can reconsider it right now."

Worried that the traumatic day had simply made her vulnerable, he searched her face, but he didn't see a single trace of lingering doubts. Grady had already passed the turnoff to the Hanson ranch, but he slammed on the brakes and turned the truck around.

Ten minutes later, he'd pulled to a stop by her house. Still clinging to the steering wheel, he faced straight ahead, not daring to look at her.

"Have you changed your mind?" he asked, giving her one last chance to back out.

"No," she said, her voice strong and not the least bit uncertain.

"Thank heaven," he murmured, leaping out of the truck and going around to catch her in his arms. He scooped her off her feet and twirled her around until they were both dizzy.

"Grady, you're crazy," she chided, laughing. "Put me down."

"Not until I can put you down on that big, old bed," he said, and headed for the house.

As if she weighed nothing, he climbed the stairs eagerly, two at a time. Her twinkling eyes met his. "If I didn't know better, Grady Blackhawk, I'd think you were as anxious as a bridegroom on his wedding night."

His step almost faltered at the image, but he managed a grin. The idea wasn't nearly as repugnant as it should have been. He'd never given much thought to marriage or happily-ever-after, but if ever a woman could turn his thoughts in that direction, it was surely Karen.

Inside the guest bedroom, where late-afternoon sun had cast a pale glow across everything, he gently deposited her on top of the colorful old patchwork quilt.

"Not being all that familiar with wedding nights," he said, studying her closely, "I can't say for certain, but you seem to me to have the radiant glow of a bride yourself."

"That's how I feel," she admitted in a whisper. Her eyes swam with unshed tears. "Oh, Grady, how did this happen? I never expected it, not in a million years."

"I didn't either," he told her candidly. "But I don't regret it. Do you?"

"No," she said fervently. "How could I, when I feel so incredibly alive?"

"Oh, darlin', just you wait," he said as he stripped off his boots and shirt, then joined her on the bed.

He cradled her in his arms, giving both of them time to adjust, time to prepare for the step they were taking. He knew that despite all her brave declarations, Karen was still harboring doubts. How could she not? She had loved her husband, a man who had considered Grady his enemy, even if that thinking had been the irrational bitterness of a boy carried over into adulthood. Grady understood all of that, which made the fact that Karen was with him all the more precious.

He stroked her cheek, rubbed the pad of his thumb across her lower lip, felt the heat begin to rise in her... and in him. Her soft moan was too much, an invitation for the kiss he'd been deliberately postponing.

When his mouth settled over hers, tasting, savoring, coaxing, she responded with more abandon than she ever had before, her lips parting, her tongue sweeping across his lips. She moved restlessly beside him, an invitation for more adventurous exploration.

Beneath the wool of her sweater, her skin was hot and soft as silk. Inch by tempting inch, he slid the sweater higher, pressing kisses in its wake until she trembled. Impatient now, she ripped the sweater over her head and tossed it aside, but when she would have unclasped her bra, Grady stopped her.

"Not just yet," he said, his gaze feasting on the swell of breasts concealed by plain white no-nonsense cotton. Somehow that image seemed to epitomize Karen, a devastating mix of fiery sensuality and practicality.

He ran a finger along the edge of the fabric, where pale skin burned beneath his touch. He skimmed a caress across her nipple, which thrust against the soft fabric. When he could stand it no longer, he bent and drew that hard, tight bud into his mouth, feeling the shudder that washed over her.

"You're torturing me, you know that, don't you?" she whispered on a gasp.

"Am I?" He was delighted by the admission.

"You needn't sound so pleased with yourself," she grumbled, then reached for the snap on his jeans. She had it open and the zipper down before he could prevent it.

And then she was touching him, adding to the pulsing heat of his arousal, sending him closer to the edge than he wanted to be.

"Clever woman," he said, shifting out of her reach. "But not just yet. We have places to go and things to try before we get to that point."

"Oh, really?" She seemed intrigued with that. "Tell me."

He shook his head. "I'll show you."

He resumed the concentrated attention to her breasts, finally taking off the bra and circling each tight peak with his tongue before drawing it into his mouth. Her hips bucked as he took her closer and closer to release just with that slow, suckling assault on her senses.

Satisfied that he'd distracted her, he slid off her shoes and jeans, then began working his way up a silky calf and rounded thigh with kisses meant to tease and torment. She was writhing when he slipped his fingers beneath her panties and found her slick and ready. One wicked caress, then two, and she was coming apart, her eyes wide with surprise as waves of pleasure washed over her.

"Not fair," she accused when she finally caught her breath.

"Oh, darlin', it's not over. We're just getting started."

To prove it, he shucked his jeans and jockey shorts, retrieved a condom from his wallet, then started once again to coax her toward a whole new peak.

This time he allowed her clever, wicked hands to roam where she wished until at last, knowing his restraint was at the breaking point, he poised above her parted legs. Their gazes locked, he slowly entered her, withdrew, then thrust deeper into that welcoming heat.

With each thrust, her hips rose to meet him, as her flushed skin turned slick with sweat. When he pressed a kiss to the pulse at the base of her throat, it was thundering, as was his.

Her name was on his lips when the explosion tore through him, his shudders setting off hers, rippling through both of them for what seemed an eternity, until at last they faded into quiet, exhausted satisfaction.

He rolled onto his back, taking her with him, holding her as if she were the most precious, fragile gift he'd ever been given, though he knew she would never, ever appreciate being considered anything but strong. This…everything about her…was amazing.

And then he felt a drop of moisture fall from her face onto his. One quick glance told the story: These weren't happy tears. Though she quickly, impatiently tried to brush them away, it was too late. He had seen the truth. They were tears of regret and sorrow.

Grady felt his heart break in two. How could she regret anything so perfect?

It was Caleb, of course. Always Caleb. Grady had to wonder, would there ever come a day when Caleb Hanson *didn't* share a bed with them?

13

Grady had seen her tears, felt them, Karen realized as she lay in his arms. She felt the sudden stirring of tension, saw the distance in his eyes where only moments ago there had been such fiery passion.

When he eased away from her, then turned his back, she felt as if she had betrayed two men, not one.

Eventually she slid out of bed and went to her own room, where she showered as if that could wipe away not just the evidence of their lovemaking but her regrets as well.

How could she have been so wrong? she wondered. She'd been so sure she was ready, that her feelings for Grady ran deep enough for this next step in their relationship.

And they did, dammit. She had felt alive and treasured when he'd been making love to her. She had responded in a way she never had with Caleb, without any inhibitions at all.

"Oh, God, that's it," she murmured, burying her face

in her pillow. It wasn't just that awful sense of having betrayed someone that she'd been feeling, but guilt that she had felt more, given more, with Grady Blackhawk than she ever had with the man she'd married.

The passion she had shared with Caleb had been quieter, less intense, comfortable—what a terrible word, she thought—even at the beginning. They had been perfectly matched, no extreme lows or giddy highs, just steady, *comfortable* companions, partners in the running of the ranch.

There was nothing easy or comfortable about Grady. He was a man who tested the limits, who demanded responses that reached new heights. She'd just experienced one of those amazing, astonishing highs. Now, alone in her own bed, she was crashing to its opposite low.

"I can't do this," she whispered aloud.

Being with Grady put her at risk, rocked her emotionally in a way she wasn't prepared to handle. She was afraid to trust this new passion, afraid the fire would burn itself out and she'd be left with nothing.

It had happened before. She had lost Caleb, the man she had expected to spend her entire life with. And if solid, dependable Caleb could leave her, then what guarantee did she have that a volatile man like Grady might not as well, in one way or another? She wasn't sure she could survive another loss. Or the discovery that he had merely been manipulating her in order to get his hands on her land.

Too late, a voice in her head mocked her.

Karen sighed. It was true—for better or for worse,

she was already involved with the man who slept across the hall. No matter the reason, whether she lost him now or years from now, it would hurt.

By the time the first pale slivers of dawn crept into the sky, she was no more certain of what she needed to do than she had been when she'd crawled into her own bed the night before. Nor was she prepared for a face-to-face encounter with Grady so soon.

She crept downstairs, drank a quick cup of coffee and nibbled at a piece of toast, then all but ran to the barn and saddled her horse.

It was only a little past daybreak when she rode out on Ginger. The air was crisp and smelled of approaching snow. Thick gray clouds rolled across the sky. Karen rode hard for an hour, exhausting herself, the wind whipping at her hair and stinging her cheeks.

The exercise cleared her head, but as she rode back into the paddock, all of the turmoil came back with a vengeance at the sight of Grady waiting, a fierce scowl on his face.

"Where have you been?" he demanded, even as he helped her out of the saddle.

She shrugged off his hands. "I should think that would be obvious," she said, leading her horse into the heated barn to be unsaddled and rubbed down.

"Not to me, it isn't," he snapped. "I thought we had agreed you weren't going anywhere alone until we know what the hell is happening around here."

She flinched at the worry underscoring his words. She had completely forgotten about the danger in her haste to retreat from a different kind of threat.

"I'm sorry if you were worried," she said, meeting his gaze for the first time.

He sighed and raked his hand through his hair as he surveyed her from head to toe. "You didn't run into any problems?"

"None," she assured him. "I didn't see a single soul, nor was there any evidence of more fence down, sick cattle or anything else out of the ordinary."

Some of the concern faded from his eyes then, only to be replaced by what looked surprisingly like sorrow. "Why did you run?"

She thought about that, debated how truthful to be, then settled for total honesty. "I was afraid to see you because I knew I had hurt you last night."

He shrugged. "Yeah, well, I'll get over it."

"You shouldn't have to. What I did was unfair. I went to bed with you willingly. No, it was more than that," she corrected. "I went eagerly."

"And then you regretted it," he concluded.

"But not for the reason you think, not entirely anyway."

"You're going to have to explain that one to me."

It was hard to tell him, but she knew she owed him the truth. "The reason I felt lousy was because I felt so much more with you than I ever had with Caleb." When Grady would have spoken, she held up her hand. "I'm not comparing exactly. What Caleb and I had together was wonderful—our life, our marriage, all of it. I will never forget those feelings for as long as I live."

"How reassuring," Grady said with an unmistakable edge of bitterness.

Karen saw that she was going about this all wrong, but she was still sorting through her emotions herself. How could she be expected to explain them so Grady would understand? She knew, looking into his shadowed eyes, though, that she had to try, or they would be lost before they'd even begun. He had too much pride to stay with a woman whose heart would always belong to someone else.

"You like steak, right?" she asked.

He was clearly startled by the question. "You're going to get into a discussion of beef with me?"

"Just hear me out," she pleaded. "I'm trying to say this so you'll understand. Do you like steak?"

"I'm a cattle rancher. What do you think?"

"Okay, then—are all cuts of beef the same?"

"Of course not."

"So, they're the same, but different?" she prodded.

"Yes," he agreed, though he still looked puzzled by the analogy.

"A plain old strip steak is tasty, right? Enjoyable?"

He nodded.

"But a filet takes it to a different level, wouldn't you agree?"

Understanding flared in his eyes, followed quickly by a hint of pure arrogance. "Are you saying I'm filet?"

She bit back a smile at the typically male response. "In a manner of speaking, but I wouldn't gloat about it if I were you," she warned. "I'm still not all that sure I'm ready for a steady diet of filet."

He grinned for the first time all morning. "I'll bet I can change your mind."

She regarded him with a mixture of amusement and impatience. "Men," she muttered. "Give them a compliment and it goes straight to their heads."

"Or other parts of their anatomy," Grady said, taking a step in her direction, then another, until he had her backed against a stall door.

When his mouth slanted across hers, her pulse leaped and her doubts fled. The kiss was persuasive, needy, maybe just a little desperate. But then, she was feeling a little desperate herself.

Feeling her senses swim, she was somehow reassured that last night's reaction hadn't been a fluke. Passion seethed just beneath the surface once again, ready to claim her and him.

Just not here and not now, she thought with a resigned sigh as Grady moved away, clearly satisfied by having made his point—that he could make her crave filet…crave him…anytime he wanted.

That knowledge filled her with hope, and guilt, all over again. But the guilt wasn't as sharp somehow, she realized with a sense of bemusement. And that was something she would have to wrestle with another time.

Grady needed to get away. He'd claimed a victory of sorts with Karen in the barn. He'd gotten an admission from her that she wanted him just as badly now as she had the night before, even if she had a few demons left to fight.

But the temptation to haul her back upstairs was a little too powerful. That wasn't the answer for either of them. A little time and space were called for.

He sent her in to fix them both the breakfast they'd missed earlier, then went in search of Dooley to make sure he and Hank would be around to keep an eye on things. Assured that they wouldn't let Karen out of their sight, he joined her in the kitchen.

Over bacon and eggs, he announced his intention of going back to his place to make sure his foreman had everything under control and to pick up the things he'd need for the next few days.

"Now who's running scared?" she taunted.

"Maybe I am," he agreed, then offered, "You could always come along."

He watched her as she considered the challenge, then shook her head.

"No, I have things to do around here."

He regarded her intently, then warned, "If you leave the house, make sure Dooley or Hank knows where you are. Preferably take one of them with you."

She nodded.

Grady paused by her chair and pressed a kiss against her cheek. "We're going to work this out, darlin'. All of it."

"I know," she said softly, but with more conviction than she'd ever expressed before.

Once Grady was on the road, he found that the solitude he'd wanted wasn't nearly as comforting as he'd anticipated or hoped for. Increasingly impatient, he floored the accelerator and made it to his ranch in record time. Too restless to deal with the packing he'd intended to do, he went to the stables and saddled the fastest, most temperamental horse he owned. He needed a hard ride and a challenge. He didn't miss the irony of knowing that Karen had crept out of the house that morning, feeling the exact same desire.

At the top of a rise, he dismounted and surveyed the rugged terrain spread before him. It was enough. In fact, it was more than enough for him, for a legacy.

Getting the rest had been about pride, not need. He'd accepted the mission because it had been important to people he loved, to ancestors he'd wanted to honor. But maybe it wasn't his fight. Maybe it was time to let it go and seize what mattered most to him—Karen's love and the future they could have together.

Before he could be certain of that, he needed to see his grandfather one more time.

As if the old man had read his mind, he was waiting for Grady when he walked into the house after his ride. Glad as he was to see him, Grady was suspicious about the timing.

"What do you want?" Grady asked, regarding him cautiously.

"Is that any way to greet your own grandfather?"

"It is when this is the second visit you've paid recently, after years of insisting that I come to you."

"Well, my messages didn't seem to be getting any response. I came to see why."

"What messages?"

"The ones I've been leaving on that infernal machine of yours for days now."

"I must have missed them. I just got in. Is there a problem of some sort?"

"Why don't you tell me? I've been waiting for you

since dawn. Either you went out very early or you never came home last night. I thought I heard your truck earlier, but you didn't come inside. Have you been with the lovely widow Hanson?"

Grady scowled. "Why do you insist on calling her that?"

"To remind you of who she is."

"Believe me, I grapple with that every minute of every day."

His grandfather's gaze narrowed. "But something's changed, hasn't it? You've finally realized that you're falling in love with her."

"Perhaps," Grady agreed.

"And how does she feel about that?"

"She's struggling a bit with it."

"Yes, I imagine she would be. Her loyalty to her husband's memory is to be admired."

"It's damned inconvenient," Grady retorted, then sighed. "And admirable. Now let's get back to my original question. Why are you here?"

"I've been worried about you. I was afraid you might not recognize what was in front of your face until it was too late." He smiled, his expression satisfied. "I was wrong, so I'll be going."

"You want me to choose Karen over the land, don't you?" Grady said with some surprise. "That's what these unexpected little visits have been about."

"Getting the land always meant more to you than it did to me. And, yes, I think love is always more important than anything else. Your father knew that, even if he was unwise."

"You knew about him and Caleb's mother?" Grady asked, surprised by that.

"Only after the fact."

"How would you have counseled *him*—since you believe so strongly in love?"

For the first time in Grady's memory, his grandfather appeared at a loss. "Weighing love against a father's duty to a child is not a choice I would want to make. It turned out that everyone lost. That's the real tragedy."

He reached for Grady and gave him a fierce hug. "But you...you make me proud."

Grady's heart filled, his eyes stung. He had always hoped to hear those words, always believed that the way to earn them was by reclaiming the land that had been stolen so long ago. But Thomas Blackhawk had surprised many people in his lifetime. Now Grady was among them.

"Thank you," he said, his voice husky with emotion.

"Just be happy."

Grady nodded. "I'm beginning to believe in happiness, Grandfather."

"And in love?"

"That, too." He just prayed that Karen would find her way to the same conclusion.

"How could I do it?" Karen asked, feeling miserable.

Uncomfortable with her own thoughts, she had called the Calamity Janes to come to her rescue. Those of her friends who were available had been at the ranch

within the hour. To Karen's surprise, Lauren had arrived with Gina, claiming that she had a day off from
shooting her latest movie and had wanted to check
up on everyone back home. Only Cassie was missing,
though she'd promised to drop by the second her shift
ended at Stella's.

Now they were all seated around the kitchen table,
cups of coffee in front of them, along with warm slices
of a coffee cake Gina had whipped up within minutes of walking in the door. It was just like old times,
though back then it had been brownies and chocolate
chip cookies coming from the oven.

"How could you make love with a man as gorgeous
as Grady?" Emma asked, forcing her to spell out what
had her in such an emotional tizzy.

"How could I betray my husband is what I meant,"
Karen responded, changing the spin but not the reality.

"Caleb is dead," Gina reminded her gently. "And he
wouldn't want you to be alone."

"Maybe not," she agreed. "But he wouldn't want me
with Grady, not in a million years."

"Sorry, sweetie, but the choice isn't his to make,"
Emma said. "It's yours. Are you in love with him?"

Karen nodded. If she could tell the truth to anyone,
it was these women who'd stood by her for years now.
"I didn't want to be. I shouldn't be, but I am. There's
no point in denying it anymore."

"Is he in love with you?" Gina asked.

"How can I know that? This all started over the land.
How can I possibly trust him?"

"Sell me the land," Lauren said, repeating the offer

she had made weeks ago. She scowled impatiently at the others. "Don't look at me like that. I'm serious. Being back here has reminded me of who I really am. Why do you think I keep turning up? I want to come home for good."

Karen considered what her friend was offering. Despite Lauren's insistence, Karen didn't believe for a minute that Lauren really wanted to own a ranch... but Grady didn't have to know that. She could tell him she planned to sell, see how he reacted. It would be the ultimate test of his feelings for her. She would finally know which mattered more to him—the land or their relationship.

"What's going on in that head of yours?" Gina asked, regarding her worriedly.

"I was just thinking about Lauren's offer."

Lauren's expression brightened. "Are you going to take me up on it?" she asked.

She sounded so eager that for a minute Karen almost believed that's what her friend really wanted.

"You could finally travel the globe, do all those things you dreamed about doing back in high school. And you'd have a place here anytime you wanted it," Lauren added.

In her enthusiasm, Lauren didn't seem to be aware of the shocked gazes of the others, Karen included.

"Okay, Lauren, what's going on?" Emma demanded. "Why are you really pushing so hard for this? It doesn't have anything to do with helping Karen out, does it?"

"Of course it does," Lauren said indignantly.

"And?" Gina prodded. "What else? Why are you

so anxious to flee Hollywood? What are you running away from? Is there another broken romance you haven't told us about?"

"I'm not fleeing anything. And I haven't been involved with anybody since my last divorce. I'm just thinking of embracing a different lifestyle."

"Why?" Gina repeated.

"Why not?" Lauren said with a shrug. Because she was such a good actress, she even managed to carry off the air of nonchalance, but none of them were buying it now.

Emma, who knew her best, finally sighed. "I guess we'll hear the real story when she wants us to know. We might as well stop badgering her."

"Good idea," Lauren said approvingly. She turned her attention back to Karen. "So? What have you decided? I've got my checkbook with me."

"I'm not going to sell the ranch to anybody," Karen said, feeling guilty at the disappointment that spread across Lauren's face. "I'm just going to let Grady think I might."

"You're testing him?" Gina asked, looking uneasy. "Do you think that's wise?"

"That could be the only way she ever finds out for sure what he really feels for her," Emma said, her expression thoughtful. She hesitated, then said slowly, "I say go for it."

"If he asks me, I'll back you up," Lauren agreed.

Karen turned to Gina. "Well?"

Gina sighed. "Do what you have to do," she said with obvious reluctance. "But lying has a way of backfiring. If it were me, I'd take a different route, but then I've had a lot of bad experiences with liars lately."

"Care to explain that?" Emma asked.

"Nope," Gina said. "Let's get one life straightened out at a time. Mine can wait."

After making that ominous declaration, Gina excused herself and departed, leaving the rest of them staring silently after her.

"It has something to do with that mysterious man who's been hanging around," Lauren said. "I know it does."

"Pestering her for answers won't do a bit of good. When it comes to being tight-lipped, Gina's even worse than Lauren," Emma said, grinning across the table at the woman she'd just accused of keeping too many secrets.

"Spend a little time having your life splashed across the front pages of the tabloids and you'll keep your own counsel, too," Lauren retorted. "Come on, Emma, my ride just abandoned me. Take me back into town. I think we ought to be long gone before the sexy Mr. Blackhawk returns. He might come to the conclusion we've been out here conspiring against him, especially when he hears what Karen has to say about selling the ranch to me. I don't want to be around when he concludes I've stabbed him in the back. He doesn't seem like the kind of man to take defeat really well."

Karen hugged her friends goodbye, straightened up the kitchen and put a roast in the oven for dinner. She might as well feed Grady well before she broke the bad—albeit false—news to him.

* * *

It seemed to Karen there was something different about Grady when he got back to the ranch shortly before supper time. He looked relaxed, more at peace in some way she couldn't quite define. The kiss he brushed across her lips was lighthearted, as was his teasing "Hi, honey, I'm home."

She regarded him intently. "You certainly seem to be in a good mood."

"I am," he said.

And she was about to ruin it, she thought despondently. Oh, well, it had to be done.

But maybe not until after dinner.

"Put your things away. Dinner will be ready in about fifteen minutes."

"Smells delicious. What are we having?"

"Roast beef."

He grinned. "Not filet?"

She chuckled at the taunt. "That remains to be seen."

All during dinner she struggled with herself, trying to force the lie about an impending sale past her lips, but the mood was too special, too sensual, too emotionally charged, to deliberately ruin it. At least that's what she told herself when she stayed silent right on through dessert and afterward, when she found herself once more in Grady's arms.

"Make love with me," he whispered as he held her.

Karen gazed into his eyes, saw the heat and longing there, and couldn't resist.

His touches were magic, just as they had been before. Her body pulsed and throbbed and burned with each increasingly intimate caress.

And when he entered her, she felt that same astonishing sense of fulfillment even as her senses spun out of control.

In the peaceful aftermath, Grady held her. Tonight there were no tears to spoil the closeness, just the dread of a lie she was determined to tell.

Finally, when their breathing had eased and their bodies had cooled, she dared to broach the subject of the ranch.

"I had an offer on the ranch today." That much at least was true, which made the words easier to get out. Yet guilt flowed through her when she felt his body go still.

"Oh?"

"Lauren's interested."

Grady didn't seem nearly as shocked by that as she might have expected. Or maybe it was just that he was totally focused on what the news meant for him and his determination to restore the land of his ancestors to Blackhawk control.

"Have you accepted?" he asked, his voice neutral.

"I'm considering it."

"I see. Mind telling me why you'll consider her offer and not mine?"

Karen hesitated. This was tricky territory, even trickier than the blatant lie she had just told. He deserved honesty, though, at least about this.

"You know why," she said.

"Because of Caleb. Even though you know that his animosity toward me wasn't justified."

She nodded.

Grady met her gaze, his expression sad but accepting. "I think what you and I have found these past few months is something special, but he's always going to be between us, isn't he?"

"No," she said. "Not Caleb. The land. I'm afraid to trust what you and I have because of the land. I know how badly you want it, and if it were mine alone to give, it would be yours. But it's mine only because my husband died trying to protect it. I have to consider his feelings."

For a moment he seemed to be struggling with himself over something, but then his expression hardened.

"So sell it," he said bitterly. "Get it out from between us. Then we'll see where we go from there."

She didn't know how to interpret his expression or his words. She did know that when he left the bed and the house, her heart went with him.

14

Grady had struggled to keep a lid on his temper when Karen had made her big announcement about possibly selling the ranch to Lauren. He'd seen straight through the ploy. Maybe Lauren had made an offer on the land, maybe she hadn't, but Karen had been deliberately testing him. Looking back on the exchange, he was pretty sure he hadn't passed it with flying colors.

Oh, he'd told her to sell it, but he'd said it grudgingly, no doubt about it. He'd set up a test of his own—sell and then we'll see if there's anything between us. They were quite a pair. Despite everything they'd shared, trust was severely lacking. He wondered if they'd ever have any faith in each other's motives...in each other's love.

Why hadn't he simply countered with an announcement of his own? Why hadn't he told her of the conclusion he'd reached earlier in the day, that she mattered more to him than the ranch?

That one was easy. Because, despite knowing that a

relationship with her was more important, it had hurt that she was deliberately trying to back him into a corner, to rob him of something she knew he had valid reasons for wanting.

He rode hard over his own acres for the next few days, trying to push Karen out of his head, but she wouldn't go. He made almost hourly calls to Dooley and Hank to make sure that she was safe, that there had been no new incidents. He'd been careful to skirt the real reason for his absence, letting them conclude that he'd had sudden business to attend to at his own ranch. Dooley grumbled that they weren't getting a lick of work done with all the babysitting they were doing.

"I suggest you not describe sticking close to Karen as babysitting," he suggested wryly. "I doubt she'd appreciate it."

"Nope," Dooley agreed, not sounding the least bit remorseful. "And to tell the truth, she's getting tired of seeing our faces around all the time. When are you coming back over here?"

"I'm not sure," Grady said honestly.

"Well, hurry it up. Hank and me have real work to do now that the weather's beginning to turn for the better."

"I'll try to wrap things up over here soon," Grady promised. Just as soon as he finished kicking himself in the butt for walking out on Karen in the first place.

At the end of the week, when he turned up alone at Stella's, craving company as much as food, Grady weathered the stormy expression in Cassie's eyes when he slid into a booth at the back.

"Why aren't you at the ranch with Karen?" she demanded. Evidently she was unaware of the fact that he'd been gone for days now. She regarded him with an accusing look. "When she refused to stay with Cole and me, you promised to keep an eye on her."

"Hank and Dooley have everything out there under control," he assured her. "I checked with them less than twenty minutes ago."

"I hope you're right," she said direly. "Because if anything happens to her, Grady Blackhawk, you'll have all of us to answer to."

Grady took the threat seriously, but it was no match for the guilt he would live with for the rest of his life if something went wrong because of his own stupid pride. He sighed. It was time to face the music.

"Make that meat loaf to go," he said, sliding back out of the booth.

"I hope it wasn't something I said," Cassie told him with total insincerity.

He frowned at her. "You know damn well it was. In fact, double the order. I might as well take a peace offering with me."

She grinned. "Take the roast chicken instead. It's her favorite."

"Whatever you say."

He packed the two dinners into the truck and headed toward Karen's, anticipation mounting with each mile he covered. He envisioned a little fussing and feuding when she first spotted him, but he ought to be able to get around that with an abject apology. Hell, he'd even help her draw up the papers to sell the ranch to Lauren, if that was what she really wanted.

And once Karen had accepted the sincerity of his apology, they could make up the way men and women had been getting back on track for years—in bed. The prospect had him stepping down just a little harder on the accelerator.

Grady was less than a mile away from the ranch when he thought he smelled smoke. As he rounded the last curve in the road, he spotted an orange glow on the horizon that had nothing to do with the setting sun. Panic crawled up his throat and made it impossible to swallow.

Sweet heaven, he thought, just as a car made a squealing turn out of the driveway onto the highway, nearly sideswiping the truck, before speeding past him in a blur. Shock had him hitting his brakes and staring, first in one direction, then the other.

There was no question about it, the ranch was on fire.

And the person most likely responsible had just come within inches of running him off the road.

Karen had just gotten out of the shower and pulled on her old flannel pajamas when she thought she smelled smoke. No sooner had the thought registered than the smoke detectors downstairs went off in a simultaneous blast of sound.

She jammed her feet into a pair of shoes, grabbed her robe and raced for the stairs. Thick gray smoke was already swirling at the foot of the steps.

"Think," she ordered herself. "Take just a second and think."

There was a rope ladder by the bedroom window. She could get out that way. It was safer than risking running straight into the fire the second she reached the first floor. And judging from the number of alarms blaring at once, the fire was already too widespread for her to be able to put it out herself, assuming she could even get to the fire extinguisher she kept in the kitchen.

Turning back to the bedroom, she paused long enough to grab the cordless phone and dial nine-one-one.

"It's already bad," she told the emergency operator. "I can't see the flames, but the smoke is all through the downstairs."

"Can you get out?" Birdie Cox asked, her manner calm and reassuring, even as she was barking directions to the ranch into a speaker that would rouse all the volunteer firefighters in the area. "Are you on a portable phone, hon?"

"Yes and I'm going out the bedroom window," Karen said. "I have a rope ladder. I'll be fine."

"Look below," Birdie advised. "Make sure there are no flames coming out of the windows downstairs. Now you leave this line open, tuck the phone in your pocket and go. I want you to tell me when you're safely on the ground, you hear me?"

"You'll be the first to know," Karen promised as she dropped the ladder out the window after first looking to make sure it was safe. Smoke was billowing out, but there were no flames.

Taking a deep breath, she forced herself to climb through the window and onto the ladder. It wasn't a long drop, but she didn't look down again until she felt the ground under her feet. Then she stepped back and took a good, long look at the house, trying to assess where the worst of the fire was located.

"Birdie, I'm outside and I'm okay," she reported. "It looks to me like the worst of this is in the front of the house."

"I've got two fire engines and a dozen men on the way. Don't try to be a heroine. Sit tight and let them handle this."

Even as Birdie spoke, Karen could hear the distant wail of a siren and something else—the frantic shouting of her name.

"Dammit, Karen, where are you?"

Dear God, it sounded as if it was coming from inside the house, and there was no mistaking the fact that it was Grady. She raced toward the front door, screaming as she ran.

"Grady, I'm outside. Grady!"

She was halfway up the front steps when she spotted him silhouetted in the thick smoke. He turned slowly, then bent over, coughing. Frantic, she almost ran toward him, but he began moving again, dodging flames and falling debris.

He was still coughing when he reached her, and there were streaks of ash on his face and holes made by burning cinders on his clothes, but she'd never been so glad to see anyone in her life. She threw herself into his arms. They tightened around her at once, and she could feel a shudder course through him.

"Thank God," he murmured. "I saw the flames just as I turned in." He held her away from him. "Are you okay? Were you inside? What happened?"

The rush of adrenaline that had kept her on her feet suddenly evaporated, and her knees went weak. She sagged against him.

"Oh, darlin'," he whispered, holding her. "It's okay."

Feeling safe at last, she finally dared to look at the house, where flames were roaring through the roof even as volunteer firefighters began swarming everywhere. Tears stung her eyes and spilled down her cheeks. All of her memories were in that house and they were being completely destroyed in that terrible inferno. It was as if her life were going up in flames. How could anything ever be okay again?

The streams of water being directed at the house merely sizzled and steamed in the heat, doing little to dampen the blaze.

When she moaned at the sight, Grady scooped Karen up and carried her to his truck, tucked her inside, then turned on the heater. He found a blanket in back to wrap her in, then climbed in behind the wheel.

His fingers slid into her hair, and he caressed her cheek with the pad of his thumb. "Talk to me, Karen. Are you okay? You're not hurt, are you? Did you get burned?"

"No," she whispered, her voice choked. "What happened? How did this happen?"

Grady's expression turned grim. "Maybe we ought

to wait and see what the firemen have to say about that. And Michael should be here soon. I called him."

She regarded him suspiciously. "Why did you call the sheriff? You think this was deliberately set, don't you?" she said, without waiting for his reply.

"Don't *you?*" he asked mildly. "Or did you leave the stove on? Or maybe forget to put the screen in front of the fireplace? Or was there a short in some wiring?"

She frowned at his mocking tone. "It could have been any of those things," she said, not ready to believe the alternative—that someone had deliberately burned down her home.

"Really?" he asked with blatant skepticism.

"Okay, no, I hadn't turned the stove on all evening. And there was no fire in the fireplace. But it could have been the wiring," she insisted stubbornly. "It's old."

"Whatever," he said. "Where are Hank and Dooley?"

"I haven't seen them since before supper time," she said. "I told them to take the night off."

He stared at her incredulously. "Why did you do *that?*"

"Because they'd been watching me nonstop for days now. They needed a break."

"Sit here," Grady ordered, looking more furious than she'd ever seen him.

She was shivering too badly not to comply. Even with the heater blasting and a blanket wrapped around her, she was cold. An aftereffect of the shock, she supposed.

"Where are you going?"

"To check the bunkhouse, then to take a look around. Maybe they've pitched in to help the firefighters."

She nodded and watched him go. Only as he walked away did she wonder at the coincidence of Grady arriving for the first time in days just as a fire destroyed the ranch that stood between them.

Grady was furious enough to knock some heads together. Dooley should have known better than to leave. Hadn't they talked about this a dozen times a day? Karen was never to be left alone, not even if she insisted.

When he reached the bunkhouse, there was no sign of either man. Of course, if they'd been on the property in the first place they would have heard the sirens, if not smelled the smoke, and run to help. Which meant they'd left, probably for a night on the town.

On his way back to the truck, he kept an eye out for either of the hands, but he was within sight of Karen when he spotted the two men climbing from Hank's pickup, horror evident in their expressions as they stared at the charred, smoldering ruins of Karen's home.

"What the hell happened?" Dooley asked when he spotted Grady.

"That's what I intended to ask you. Why were the two of you away from here tonight?"

"The boss insisted," Hank said defensively.

"I told you we shouldn't listen," Dooley grumbled. "We should have stayed right here, just the way Grady told us to."

"Where'd you go?" Grady asked.

"Into town."

"Winding River?"

"No, the other direction, over to Little Creek. There's a bar over there with country music on the jukebox and some pretty waitresses. It's usually packed with hands from all over," Hank said. "We didn't stay long. We had supper and came straight back, because Dooley here was nagging me like an old woman." Hank's gaze strayed back to the fire. "Guess he was right to be worried."

Grady paused, thinking about that. "See anyone you recognized?"

"The place was packed. It's Saturday night, payday for most of the men around here," Dooley said.

"Think," Grady said. "Was there anybody in there you knew?"

For a long time neither man responded. Then Dooley glanced at Hank. "Didn't I see you talking to Joe Keeley?"

"Who's that?" Grady asked.

"He works for the Oldhams," Hank said.

So, Grady thought, the Oldhams could have known that Karen was here at the ranch unprotected. One glance at Dooley and he saw that the old man had reached the same conclusion.

"You thinking what I'm thinking?" Dooley asked.

"We should tell the sheriff and let him deal with this," Grady said, though he was itching to take on the task himself. The image of Karen's tear-filled eyes and heartbroken expression was the deciding factor.

"Let's go," he said grimly. He faced Hank. "Karen's in my truck. You go over there and sit with her. This time I don't care if she tries to bribe you with a million bucks, you don't let her out of your sight until we're back. Is that clear?"

Hank nodded. "I'm sorry about what happened," he said, casting a devastated look toward the house. "It's been so peaceful around here lately, I thought it would be okay."

"I know," Grady said.

"If she asks where you've gone, what do I tell her?" Hank asked.

Grady smiled ruefully. "I suppose telling her not to worry her pretty little head about it is a bad idea."

"Real bad," Dooley concurred. "At least if you expect her to be talking to you again."

Grady nodded. "Then tell her we've gone to visit a neighbor and that we hope to come back with some answers about what happened tonight."

"That's going to bring her running right after us," Dooley pointed out.

"Not if Hank does his job," Grady said grimly.

"Yeah, well, sometimes the boss has a way of sneaking around the best intentions," Dooley said.

Grady exchanged a look with Hank. Satisfied, he said, "Not this time."

He was counting on her staying put, just where he'd left her. Later they could argue about how macho and chauvinistic his behavior was. In fact, he'd be happy to discuss it with her for hours on end, once they were both safely tucked in his bed.

* * *

"He went *where?*" Karen's shout echoed in the cab of Grady's truck. It had gotten too hot some time ago, so she'd turned off the engine. The temperature had climbed another ten degrees just since Hank had made his announcement about Grady taking off to do a little informal investigating.

Hank winced under her accusing scowl. "To see a neighbor."

"Without discussing it with me," she muttered, mostly to herself.

"He was in kind of a hurry," Hank said, defending Grady's sneaky departure. "Dooley's with him. He'll be okay."

"I'm not worried about his safety. In fact, I'm considering strangling him myself. Didn't he think for one single second that I might have a right to be in on this little visit?"

"Actually that did come up," Hank said. "He thought you'd be better off here."

Fury had her seeing red. "Oh, he did, did he?"

"I think he knew you might not like that," Hank said, clearly trying to help by pointing out Grady's deep understanding of her psyche.

"But he didn't stop for one minute to reconsider, did he?" she snapped.

"No, ma'am."

"Okay, then," she murmured. She would just have to take matters into her own hands. "Hank, start the truck."

"Ma'am?" He looked as if he'd rather climb on the back of a horse straight out of the wild.

"Which part of 'start the truck' did you not understand?" She reached for the key and gave it a twist. The truck sputtered, but didn't start. "Get the picture?"

"Yes, ma'am, but I think it's a really bad idea."

She frowned at him. "Why is that?"

"Because Grady's counting on you staying right here."

"I'm sure he'll learn to live with his mistake," she snapped. "Start the car, Hank, or get out of my way."

With painfully obvious reluctance, Hank started the truck, then put it in gear. "Where are we going?"

She frowned at the question. Hank had been very careful not to indicate which neighbor Grady suspected of involvement in the fire. She was reasonably certain he didn't intend to share that piece of information now, which explained the deliberately vague expression on his face.

"If you don't take me wherever those two men have gone, I swear to you I will not only fire you, but I will destroy any chance of your getting a job on any other ranch in Wyoming. Hell, I'll make sure you don't work anywhere in the whole damned country."

Hank regarded her with an injured look. "I'm just trying to do my job, ma'am, the way Grady told me to."

"You don't work for Grady," she reminded him, clinging to her patience by a thread.

"Maybe not, but the last time I ignored one of his orders, look what happened." He stared miserably toward the smoldering remains of the house.

Karen sighed. "Turn off the engine."

Hank nodded, looking relieved. "Good decision, ma'am." His expression brightened. "And just in the nick of time, too. Here comes the sheriff."

Karen glanced outside and saw Michael approaching the truck, his step weary.

"You okay?" he asked, when she stepped outside to greet him, still swaddled in the blanket.

"I've been better," she said honestly. She nodded toward the house. "What's the verdict?"

"Arson," he said succinctly. "Not much doubt about it. There was evidence of gasoline about thirty yards from the living room window, along with some scraps of rags. Whoever did this probably tossed a firebomb into the house. I'm surprised you didn't hear glass breaking."

"I was taking a shower when it started."

"Lucky for you you were upstairs. It gave you time to get out before the fire spread. Looks as if it moved pretty quick through the downstairs." He glanced into the truck and spotted Hank. It seemed to take him by surprise. "I thought Grady was with you."

"He was here until a little while ago."

"Where is he now?"

"He and Dooley are checking into something," she said evasively.

"You sure about that?"

"Of course," she said, ignoring that brief flicker of doubt she'd felt earlier. This was no time to be discussing coincidences with the sheriff.

"You don't think maybe he got nervous watching me poke around out here?" Michael asked.

"He's the one who called you," she reminded him.

Michael nodded, though he didn't look completely satisfied. "So he did. Where did he go to do this checking?"

"I'm not sure," she said truthfully.

"Well, I'm going over to have another word with the fire chief." His somber gaze locked with hers. "I'd suggest you track down your friend and get him back here, because if I have to go hunting for him, he's going to pop right back to the top of my list of suspects."

She watched as Michael walked away, then turned back to Hank. "You heard?"

He nodded.

"We have to warn him, Hank."

The young hand sighed heavily and started the truck. "Let's go."

Karen climbed back in and patted his knee. "Don't worry. You're doing the right thing."

"If you say so."

"I do. It'll be so much better if I wring his neck, instead of waiting for the sheriff to do it."

15

The minute Grady saw Jesse Oldham's car parked behind his barn, instinct told him that it was the same car he'd spotted earlier leaving Karen's. Even though it was cold enough to cool an engine quickly, he touched the hood. Was there a lingering trace of heat? Or was that merely wishful thinking after all this time?

"What do you think?" Dooley asked.

"Nothing yet. I'm keeping an open mind," Grady insisted as he opened the unlocked car and sniffed the air. This time he knew it wasn't his imagination playing tricks when he caught a whiff of gasoline. Just in case, he called Dooley closer, then stepped aside. "Lean in there. What do you smell?"

"Gasoline, plain as day," Dooley said, his blue eyes snapping with indignation. "I'm gonna murder that man with my bare hands."

"Not without my help," Grady said grimly.

They stalked across the yard. When Dooley would have politely knocked on the fancy oak door, Grady shouldered it open, shouting for Jesse as he entered the dimly lit foyer.

"What the hell's the ruckus?" Jesse demanded sleepily, all but stumbling from a room on the left where the flickering of pale light suggested he'd been comfortably watching TV. For just an instant, alarm flared in his eyes when he spotted Grady.

"What are you doing here?" he asked.

"Can't a neighbor pay a friendly visit?" Grady asked.

"You just about broke my front door down. What's friendly about that? Besides, you're not my neighbor. If there's any justice in this world, you never will be."

Grady regarded him silently for a full minute, watching his nervousness increase. "Oh?" he said finally. "Why is that? Surely you don't think I care whether there's a burned-out house on the land I've had my eye on."

Just as Grady had expected, Jesse didn't show so much as a hint of surprise at the announcement. "You don't seem shocked," Grady noted.

"About the fire?" Jesse said with a shrug. "Why would I be? The police scanner's been blaring the news for the past couple of hours now. Never heard such a commotion."

That was one explanation, Grady thought, impressed by the man's quick thinking. "I imagine it has," he agreed. "But I'm thinking there might be another reason you know all about Karen losing her home tonight."

Jesse regarded him defiantly. "Such as?"

"Being there when it started," Grady suggested.

"That was you who almost ran me off the road tonight, wasn't it?"

Jesse's expression faltered just a bit at the accusation. "I wasn't anywhere near the place. I've been in there right smack in front of the TV all night long."

"And your wife can vouch for that?"

"She went to bed early. Had one of her migraines. Started round about supper time."

"What about Kenny?" Dooley asked. "Where's he been tonight?"

"I don't keep track of my son's comings and goings. He's a teenager. They roam all over the place. I know for certain that he's in his room right now. Heard him come in."

"When was that?" Grady asked. If Kenny Oldham had returned at any time in the past two hours, that would leave him wide-open as a suspect. Jesse seemed to be struggling to do the math.

"Beats me," he said at last. "I fell asleep." His smile suggested he was proud of his ingenuity.

"Really? Yet you heard all about the fire on your scanner?"

Jesse nodded, that smile fading into feigned sympathy. "Felt real bad about it, too."

"But not bad enough to get your son and go over there to help out. You are a volunteer firefighter, aren't you?" Grady guessed, knowing that most of the men around here were. At the very least, they pitched in to help save a neighbor's property when a tragedy like this struck.

"Nope," Jesse said, tapping his chest. "Bad ticker. Used to help out, but no more."

Grady was about to demand that Jesse call his son down to be questioned, when the front door burst open again and Karen came in, trailed by an apologetic-looking Hank.

"Sorry," Hank said. "There's a real good reason we're here."

Grady scowled at the pair of them, but his gaze rested longest on Karen. There were dark smudges under her too-bright eyes and her complexion was still very pale.

"What might that be?" he asked.

Karen looked from him to Jesse and back again. Whatever had brought her running over here seemed to have been forgotten. She faced her longtime neighbor.

"Did you do it?" she asked bluntly.

Jesse returned her gaze uneasily. "Like I told your friends here, I haven't left the house all night."

"Unfortunately, he's not quite as capable of accounting for his son's whereabouts," Grady said.

Karen looked shocked. "Kenny? He used to sit in my kitchen and eat cookies while I visited with his mother. Surely he wouldn't set my house on fire."

"He would if he was real anxious to get his daddy's approval," Dooley said, speaking up for the first time since Grady's interrogation had begun in earnest. "That boy's always been crying out for some man to look at him like he's worth something. Jesse here's been too busy to give him the time of day, since he's not big enough or strong enough to play football, isn't that right, Jesse?"

Even as Dooley made the accusation, Grady thought he saw movement on the stairs. He glanced up and caught sight of Kenny, hovering on the landing. Given what Dooley had just said about the teen's relationship with his father, he felt a stirring of pity for him.

"Come on down here, son," Grady said.

Kenny crept down the stairs, his terrified gaze locked on his father. As Dooley had said, he was slight for sixteen, his body not yet filled out. At the foot of the steps, he instinctively edged closer to Karen. She reached out and took his hand, then gave it a squeeze.

"Kenny, did you start that fire?" she asked, her voice filled with hurt.

Tears welled up in the boy's eyes, but he nodded, his gaze never leaving her face. "I'm sorry," he whispered. "I didn't know it would be so bad. I swear I didn't. I just thought it would scare you, the way Daddy said. He said we had to have that land or we'd never be certain whether our herd would have water. Mama argued with him. She told him you would never cut us off, but he said you'd be selling out soon enough and the new owner might not be nearly so concerned with an old piece of paper drawn up between friends. It wasn't even notarized."

Even as she held the boy's hand, Karen scowled at his father. "You coward," she accused. "You didn't even have the guts to do the job yourself. You counted on Kenny's need to please you. What kind of father are you? You're not even a man. You're scum. And if you were worried about those water rights before, you'd better be on your knees praying now, because I'll see you in hell before I ever let your herd near that creek again, paper or no paper. I'll find some way to see that it's voided."

When she swayed on her feet, Grady stepped closer, but she steadied herself, then took one last, scathing look at Jesse Oldham and turned to leave.

"Let's get out of here before I'm sick to my stomach," she said. She touched Kenny's tearstained cheek. "Thank you for having the courage to tell us what really happened tonight."

"Hank, how about sticking around here till we can get the sheriff over here?" Grady asked. "Somebody ought to keep an eye on things." He lowered his voice. "Make sure Oldham doesn't do anything to that boy, all right?"

"I'll stay with him," Dooley said. "He'll need a way home."

Grady nodded. "I'll call the sheriff. Then I'm taking Karen home with me." He glanced at her for a reaction, but her face was expressionless. He took that for agreement, or maybe she was simply too wiped out to object.

"We'll see you in the morning," he told the two men. "And, Dooley, thanks for helping me out tonight. You be sure and tell the sheriff how helpful Kenny was."

"No problem. I just hope a court can distinguish between a mixed-up boy who set that fire and the man who put the notion into his head."

Grady nodded. "We'll see that they do."

He led Karen to the car and settled her inside, then

felt his heart clutch at the despair on her face. He couldn't help feeling he'd set all of this into motion by making it so plain to one and all that he intended to buy her ranch. Maybe that was what had set off Jesse Oldham's paranoia about those water rights.

"I'm sorry," he said.

She glanced up, clearly startled. "Why? You didn't have anything to do with this."

"Jesse might not have tried anything if he'd thought his water rights were safe," he said.

She shook her head. "This started long before you came into the picture. He didn't trust Caleb to honor them either, remember?"

That was true enough, Grady supposed, but it didn't seem to lessen his own sense of guilt. He was silent for the entire drive to his ranch, though he couldn't help sneaking a glance at Karen from time to time. He'd never seen her looking quite so lost.

At his house, he led her inside, then pointed out the master bathroom. "Take a warm bath, why don't you? I'll call your friends and let them know what happened and that you'll be staying here for a bit. There's a robe on the back of the door. It'll be too big, but it'll keep you warm enough."

She nodded, then retreated into the bathroom and closed the door. Feeling unbearably tired, he stood there listening to the sound of water running. Only when it had cut off and he heard the subtle splash suggesting that she'd climbed into the deep tub did he go back to the kitchen and put a pan of milk on the stove.

Maybe a cup of warm milk would help both of them get some sleep.

Then he called Cassie's house. He was relieved when Cole answered. He explained what had happened.

"We can be over there in an hour if she needs us," Cole said.

"I think she needs a good night's sleep more. Come in the morning, why don't you?"

"We'll be there," Cole promised. "Cassie and I will call the others."

"I'd appreciate it," Grady said, relieved not to have to go through the explanation of the night's events again and again.

"Grady?"

"Yes?"

"I'm glad you're there for her. She's going to need you."

"I'm not so sure about that," Grady said. "I can't help thinking that when she thinks it through, she'll blame me for setting it all into motion."

"No," Cole said. "She's going to blame herself for not protecting Caleb's legacy. It's up to all of us, you included, to make sure she understands how wrong that is, that this was out of her control."

With Cole's words still echoing in his head, Grady was less surprised when Karen walked into the kitchen, her face drawn, her eyes dull. She accepted a mug of warm milk, then sank wearily onto a chair.

"I've been thinking," she said dully. "I have to rebuild. It's what Caleb would want."

Grady wanted to shout that Caleb was dead, that his

wishes no longer mattered, but he couldn't. She wasn't ready to hear that.

Instead, he simply asked, "What do you want?"

She blinked in surprise at the question. "To rebuild," she said a little too readily.

"Really?"

"Of course."

He started to point out that the ranch was draining the life out of her, just as it had from Caleb, but he kept silent. She wasn't ready to hear that, either. To his deep regret, he realized that maybe she never would be.

Karen spent the night wrapped in Grady's arms. He didn't make love to her, as if he understood that her emotions were too fragile right now to bear it. She loved him for understanding that much about her. In fact, she loved him for being beside her all during the long ordeal of the fire and its aftermath. The truth was, she would probably go on loving him forever.

Unfortunately, she couldn't tell him that, or be with him. She had a duty to Caleb to honor first. It seemed she might never be free of that terrible sense of obligation.

In the morning, when Cassie, Cole, Gina and Emma arrived together on Grady's doorstep, she was passed from embrace to embrace. She felt as limp as a rag doll, but she forced a smile to reassure them all that she was okay.

"Okay, then, what are your plans?" Emma asked briskly as they sat around the table, while Gina instinctively moved to the stove to whip up a hearty breakfast.

Grady looked at her across the table. "You can stay here for as long as you like," he said.

She was tempted. Oh, how she was tempted, but she shook her head. "There's another room in the bunkhouse. I'll move in there while the house is being rebuilt."

When everyone stared at her incredulously, she returned their gazes with a touch of defiance. "What?" she demanded.

"Why are you doing that?" Cassie demanded. "You know you don't want to."

"Of course, I do. Caleb—"

"Is dead," Cassie snapped, then cast a belligerent look at the others. "I'm sorry, but it's true and it's what the rest of you are thinking."

"Still, I owe it to him," Karen insisted. A glance at Grady made her sigh. He looked resigned. No, worse than that, he looked unbearably sad.

"I'm sorry," she added in a whisper meant for him alone.

He gave a curt nod. "I know."

No one seemed to know what to say after that. Gina's breakfast cooled on the plates in front of them, until she finally stood impatiently, gathered up the plates and scraped the leftovers into the trash.

"Leave the dishes," Grady said. "I'll do them later."

"Then I guess we should be on our way," Cole said, casting a sympathetic look at Grady and a worried one toward Karen.

"Can you give me a lift home?" Karen asked him.

"I'll take you home," Grady said tersely.

"But—"

"I'll take you," he repeated.

She nodded, then hugged the others. "Thanks for coming over."

"If you need anything, anything at all, call us," Emma said fiercely. "And I expect you in town later today to go shopping. You'll need some clothes."

Karen realized that hadn't even occurred to her. She didn't own so much as a toothbrush. Suddenly it was all too much for her. The last bit of stoic resolve collapsed. The tears she'd been battling since last night poured down her cheeks. Great, gulping sobs welled up deep inside.

It was Grady who gathered her in his arms. Grady who murmured soothing reassurances when the others reluctantly left. Karen cried until there were no tears left, until Grady's shirt was soaked and her face was swollen.

"Oh, God, I must look awful," she said with a hitch in her voice.

"You look beautiful," he said.

"Liar."

"Not about that," he insisted. "You will always be beautiful to me."

She lifted her gaze to his, saw his heart in his eyes. "I love you," she said. "But I have to do this. Please tell me that you understand."

"I don't," he said, wiping the tears from her cheeks. "Not really. But it doesn't matter. It's enough that you believe this is what you have to do."

"I don't know what will happen," she told him honestly. "I can't ask you to wait. In fact, you should probably give up on me."

He smiled at that. "Never." His caress lingered on her cheek. "When the house is built and you're ready to move on with your life, I'll be waiting."

The promise gave her strength. Maybe what she was about to do was sheer folly, but she knew that she wouldn't be free until she had done it. A new house, a thriving ranch, would be her gift to Caleb's memory. Maybe then she would finally be able to walk away and into the life with Grady that she so desperately wanted.

Grady was bombarded by information on the progress of the new ranch house. What Dooley and Hank didn't report, one of Karen's friends did. They kept him so completely in the loop that he knew the instant the paint had dried on the new kitchen walls. He knew within seconds when the last workman had left.

"Go over there," Cassie pleaded, not for the first time.

"No," he said flatly, regretting his impulse to have dinner at Stella's.

Cassie ignored his scowl and slid into the booth opposite him. "She loves you. I know she does."

"I know it, too," he agreed.

"Then why won't you go to see her?"

"She has to want what I'm offering bad enough to come to me."

"What exactly are you offering?" Cassie demanded.

"A future," he said.

"Does she know that?"

"Of course she does."

"Really? Did you propose to her? If so, I must have missed it."

He frowned again. "Not in so many words," he mumbled.

"What was that?"

"I said I didn't propose in so many words."

"Well, then, is it any wonder she hasn't come to you? You've ignored her for four months. She probably—no, make that definitely—assumes you've lost interest. Not that she'd ever blame you. Isn't that precisely what she told you to do, to forget about her?"

"She told you that?"

Cassie sighed. "No, she doesn't say much of anything. She just works day and night. She's going to keel over if somebody doesn't stop her."

"And you think I ought to be that somebody," he guessed.

"If you love her the way you claim to," she challenged. "None of the rest of us are getting through to her."

He scowled at her, but she didn't back down. "Okay, okay," he said, tossing his napkin on the table. "I'll go to see her."

"With an engagement ring," she called after him.

"No, something even more convincing," he retorted, and let the door of Stella's slam behind him before Cassie could demand details.

And before she realized that he'd just stuck her with his bill. He figured she owed him the meal, since she hadn't let him eat it in peace.

He rode out to the ranch, walked into the den and picked up the paper he'd had drawn up months ago, along with another packet that he'd been holding for the right time. For good measure, he also grabbed the little jewelry box that had been tucked into his desk drawer just as long. The latter would definitely have made Cassie happy if she'd known about it. He had a feeling, though, that it was the papers that were going to make the difference with Karen, if anything did.

He was about to leave when his grandfather stepped through the front door. He took one look at the papers and the box in Grady's hand and gave a nod of approval.

"About time," he said, heading for the living room and lowering himself heavily into a chair, groaning a bit with the effort. He was playing the role of aging family scion to the hilt.

"Make yourself at home, why don't you?" Grady said sarcastically.

"I intend to, and this time I'm not leaving until you've talked that woman into marrying you. I'd like to see one great-grandbaby before I die."

Grady grinned at him, impressed with the performance. Last he'd heard, the family doctor had said that Thomas Blackhawk would outlive them all.

"With any luck, we'll give you half a dozen," he promised. If this was what his grandfather really wanted from him, he was all too eager to grant the request.

"Not unless you get the woman to say yes," the old man said wryly.

"I will," Grady said with confidence. He'd been waiting too damned long to take anything less than a yes for an answer.

Karen was hanging laundry when she saw Grady's car leave the highway and tear up the driveway creating a swirl of dust. Her heart went still and her hands rested motionless on the clothesline. The late August sun burned her shoulders.

She watched warily as Grady came toward her, his gaze seeking hers, that incredible swagger making her blood run hot. It had been far too long since she'd seen it. More than once, she'd wondered if she would ever see him again.

When he neared, he didn't reach for her, didn't change expressions. He simply handed her a single page of white paper with a few typed words, a scrawled signature and a notary's stamp.

"What's this?" she asked, her gaze on him, not the paper.

"Read it."

Her fingers trembled as she took the page and began to read.

"Should Karen Hanson agree to marry me, I hereby relinquish any claim whatsoever against whatever property she might own at the time of our marriage. Such property shall be hers to do with as she chooses."

Stunned, she searched his face. "This is real?"

"They tell me it's legal," he said. "This time I had Miss Ames at the bank look me in the eye when I signed so there would be no mistaking that it was me.

Nate Grogan was there, too. They still have a lot to make amends for after that last fiasco."

For a moment she was distracted. "Did they ever figure out who forged those papers?"

"No, and I told 'em to drop it. I'm convinced it was Jesse Oldham or someone he hired, but we might never know for sure no matter how much investigating is done."

She glanced again at the paper she held. "When did you do this?"

"Look at the date."

To her shock, it was dated back in the spring, long before the fire. Her hand went to her mouth. "Oh, Grady," she whispered, thinking of all the months he'd waited to show her this proof that she mattered more to him than the land. In all that time, he could so easily have changed his mind.

But he hadn't, she thought, lifting her gaze to his.

"It says something in here about marriage. Are you proposing?"

A smile tugged at his lips. "I suppose I did go about this a little backward, but I wanted you to be sure of one thing before we got into the other."

"Sure of what?" she asked, though it was clear as the blue Wyoming sky.

"That this is about the love I feel for you, about me wanting to spend the rest of my life with you." He reached into his pocket and withdrew a jeweler's box, then held it out to her. When she made no move to take it, he flipped it open to reveal a diamond solitaire, elegant in its simplicity, stunning in its confirmation that the proposal was for real. That diamond, its facets sparkling radiantly, all but shouted forever.

"Now, there's one more thing I want you to see before you decide yes or no," he said.

He reached into his back pocket this time and handed her a thick packet. When she opened it, she found airline tickets inside, two of them, to London. The date for travel was open, but the date of purchase, once again, was last spring. Her gaze flew to his.

"I thought it might be a good place to start our married life—someplace neutral, someplace romantic, someplace where I can show you that you're the only thing that matters to me," he explained.

"London," she breathed softly, tears stinging her eyes. "Oh, Grady, how did you know?"

He chuckled at the question. "That you wanted to go to London? The stack of travel brochures on the kitchen table way back when was my first clue, that and the fact that you've mentioned that dream a time or two. It wasn't hard."

"Not about London," she said, as she moved into his embrace and lifted her mouth to his. "How did you know the way to my heart?"

"Even easier," he said. "I looked into my own."

His mouth settled over hers then, coaxing, persuading, until she pulled away. Her heart thrumming, she glanced toward the ring he was still holding.

"I'm ready," she whispered. She had been for weeks, but she'd been too scared, too afraid that it might be too late.

His tanned fingers shook as he slid the ring onto

her hand, then raised it to his lips. He gazed into her eyes, and only then did she see the hint of vulnerability fade, the quick rise of joy.

"For a while there, darlin', I was beginning to wonder if you ever would be."

"I'm sorry I took so long."

"You were worth the wait," he said, and then his mouth claimed hers once more.

Enemy, friend, lover…and now, one day soon, Grady would be her husband. Karen felt the familiar heat begin to build between them, felt the sharp tug of passion, and knew that this was right, that it was meant to be.

Epilogue

Karen gazed into the face of her son and felt an indescribable sense of joy steal over her. With his black hair and dark eyes, Thomas Grady Blackhawk was the most beautiful baby she'd ever seen.

His great-grandfather agreed with her. He'd been hovering over the two of them for days now, eager to take over feedings, even diaper changes. Watching the two of them together had been a revelation. Until then she had been just a tiny bit intimidated by Grady's grandfather. Now she knew that beneath that quiet, solemn, wise demeanor he was a real softie.

She also knew what she had to do. In fact, she had already talked to a lawyer and today, now that the christening was over and the guests had left, she would tell Grady and Thomas what she had decided.

There was a soft knock on the door of the nursery and both men came in. The baby whimpered as if he knew that his great-grandfather was in the vicinity. Only when she had handed him over to the old man did baby Thomas quiet down. She rose and gave them her place in the rocker, then walked over to the dresser to pick up the papers she had left there.

"What are those?" Grady asked.

She grinned as she handed them to him. "Why not read them and see for yourself?"

Regarding her with a puzzled expression, he took them and began to scan the contents. He'd barely read a page, when his gaze shot to hers. "You want to do this?"

"It's done."

"What is it?" Thomas asked.

"She's donated the ranch to the Bureau of Indian Affairs," Grady said. "It's to be a working ranch for Native American boys who need a second chance."

"The Blackhawk Ranch," she said quietly.

"But Caleb's family," Grady protested. "They'll hate this."

"I talked with them. I explained what I wanted to do and why. It was one of the most difficult conversations I've ever had in my life, but I told them I was prepared to go ahead with it whether they approved or not."

She reached for Grady's hand and pressed a kiss to his knuckles. "Do you know what his father said?"

Grady shook his head.

"He said it was the right thing to do, that if he hadn't been so blinded by his own anger and hurt all these years, he might have thought of it himself, that maybe if he had, Caleb would have been free to pursue a different life, that maybe he'd still be alive."

"And his mother?" Grady asked. "What did she say?"

"Not much that first time, but she called me the next day and told me it was okay. She said that loving your father might have been wrong, but that he had been a good man and this would be a fitting tribute to him. She also wanted me to ask if you could ever forgive her for blaming you for what happened the night your father died. She said it was a burden you never should have carried." Her eyes filled with tears. "After all this time, I think she and I have finally made peace."

"It's a fine thing you've done," Thomas said quietly. "But I think there's one change needed."

"What's that?" Grady asked.

"I think it should be the Blackhawk-Hanson Ranch. That would make it the real tribute it ought to be."

Karen had considered that, then dismissed it, fearing that it would negate the meaning of the gesture to Grady's ancestors. "Are you sure?" she asked, kneeling beside him.

Thomas Blackhawk rested his hand on her head in a gesture that was part blessing, part affection. "I'm very sure, child. No tribute to the past is complete if it ignores part of the history."

"Then the Blackhawk-Hanson Ranch it is," Grady said. "Maybe one day our son will grow up to run the place."

All three of them looked at the boy sleeping so peacefully in his great-grandfather's arms. He had quite a legacy to live up to, Karen thought, gazing from his father to his great-grandfather.

Then she grinned. The men in her life were really something. And with Kenny Oldham spending so much of his time with them these days in an attempt to make up for his part in the fire, she was surrounded by males. She needed a daughter to even things up a bit. She met Grady's gaze.

"I think your grandfather has things under control in here," she began.

Grady grinned. "Absolutely. What did you have in mind?"

"Don't tell him in front of me," Thomas said. "I'm an old man. I don't need to know the details."

She winked at him. "Don't worry. I'll whisper my plans after I get him all alone."

A smile spread across the old man's face. "If he doesn't know without you spelling it out, he's no grandson of mine."

"I agree," Grady said, leading her from the room. "Talk is highly overrated."

"Then I'll show you," she said, closing their bedroom door securely behind her.

She was pretty sure he'd gotten the message even before her blouse hit the floor.

* * * * *

REQUEST YOUR FREE BOOKS!

2 FREE NOVELS
FROM THE ROMANCE COLLECTION
PLUS 2 FREE GIFTS!

YES! Please send me 2 FREE novels from the Romance Collection and my 2 FREE gifts (gifts are worth about $10). After receiving them, if I don't wish to receive any more books, I can return the shipping statement marked "cancel." If I don't cancel, I will receive 4 brand-new novels every month and be billed just $6.49 per book in the U.S. or $6.99 per book in Canada. That's a savings of at least 19% off the cover price. It's quite a bargain! Shipping and handling is just 50¢ per book in the U.S. and 75¢ per book in Canada.* I understand that accepting the 2 free books and gifts places me under no obligation to buy anything. I can always return a shipment and cancel at any time. Even if I never buy another book, the two free books and gifts are mine to keep forever.

194/394 MDN GH4D

Name   (PLEASE PRINT)

Address   Apt. #

City   State/Prov.   Zip/Postal Code

Signature (if under 18, a parent or guardian must sign)

Mail to the **Reader Service:**
IN U.S.A.: P.O. Box 1867, Buffalo, NY 14240-1867
IN CANADA: P.O. Box 609, Fort Erie, Ontario L2A 5X3

Want to try two free books from another line?
Call 1-800-873-8635 or visit www.ReaderService.com.

* Terms and prices subject to change without notice. Prices do not include applicable taxes. Sales tax applicable in N.Y. Canadian residents will be charged applicable taxes. Offer not valid in Quebec. This offer is limited to one order per household. Not valid for current subscribers to the Romance Collection or the Romance/Suspense Collection. All orders subject to credit approval. Credit or debit balances in a customer's account(s) may be offset by any other outstanding balance owed by or to the customer. Please allow 4 to 6 weeks for delivery. Offer available while quantities last.

Your Privacy—The Reader Service is committed to protecting your privacy. Our Privacy Policy is available online at www.ReaderService.com or upon request from the Reader Service.

We make a portion of our mailing list available to reputable third parties that offer products we believe may interest you. If you prefer that we not exchange your name with third parties, or if you wish to clarify or modify your communication preferences, please visit us at www.ReaderService.com/consumerschoice or write to us at Reader Service Preference Service, P.O. Box 9062, Buffalo, NY 14240-9062. Include your complete name and address.

SHERRYL WOODS